Praise for the novels

"I was going to finish this tomorrow but I just couldn't stop reading. Great story."

- J. Bowers

"Solid sci-fi spy thriller. One thing I particularly liked is that many of the supporting characters are well developed, atypical, and just plain fun. ...I recommend it to anyone who likes sci-fi, thriller and/or [espionage] combinations. I'll definitely be buying the sequel."

- S. Barnes, Editor of NewMyths.com

"...you hit the ground running and you're compelled to turn the page. I'll conclude with a final warning to potential readers of this book: Jake Dani is addictive."

- R. Murray, speculative fiction writer

"...a beautifully woven rug, every piece of the story, yet complex, fits perfectly with the other pieces."

- T. Khan

"The story drew me in early and maintained its pull on my imagination as the plot included many twists and turns and surprises. I especially liked the way

- D. Sainsbury

Novels by Victory Crayne

FREEDOM

HUMANS ONLY

For free short stories, sign up for a free mailing list. This mailing list won't clutter your inbox since I'll use it primarily to announce new books. See www.crayne.com for details.

For the first five chapters of each novel, see www.crayne.com.

Humans Only

by

Victory Crayne

Cover design by Greg Banks.
Victory Crayne
Laguna Woods, California
Visit our website at www.crayne.com.

ISBN-10: 0988690586
ISBN-13: 978-0-9886905-8-5

ACKNOWLEDGMENTS

I cannot give enough thanks to Scott Barnes for his critiques and content editing and for buying two of my short stories for his great ezine, "NewMyths.com." Thanks to Greg Banks for his cover art and interior design work. Scott and Greg are like geniuses but don't know it yet. And don't you dare tell them. They'll get swelled heads.

Thanks also to Myra Posert for her copy editing. She spotted several mistakes that I overlooked.

This story took many cooks and I'm grateful for the aid of these professionals. I wrote the basic story and learned from them how to make it shine. Any errors that remain are entirely my responsibility.

CHAPTER 1

Leanna and I had just passed Gate 4 when the bomb went off.

I was watching the six humanoid robots and their human guards when the flash backlit them and the blast slammed me backwards against the beige cement wall. Dazed, I tried to catch my breath as I surveyed the scene—the robots had disappeared, but the ground around them was littered with body parts.

Leanna was my ex and our daughter was due to arrive in sixteen minutes at Gate 7.

Leanna had on a light brown pantsuit, yellow lace shirt, and matching brown low-heeled shoes. I had strode beside her in jeans, white dress shirt, and work shoes. We had left our weapons in the car. We'd just have to give them up passing through Security.

There was no sign of the dozen human males in green uniforms who had escorted the robots. Nor of the taller robots themselves.

What the hell?

The scene near the gate was chaos. Sounds stopped. Body parts and blood lay scattered everywhere. Faces appeared to scream in the absolute silence.

There was nothing where the six bots had been. Nothing. Nor was anything in a radius of twenty feet. Bright red lights flashed from exit signs over the doorways. Fresh cool air streamed in from the broken windows that overlooked the landing strip.

A bomb had gone off?

My eyes opened wider as I struggled to peer through the smoke. Dozens of people near me lay injured or still—and probably dead. I smelled cordite from the explosion.

Destruction and death lay around me.

But no sound came. Everything was quiet.

Hands pushed on my sides. My ex-wife Leanna lay behind me, pressed against the hard wall by my body.

I struggled to move away from her. My limbs didn't want to obey my commands.

Her lips moved and she had a glare in her eyes I had not seen in a long time, with eyes lit up like the fiery ends of ecigs. After ten years of marriage, I recognized the signs of anger.

"Sorry," I said but only the vibrations of my voice rattled through my skull. My ears ached in the silence.

Wonder how long it will take for my hearing to return.

As I moved off her, her straight brown hair flopped on the sides of her head. Her eyes gazed behind me and opened wider. Her jaw slid down as her mouth opened.

I examined at my clothes. Blotches of red lay on my gray pants and suit jacket. Somebody's blood. A human finger stuck on my white shirt.

Yuck!

Despite the daze in my head, I forced two of my own fingers to grasp the finger and throw it off. It landed next to a robot hand with wires dangling from its wrist.

Then I realized my daughter might be hurt.

Alena!

My gaze snapped to Gate 7 where she would arrive in a few minutes, but folks at Gate 6 blocked my view. Dozens at Gate 5 lay still. The explosion had not gotten as far as her gate.

My daughter had escaped the worst.

Movement on the floor near me grabbed my attention. Four people tried to sit up but most of the others lay still. All wore the red of blood. Most of the people close to the blast stayed prone, without motion of any kind.

It dawned on me that the dozens of people between us and the blast had saved Leanna and me.

A woman reclined in a nearby chair. She sat still with unblinking eyes gazing at the carnage. A blue scarf covered her hair and I saw blotches of red on the blue. In her arms a baby rested with its mouth open and frozen in a scream.

Was it the father who had died?

Another movement caught my eye. A man with clothes covered in red sat up from the floor and stared without expression on his face. Then his eyes closed and he fell. Blood poured from his mouth. Another victim.

Other bodies lay shattered beyond recognition, a pile of arms, legs, heads, and torsos. A sea of blood covered most everyone near me. Blood that just a short while ago was deep inside a living, breathing human being and now was outside, where it didn't belong.

In one bent chair rested a green and black backpack, miraculously free of red.

Had its owner left it to greet a loved one coming off a plane?

He was lucky. Perhaps he had gone to the men's room instead and had lived.

The odor of fresh blood hit my nostrils. It could be from the goo on my clothes or from the sea of red in front of me. I tasted salt and spat out something red.

Was that mine or someone else's?

Since I felt no pain, I assumed I was uninjured, but experience had taught me that sometimes I didn't feel pain immediately, even if I had been shot.

Leanna's eyes opened wide. Her lips moved and I read the name "Alena."

Motion caught my attention. I looked up as police and airport security straggled in one by one from the hallway in their blue and green uniforms.

I had never been this close to a terrorist bomb.

Instinct took over and I wanted to get away. So I pulled Leanna up and led her away from the chaos toward Gate 7.

As we went past people with eyes drawn toward Gate 4, many stared at the blood on my clothes. One lady rushed her hands to her mouth.

I still couldn't hear anything.

On the way, I passed an overhead sign of "Restrooms." So I halted Leanna and pointed first to my ears, then at the blood on my clothes and then to the men's room.

She watched my motions and nodded. Then she crossed her arms and leaned against the wall.

Inside, I washed off as much blood as I could.

When I came out, a cop in a blue police uniform blocked my path.

What the hell is this? Does he think I did it?

His lips moved. I shook my head and pointed to my right ear. With his right hand he grabbed my arm. At least he hadn't pulled his gun.

As the guard led me away, Leanna pushed away from the wall.

"Leanna!"

The sound pierced the bones of my skull but I heard nothing.

I pointed with my finger in the direction I walked. She nodded, put her arms down, and walked away toward Gate 7. At least she wasn't splattered with blood. It was a good thing I was in front of her when the explosion occurred. I wondered if she could hear.

I felt a jerk on my arm. My cop nodded his head in the direction we had been going. There was no sense in fighting him so I let myself be herded back toward Gate 4 and the other people.

On the way, I scooped up a leaflet someone had discarded and read as we walked.

The words across the top of the page stated, "Rossa is for humans!"

In the first column, I read "We all came here to get away from the damned robots on Earth. Since the middle of the twenty-first century, robots have taken over our jobs and the military. Now they want our bodies as more and more people have artificial body parts. Where will this madness end? When they take over our souls too?"

The angry face of Guy Coocher filled the left column. He was head of the Human Only organization and an elected member of Parliament.

"We came to Rossa to get away from the sameness of Earth. We came here to get away from the damned hybrids and the robots. We came here to get away from half-human half-robots. Let us keep our humanity. It's precious. We deserve a place to call our own. We deserve Rossa to be free of robots and aliens."

Quite an appeal.

I read on.

"If we let the damned robots come here, we're just inviting the Devil to dine with us."

The Devil?

I must have stopped because I felt the cop tug on my arm. As we walked past Gate 4, I peered at the carnage.

Hope there's no second explosion.

CHAPTER 2

As I strode back with the guard, a crowd rushed in the opposite direction. Wondering what I had missed, I glanced their way.

At Gate 5 two black aliens, mercons, stared at the crowd as it got closer to them. Shorter than adult humans and with almost black skin, their nose slits came up to the spot between their eyes.

I wish I could hear, damn it!

As the crowd got near the mercons they blocked my view of them. Arms waved in the air. A few carried signs but I couldn't read them from my angle. They acted like a mob.

I must have stopped because the guard grabbed my arm and pulled me in the opposite direction.

Pushy little bugger.

He led me down the hall to an open area crowded with people. A man got up from a chair and I was about to sit on it when I noticed an older woman entered the room wobbling on a cane. So I surrendered the seat to her and sat on the floor next to a blue wall with my knees tucked up under my chin.

She mouthed, "Thank you."

Maybe she had lost her hearing too.

I bobbed my head a couple times in reply.

Over the next a few minutes, the guards and staff got organized. Nothing like this had ever happened in York. Maybe they were more used to it next door in Algebra, where immigrants settled from the Mideast, but we weren't used to it here.

With nothing to do, I checked my comm, figuring I could learn more about the explosion. But before I could read much, a guard positioned himself in front of me and covered my comm. He pointed to the top of a digital pad in his hand, where I read, "Your comm will be returned to you after you are interviewed about your experience."

I sighed and presented my left arm. He pulled off my comm and attached a rubber band and sticker to it with a number. He presented a clipboard. I printed my name in block letters next to the number on the pad and memorized the number, thirty-seven.

Great. That meant I would have no idea how bad the damage was or how many had been killed.

Spies like to know that stuff. But I could understand his point. Someone wanted my report before I interpreted my responses based on what I learned from my comm.

I remained on the floor, bored, and in silence. A clock on the wall showed the time, fifteen minutes past ten. Ever notice that no matter how you try to speed up the second hand, it still maintains its sluggish but relentless pace? You can't slow it down nor speed it up. Time is like that. Seconds slip by and turn into minutes, minutes into hours, and soon a day is gone. Forever.

I read someplace that ten thousand days pass in about twenty-seven years. That meant I was working on my second ten thousand.

When a man sitting in a chair along the wall opposite me rose and made off, I took his seat.

Beats sitting on the floor.

Two minutes later, a guard in a green uniform drew near me. He motioned with his finger that I should go to my left. I rose and went as directed to a gray plastic chair next to a gray desk. A black male nurse took my blood pressure, pulse, and temperature. Then I got in line to get my photo taken, bloody shirt and all, and in yet another line to be interviewed.

Waiting is not my favorite game.

Finally, they let me have a seat in a chair with black plastic for the seat and back, and with stainless steel legs ending in rubber feet. The kind you see in school auditoriums. Must be easy to clean, easy to stack.

On a bench opposite me a boy rested with a dark-green toy army man in his lap. The boy's pants and shirt had red blotches and he stared tearless. Probably in shock. I waved my hand and grabbed his attention. I pretended to duck and fired a finger-gun at him. He smiled in return. Somebody was playing with him.

I remembered myself as a little boy after my older brother Ken had been killed. That happened a long time ago, but it was one of those key moments in my life that changed me forever. It drove home what it meant to be a Binger and face discrimination.

Years before I came into this world, Dr. Bing inserted snippets of mercon DNA into human children to copy some of the alien strength and intelligence into humans. The children of those experiments became known as Bingers.

That was during the war against the alien race who lived on the planet Durr, at about the same distance from Earth as Rossa. The three planets' stars formed an equilateral triangle with its corners spaced twenty-five light years apart.

My father was a full-blood Binger and my mother a full human. So I had half my DNA altered. Most people on Earth treated Bingers as part-alien. The resulting discrimination was hard for a boy of twelve to grasp until the day I learned Ken was dead because someone suspected he was a Binger.

Two seats down and across from me, a girl sat next to a woman with the woman's left arm wrapped around her. The girl had puckered lips and her body shook. I figured she was crying. On the floor a few feet away lay a stuffed giraffe. I stooped, picked up the giraffe, and held in out in front of the girl. She reached out with her arms and pulled the toy animal close to her body. I detected a brief smile on her face. Then she spotted the blood on my clothes. In seconds, the edges of her mouth turned down and her jaw dropped. Her eyes squeezed shut. I figured she cried again.

The mother mouthed, "Thank you."

I pointed to my ears and her head went up and down an inch. She was probably deaf too, another victim of the explosion.

The boy on the bench across from me waited until I parked in my chair. Then he used his fingers to fire back. I grabbed my chest and winced. Another smile was my reward. He fired again but a woman in white came up in front of me and grabbed my arm. It was my turn for interrogation.

As I rose from my chair, I waved to the little boy. He gave a small wave back. At least I had broken his loneliness for a few seconds with playtime.

All this happened with the ringing in my ears as the only sound I perceived. Weird.

This time I parked my behind in a brown metal folding chair while a middle-aged woman wearing a Zor-Franken Airport badge on the front of her green uniform asked me questions via a digital pad. She took my blood pressure and pulse. Why they did that twice I didn't know. Then my training kicked in. They were checking to see who went into delayed shock.

Being deaf put me at a disadvantage. So I scanned around me every ten seconds to see if anyone came up behind me.

The nurse spoke into a microphone and her words appeared on her digital pad.

"Is there something you're worried about?"

"Yeah, being killed."

"I assure you, Mr..." She paused to read my name from her pad. "...Snyder, you're safe. Try to relax."

Easier said than done, sister. You're not a deaf spy.

We'd received a tag a few hours ago that our daughter would land at the airport from the Meda Space Elevator and needed a ride.

Which was a shock to both Leanna and me. We had kept Leanna's presence on Rossa a secret from Alena. We never expected her to come to Rossa.

"Serves us right," Leanna had said, "for deceiving her like this."

Before Leanna and I had left for the airport, one problem had been what names to use. I didn't think it was wise to give our own names "in the open." Leanna agreed. But what to do with Alena's last name of Dani?

I had searched for a name to call myself and hit upon Snyder. Ralph Snyder was the protagonist in the current novel I was reading. The name sounded nice.

I had suggested to Leanna that she use Ebonta Snyder. We could say Alena Dani was her daughter from a former marriage.

I had Vincent cook up fake identities for both of us. Mine said I worked as a private investigator as a consultant. Which was true. Leanna didn't like pretending to be married to me—again. But I thought it was better to travel as a married couple.

The nurse used a black funnel on a handle to peek into both of my ears. When she finished, I read her words from the digital pad. "You're fortunate. There's no damage to your ear drums. Your hearing may return in two weeks."

That was the first bit of good news since I had arrived. I expected my hearing to return sooner than that, a gift of my Binger genes. We healed faster than mundanes, the name we used for "normals."

The whole experience of being deaf made me realize what it would be like to be deaf all the time. The quiet was nice but not being able to hear conversations was a bitch. I was an outsider trying to eavesdrop without success.

My interrogator asked more questions on her pad. At one time, she wanted my ID and I showed her my PI card. She asked, "Gun?" with her index finger thumb extended and her thumb closed on an imaginary hammer.

I replied, "In my car."

My voice still sounded muffled through the bones of my head.

She looked in my eyes and mouthed the words, "Why are you here?"

I answered, "To pick up my daughter at Gate 7."

"Her name?"

"Alena Dani."

"Spelled that, please."

"A-L-E-N-A space D-A-N-I."

A few clicks on her keyboard showed that name on her monitor.

She asked, "What did you see at Gate 4?"

"Six humanoid robots, each seven feet tall, came out of Gate 4. They were accompanied by a half dozen humans in light green uniforms. The robots looked like humans with flesh-colored skin and wore blue and white clothing. The edges of white shirts were visible near their collars.

"Then a blast came from behind them."

She asked another hundred questions. At least it seemed like that many.

The nurse reached in a box and searched for a tag with a number attached to a comm.

I said, "Thirty-seven."

"I know," she added. Her words appeared on the ereader in front of me.

When she found mine, she removed the tag and handed it to me.

She pulled out another piece of paper. It said, "You must go to the hospital to get x-rayed for metal pieces stuck in your body."

I replied, "But I don't feel anything."

She mouthed, "Go anyway."

She jerked her thumb in the universal sign of "You can leave now" or "Get outta here." I couldn't tell which but I got the message.

She wiggled her right index finger three times to a guard standing nearby to bring the next person in line to come sit in the chair.

I put my comm on my left wrist and I proceeded out of the roped off area and through a crowd sitting on benches. Some had the red of blood on their clothing. As I went on foot by them, I wondered if they expected the hundred questions. Didn't matter. They'd get asked anyways.

Then I strode toward a crowd of gawkers beyond a rope. A guy in a light green uniform opened the rope for me to pass.

When I got beyond the gawkers, I saw two familiar faces sitting on a padded bench. My ex and my daughter.

Leanna and Alena rose as I got near them.

I had last seen my daughter several years ago when I left LA to come here. Alena no longer was a skinny and clumsy teenager. She was a woman now.

But the look on her face wasn't warm. Her lips were pursed and narrow. Her eyes glared under lowered eyebrows.

A beige sweater hung over her left arm. She had on black slacks and a beige short-sleeved blouse. On her feet were low-heeled brown shoes. She stood beside a luggage carrier. On it were six large suitcases. Four were of the same blue color and hard-shells. The other two were dark brown with cloth covers.

She was an inch taller than me and about my weight but with muscles bulging in her short-sleeved blouse. She might be 210 pounds. Good for her but she would stand out on Rossa.

You could tell who came from Earth by their height. With the fifteen percent higher gravity on Rossa, those born here did not reach the heights of most Earthers.

When I approached, Leanna smiled and said something. "…daughter…."

I looked my daughter over while she held her arms out. She took one look at my bloody shirt and shook her head. She decided against a hug.

Can't say I blame her.

I said, "I have a lot of questions."

Alena said something.

I pointed to my ears and shook my head.

"I can't hear. Comm," I ordered. "Use subtitles for translation."

Thank heavens for voice recognition software.

I pulled Alena's luggage cart while the two women strolled ahead of me.

As we entered the garage, the air felt muggy. Rain was coming.

When we got to my black sedan, I put her luggage in the boot while Alena sat in the rear seat behind her mother. I put on a spare shirt from my trunk. There was blood on my slacks but not as much.

When I sat in the driver's seat, I said, "Car. University of Zor. Unlock seat."

I felt the click as my seat came unlocked and I swiveled to face my two women.

"Did the news say how many had died?" I asked of Leanna.

She looked at me with a frown. "You didn't use your comm?"

I had to look at my comm to get her message.

"They took it from me. I didn't get it back until a few minutes ago. Guess they didn't want me to read the news before I told my experiences."

"They said that over fifty people were killed." She said that so fast I asked her to repeat it. She flashed her hands with her fingers spread five times and then stuck out her tongue on one side of her mouth and tilted her heads sideways with her eyes closed in a pantomime of someone dead.

"No robots?"

She raised one eyebrow. "Silly."

Guess robots don't count as people.

I wondered how long that would last.

CHAPTER 3

We loaded Alena's luggage into the BIS van. As we drove out of the garage and onto the main streets, I saw sprinkles of rain on the windshield.

Warm air blasted out of the vents and soon the windows fogged. That didn't last long as streaks of clearness expanded between tiny black wires on all the side and back windows. On the windshield, I saw a growing clear view expand upward from the dashboard.

We soon came to a stop light and more rain hit the windows. I didn't mind because we needed the rain. Zor was in the midst of a drought.

So far, nothing had been said. The tension in the air grew to be unbearable. I had to say something.

"How did you get your mother's comm number?"

From the backseat, Alena didn't answer right away. What she said made little sense until I checked. Reading their words on my comm was becoming a nuisance.

"What I'd like to know is how long are you two gonna to keep this pretense up?"

Did she mean her mother being on Rossa or our being spies?

Leanna said, "What do you mean?"

"I mean," said Alena to her mother, "how long were you going to pretend you were in Germany?"

We had had Alena's messages sent to our contact in Cologne and then be forwarded to the next courier to Rossa. Leanna had said she held a training job that required her presence in different parts of the world so she couldn't respond right away. We hoped we could delude Alena into thinking her mother was on Earth.

"I asked you a question," I interjected. "How did you get your mother's comm?"

Our daughter responded in a quieter voice as she stared out her window. "I knew she married Vincent Stone, so I looked up his business. I finagled the receptionist to give me her number."

Like a good spy. Damn it! There I went.

"Why are you both on Rossa?" she asked. "Why did you pretend the whole time?"

Because we're spies and didn't want you to know Leanna was here.

But I couldn't tell her that.

I stared at my ex and she looked back at me. Her eyebrows went up. It was my turn.

I returned my gaze to my daughter in the back seat. "We wanted to protect you," I said.

"From what? From knowing you were both here? Didn't you think I'd want to come?"

Yeah, we knew you'd want to come. That was the point.

"I'm sorry, Alena," I replied. "We were just trying to protect you. Why are you coming here anyway?"

Alena crossed her arms and answered back while staring out the window, "I'm attending classes at the University of Zor. The official reason is for my degree of xenoanthropology. Rossa is the only place where there are three species—humans, mercons, and napes. So I want to get my degree here and go on to my Ph.D."

I knew she was studying xenoanthropology. And her argument made sense. If I wanted to get a Ph.D. in alien lifeforms, I'd want to come here too.

"And the unofficial reason?" I asked.

She peered out the window. "Because my Mom and Dad are here."

"Why didn't you tell us you were coming?"

She fired back as she fixed her eyes on both of us, "You didn't tell me. Why should I tell you?"

Silence. That would explain why Leanna had received no emails from our daughter in two weeks. Travelers on their way to Rossa, or back to Earth, cannot send or receive emails for two weeks.

"Why couldn't either of you come to my graduation for my bachelors?" Alena asked.

I looked at my ex and sighed through pursed lips. Alena was hitting hard with her questions. Maybe she had them stored up.

"You surprised everybody by graduating from college in two years," I said. "I was busy here, organizing my team."

"And I was busy in training school," answered Leanna.

I kept my eyes glued to my comm as I tried to keep up with the three-way conversation.

"Spy training?" Alena asked.

Leanna and I glanced at each other.

"What are you not telling me about you?" asked Alena. "I can see it on your faces."

I answered, "Nothing."

"Right. Do you expect me to believe that after you lied about being on Rossa? Great-uncle Berry told me he knew both of you were on Rossa. Every Binger knows he's the head of BIS." She looked back and forth at her parents.

"Are you spies for Uncle Berry?"

Leanna turned her eyes to me. "Jake?"

I studied my comm to catch up on what Alena said.

I inhaled a deep one.

Here goes.

"I guess you'll find out soon enough. Yes, I'm a spy for BIS. And so is your mother. She works for me here. I'm the station chief on Rossa. And now that you know, you're in danger."

Alena leaned back with a smile. "That is so cool."

She crossed her arms and stood silent for a few moments.

"I wanna be a spy too."

I stared at her.

"It's not all glamor. Ask your mother. Sometimes it's boring and sometimes it's dangerous. I was captured a year ago and tortured. I thought I'd die. The explosion we saw back there is a good example. We often go for long periods of time with little danger, and then we are frantic with fear as we deal with a problem."

My daughter snapped back, "But you do good work, too, don't you?"

Leanna spoke next. "Alena, your father's right. It's dangerous work. And you never know when it could get more dangerous. We become paranoid."

"Uncle Berry talked with me about it. I already know all that. He let me see training vids. I know it can be dangerous. But I want to fight prejudice and find out the truth."

I had to respond to that. "You'll have plenty of opportunity to do that in your research."

Leanna added, "You may have to kill someone. Have you thought of how you'd react to that?"

Silence.

So she had not thought about it.

I had to change the subject.

"The trip here is expensive. How'd you manage it?" I asked.

Alena stared out the window.

"Scholarship. Uncle Berry provided some help, too."

So he could get his hooks in her.

She returned her gaze to me.

"I still want to join," she added.

"Oh no you don't!" I exclaimed. "It's far too dangerous."

"Listen to your father for a change," said Leanna. "He's right. It's very dangerous."

I asked the question on every father's mind.

"Got a boyfriend?"

"Nope. I want to get my Ph.D. first. Boyfriends can wait."

Which meant a family of her own. Then it hit me.

Good grief! I might become a grandfather in a few years.

My car turned to the right at the light onto University Avenue.

It said, "Destination, please."

"What's the address of your dorm?" I asked.

Alena told me.

Our BIS van's AI Chima acknowledged, "We should be there in two minutes twenty-five seconds."

The rain turned to a few sprinkles now and then.

I asked my daughter, "Do you have a local comm number?"

She nodded.

"Let's share comm info," I said.

We touched our three comms together.

We turned left at a light and soon pulled into a parking lot with dozens of cars. I turned my car seat back to the front and when we stopped, I got out. The rain had let up. For now. Dark gray clouds filled the sky from horizon to horizon. The air felt sticky with humidity.

I looked around but couldn't see Alena.

Where is she?

Soon she came out a door pushing a luggage cart. I hefted all six of her pieces onto the cart and was about to push it when Alena stopped me.

She fixed her eyes on me and we embraced again. This time was warmer. Leanna came next for a long hug from her daughter.

"I'll tag you after I get settled in," said Alena as she pushed her cart up the ramp and into the building.

I watched her as she strolled away, pushing the cart.

My daughter was on Rossa.

I said, "Well, she's here now."

"She's changed."

I nodded. "Not a kid anymore."

"Do you think she'll contact Acorn?"

"I doubt it."

"He won't stop trying, you know."

I sighed. "Unfortunately."

* * * * *

"Chima, Gerges," I ordered. I had an unscheduled appointment there.

"Telly on."

Both of us viewed it on the dashboard. Sure enough, the explosion at Gate 4 was the big news.

I could not see the two black mercons. The mob may have taken their anger out on the two small aliens. Next came a vid of the two being rushed to an ambulance, wrapped in white with red stains. Their dark skin contrasted with the white of the bandages and the red of their blood.

Poor little buggers.

The scene changed to show the entrance to the mercon embassy as the ambulance pulled through the gate. Black mercon guards in military uniforms closed the gate.

The scene changed again to show a woman speaking into a microphone. I glanced at my comm.

"News of the explosion has spread over Rossa."

The next scenes showed angry crowds with parts of the Meda Spaceport behind them. I read the text across the bottom of the screen.

"Hundreds of flights cancelled."

Our van made a right turn at the Main Street light and a block later we pulled into the large lot at the hospital.

Inside Gerges and not knowing where to go, we stopped at the receptionist's desk just inside the front door. A gal sat behind the window in a light brown jacket and yellow lace blouse. From the dark areas under her eyes, I figured maybe her ancestors came from India or Pakistan. She moved her lips but that wasn't much help.

So I replied, "I was at the explosion at the airport. Lost my hearing so you must speak slower while I try to read your lips."

She turned to my ex and spoke.

Guess that was too much to ask.

Leanna took the directions and pulled my arm. I felt like a child brought along with my mommy.

We walked down what seemed like a mile of hallways. We made lots of turns and I lost track of where I was until we got to an overhead sign that said "Radiology."

Leanna chatted with a male receptionist seated behind a glass window through a round hole.

She turned to me. "You're supposed to get undressed before your x-rays."

She pointed to a sign over a door. "Men." Beyond it was another door labeled "Women."

I wondered what they did with aliens. Probably didn't get many.

I went into the men's room and undressed. After counting my cash, I locked my clothes in a cupboard with a plastic card that hung around my neck on a cord. To hide my nakedness, I had to don a blue hospital gown that might have weighed four ounces. I slipped my feet into matching blue thin-soled slippers.

When I entered the cool x-ray room, a sign said, "You may take off your slippers when on the x-ray table."

The monitor reported, "Please remove your comm."

So I did.

It didn't take over fifteen minutes to get my whole body x-rayed. I watched a small monitor where a cartoon man dressed in a similar blue hospital gown went through the motions. As instructed, I held my breath and froze in each position for two or three seconds before I received orders to change to another.

I had watched old vids where a human technician moved the patient before walking out of the room between x-rays. The patient was supposed to lay still in each position. That must have taken hours.

When the ordeal was over, the monitor said, "You may exit and change your clothes. Remember your comm."

I put on my comm and returned to the change room. There, I used my neck card to open the small locker. Sure enough, my clothes waited for me. Being a spy and a bit paranoid, I checked my cash and ID, but they were as I had left them.

I dressed and walked into the nearby small waiting room where my ex sat. The room had chairs and two sofas that might be comfortable for tall people like me and I wondered how short folks or children found them. Or adults born on Rossa. I guessed the hospital staff person who ordered the furniture came from Earth and was tall. The décor left a lot to be desired. Dark green upholstery on the furniture, light green walls, and speckled yellow vinyl plastic on the floor.

I must have read every damned magazine on a tablet attached to a metal cord while we waited for the results.

The junk people read these days.

Celebrities, sports, household items, cars, trucks, meds for every ailment, etc. What I wanted was news of the explosion. When I found the news button, I watched as reporters spoke in front of the screen. I clicked on the "subtitles" link and selected Amerish. I must have watched several reruns of the explosion. The cameras weren't close to Gate 4 so the explosion was in the background. Other than the big bang and the debris around the gate, I looked for Leanna and me. Sure enough, we were visible along one wall.

Damn.

This coverage would get to Earth too. I hoped no one recognized me. Being a spy means avoiding your fifteen minutes of fame in front of cameras.

My comm vibrated on my wrist. When I looked at it I saw it was a call from Ron Boscoe, fellow spy and best friend.

He asked, "How did your meeting with your daughter go?"

I showed Leanna my comm and she tagged Ron on hers. They chatted for several minutes. When she finished, she mouthed, "That was Ron. I told him about the explosion and that we're okay, minus your hearing."

Five minutes later, a guy from Radiology came in and spoke to Leanna. After he left, she turned to my face and spoke with exaggerated lip motions.

"X-rays showed no metal fragments. We can go."

I suspected the tech had said a lot more than that. My hearing couldn't return soon enough.

I appreciated how deaf people must feel when talkers don't tell them everything. It was like being a kid left out of adult conversation.

CHAPTER 4

I dropped my ex off in front of the Channel One building where she worked part-time. I stayed in the van while she walked through the glass double doors. The big "1" in a circle marked both doors. My staying existed from an old habit. Never abandon a woman until she was safe inside.

"Home."

When I climbed the steep stairs inside my apartment on the second floor above a real estate office, I found Tut, my robocat.

To my left I saw my living room, complete with a bar, and on its right was the doorway to my small office that overlooked Abby Lane. My gaze swept in a circle. On my right lay the dining room, kitchen, "guest" restroom, and a small storage room. Behind me on my right lay the guest bedroom, and on its right the main bedroom with its own bathroom. The hallway around the stairs joined the rooms.

Most rooms held prints of art. Mine was a functional home, not a decorative one. But I was a guy, so what could anyone expect?

Come to think of it, much more artwork rested on the walls of Ron's house. What art I remembered there came from photos of the buildings Tos designed. Tosten Carrel was gaining a reputation in Zor for his curved designs. The two gay men lived together. Were married, as a matter of fact.

Tut's head tilted to the left, showing me no one had visited my home in my absence. I still played back his recording at fast speed. Other than the changes of light through the windows from passing clouds, nothing moved. Tut, of course, stayed still on his cat bed at the top of the stairs. He'd appear to be sleeping and would move only when someone came up the stairs. Then he would act like a normal cat, stretching and yawning, but always keeping an eye on the human in front of him.

We spies are paranoid about being spied upon. So when I got to my office, I still checked my hidden cameras, figuring someone might have learned how to bypass a robocat's recordings.

My desk faced me with the back of my chair against the window overlooking Abby Lane. Since the office was a corner room, the wall on my right overlooked the parking lot. I used the white wall facing my desk as a monitor sometimes.

Next I reclined in my chair and checked my computer. One email message dated this morning caught my eye.

"We are as concerned about explosion at airport and mob action against aliens as you are. Maybe we can pool our resources."

The message was signed by someone named Deeter.

I avoided touching my keyboard lest I alter the message. I tagged my communications expert Zetto Teasely and explained.

I spoke into my com.

"Can't hear. My ears were damaged in the explosion at the airport. You must speak slowly so my comm can translate. Can you figure out who sent the email from Deeter?"

He already had the codes to see what I saw on the public access part of my computer.

"Give me a few minutes," he replied.

I got a cup of coffee from my kitchen and waited.

"Whoever he is, he's hid himself well," replied Zetto on my comm pad. "I can't trace him any closer than the Harper Hotel."

After thanking Zetto, I wondered about this new message. If it had not included the word "explosion," I would have deleted it. The Harper Hotel was right across the wide boulevard of Shoreline Drive from the mercon embassy.

Which brought forth memories of those two black aliens just before they went out of my line of sight with the mob descending on them.

I figured my spy boss on Earth, Acorn, would not send me new orders until another day had passed while he learned more of the incident at the airport. So I had a little time to investigate this email. Besides, from the pamphlet I picked up off the floor at the airport, it might relate to the bigger problem of the explosion.

I recorded a few notes on my afternoon's experiences, encrypted them, and sent them off to Earth. In another two hours, Acorn would receive it via the fast news couriers. Since the couriers had no humans aboard, they could speed up much faster and made the twenty-five light-year trip to or from Earth in less than two hours via the jump gates. In that way, the residents of Rossa and Earth kept in touch.

As I checked for any further emails, I read a new one.

"Let's talk. Harper Hotel, room 43. I have information you may not have."

Once again there appeared the signature of Deeter.

I doubted that was his real name. Maybe he'd recognized me standing next to the wall. The message had all the features of a trap.

Before I responded, I sent another message to Acorn to update him on this new development.

Next, I needed to find out how long I'd be unable to hear. I searched on the Net and learned the name "acoustic trauma." Left untreated, it might take two weeks for me to fully recover. Fortunately, we Bingers healed faster than normal so my hearing might return in a couple days.

Then I checked the news. The explosion at the Zor-Franken Airport captured most of the attention.

"Computer, use voice recognition. Display as subtext on the bottom of the screen."

The Humans Only organization denied responsibility for the explosion. Why would they when they were giving a talk close by and could get hurt themselves? That made sense.

But I wondered about that. They were on the other side of the security area when it happened. Far enough away to avoid injury.

And no one claimed responsibility for inciting the mob that attacked the mercons. From the photos as they were carried to ambulances on gurneys, the two aliens were dressed in white bandages that showed only a little of their dark skin. Poor guys must have taken quite a beating. Then I noticed there were five mercons in the hospital at the embassy. I saw only two being attacked, so why five? Then I read that three aliens working a small food shop in the airport took a beating too.

Since I had not paid much attention so far to the HO group I did more research. Besides, what else could I do with my time while I waited for my hearing to return?

HO opposed robots on Rossa. The face of Guy Coocher, head of HO, appeared on almost all the news reports. He was also elected to the House of Parliament from a rural district west of Zor. A short guy, he obviously didn't work out much. I deduced that from his large belly and double chin. He claimed he didn't trust doctors because they always tried to get him to exercise, lose weight, and have surgeries.

One quote of his showed up several times. "I'd rather be the way I am than have some frickin' doctor make me a damned hybrid."

It didn't take me long to form the opinion that most of HO presented a platform for hate groups. Hatred against robots. Hatred against hybrids, the people who had mechanical or computer-driven implants. Hatred against gays. Hatred against the medical profession. Hatred against Bingers. Hatred against the alien mercons and napes. You name it and they probably hated it. Except their own kind, of course.

The problems came when many folks in York believed the same things. Folks may have immigrated from Earth but that didn't mean they'd left behind their fears, prejudices, and biases. Oh no. That's what they considered part of their humanity.

I shook my head.

When will they learn?

Several articles mentioned explosions at medical facilities that provided robotic body parts and at the Nape Museum. Some even mentioned explosions at the University of Zor where classes taught tolerance of different species, including hybrid humans. In each case, the Humans Only organization denied responsibility. But the fingers did point.

The information on acoustic trauma suggested lots of sleep. When I found myself yawning, I went to my bedroom, pulled the covers back, and lay down.

I dreamt of running from an angry crowd of people waving guns and knives while carrying hate signs. Every time I looked at myself, I saw fingers pointing at my eyes. Just the fingers. No person attached. Naturally, I walked into a bog where my feet moved sluggishly and the crowd gained on me.

I woke from the little nap more exhausted than when I went into it. My body odor reeked of sweat, so I took a shower and put on fresh clothes.

Gotta do something else besides study HO and these damned mysterious messages from Deeter.

So I went to my living room and opened my comm to read a book about Daniel Snyder, spy-detective for the US Navy in New York City. Unfortunately, the novel focused on a terrorist group and my mind kept wandering back to HO. This group needed more watching.

I made coffee and out of habit, set a timer. Then I remembered I couldn't hear it so I checked it visually several times. During my first cup, I felt vibrations through the floor as someone came up the stairs.

I pulled my Snap out of its holster, crouched behind the dining table, and aimed the gun at the top of the stairs where a head might appear.

The first thing to come into view was a handgun. Then a head.

* * * * *

It was Ron Boscoe in a white long-sleeved shirt, blue jeans, and dark blue shoes. In both ears, he wore gold stud earrings.

Much relieved, I eased my gun up and stood. When he saw me, he pointed his Snap upwards.

After replacing my Snap in its holster, I saw his lips move so I shook my head and used my left hand to point to my ear on that side of my head.

He frowned and said something else as he put his gun in its holster. Since I couldn't hear him, I hunched my shoulders, turned my palms outward, and raised my eyebrows.

I strode past him to my bar and fixed us two tall drinks. I reclined in one easy chair and he in the other. While we sipped, I used the voice recognition on my comm to display our messages.

"I came over to check on you," he said.

Ron said he had not heard anything from me all day. Ever since my unfortunate experience of being kidnapped, he got anxious whenever I didn't communicate.

It turns out his new husband, Tos, had moved in with him. They had met on a spy op four years in Campbell on the island continent of Braco south of the equator. Apparently vid and audio conversations didn't do it. Or maybe it just increased their affection for each other.

From the smile on his face, I knew my buddy was now a much happier camper.

I swear Ron is as romantic as I am.

He may be gay but I trust him with my life. Had on several occasions, as a matter of fact. And vice versa.

"Need any food?" Ron asked by slowly mouthing the words.

I shook my head. "Stocked up two days ago."

"Anything else? I can go with you to talk with clerks if it would help."

"Can't think of anything," I replied.

I filled him in on what I experienced at the airport, but the parts about Leanna and Alena were highlights only, since I was not there when the two women chatted. Couldn't hear them if I were.

"You worry about your daughter, don't you?" he said via my comm.

I had to nod at that one.

In a period of awkward silence, he mouthed, "Let's watch the news."

We sipped our drinks and watched reruns on the explosion at the airport. Living through the experience again helped me see how bland the reporting was. The most interesting commentary focused on who did it. All fingers pointed to either the Humans Only organization or to RUFF, the Rossan United Freedom Fighters. Since HO had presented a rally at the same airport, and could have been injured in the blast, suspicion focused on RUFF.

Craig Horton, head of that organization asserted, "RUFF had nothing to do with this! We don't believe in terrorism."

I studied Horton's face.

Had RUFF changed from a passive posture to a more aggressive one?

A few of the folks on the news interviews wondered if the Bingers were behind the explosions.

One gal said, "By eliminating robots that might be used as soldiers against an invasion, the damned Bingers were weakening the planetary defenses of Rossa."

Of course, no one bothered to mention that the only aliens we knew about already lived on our planet—the mercons and the napes on Braco.

I shook my head. People react too easily with emotion without thinking it through.

My greatest concern was potential bigotry against Bingers. Having inherited half of my father's DNA, altered to include genes from the alien mercons, had marked me as a threat to those with much less education or tolerant thinking.

You'd think by now I'd get used to this. But having blood and a human finger on the front of my shirt brought the danger home. I could be next.

Maybe I should avoid crowds for a while.

According to the interviews on the news, most folks in the city were frightened of more explosions. Many immigrants had come here from places on Earth where bombs terrorized them. They thought coming to Rossa would be different.

I sighed at that one. People may change their address but they always bring their old customs and habits of thinking with them.

Terrorism works by instilling fear of the bully. If we give in to that fear, the bullies win.

CHAPTER 5

When I watched the telly on the third day after the explosion, I noticed everyone mumbled. Some of my hearing must have returned. The low frequencies came through but not the high ones.

Ron knocked on my door. He may have knocked on his earlier visit, but I couldn't have heard it.

The monitor showed he wore a blue sports jacket with the Zor Screechies logo, jeans, and a low-slung blue cap. He had on a yellow shirt with wide lapels, the current rage in men's fashions. The sports logo of the local baseball team showed the face view of a single screechie with its mouth open in a run from home to first base.

On Rossa, screechies were an indigenous species that looked like Earth's prehistoric velociraptors. Mean little animals, they stood two feet tall and were famous for the screeches they let out when a group of them attacked. I had been on a screechie hunt and will always remember the terror of facing a herd of them as they let out their screech and rushed toward my group of four hunters.

Ron climbed the stairs and mumbled something.

I waved him into my office. He closed the door and I scanned the room for bugs with my comm. For spies, it's always a good idea to scan every room you enter, even if you've checked it before.

Then I took the desk chair and Ron reclined in the guest one. After making sure the blinds were closed so no one could see the wall opposite my desk, I displayed Acorn's message on the wall.

"HO on Earth has become a terrorist group. They are behind explosions in public places, even in developed countries. Watch HO there closely. They could become a problem. If that happens, deal with it. My sources tell me HO on your world is planning a surprise that will upset anti-HO voters. Find out if you can. You decide what to do with the mysterious messages."

I turned my eyes upon Ron, who nodded his head and pursed his lips.

He queried, "What were the mysterious messages?"

I could not make out what he said and it was important to get it right. So I turned to my comm to see what he had said.

Then I displayed both messages from Deeter on my monitor and let Ron read them.

This deserved more thought. I settled back in my black leather office chair, placed my elbows on the arm rests, and pressed my fingers together under my nose.

My boss would see the same news broadcasts so he might ask for more information. Maybe it was time to infiltrate that organization.

But who could I ask?

Andy Warden kept busy with his hardware business. His Mourtan Security was at the top of his industry. Some say it came from his genius. He needed to be left alone as much as possible. Besides, he was too well known to become an undercover agent. All one had to do was check his name or photo against his website.

Vincent Stone worked as my software guru and would have a hard time passing. Besides, he was a hundred percent Binger. Leanna was his wife and my ex. She couldn't pretend to believe the HO line. Ron was half-Binger and gay and either could become a problem, so he wouldn't do.

Which left Zetto, my communications expert. Zetto lived alone and only wanted into my spy ring for the thrill of it. Being a hundred percent human, his DNA would allow him to pass HO inspection.

"We need to infiltrate HO. And Zetto appears to be our best chance."

Ron's words appeared on my comm. "Can't we turn anybody?"

"Do you know anyone in the HO organization? Got anyone in mind?"

He paused before shaking his head. "Just wonderin'. What about Deeter?"

"Find out what you can about Room 43 at Harper. Who rented it, et cetera."

"Vincent is better at that."

Might as well use the best brains I had on my team for hacking.

"You're right. Give it to him."

I opened my file on Zetto and studied it. My man lived alone in an apartment here in Zor and was an admitted introvert. He had no known girlfriends and considered himself asexual. As in not interested in sex.

For a moment, I wondered about that.

How could the man not enjoy the thrill of sex?

I thought his devotion to electronics came before that. He got more of a thrill tracing comm tags, a thrill that lasted days. Sex came a distance second.

He had taken part in special ops before and said he liked the sense of danger. That reminded me of Ron's getting a thrill out of B&E ops.

The real question remained. Could he go undercover in HO and pretend to be an alien hater?

* * * * *

Ash Getner sat at his desk behind the window in a gray business suit and white shirt.

He studied Alena's last name of Dani on the roster of those who had landed at the Zor-Franken Airport. He received a list, with photos, on all the people who came to York. With his two artificial legs, he was the half-man half-machine head of the York Security Agency, or YSA for short. He considered himself the master spy on York.

"Where have I seen that name before?"

Then it hit him.

"Ah ha! The spy."

To make sure no one could detect conversations by vibrations of the glass of the window, he had installed double panes with six random noise generators around the edges broadcasting into the space between the panes of the bullet proof glass.

He could change the blinds covering the window to allow light in whenever he wished to gaze out, but he seldom did that for fear that someone might take a shot at him through the window. To reduce the chance of that happening, he had the double panes offset so his image wouldn't coincide with what appeared on the outside. A shooter would miss.

The side walls had thick insulation to deaden the sounds of conversations. To reduce the chance of them being used by anyone who wished to eavesdrop, he had rented the adjacent rooms, one for storage and the other for a bathroom off his office. He didn't want to use a public restroom. Too risky.

He also used the space above and below his office for his pseudo-firm, Rossan Export-Imports, Ltd.

The walls of his office held photos of politicians and himself. He was most proud of the photo of the current Prime Minister Pierre Klava shaking hands with him in front of the flag of York. For security purposes, he preferred to use his monitor for displaying any images from the Net rather than use the wall opposite his desk. On that wall rested landscape images of York, something peaceful to calm his nerves. Being the head of YSA provided plenty of stress.

With a few right-eye blinks he went to the background file on Jake Dani but saw no reference to a daughter.

Could they be related?

Next he checked the interviews of witnesses to the explosion. Sure enough, there stood the name Ralph Snyder. But the photo yelled out at Getner. This was Jake Dani, the BIS spy. He had come to the airport to pick up his daughter Alena, accompanied her mother, Ebonta Snyder.

Getner leaned back in his tall black office chair.

Well, well, well. Has Fortune smiled on me or what?

He knew Jake was a spy for BIS but the real question became were this Ebonta Snyder and Alena Dani also spies? Since Alena was only twenty years old, she seemed too young.

He checked his databases for Ebonta Snyder but couldn't find anything. Puzzled, he checked her photo image from the airport records. In ten seconds, his computer found a match from his private files.

Well, well. If it isn't Leanna Stone.

With a few taps on his keyboard he brought up the information on her. She came to Rossa a year ago and was married to Vincent Stone. That name Getner knew. The artificial limb guy. Getner's own legs had been replaced just four years ago with a pair from Stone Industries. Naturally the head of YSA had used another name on his visit to Earth to have his legs upgraded to the newer model from Stone. Vincent Stone was a genius and got artificial limbs after his own legs became useless from a car accident.

Hmm, could Vincent Stone be a BIS agent too?

There was no quick way to find out. The display of information on his monitor gave no hint of Stone's being a Binger or part-Binger. Everybody in the Earth-based American CIA and the Rossan-based YSA knew of Berry Dani's recruitment of every Binger he could get his paws on into the Binger Intelligence Service. Getner wouldn't be surprised if Berry Dani resorted to blackmail. He knew he would in the same circumstances.

Getner spent the next fifteen minutes revising his plans on how to use this new information.

He made a mental note to ask for more money at his next session in front of the Senate Committee on Security. Conservative people were more willing to spend money on espionage and the military. He looked forward to reaping the rewards of his helping Coocher and HO.

Ash Getner was the son of Ashton Stephen "Steve" Getner, a wealthy industrialist from Cleveland in the State of Ohio in the United States on Earth. His mother, Mary Love Beadley was a hard driving woman. She had been a beauty in her youth, and the elder Getner and she had found each other to be complimentary in needs and resources. Her family had lots of money, which Steve used to launch his companies. A genius, Steve built an industry around making computer parts used by hundreds of millions. Steve and Mary had two children and when the young sister, Louella Getner developed brain cancer at age ten and died a year later, they focused their attention on young Ash.

Mary molded the personality of Ash, driving him on to succeed at any cost. She was a sociopath in that she couldn't feel others' emotional pain—physical or emotional.

Young Getner graduated from Yale summa cum laude and went directly into the American CIA. Being only five feet seven and a frail youth, he tried harder in everything. After one drunken party, he crashed his motorcycle and ended up with paralysis of both legs. His father poured money and time into helping his son become whole again.

Being full of ambition fueled by his parents, Ash made a decision that changed his life. Getting around on useless legs with the aid of half-crutches wouldn't do for a man with ambition, so Ash had elected to have his legs amputated and replaced with not two but four artificial ones. Since four would be noticed, he didn't bother to make them look like human legs and chose a metallic appearance. It was impossible to knock him over and he could flaunt his uniqueness. He had also chosen to have longer legs so he could tower over everyone else at seven feet.

Four legs soon became a handicap, however, since any presence in public drew attention, which the CIA frowned upon. So he returned to Stone Industries to get the newest model of two legs. But he had liked being taller than everyone else, so he chose legs that would put his height at six feet even.

When the York Security Agency formed in 2100, Ash migrated at the age of 38 to Rossa on a First Class ticket, courtesy of his wealthy parents. There he grew the agency.

Six years later, with a black budget rumored to be over fifty million sols, Ash preferred to keep a low profile. He rented space outside the federal building under the name of Rossan Exports-Imports, Ltd.

Today, Getner made the first of several moves to expand his empire. Then he called in his top field guy, Ben Portal.

* * * * *

Ben was a big man, six four and two hundred and sixty pounds. He worked out to keep in excellent shape. He spent another half hour each day at a shooting range and took pride in being the top field operations man on the planet. Or so said Getner on many occasions.

Ben entered the outer office of Rossan Imports-Exports.

Getner's assistant, Shirley, recognized him. "Please take a seat, sir. He'll be available shortly."

A scan showed he was the only one other than Shirley in the office. She wore a light blue top with long sleeves. He wished he could get a glimpse of her legs but they were hidden behind the front of her desk.

He took a chair without arms since he hated to squeeze between the arms of the others. Today he wore a gray suit jacket and slacks. His shirt was a pale yellow with wide lapels, which he thought would help him fit right in with current fashions.

She stared into space as she said, "Mr. Portal is here, sir."

Portal figured she was wearing an earpiece inside her ear cavity. Ten seconds later, she looked at him and pointed with her hand that he was to go through the double doors.

Ben rose to his feet and made his way into the inner office. Once inside, he first noticed the blinding light from the windows with his boss silhouetted against the light, standing his full height of six feet.

Getner motioned with his head that Portal was to sit.

Then his boss told him his newest assignment.

CHAPTER 6

At six o'clock I put the evening news on my office wall. Channel One often had something interesting. And having another chance to watch Sheila Fish was always a pleasure.

Sheila said on my screen, "We now take you to the Zor-Franken Airport."

The scene changed to show police preventing gawkers from getting closer. I recognized the mezzanine. The camera view zoomed in on a man and a woman hanging from an overhead rail. Signs of "Binger" hung from each of their necks. The reporter then showed the mug shot of another man in Satchel Prison who was killed because he was a suspected Binger. I didn't recognize any of them but all three had large skeletal frames.

When I read the subtitles, I thought of my brother Ken. When I was twelve and lived on Rossa, my brother was falsely arrested for theft and while he waited in jail, several bigots accused him of being a Binger and stabbed him to death.

* * * * *

I was in class when my Dad burst through door. He scanned the room and when he saw me, he rushed up to my desk and said, "Come on. We're going home."

I didn't know what to do. I looked down at my open book of algebra problems.

"Come on!" my Dad repeated. "No time for that now. We're going back to Cleveland."

My teacher riveted her eyes at both of us but didn't say a word.

Suddenly, my homework didn't seem so important. My Dad placed his hand on my arm and pulled. I ran to keep up with him as he pulled me by the arm from the classroom, down the hall, and out the front double doors to his car parked on the street outside. He opened the back seat door and shoved me in. I saw Mom in the front but no Ken, my older brother.

"Where's Kenny?"

That's when I saw Mom's face, scrunched up with squinted eyes full of tears.

When Dad got in the driver's seat, I yelled from the back seat, "Where's Kenny?"

"Your brother is dead," he yelled as he closed the door.

Soon the car lurched forward and raced down the street. We stopped only for traffic lights.

At one stop, I uttered, "Kenny is dead?"

Mom nodded and cried some more while burying her face in tissues. I looked to my father's face in the rear view mirror.

"Ken was murdered in jail," he said. "Some inmates called him a Binger and stabbed him. I found out an hour ago." Dad spoke with that don't-bother-me-with-questions voice. "Now be quiet. Fasten your seat belt."

I shut up and busied myself with my belt.

Dad replied, "I bought tickets for the airport. We're going home to pack."

When we got home, I went upstairs to the room I had shared with my brother in our small two-bedroom apartment. As I laid my only suitcase on my bed and pulled clothes from my dresser, I looked at Kenny's guitar hanging on the wall. Well did I remember his strumming it as he learned a new song, while studying the sheet music in front of him on the stand. I expected him to walk in the door.

"Hurry up!" yelled my Mom. "We're almost ready."

I finished as fast as my little fingers and hands would allow me. All I remembered was it was hot in Cleveland. So I packed some of my summer things. As I struggled to lift and carry the heavy case out of my room, my Dad came up to me and grabbed it. I followed him down the stairs while he lugged two suitcases. Mom followed me with two more.

My parents and I went out the front door. Dad put the cases in the boot of the car while Mom and I opened the side doors and got in.

My father drove faster than I've ever seen him. When we got to the Zor-Franken Airport, Mom held my hand tightly as we stood in three separate lines. One to drop off our luggage, another to walk single file through the scanner, and finally to stand in front of Gate 17.

"What about my toys?" I asked Mom.

"We'll get you some new ones when we get home."

Something told me to be quiet and not ask questions.

Sitting between Mom and Dad as we waited seemed like forever. I studied both their faces. Mom's was wet with tears. Dad had his jaw locked tight and stared ahead.

Finally, a man said, "Those with small children may board now." All three of us got out of our seats and went in the line. Dad went first and presented his comm to the guard and we rushed down the long hallway.

I sat next to Mom on the plane and Dad took another seat several rows behind us. At one point, I looked over the back of my seat and saw him. He waved and blew me a kiss. I returned the air-kiss.

"Fasten your seat belt, Jake," said Mom.

Hours later, we got off the plane and went inside the humongous terminal at Meda. We ate at a fast food place. I went into the gent's room with Dad and relieved myself.

Next we stood in line and entered a small room with lots of seats. I put on the seat belt when I saw Mom put on hers, she on my right and Dad on my left.

Fifteen minutes later, we rose up. And up. And up. Outside the few windows I saw clouds as we passed through them. The sky got dark and stars came out. The trip up the Space Elevator took two long hours.

When we slowed, I felt vertigo while my arms floated in front of me. I knew the feeling from my previous journey to Rossa. We were in weightlessness. I followed Dad as we used handrails to make our way forward in the small elevator car and down a hallway.

My parents were by my side all the way.

We finally entered a small cabin and Dad closed the door.

"Are we leaving Kenny?" I asked.

Dad looked at Mom, but she bowed her head and cried. He looked at me.

"Ken is dead. We won't see him again. You're all we got now. You've got to protect yourself."

I wanted to enjoy the feeling of weightlessness but Dad's words kept going through my head. "Ken is dead."

I grew up a little that day.

* * * * *

It took another twenty-four years before I came back to Rossa.

I transmitted a message to Acorn asking him if he knew of any Bingers here other than my team. He replied four hours later, keeping it short to frustrate decoders.

"You are only ones I know, other than twenty on Braco. How is your infiltration?"

Gancha Morentoss was half-Binger and ran the drug rackets in Zor, so I knew his information was out of date. I knew of the small group on the western edge of Braco who were trying to set up a colony for Bingers. I sent back information on Gancha but did not answer his question.

By Saturday, my hearing recovered to almost normal. I still had ringing in my ears but I could understand people when in face to face conversations. When I received a tag, I increased the incoming frequencies by a few decibels on my comm and it helped..

Being alone in my apartment for days on end stressed me out. I found myself watching the telly more than usual. Coverage of the explosion had passed off the top story. Even the Net showed less interest.

One segment showed MP Guy Coocher.

"We have to have government control of the jump technology. It's too important for the human race to be left in the control of corporations."

He meant Space Services, a conglomerate of major corporations. I wondered how the government would do any better.

The news from Earth got more alarming every day. Dale Avan, the lead male anchor from Channel Four reported, "Fighting continued in northern Pakistan after the seizure of the most of the Kashmir state by Indian troops."

Vids showed artillery firing in the background. Another showed drones engaging in aerial combat with each other in the mountains.

"IIAP, formed by the mergers of Iraq, Iran, Afghanistan, and Pakistan waged war with India with no end in sight." Vids showed the devastated ruins of an unidentified city. "Radiation levels remain high in Mumbai and Karachi. Fortunately, they were the only cities hit with nuclear weapons in this conflict."

The map changed.

"Meanwhile, the war in eastern Europe continues with Polish troops from NATO reported taking over Brest, Belarus from the Russian Third Army and German and Slovakian troops from NATO taking over Lviv, Ukraine from the Russian Fourth Army. Western Europe and the United States have increased their production of robot soldiers. There are no reports from Moscow. So far there is no progress in peace talks in Geneva."

A vid showed animated conversations across a large table and both sides shouted.

NATO robotic soldiers had a decided advantage on the battlefield. I suspected they came from America. The robots could not be destroyed by simple gunfire unless hit in a vital spot and were not afraid to charge human soldiers. The most effective strategy was guerrilla warfare, with humans planting bombs wherever robot soldiers traveled. When NATO robots met Russian robots, fighting was fierce.

I grew tired of news of war and changed to Channel One.

Vids of a herd of six-legged beasts appeared. Sheila Fish reported, "Carl Nelson of Campbell, on Braco, announced success in cross-breeding Earth cattle with bopums." A vid ran of several people in a restaurant, wearing the pointed hats typical of the inhabitants of Braco, with smiles on every face. Sheila continued, "Even though the new animals are sterile, meat from them appears to be a lot easier to chew."

Next came the weather report.

The weather gal said, "Up to six inches of snow are predicted in the eastern mountain regions." She stepped back to the left to reveal an overlay of York with the jet stream dipping down from the north. "We can expect cooler weather in the weeks ahead."

The scene changed to show rows of trees with electric heaters between the rows. Energy was cheap in York with so many solar panels covering public parking lots and most buildings.

"Fruit prices are expected to rise since the garnot and other crops may experience frost overnight."

Garnot was a cash crop grown in the temperate climates of York. The small brown-skinned fruit tasted between that of a plum and a peach.

After a sigh, I switched off the telly. This was another of the quiet spells. You'd think I'd get used to this by now. Being a spy meant long periods of relative calm, followed by maddening tension as we dealt with a crisis.

CHAPTER 7

Ron tagged me and wanted to chat on vid.

I said, "Computer, put Ron's vid on the wall." In less than a second, I saw Ron's face. From the background, I figured he was home. Today he dressed in green slacks with a yellow and green polo shirt. I had on brown slacks and jacket with a white shirt. Obviously, we didn't have the same mother at home. Grandmother yes, mother no.

"Leanna said you might be interested in getting another pet," he said. "A live one this time. She saw an advertisement for a moncat and sent me the link."

On my monitor, I clicked on Cyclopedia and looked up "moncat." They were bred from the DNA of a cat and a monkey. There was only one on Rossa, owned by a wealthy private zoon owner, and named Monk. The word "zoon" brought back painful memories of the time I was a slave. Zoons were the large agricultural areas, usually owned by one person and much like old plantations back on the home planet. I shook my head and focused on the rest of the article.

There were five of the critters back home on Earth. One lived in Berlin. Four resided in New York City where the experiments had started. All came from DNA experiments, not from cross-breeding and were male and sterile.

Guess that rules out Monk getting a girlfriend.

The Cyclopedia said, "Moncats eat nuts, fruits, and vegetables, but can also eat scraps of bopum or chicken."

The article recommended a special toilet that a moncat could use by himself. They showed a diagram of how to connect it to the main toilet's plumbing so it can be flushed. I shook my head.

What they won't think of next.

I clicked on the link to the Zor Animal Shelter.

"Wanted: a home for Monk. This cute little moncat is scheduled for euthanasia in a week. An owner who couldn't care for him anymore had dropped off Monk and the zoos wouldn't take him."

It showed a vid of their moncat eating peanuts with his two hands while resting on his side. Four legs showed. "Monk has two arms and four legs." I had to admit, his soft brown long fur looked smooth and very pettable. "Monk was trained to use a toilet designed for him." It got better as I read.

I watched the vid of Monk over and over again. Something about the littler critter appealed to me. But I wondered how he'd take to my robocat. I wasn't concerned about Tut. His programming could be adapted to living with a live cat. Or moncat, as it were. It was the live critter I wondered about.

The part in the ad about euthanasia pulled on me. Being part Binger myself, I understood why this small critter would be put to sleep. There must not be much demand for recognizable hybrids. Specially these days.

I look at Ron's face on the wall. Something must have shown in my face because he smiled.

"Shall we take a look at Monk?" he asked.

I pursed my lips and pressed my lips upward, while nodding.

What the hell?

* * * * *

Ron drove his little red sports car with the two seats. Today he had the top in place since the air was chilly and windy.

The first thing that caught my attention in the shelter was the smell. Not just the mixture of cats and dogs but of urine, feces, and food. You'd think this animal shelter would get more customers if they used stronger air recycling. Then again, maybe they kept the air foul so visitors might think they were rescuing an animal from all this.

"I came to see the moncat," I told the guy behind the desk.

He turned and yelled, "Carl, they want to see Monk."

Ron and I followed Carl through a door marked "Miscellaneous." The air had the aroma of birds. In one cage I saw a four-winger resting on a tree limb using its claws. These birds were native to Rossa and could hover and quickly change direction. Local farmers liked them because they ate a lot of reddoes. Their second set of wings was toward the rear and they had two legs with claws. Long and mean-looking claws too.

Reddoes were a scourge for farmers since they ate crops. These red lizard-like critters had six legs, as did most of the animals native to the planet. Six inches long and with a dark reddish skin, they preferred to eat bird eggs and rats, but would eat some crops. Their predators were four-wingers and screechies. And cats. The farmers who could afford cats often kept them as household pets to keep the reddo population down. Unfortunately, cats drew screechies, who would just as soon eat a cat—or a small child.

On Rossa, Nature ruled everywhere except the cities like Zor.

The caretaker led us to a far door and through it.

"We don't get many requests for moncats," he said.

I spotted Monk in one cage. When the little guy looked up into my eyes, something clicked in my heart. We were buddies. I had to get him out of here.

When the caretaker opened the cage and lifted Monk out, he came to my arms at once.

He was like a baby and a cat rolled into one. When I stroked his fur, he looked up at me with a grin on his little monkey face. What can I say? We bonded right there.

"I'll take him."

At the front desk, I used my credit card and paid three hundred and fifty sols to get Monk. Ron carried the accessories and placed them in the boot of his car. I held Monk inside my jacket to protect him from getting cold.

When I walked up the stairs inside my apartment, Tut greeted us. Monk screeched and held on tight to me.

"The two of you might as well get used to each other."

I parked both Monk and me in an easy chair in my living room. I petted Monk for a few minutes, while Ron put his toilet in the bathroom off my bedroom. It was not the kind that connected to the plumbing. So I would need to empty his waste bins.

I made a mental note to have a plumber in to attach it. I made another mental note to have one of my team build a similar toilet for use at the operations center for the times when Monk would stay there.

Monk stared at Tut the whole time. After five minutes, he got on the floor and sniffed my robocat, who looked like a regular cat. That was a key reason why I bought him. In five seconds, Monk turned his back to Tut. I guess he decided Tut wasn't a threat after all.

"Tut. Reprogram to allow Monk in this apartment. This is his home now."

Both eyes on Tut blinked twice at me in recognition of his revised programming.

Ron, Tut and Monk played chase around my apartment. Most of the time, Ron chased the two cats. Then Ron took a break to recline in the seat near mine while Monk chased Tut some more. Guess he wanted to show who was boss. Tut didn't mind, of course.

My comm vibrated with a message from Acorn, my spy boss on Earth.

"Ron, if you could tear yourself from playing with Monk long enough, you might as well hear this. It's from your dad."

Monk busied himself exploring the stuff in my home while we went to my front office.

CHAPTER 8

It was four days after I got the first message from Deeter when I got a third one.

"Were you affected by explosion? More may come. We need to talk. Harper Hotel, room 43."

The sender's persistence meant I couldn't ignore it. More might come. I brought up his two earlier messages.

The message continued, "We are as concerned about explosion at airport and mob action against aliens as you are. Maybe we can pool our resources."

And

"Let's talk. Harper Hotel, room 43. I have information you may not have."

Acorn had given me leeway and I felt the need to check into it.

But I didn't want to go alone. So I texted Ron to come to my home.

He must have been off work because he replied two minutes later.

"On my way."

I didn't have long to wait when I heard a knock on my door.

Ron came up and we went into my office. He closed the door behind him and I replayed Acorn's message on the white wall.

He nodded at the words "mysterious message."

"I suggest we reconnoiter Harper Hotel."

"Shall we take my car?" Ron asked.

"Might as well. Let's go to the parking lot in front of the prime minister's residence."

We both wore blue jeans, black gloves, and jackets. Today we needed the extra wear. The wind was chilly and brisk. I didn't look forward to snow as we approached the end of the year. Usually it fell in early November and stayed until April, making the air quite cold.

I swear Ron's car kept getting smaller every time I got in it.

"This your new pimp-mobile?"

"You bet. But don't worry, you're not my type."

"That's a relief." I had to lengthen the seat beat while I fastened myself in. "Last guy must have been small."

Ron grinned. "In that way, yes."

I had to chuckle at that one.

It took a half hour to get to the PM's house, despite our taking a loop to check on any tail. Traffic was light on this Saturday.

Ron walked sixty yards behind me to check on any tail on foot as we made our way on the sidewalk on Shoreline Drive to the Harper.

In the main lobby, I studied the directory. All the three-digit numbers started with a one or higher, so I figured ours was in the basement. When Ron entered the lobby and scratched his head, indicating that no one had tailed me, I went to the stairwell and descended. I walked as quietly as I could, alert for a trap as I walked, alone on the stairs.

I got to the basement level and looked toward the elevators.

In a minute, Ron came out of one and walked in my direction. I looked both ways, but no one else appeared in the basement. We examined the room numbers and when we came to 43, we put on gloves, drew our Snaps, and stood on both sides of the door. Ron on the left and me on the right. I knocked with my left hand and didn't get an answer. I turned the knob to find it locked. Out came my trusty tool. I inserted the tip into the lock and watched the lights. In forty-five seconds, the green light on my pick came on. I pulled the door open. Darkness greeted me.

Ron pulled out his flashlight and extended its telescoping flexible arm. He pushed the arm into the room while remaining outside it. The tip of the arm had a light and a camera. He studied his monitor as he maneuvered the arm to scan the room. The movement of the tip of the flashlight must have activated motion detectors in the room because the walls of the room lit up on their own.

Ron looked at me and said, "Nobody there."

Boxes lined three of the four walls. In the center was a ping-pong table, complete with four pairs of paddles and two white balls. Maybe hotel workers used the room for recreation.

Ron went in and searched the room for anything that transmitted a signal. In a minute he said, "Clear."

I entered and closed the door.

Where was Deeter?

One wall had a dark rug hanging over it with a pile of boxes in front of it.

"Strange place to hang a rug."

Ron nodded and removed boxes in front of it while I guarded him with my Snap. In seconds he cleared access, and I pulled the corner of the rug aside. There stood a door with a numeric keypad lock. Above the lock was a note on paper saying, "245613. Please destroy this note."

Ron held the rug back while I took an image of the note on my comm. I didn't want to press the keys on the keypad with my finger lest one of them contained something poisonous on a needle. I used the nozzle of my Snap to enter those digits and heard a click. With one gloved hand, I pulled the note from the door and tucked it in my jacket pocket.

Taking positions on both sides like before, I turned the knob and shoved the door open to see darkness again. As the door swung open, the walls of the room glowed with light. It was empty.

I went in while leaving the door open with the rug hanging over it. We might need a quick exit.

We searched the small room for any clues when I felt a sting on my neck. I spun around to see where it came from. Ron fell to the floor and whatever was in the sting made me woozy. I joined Ron on the floor.

* * * * *

When I came to, I found myself strapped in a small box car as it sped along a rail in a tunnel, my ankles and wrists in metallic straps. Every twenty feet an overhead light appeared as I moved along the rail. The way the tunnel turned frequently and went up and down, along with dizziness from the drug, I could not tell what compass direction I was headed in. The tunnel appeared to be a foot wider than the car I was in so it was a tight fit. No room for two-way traffic. The walls looked like they were made of rocks with lighter strips of dirt or sandstone.

I glanced at to my left wrist and did not find my comm. So I could not trace this route later from its positioning software. The tunnel walls might have made that impossible anyway if they acted like a Faraday cage, blocking all signals.

The turns were gentle but frequent. I doubt if I traveled more than two hundred feet in a straight line.

I heard a moan and twisted around just enough to glance over my shoulder. Ron sat behind me, also bound.

"Are you all right?"

"I dunno. My head is fuzzy," Ron replied.

We didn't have to wait long before our ride slowed and stopped.

Four small black creatures appeared on the walkway to my right. Bipedal like us. This close, I estimated their heights at around four feet tall. Black skin. I recognized them right away.

Mercons.

They all wore the same dark blue uniforms with shiny buttons. Definitely not field uniforms. More like formal attire. On the hip of one I spotted a holster with its gun. At least I thought it was a gun, although it was green from what I saw.

From my memory, I could see that all four were males. Very dark skin, almost black. They had evolved on a planet with little sunlight and most of that in the wavelengths that tanned skin. Their eyes were larger than those of humans and each had a prominent nose with nostrils more vertical than mine and longer and farther up from their mouths just shy of the bridge between their eyes.

The mercons were bipedal in that they walked on two legs and had two arms each, topped by a head. But the resemblance to humans ended there. From my study on the Net, I had learned the average male mercon stood four and half feet tall and weighed one hundred and twenty pounds. The females were smaller at just over four feet and one hundred and five pounds on average. They had very strong muscles for their size. So they looked almost like puffed up little people.

Both genders had five fingers on each hand, and five toes on each foot. So they were a smaller version of us.

Except for their hands. They had two opposing thumbs.

Three of the four in front of me stood at attention while the fourth studied us. The taller one appeared to be the officer in charge and held a small device in his hands. He looked at it and pressed a button. With a click, my metal bindings opened and receded into the arms of my chair.

I checked for my chest Snap and found it gone. I reached down and checked my right ankle. That smaller Snap was also missing. I turned to check on Ron. He shook his head at me.

He said, "No guns."

The head mercon guard pointed to my left, down the hallway. All four aliens moved in that direction, leaving Ron and me alone. I looked behind us at the tunnel. I saw four box cars with two empty ones behind the two we used. The lights in the tunnel were out and a black hole appeared to recede in the distance.

The taller mercon reappeared and waved us to follow.

"I think we're under the mercon embassy. It appears we've been invited."

"Some invite," said Ron as he rubbed the back of his neck.

We climbed out and followed the little fellas through a doorway and up a stairs. We walked up four flights before our guides split into two pairs, one pair on each side of a doorway.

The mercon in charge stood closest to the door and opened it. He entered a hallway with Ron and me in tow. The ceiling was low and I ducked to avoid scraping my head.

When we got to the end of that hallway, I saw another door. The mercon waited beside it and stood at attention. The look was universal.

When I approached him, he glanced at the knob and nodded.

I twisted the knob and opened the door.

"Come in," said a male mercon sitting at a fireside. He pointed to two comfortable looking high-back chairs, upholstered in red.

"Have seat. Jake. Ron."

I studied our host and recognized the ambassador himself. Gliituk. His gray hair extended down the sides of his small head and I could see part of his scalp on the top. The contrast of gray hair on black skin was stark, like crabgrass fighting to cover a black rock.

It must be a bitch to get old, when you see your body breaking down, things not working like they used to. It all happens so slowly, day by day, that you don't notice much. Then one day, you look, really look, at your hands and they're different, like an older persons. Like you used to see on your parent's hands. I examined my hands and saw wrinkles.

Oh dear. It has started.

Gliituk wore his trademark long robe of iridescent orange which flowed over his legs like water over a dam.

Wrinkles on his face on either side of his long vertical nose and his mouth verified he was old. From the news blurbs about him, I knew him to be around sixty-four of our Earth years old. I was fifty-one. Mercons aged faster and the average seldom got to sixty.

"I'm sorry for inconvenient way I brought you here," said Gliituk. "You didn't let me know you were coming."

CHAPTER 9

I took one chair and Ron the other. The fire cackled behind a black screen as I scanned the room. All the comforts of home. Which made me wonder how much of this setting was for our benefit, to make us feel comfortable.

Paintings or holographs of mercons lined the walls. One tall image showed a male in formal attire, complete with a crown and lots of jewels on his clothing. From where I sat I could not make out the name plate below him, not that I would have understood what it said.

The decorations in the room were mostly dark but the walls glowed as usual to give light. I glanced at the nearest of the two windows and saw a random wavy checkered pattern. So our host knew of sensors that could detect tiny vibrations from the voices inside that might reveal conversations. This might also mean his window faced an outside wall where such precautions might be necessary.

In the center of the room rested four chairs, two for Ron and me. Two others were closer to the floor. The ambassador sat in and I wondered who might join us. Each black leather chair had a tall back and two arm rests. The floor consisted of dark wood.

Gliituk raised his glass. "Care for wine? I assure you it is not drugged. I had it purchased for guests. Myself, I prefer local brew made from Durran fruit."

His voice was higher pitched than mine, but then again, his body was smaller.

I shook my head.

From his chair Ron added, "No, thanks."

"We scanned both of you before you were brought here. You don't have tracking devices. We'll give you your communicators and weapons back when you return to hotel."

"Why have we been brought here?" I asked.

"My apologies for mysterious way you were transported. But I did not want you to see path from hotel underground. Let's keep that our little secret, shall we?"

The ambassador spoke our language well, except for the definite articles, but then it would behoove him to learn how to speak the human tongue in his official role.

"You still haven't answered my question," I said.

Gliituk nodded and took a sip of dark liquid from his glass.

"I had DNA samples taken from both of you. Earlier this week you received invitation to Harper Hotel."

Ah, the mysterious Deeter.

"Why?" I asked.

"I had suspected you were Bingers, or at least descended from Bingers. DNA tests confirmed that. I had to be sure before I brought you here."

I had to ask. "Which begs the question again. Why are we here?"

Gliituk stared back into my eyes. "What I'm about to tell you should remain between us."

A deadly silence ensued. Ron followed my example by keeping quiet.

"Do I have your word on that?" asked the ambassador.

"I don't know yet. Depends on what I learn next," I replied.

"Fair enough." Gliituk picked up a tiny bell and rang it. In seconds, I heard a door open opposite the fireplace and a single dark-skinned male mercon entered wearing a long light green robe and matching pants. He took a chair to the right of the ambassador and appeared to be the same height. What I could see of his "shirt" was a dark red.

Gliituk pointed toward the new mercon. "This is Tettar, head of our intelligence service."

Tettar spoke. "I am concerned about the explosion at the airport. There will be many humans who will blame us mercons."

The ambassador said, "I think it is in your best interests as Bingers to join us in our investigation. Whatever fallout could land on you as well."

Tettar added, "What the ambassador is suggesting is that we pool our resources. It must be done carefully, of course. Any hint to the press of our cooperating could harm you as well as us. You are free to move about among the human population. We stand out too much. What we can offer is our resources, limited as they are."

I noticed the spy chief spoke better English than our host. I had to ask, "What resources?"

Tettar added, "We have several subcontractors who provide us with goods and services. We hear things now and then. If we can pool our networks, we both can learn more."

Gliituk took another sip of his wine. "Perhaps it would help if we told you little of history of our people. What I'm about to tell you must remain between us."

"Okay. We agree," I replied.

Gliituk paused before adding, "We've been to Rossa before. And to Earth."

Son of a bitch.

My mouth dropped.

I recovered from my shock and added, "In the negotiations of the Alcott-Gortush Treaty, the mercon representative said that mercons had never been to Rossa or to our home world."

Tettar said, "The negotiators spoke the truth—as they knew it."

Gliituk spoke next. "Like I said, perhaps it would help if we told you some of lore we have been able to retain over millennia. There is society among us—secret society—that has kept records going far back in history. Have you ever heard of Mattons?"

I shook my head.

Tettar leaned over to his left and whispered something in the ambassador's ear.

"Mattons have records of many cycles," added the ambassador. "By cycle, I mean one up and down in volatile tendency to expand and build, then break out in civil war and destroy everything. Survivors picked up pieces and created another cycle of development, followed by yet another civil war."

I asked, "How many cycles have there been?"

Gliituk took a gulp of wine before responding. "We don't know for sure. At least several hundred. Our records go back only hundred thousand years. After each collapse, both skolanders and bemanders falsely believed that by destroying all history records they could prevent another collapse."

"Skolanders? Bemanders?" I asked.

Gliituk nodded to Tettar, who explained. "The skolanders are the more conservative political group. Both the ambassador and I are skolanders. The bemanders are the more liberal party."

"And which party is Picka'tor?" I asked.

"A skolander," replied Tettar. "He's also the head of the Mattons."

"Are both of you Mattons?" I asked.

The ambassador nodded.

From the Net, I had learned Picka'tor was the current head of the mercon government on Ensam. After the Alcott-

Gortush Treaty, the mercons remaining after the nuclear holocaust on Durr numbered fifty thousand. They approached the United Earth Federation to negotiate a place to live. The dessert island continent of Braco in the southern hemisphere had only a few hundred humans living on the eastern side of the island. They were moved elsewhere and the mercons moved in.

Gliituk added, "That is something we hope you will keep to yourself. If bemanders learned we three were Mattons, there could be another uproar, maybe even collapse of our government. It could mean civil war. Not all mercons are happy with treaty. Few still live on Triina, moon orbiting Durr. Conditions are touchy right now among us. It wouldn't take much to set off another war between us. That's major reason why you have to keep this secret."

I glanced at Ron who took in a deep breath and let it out slowly, while he looked at me with raised eyebrows. My sentiments exactly.

"You've given us a lot to digest. I must discuss this with my team and my boss back on Earth."

"So you report to the CIA?" asked Tettar.

"Not exactly." I had to smile. Apparently there were holes in their intelligence sources. Either that or they were playing with me to see what they could learn.

I debated what I should reveal but thought telling even a little about Ron and me would make for more cooperation. At least as long as we were held here. You gotta be nice when you're captured in the hope of gaining release.

"No. I report to the head of the Binger Intelligence Service."

What the hell. He'd been open with me. Might as well go all the way.

"I'm only its head here on Rossa. You mentioned that mercons had visited Rossa and even Earth."

Gliituk glanced at Tettar. Maybe my admitting I was head of BIS was news to them or was just confirmed. From their faces I could not be sure. Dang. I wish I knew more about their expressions.

Gliituk spoke next. "During high point in one cycle we had space travel and visited Earth. At that time, we believed we were First Race of intelligent people in our galaxy. That was conceit since we had explored only tiny fraction of galaxy. Mercons visited Earth about three hundred thousand years ago but saw only primitive animals. No technology.

"We left observation post that reported on a powerful volcano in Indonesia. We thought primitive bipedal creatures would be wiped out. After six revolutions around your local stellar object, cloud cover parted enough to show lots of snow covering planet. Over time, oceans thawed and ice broke up. We were," he turned toward Tettar, "what's the word?"

"Happy," said Tettar.

"Yes, happy to find some of our ancestors still alive.

"A group of scientists of Mattons Society inseminated some of early bipedal creatures to alter their DNA. Perhaps your Dr. Bing would have been a great student of theirs. These early experiments later became modern humans."

Ah, so he knew of Dr. Bing. Wait a minute! What did he say? That humans were descended from mercons?

"During later up cycle, we developed space travel again and visited Rossa. We tried to inseminate napes with fragments of our DNA to stimulate their development. Virus later altered that DNA to keep them from evolving as fast as humans. So we have been keeping eye on humans for long time."

"Off and on," I added.

"Agreed. For tens of thousands of years, no mercons visited Earth or Rossa. We experienced many cycles. Humanity and napes continued to evolve. Later, some robot space ships from your Earth encountered some of our military outposts. Durr-Earth war resulted. Rest is history."

Like most mercons, he preferred to call the war with his home planet first.

Tettar spoke, "We were very surprised to see how well the humans fought. Some Mattons suspect humans are going to succeed better than we will. Especially the Bingers. You can imagine our surprise when we learned that humans had established a colony on Rossa."

"Humans and mercons have much to learn from each other," said Gliituk.

"Like I said," I added. "You've given us a lot to think about."

"We understand. There is no hurry," said Gliituk. "Please do me honor of keeping what we've told you away from your government and press."

I nodded. "We can do that for a while. Can we go now?"

The two mercons exchanged looks and Gliituk answered, "Yes. Tettar will accompany you to tunnel. Your communicators and weapons are in room where you left them in box. Tettar will give you password."

All four of us stood and Gliituk added, "I'm glad we had this little talk. Perhaps we can avoid another war."

With total disaster for the mercons. Humans now numbered in the billions, mostly on the home planet. To the best of my knowledge, after their nuclear holocaust, their population came to maybe fifty thousand. During the war, humans outnumbered the residents of Durr but now the ratio was much, much higher. Another war might exterminate the remaining mercons. Poof. No more mercons.

I extended my right hand and met Gliituk's. His skin was warm and dry. Our upper thumbs crossed, but I felt something odd as his lower "thumb" wrapped around my four fingers.

Next I shook with Tettar. I saw Ron shake hands with Tettar and Gliituk. Tettar then walked out the door we came in.

We followed him and when we got to the tunnel, Tettar added, "Please give some thought to our request. It will mean a lot to us. The password to the box with your weapons is Rossa21."

We shook hands again. I climbed down into the front seat as Ron took the second car. The rail cars now faced in the opposite direction.

Soon after we sat, the rail cars moved. At least we could travel the rail without our limbs anchored.

When we stopped, a panel slid open to show an empty room. We got out. In one corner of the room rested a gray box with a keypad.

I pressed the pad with the password from Tettar and heard a click. I pried open the box to see our comms and weapons. We put them on and went through the door with the rug over it.

I said, "The questions are, why did the mercon ambassador provide so much information and ask us to help him?"

"They are frightened of the rumors that the mercons are behind the explosion at the airport."

"Could be. And maybe this is a chance to enlarge their network among humans by getting us to work for them. Which means I have to find a way to get them to work for us."

Ron said, "That's why you get paid the big bucks."

"Will you cut that out?" As the son of my boss, Ron seldom missed a chance to show his jealousy of my having been selected station chief on Rossa over him.

* * * * *

Ben Portal listened to the recording from his eavesdropping device embedded in the rug in the small room next door. "So they went to the mercon embassy and met the ambassador. Ash will love this."

He waited for ten minutes after Jake and Ron passed by his room 41 in the basement before he slipped out.

CHAPTER 10

Zanuck, Gliituk's personal assistant, came into the room wearing a purple gown that flowed onto the floor behind her. On her head rested a purple double-pointed hat in the same color preferred by her husband, Picka'tor. She raised her head and sniffed several times. Her larger than human nostrils wavered as she tested the air. In the mercon language, she said, "Humans have been here."

Gliituk smiled. He had noticed their odor too, but as an ambassador he avoided commenting on it while they were here. He responded in his native tongue, "Right, as usual. If you will excuse us for a few minutes, we have issues to discuss."

After Zanuck closed the door behind her, Tettar said, "She will report that to her husband, you know."

"Of course. That's why we need to talk about our little meeting and I need to send a report to Picka'tor first."

He reached over to a black box on his desk and pressed a button.

"Gondaroo, remove the two tall guest chairs in my office and have them cleaned."

He leaned back in his chair, relieved that this new position helped with the pain. For the ambassador had nyteen, a condition most humans would describe as spinal arthritis. Gliituk didn't know how much longer he'd live.

"What do you think our two humans will do next?"

Tettar replied, "It's difficult to tell. I wish I knew more about human expressions and body language, but I think they'll help us."

"Do you think they suspect our other motives?"

"No. I don't think so."

"What can you tell me about the bemanders on Ensam?"

He referred to the eastern part of Braco his fellow mercons called their new home. A tall mountain range on the west coast of Braco prevented rain clouds from getting to the desert in the middle of the island. In the east, another smaller and older mountain range rose from the desert. Called the Merco Mountains, it separated the human side from Ensam, home of those mercons who managed to escape the radiation on Durr. On the western side of the Merco Mountains lay Braco Lake, fed by the Sabine River. The lake provided much of the drinking water for Ensam, pumped over the Merco Mountains.

Very few mercons settled in the mountains because it was too cold. Normal temperatures there were forty to sixty degrees cooler than on the desert. The temperatures on Ensam were more moderate.

The largest city in Ensam was Stavros, at the eastern end of the Braco Railroad. That rail line went from the western end of the island in the village of Telmot, where some humans and Bingers lived, through Campbell where only humans lived.

Tettar replied, "Near as I can tell, the bemanders have stockpiled personal weapons. Nothing major that would be detected by the roving human inspectors. There is a lot of resentment about the Gortush-Alcott Treaty."

"Have they heard about the explosion?"

"Most have. They're frightened that the humans may act against us."

Gliituk said, "Which is one more reason why we need to connect with humans."

He took another sip of his wine and stared at his chief of intelligence.

"What about our own weapons?"

Tettar grinned in return.

* * * * *

After he dropped me at my apartment, Ron made off to the house he shared with Tosten.

When I got inside, my robocat Tut rested at the top of the stairs. His head tilted to the left indicating no one had entered my place in my absence. Monk was nowhere in sight. Probably sleeping on my bed.

The first thing I usually do when returning home is scan my apartment for any bugs. Tut indicated I had no visitors. So I went first to my kitchen and ordered my AutoCook to make coffee. With that in hand, I went into my office, where I repeated my scan for eavesdroppers. We spies can be so paranoid.

I tagged my team for a virtual meeting. I gave a report on our meeting with the mercon ambassador and their head of intelligence, Tettar. Despite Gliituk's request to keep everything as a secret, I told my team all we had heard. Since Tettar was a spy chief himself, I thought he would understand.

Leanna inquired of Gliituk's and Tettar's reactions but I expected that from my favorite profiler.

Her hubby Vincent popped a question, "So, if the mercons go through cycles of development and bust, they are now in another cycle of development."

I said, "Which means we have to watch them closely to see what weapons they develop down on Ensam."

"Which they surely will," contributed Vincent.

Zetto asked the million sol question. "What do we know about their weapons development?"

"Absolutely nothing," I replied. "I figure we'd better help them so we can get some leverage into finding out the answer to that question."

Andy Warden had nothing to add. The others nodded in their sections of my wall.

I added, "Gliituk is excited that maybe they've broken their pattern of cycles this time. Only two previous cycles had space travel, the one that seeded humans and the one that seeded the napes. But the human one happened so long ago they had few records with any details."

Leave it up to Vincent, possibly the smartest man on my team, to put his finger on the key issue. "If they develop weapons down there, and that leaks out, the human population on Rossa will go berserk."

I added, "And could go on another witch hunt for Bingers."

Leanna asked me, "Have you told you-know-who?"

"He's next," I replied, knowing she referred to Acorn.

Vincent brought up an old problem. "I hate to mention this now, but having the mercons here on Rossa presents an opportunity for the Binger community."

Ron said, "What kind?"

Vincent replied, "We have always wanted a place to call our own. Maybe a piece of Braco could be it."

Ever since the persecution of Bingers on Earth there had been talk of finding a place where Bingers could migrate to and call their own. Where they could be free of persecution, where they would not have to hide their DNA or their extra strength. A place they could call Home.

I brought up the major objection as I saw it. "You think the residents of Braco would be willing to give up part of their island for Bingers? With Bingers on the western side and mercons to the east, they might not like being in the middle of such a sandwich."

Ron was quick to add. "Gliituk and Tettar feel more comfortable with us than most non-Binger humans. Remember what they said about visiting Earth long ago? I think they feel humans are their descendants, or at least cousins of a sort."

No one said anything for a minute. I could tell the idea had appeal.

CHAPTER 11

After I closed the joint session on my wall, I pondered Acorn's recent request. Then I got a surprise tag.

I flared my nostrils to answer. Those who had control over their nasal muscles could open a comm call with such action. Otherwise, they had to tap one nostril to open the tag and two to close.

"Hi Jake. Gancha Morentoss here."

Whoa!

I had dated Gancha before I met Leanna. She and I had broken up because I wanted a longer term relationship and she wanted her freedom. Now that she was on Rossa, she wanted to start up again.

After the death of my current flame, Gancha and I had dinner at the Top of the Town in the penthouse of the Embassy Suites. She had inherited the criminal empire of James Venisio and, since she had a small fortune now, paid for the meal.

I had to hand it to her. She was a half-Binger like me and one helluva tough woman. She could handle guns well and kept in shape. Two big pluses.

During our chitchat over a meal, she had asked if I was a spy. Every Binger knew that my uncle tried to recruit every Binger. I had toyed with idea of inviting her to join my BIS team but had avoided telling her too much.

We shared a goodnight kiss before I walked out of Venisio's house. Correction, her house now. Another correction. It was a terrific kiss.

"What do you want? I'm kinda busy," I replied. Not really but the habit of lying was hard for this spy to break.

"I moved out of the large house in Beverly Hills into a smaller one in Corey. Sold the big house too, along with much of his old artwork. The rest I gave away to the Zor Museum of Art."

I remembered last year when the voters in the unincorporated area elected to start a new city as a suburb of Zor.

"Still head of an empire?"

"No. Well, sorta. I sold all but the drugs and gambling. Those two provide a rich source of income. Which brings me to my point. Care to eat out? My treat. I have oodles of money now. You name the place. We'll go."

I thought of Alena's being on Rossa. At the moment, things were quiet.

One thing for sure, I still wasn't convinced that I should let Gancha back into my life.

"I don't know, Gancha."

"I have a proposition for you I don't think you'll be able to reject."

"If you're thinking of marriage, that's out."

"Nope," she replied. "That's not it."

What the hell?

* * * * *

Since he came late, Zetto Teasely sat in one of the dark brown metal folding chairs near the back of the community center hall. The room was cool so he was glad he'd kept on his brown jacket and thicker brown slacks over his white short-sleeved polo shirt.

Stenton Duran stood on the stage dressed in dark blue. He must have been wearing one of those lapel microphones because Zetto could hear him clearly across the fifty yards between them, despite the hundreds of people in the room. He located eight black speaker boxes hanging from the walls.

Duran said, "And now let's hear from our founder, the honorable Guy Coocher!" He clapped his hands and everyone in the audience followed his example.

Coocher came up to the center of the stage, also dressed in dark blue. As the clapping diminished, he continued. "Thank you for your warm greeting."

Zetto heard him speak with power, like old Texan money, in a slight southern drawl worn down by years of addressing crowds.

Coocher continued. "We came to Rossa to get away from the sameness of Earth. We came here to get away from the damned aliens and the robots. We came here to get away from half-humans, half-robots. Let us keep our humanity. It's precious."

He paused before adding, "We deserve a place to call our own. We deserve Rossa to be free of robots and aliens!"

Zetto found his view blocked as many of the guys in front of him stood to give Coocher a standing ovation. He pulled himself up and joined in.

He scanned the crowd. Being six foot five helped. Three men along the walls studied the crowd and did not join in the clapping. One of them scanned the crowd and focused on him. Thinking they might be scouts, Zetto raised the rate of his clapping. He cupped his hands over his mouth so his voice would carry farther and cheered.

"You tell 'em!"

He returned to his seat when the rest of the audience sat and listened to Coocher's litany of hatred toward hybrids, aliens, and Bingers. At the mention of Bingers, Zetto nodded in agreement and raised one clenched fist with a thumb up as if to say, "Right!"

The speeches took another half hour, and he followed the crowd as they exited the hall.

He stood in line at the buffet to pick up a paper plate and grab some mushrooms, meatballs, vegetables, and BBQ beans. He tasted one of the meatballs. Sure enough, it was bopum and tough to chew. The flavor of the sauce was good though and he managed.

He grabbed a gray metal folding chair at a card table at the edge of the huge room. The other three men sitting there enjoyed the hors d'oeuvres. The noise level was high, though. Zetto looked around. Cement walls and floors, metal doors, flat metal pieces in the ceiling. Nobody said much and kept busy eating. As he finished and leaned back, someone tapped his shoulder.

Two men in gray suits stood next to him. One said, "Can we speak to you for a minute?"

He nodded to his left and Zetto left his plate to follow them.

The guy went into a small room and his partner closed the door behind him. The noise level dropped.

"We noticed you're new here," said the leader. He extended his right hand. "I'm Jan Teller." Jan had a belly on him and nodded to his right. "And this is Bob Backhurst."

"Yates Smythe," Zetto volunteered.

"Like what you hear?" asked Jan.

"Yeah! That guy Coocher's right on," replied Zetto.

"We agree. Is there anything you liked the most about what he had to say?"

"The part about the damned Bingers."

"Oh? And why's that?" asked Jan.

"I got passed over for a promotion once. I think the man who got it was a Binger."

Jan looked at his partner and back to Zetto. "Is that so?"

"Yeah. I hate those bastards."

"Why'd you think he was a Binger?"

"Big sucker. Broad shoulders. Stood about here," Zetto raised one hand flat out at the height of his nose. "They don't make them that big on Rossa."

"You're pretty tall yourself. Come from Earth?"

"Yep. Came as a teenager with my parents. Dad and Mom had to get away from all those robots and such. Hated to leave my friends behind but family is important."

Jan nodded. "You got that right. May I ask what you do for a living?"

"I repair computers," Zetto replied and grinned. "But what I really like is communications."

Jan looked at Bob.

"Yates, we're having a private meeting in a couple days. Care to join us?"

"Sure!" replied Zetto with lit up eyes.

An hour later, he left the parking lot.

Thanks for the practice sessions, Jake.

* * * * *

Donned in casual clothes like most students these day, Alena Dani had on maroon slacks and a white T-shirt with the words "I love my attitude problem" in black letters and with a heart in place of the word "love." Alena was an exceptional student and liked being thought of as "different."

After her biology class with Dr. Albert K. Albert, she approached the professor at his desk next to the lecture table. On the table lay an assortment of the artifacts he had brought back with him from Braco when he visited the nape reservation. A club, a spear, a knife, two baskets, a pouch made of bopum leather, and finally, three nape dolls, complete with long black hair. He wore a white lab coat and under it, gray slacks and a white shirt.

"Dr. Albert, do you remember me?"

He looked up and adjusted his glasses. "Of course. You're Ms. Dani, aren't you? The one who's always asking questions?"

"I hope you don't mind my asking them."

"Of course not! It shows you have an interest in xenobiology."

"I'm pursing my Ph. D. in xenoanthropology."

His face grew more serious. "Then I'll be your advisor. That's my specialty. I came to Rossa ten years ago to study the napes. I find them very fascinating."

He waited while she paused. "Is there something else you want to ask me?"

"Yes, there is. The girls in my dorm are only interested in boys and parties. I find it hard to study when they're around. What do you recommend I do?"

"My wife Francine and I have a three bedroom house. I use one bedroom for my home office and the basement for my lab. I'll ask her if she's interested in your staying with us."

"Would you?" Alena's eyes lit up. "That would be great!"

She savored the chance to ask him questions. Maybe she could wiggle an invitation to visit the napes on Braco on one of his expeditions.

That would be so cool!

CHAPTER 12

After alerting Ron and Zetto to my dinners date with Gancha, I put on my dark blue outfit of slacks, business jacket, and shoes. And a pink shirt. Any guy who commented on my attire risked a busted nose. I wouldn't hit a woman.

Naturally I put on both Snaps. I'd feel naked without them. The shoulder holster fit snugly under my left arm and the smaller Snap on my right ankle was light.

I pulled up at the gate of the new home of Gancha, a residential house in the suburb of Corey, off Indio Road and east of Ambassador Boulevard. I presented my ID, received a wave, and advanced into the lush community. Everywhere I turned were trees. The dark orange flowers on the trees informed me they were native to this planet.

Her house looked expensive, standing two stories tall and surrounded by a wall of gray stone masonry.

After parking in her driveway, I walked up her cement steps and rang the front door bell. In a minute, the door opened to show a dark-skinned woman in a soft dress with diagonal stripes of purple and yellow. Gancha wore a dark purple knitted shawl over her shoulders. Her hair was wavy and black. She must have remembered how I liked to caress her hair. She wore low heeled shoes. Maybe she didn't want to be taller than me.

I steered up Indio Road and made a left on North Central Park Avenue.

She said, "I thought a lot of my future. I've sold the big old house of my grandfather's. Do you like my new place?"

"The outside looks very nice," I replied.

"Maybe I'll get a chance to show you the insides later."

Maybe she had more in mind.

We chatted little as I drove to the Embassy Suites. You could cut the tension in the air. Perhaps neither of us was willing to say any words, lest we regret them. I know I felt that way.

Once we got to the Top of the Town, our hostess led the way to a booth and I sat opposite Gancha. To my left I saw the lights of the city, including the red lights going north over the dark patch of the Oreo River and the brighter white lights going south. Soft piano music played in the background. Perfect for an easy night out with a date.

She had a glass of Chardonnette, the Rossan equivalent of Chardonnay. I had Merlotte, the Rossan equivalent of Merlot. She ordered lobster. It was expensive since they hadn't figured out a way yet to get the crustaceans to grow in the waters on Rossa. They had to be transported live from Earth. Guess she still felt flush with her wealth.

I had sirloin tip, made with real cattle from Earth. I wasn't ready to try the new bopum yet, despite its claim of being easier to chew than ever before.

"You look gorgeous tonight," I said as I lifted my glass of wine.

She brought hers to mine and we touched them. I read someplace that the old custom of clicking glasses came from the Norse who thought that by doing so they would chase away the evil spirits in their beer mugs. Maybe that was an excuse they made up for more drinking.

It's funny how we retain habits way past their usefulness.

"You look good, too," she replied as she grinned over the top of her glass.

After she rested hers on the white tablecloth, her head tilted down. "I've been doing a lot of thinking. I miss my old life back on the home planet. All this wealth," she raised her head and waved her hand, "came as a surprise. Out of the blue, so to speak."

"You'll get settled in. Give it some time."

She shook her head and sipped her wine. "Don't think so. I sold the big house and a lot of the stuff in it and I divested myself of some of my grandfather's empire. I retained the gambling and drugs. Like I said, they provide easy income. On the legit side, I've retained a few small businesses and my share of Channel One. Thought that might come in useful someday."

She stared at her glass of wine. "What I mean to say is, I want to get back into some action." She lifted her gaze to look me in the eyes. "I want to join your spy ring."

Whoa.

Not only had I never admitted being a spy, I wasn't sure she could fit in. She had good qualities though. Fast thinking on her feet. Kept in physical shape. Was used to breaking into places. And she was a Binger, so she could carry a lot of stuff.

I must have been lost in thought because I didn't notice the silence until our waitress brought our food. That kept us busy for a few minutes.

"What do you think?" she asked when we were alone again. "I know you're a spy. I've kept that to myself, by the way. Good ol' Berry tries to recruit every..." she paused and looked around, "one of us."

It was no use pretending any longer. I nodded. "You're right. But having you on board could be a problem."

"So? I could be a consultant. You could use me on your special operations. That's what I really want anyway. Besides, I'm going nuts being rich with nothing to do."

I cut off a piece of my steak.

"I can't go back to Earth," she said. "Jimmy Dice got off with only two years. He was my former boss."

She put on her plastic bib to protect her dress and used her strong hands to break open one claw of her entrée. As she slid out the pink meat inside, she continued.

"That means he plea bargained. Maybe he gave up information on me to get his own sentence reduced. After all, I wasn't around anymore. And since York has an extradition treaty with the USA, if the cops here ever learned of the warrant, I could be deported back to Earth. That means a possible death sentence, or at least decades in a cage." She paused and looked in my eyes.

"I hate cages. Been there, done that. It's not for me. I'd rather die."

I nodded and cut and placed another piece of my steak in my mouth.

"But I miss the action," she continued, "The thrill of risk."

She inserted a piece of the pink meat in her mouth and closed her eyes while chewing. When she swallowed, she said, "I haven't had lobster in a long time. Too long."

Her next words came with a small problem.

"Unipol has a warrant waiting for me. So I can't travel to Earth. That means no spy school on the home planet."

That also meant no spy training other than what we could provide here.

I put a piece of my beef in my mouth and savored the flavor. There's nothing like the real thing. Next came a sip of Merlotte to wash it down.

She reached across the table and put her right hand on top of my left. "There's a bonus in it for you."

We both knew what that meant.

"I'm still not sure," I said.

She withdrew her hand.

Was that a sign or what?

"I'll have to discuss this with my team."

"You don't make those decisions by yourself?" she asked.

That one I preferred not to answer.

She dug out lobster meat with her tiny fork.

We spent the next hour going over old memories, aided by the lubrication of the wine.

Time glosses over the bad memories and turns the good ones into gold. We talked about our walks on the piers, the national parks, and the walks arm-in-arm from one street lamp to another.

We laughed at being surprised by a street gang on one of our walks. They popped into view brandishing knives. But I had time to pull my gun out. She searched in her purse and pulled out a .38 Special. We pointed them at the gang leader, whose eyes opened so wide we could see the whites on his dark face. It was obvious he had not expected our response. He turned and ran away, followed by his three compatriots.

We laughed afterwards. Recalling the memory brought grins to both of us.

When the waitress came for our dessert orders, we both declined. Then the waitress pulled out her digital pad and handed it to me. The bill. I handed it over to Gancha.

She put her comm next to it, she scribbled her name on its surface, and paid for the meal with her credit card.

I figured she had one of those black cards with no credit limit.

We moved out of the booth and she raised her shawl to cover her shoulders as we walked out into the cool air.

We didn't say much as I drove her home. Of course, her hand in mine said a lot. From time to time, she squeezed mine.

When we arrived at her gate, the guard let us in right away. Apparently, Gancha's comm had broadcast her ID to the computer there.

I stopped in her driveway with its arch of red brick. She stayed in the car while I went around and opened her door.

Was that a deliberate show of leg?

She stood and came close to me.

"Fraternizing with the boss is not a good idea," I said with a smile.

She grinned. "I'm a woman with active hormones. You're a good looking guy. What could be more natural?"

She had a point. Besides, it had been too long for me.

We entered her home with my hand on her waist.

The side door opened to the kitchen. Off to my right was a small pantry where one door stood open to show rows of canned goods and a few boxes.

Her kitchen had a black-topped island. The whole ambiance yelled luxury and convenience. A small family room stood beyond it. On the right was a short hallway. As I looked down it, I could see stairs on the left. To the right was an immense formal dining room, complete with high-back chairs upholstered in black leather and a long rectangular table. A chandelier hung above the table. The only things missing were glass-doored shelves with stacks of dishes and it would have been a perfect old English dining room.

Gancha came up to me as I felt her body on my hip. She looked up into my eyes as she pressed her body to mine. Her eyes stared at my mouth.

What a signal.

I took the hint, wrapped my arms around her, and pressed my lips on hers.

That led to one thing after another. She was right. This was natural. Dogs do it. Bees do it. And we humans love to do it too.

Later, in bed, she looked into my eyes. "I'm serious, Jake. I'm ready."

For what she didn't say and I wasn't about to ask her to clarify.

So I kissed her again.

The second time was even better. We both knew we wanted it and we took it.

* * * * *

On my way home the next day, I debated about dating Gancha.

Had she really changed?

People don't change that easily unless driven by powerful forces. Like fear of death. She said she was afraid of being arrested and sent back to Earth to face certain execution or spending time in a cage, both of which she hated.

Could that be enough to force her to change?

It's amazing how facing death can clear your priorities.

She was also getting older and had expressed an interest in having a baby by me. That's a lot of change. Could she settle down to raise a child?

For that matter, could I?

And what kind of child would come of our joining? Being both half-Bingers, it was likely the boy or girl would be a half-Binger. It could be a normal child or a full Binger. Which meant a lifetime of discrimination, right out of the womb.

But I had survived and so had Gancha. Its parents would be brighter than average, which was always a plus.

I've got to stop thinking of the baby as an 'it.' I would have a boy or girl, not an 'it.'

Then it dawned on me.

I could become a father again!

If Gancha came on board as part of my spy team, how would that affect her? And me. But Leanna was part of my team and that didn't affect me very much.

Come to think of it, would the two women fight? Leanna had Vincent now. Would that be enough to make a difference?

This is a lot to think about.

* * * * *

Gancha thought over her conversation with Jake. One positive of having a crime empire was the cash flow. That was very good indeed.

But, and this was the gotcha for her, if the cops ever arrested her for anything those below her in the org chart did, they might check with Earth and find an open warrant on her—for murder. Since murder would trump anything they had, they would send her back to Earth. And that would be a death sentence. Or a lifetime in a cage. Both of which she hated with a passion more than life itself. She'd rather kill herself than go back to Earth. Very few people faced such strong choices. It certainly cleared her priorities.

So she had one decision. Sell her remaining crime empire. That would mean going legit.

Hmm, something new to consider. Could I stay within the law?

Well, if she went on ops for Jake that might satisfy her need for an occasional adrenaline rush.

Then there was the whole idea of a romantic relationship with the man of her dreams.

Yes, something to consider.

The next day, Gancha made up her mind. She tagged Jat Keepen.

"Whatcha want?" he asked.

"How much would you pay to buy my share of the drug trade?"

"You sellin'?"

"Just checking." She knew from experience that being too eager would mean a lower price for her goods.

"I dunno. Let me think about that. What do ya want?"

"Three hundred twenty mil."

"Ouch! That's steep."

"Think it over," she replied. "You could make that up in a couple years. Sooner—if the flood of immigrants keeps up."

She disconnected from Keepen and placed three more tags to the other crime bosses in Zor. One of which was interested in her gambling businesses.

Two days later, she got a tag from Keepen.

"Your price is a bit steep. Can you come down?"

"Nope. I've got other nibbles."

"Okay." He paused before adding, "I can handle your price."

"Told ya," she replied.

By the end of that day, she had sold off her gambling interests too. She used some of the cash to buy legitimate businesses. Even a bank. She had to smile at that one. Many years ago, she had robbed a bank in broad daylight in Santa Claus, Indiana.

When she paused to ponder what she had done, a cool five hundred million plus sols sat in a string of Certificates of Deposit, while another hundred million in stock provided an average income of one and a half million sols a month. Selling Venisio's house and buying this one had netted her a half mil. The profits from her legit businesses came on top of that.

With her house paid for and a part of her income set aside for housekeeping, she smiled at herself. She wondered what her crime boss grandfather would think of her decisions, but he was gone now and not part of the picture. Life was for the living and she was busy looking out for herself.

Birds do it. Snakes do it. Even insects do it.

Without a conscious thought, Gancha busied herself cleaning up her life. And building a nest.

CHAPTER 13

Alena spent the two hours before her next class thinking of how to get a sample of mercon DNA for her experiments. First she needed a cab, so she tagged one. When the autocab arrived, she inserted her student ID credit card for the student discount. Once inside the cab, she gave instructions for her destination, "Franken Mall."

Like many college students, she wore a short tight orange skirt with black hose. To complete her outfit, she wore a green long-sleeved sweatshirt bearing the logo of the Rockets, the University of Zor basketball team. The colors matched that of the University. Her reddish-brown straight hair fell over her shoulders.

The cab delivered her to the curb outside Omar's Department Store. She walked through the department store, ignoring the robots who tried to get her attention. At one time, she had to step around them. They seemed to be everywhere.

"We have a wide assortment of purses. Some very affordable," said one female bot with many purses hanging from both arms.

Once inside the open space, she went first to the directory. The mercon restaurant was on the ground floor. She looked for an escalator since she was on the second floor.

Happy music echoed from the walls.

Is that a version of Jingle Bells?

The smell of baked dough hit her nostrils. She looked to her right to see a bagel shop.

Many women, with children alongside, walked the halls. Here and there she spotted a young couple. She wondered how they could afford all this. Most of the shops catered to the wealthy.

Off in the distance she spotted an escalator going down.

Even on the escalator, she found herself subjected to advertisements on the overhead vids. "Buy this at Omar's," "Buy this at Franken's," "Enjoy a break at Kindell's Ice Cream Parlor. You deserve it."

No mention of price, of course. If you had to ask, you didn't belong here.

When she got to the ground level, she turned to walk back toward the mercon restaurant. According to the directory, it was along her left side. She looked for the sign.

As she walked, another fembot wheeled up to her.

"Care to try a makeover? It's free!"

She ignored the bot. Then she saw it. The mercon restaurant was two shops away. With a line outside.

Rats.

A glance at her comm told her she might not have enough time to stand in line.

So she walked into the mercon gift shop next door and proceeded deep into the store to get beyond the gawkers who waited out their time to get into the restaurant.

The smaller "people" behind the counters had dark skin. Much like those from the sub-Sahara parts of Africa. The mercons were bipedal and thus stood on two legs. They heard with two ears on the sides of their heads but from the long black hair on those behind the counter she couldn't see their ears.

From the length of their black hair and the bright colored capes they wore, Alena assumed these were females. She had heard that women were chosen for sales jobs because her own species thought they were less aggressive. Too many memories still remained of the warlike males.

She could see a resemblance with the napes, but these mercons were taller.

The most striking feature on their faces were their noses of long slits. The slits started wide just above their small mouths but got narrower as they rose up between the eyes. All the clerks wore plugs in their noses. Alena had heard they had a great sense of smell and that most human odors were offensive to them.

Seeing one of them with nose plugs made her conscious of her own body odors. She had taken a shower this morning but that was five hours ago.

Would I offend them?

Not wanting to take a chance, she stayed away from the edge of the counter as she approached one mercon standing with an assortment of ornaments behind her. The first thing to catch Alena's eye was a doll with dark long hair that flowed almost to the doll's waist. It was marked "75 sols," a princely sum for a student. But she had to get her hands on that hair.

Also from the Net she learned that mercon dolls were made of native materials and used native hair. Which meant mercon DNA.

"Can I show you something?" ask the clerk with a slight accent.

Taken aback by the flawless speech in her own native tongue, Alena paused. "I'd like to see that doll there." She pointed. "Do you have one that human customers haven't touched yet?" It took two tries to get that across to the non-human clerk.

The mercon went to the back room and came out with three dolls.

"These were all made by one woman in a village in the mountains," she added. "And I assure you, no human has touched them."

When Alena saw black hair on all three, she could hardly restrain her excitement. Without touching them, Alena pointed to one and said, "I'll take it." She handed over the credit card from her dad.

"Gift wrap?" asked the clerk with the same accent.

"Please," replied Alena with a nod.

All the better to protect it from contamination.

In the autocab, she wanted to touch her new possession but realized she couldn't until after she had run her tests.

She resisted the temptation until she got back to her science lab. There she put on a lab coat, white sterile gloves, and a face mask. With great care to avoid letting her precious samples touch a non-sterile surface, she spent hours analyzing the mercon DNA. When the results perplexed her, she repeated the entire experiment with fresh clippings of mercon hair.

* * * * *

Alena pondered her next problem. She didn't want to use her own DNA because of her Binger ancestry. That might reveal too much, especially in this climate of bigotry. She much preferred to use tissue from a pure human.

You'd think getting samples of human DNA would be the least of my problems, surrounded by non-Bingers as I am.

But she didn't want to reveal her reasons. Would anyone agree to give a few hairs if they knew their identity might be published in a paper someplace, especially a controversial one?

She considered this problem one night while sitting on the toilet. Two humans slept in beds nearby. All she needed was a few hairs. Like from a hairbrush.

Just like that, the solution to her problem popped into her head.

Sometimes Mrs. Albert used the second sink in the guest bathroom to brush her hair. Right within five feet of Alena was the solution. After washing her hands, she went into her own room to get a plastic bag. She returned to the bathroom and pulled out a pair of metal tweezers from her own drawer and sprayed them with an ethyl alcohol mist. Using the tweezers, she pulled three long hairs off the translucent brush used by Mrs. Albert. She wrote "Mrs. A" on the outside of the bag.

When she crawled back into bed later, she reviewed her next problem. Getting nape DNA.

That evening, after dinner with her two hosts, she stayed in her seat at the dining table. The professor often returned to his university laboratory for his own research.

After he left, Alena realized her opportunity. She recalled a saying from her reading. She couldn't remember who said it. Actual difficulties can be overcome. It was only the imaginary ones that sometimes couldn't.

She left the table and went to her room to get a pair of plastic gloves, which she stuffed in one pocket of her skirt. Then she returned to the dining room and spoke to Mrs. Albert.

"I left my notes in his office."

With that, she climbed down the stairs to the basement lab of Dr. Albert.

Even though her notebook was in plain sight on the professor's desk, she went to his glass case and glanced up at the stairs. The sound of running water greeted her ears. Mrs. Albert was washing the dishes.

Returning her gaze to the glass case, she stared at four dolls and a knife in a sheath that Dr. Albert said he received on his last expedition to the nape reservation on Braco.

With one more nervous glance at the stairs to make sure Mrs. Albert wasn't coming, Alena rushed to the front of the professor's desk. She opened the right side second drawer and saw the red box. With care, she brought the box to the surface of the desk and removed the lid. Inside was an assortment of keys. She studied the tags on them until she saw the one labeled "Doll Case."

After another quick glance at the stairs, she heard only the sound of running water and the occasional clatter of ceramic dishes.

Alena reached in so as not to disturb the other keys and took the one she needed. She stole quietly to the case and used the key to open the sliding lock. She pulled the glass door aside gradually so as not to make a sound. Then she remembered her surgical gloves and put them on. She pulled out a doll and with strong fingers, broke off three of the long black hairs and held them up by the ends. Carefully, she placed the hairs in a plastic bag from her pocket and sealed it. With shaking hands, she used a black pen and wrote "N" on the outside of the bag. She placed the bag inside her skirt pocket.

Then she returned the doll to its original position, slowly slid the glass door shut, and removed her gloves. After locking the case, she returned the key to the same position in the red box, making sure to slip it under the key above it as she had found it. She replaced the lid and keeping the box level, put it back into the desk drawer and shut it.

Alena stepped around to the front of the desk, picked up her notebook, and clutched it to her chest. Turning on her heel, she took one more look at the hobby case. This was the closest she'd get to real napes in months, maybe ever.

Only then did she relax. She proceeded up the stairs.

Mrs. Albert stood before the kitchen sink.

"Want to lend a hand?" Mrs. Albert asked.

The older woman looked down at the plastic basin of soapy water. She was old-fashioned in that she did her dishes by hand.

"Sure," replied Alena. "Give me a minute."

Alena set her notebook on the dining table and proceeded into the kitchen. She tried to calm herself as she dried each dish and placed it in the cupboard. It would not do to drop one out of nervousness.

CHAPTER 14

That night it was hard for her to get to sleep. When morning finally came, Alena pulled on orange hose and added a brown tight skirt, and a white long-sleeved top. Then she rushed to the Science Building.

Dr. Albert's lab was on the second floor and overlooked the parking lot. He was not in since it was time for his lecture in the main auditorium on Introduction to Alien Culture 102.

After donning her white lab coat, Alena analyzed her samples of DNA from mercons, Bingers, napes, and humans. As she stared at the results, her eyes opened wider and her lips parted.

"Whoa!"

She spent the next four hours writing up her results in the proper format for publication, not stopping to eat. Food could wait. She emailed a copy of her paper to her advisor and washed her labware.

Her comm vibrated and she answered with a tap on her nostril.

"Are you coming to dinner?" asked Mrs. Albert.

"Oh my gosh! Is it that time already? I'll be right there," Alena answered.

At the dining table that evening, Mrs. Albert spoke up and asked how her day was.

"Okay, I guess," replied Alena. She didn't mention her lab work. "I'm taking Chem 201 and I'm bored to death. I had all this stuff back on Earth. But I have to take it again to get credit for it."

"I looked at your paper," the doctor said. "Even though I read only the first three pages, I think it's very good. How did you get samples of the Binger DNA?"

Damned if I'll tell you.

"Can't tell you that. My source insisted on secrecy."

"I can understand that with all the anti-Binger gossip going on," he replied. "Listen, I think your paper should be published in 'The Journal of Rossan Biology.' It's unusual for an undergrad to be listed as an author and I think it would have more credibility if my name appeared first. But I insist that your name be next."

Alena grinned. "That would be great!"

* * * * *

That night, Dr. Albert knocked on her door.

"Come in."

After he entered, he said, "I read your full paper on DNA."

"What'd you think?" she said with a grin, expecting praise.

He shook his head. "I'm not sure you should use my name on it."

"What?" The edges of her mouth dropped. She looked at his furled eyebrows. He was serious.

"Come on, this is groundbreaking," she added. "You'll be famous."

"That's what I'm afraid of," the professor added.

"What's there to fear?"

"My peers are conservative. I'm afraid this paper of yours won't get past them. To suggest a connection between human and mercon DNA would only add fuel to the roaring blaze of public attitude right now."

"Oh boy. If you don't publish this, when your name is mentioned one hundred years from now, people will laugh."

"At you or me?" he replied.

"Sheesh. Think of all the great scientists of history."

He shook his head. "I'm thinking of all the great fools of history."

"Well," she added. "If your mind is made up then, I'll send it in on my own."

"If you do, I'm not so sure I want to stay your advisor."

When Alena got back to her computer, she removed her advisor's name and sent the article with the accompanying images, to the editor of "The Journal of Rossan Biology." Even though it might take days, maybe weeks if Dr. Albert were right, she looked forward to the fame it would bring.

She picked up her schedule.

Damn.

A test in Differential Equations tomorrow. Time to put her research aside and study. Her father's word echoed in her head.

"One thing at a time."

CHAPTER 15

Guy Coocher opened the email from his scientific advisor, Stenton Duran. Duran subscribed to every scientific magazine related to research on Rossan life forms and passed the articles that might interest him to Coocher.

The email said, "Read the article by Dani on 'DNA of napes.' Even though this is preliminary to the paper to be published online later, it might get on the news."

Coocher didn't like reading scientific papers, especially this one. They were hard to digest and full of words he didn't understand. He skimmed over the introductory material and stopped when he saw a figure with the caption "Comparison of human and nape DNA."

He reread the section on humans and napes for the second time and slammed his fist on his desk.

One of his priorities when he became the prime minister was to stop such wasteful research. That meant research on Bingers and napes too.

Why couldn't they stick to safer subjects, like the lives of insects and other animals on this planet? There's plenty to be learned right there that we could use. Rossa is full of the critters.

Since the major funding for such research came from the York Science Foundation he'd have little trouble getting those funds turned off. The YSF received ninety percent of its funds from the federal government and as the prime minister from Zor, he'd be on that committee. Most of the time, he'd send a representative. But for this funding decision, he'd go himself. His opinion would carry a lot of weight.

The name on the paper sounded familiar. Alena Dani. The daughter of a private investigator here in Zor, according to Duran.

The tone of the article was fresh and Coocher had little doubt most of it came from this Alena Dani. He pondered this new development.

Something has to be done about her before it's too late.

* * * * *

Borner Hoskins yanked the rope tighter between his gloved hands but it didn't help. It lacked that "personal" touch. What he needed was a human neck in the garrote.

The nervousness was like an old friend. It was time to hunt again.

His father had tied his mother up during sex and she liked it when he strangled her just short of death. But the last time he did that she died. He would always remember the look of rapture on her face before she passed out. The young Borner ran from the house, afraid his father would turn on him.

His father ran away instead and never returned. The years right after that were a blur to his young mind. He was the son of a murderer. So Borner spent the years of his youth in orphanages in rural Romania near the town of Deva. With a weak name of Borner Hoskins, he learned how to be tough, how not to seek affection from anyone else. None at all. The time he slugged a smaller boy and saw the fear in his eyes was an education. Being tough and ready to hurt others would bring the respect he wanted.

He knew being caught by the cops "doing his thing" could result in years in a cage or a firing squad. They just didn't understand his needs at all. So he learned how to hide his "hobby" from the eyes of the police. Over time, it had become a need.

Which was a major reason why he got the nickname "The Rat." He could scurry for cover whenever people with a badge came near. Any witnesses against him disappeared, sometimes under unusual circumstances.

A man's gotta protect himself.

He tied the scarf around his mouth and nose and pulled it down. Then he coiled his favorite garrote, the one made of nylon cord with two wooden cross pieces for his hands, and inserted it into the inside pocket of his black bopum-leather jacket. He had purchased the cheap nylon cord at Beta Hardware so it would be hard to trace if any of it remained on his victim.

Knowing full well he could kill someone today added to his excitement and he quivered.

"Gotta be careful to not leave any evidence that could be traced back to me."

Hoskins put on his leather gloves and got in his car. It had been too long since the last time. The need to kill pulled on him, tensing every nerve. The excitement, the overwhelming tension, had grown in recent months. It wouldn't let up until he satisfied it. More and more, his thoughts turned to using his garrote.

He turned on his headlights to drive away the darkness. He manually drove the vehicle to the parking lot at the northern edge of the Franken Mall and pulled into a spot along South Central Park Avenue. The edge of the jail on North Central Park Avenue was visible between the Natural History Museum and the Parliament Building. He shuddered to think of himself being stuck there.

The air was brisk but he expected that since it was autumn on Rossa. Winters came faster here than in Nantes on the west coast of France where he spent a decade. Even after seven years on Rossa, he still found the air chilly this time of year.

He wore soft-soled athletic shoes as he walked along South Central Park toward the train station. He had purchased them two months ago at a discount store so they'd be hard to trace.

Monday evenings were the best time of the week. Many folks were tired from not having slept enough the night before. Their guards were down and they might take shortcuts.

He spotted his prey. A woman walked in bright pink slacks, her head covered in the pullover hood on her beige trench coat. She carried two bags with the logos of Omar's and Alton's, two of the biggest stores in the mall.

Not sure what she might do, he walked fifteen paces behind her and raised his scarf to cover his mouth and nose.

Her left hand was not visible from behind. Maybe she carried her purse in it.

But her right hand interested him the most. The "almost" flesh color brought a smile to his lips. She had an artificial hand.

Excellent!

That would make it harder for her to pull on his garrote.

Will she take the shortcut through the alley to the railroad station?

He eased back to give her more room. His heart beat faster in anticipation as he followed her. When she turned to see who might be following her, he put his head down and raised his hand to his ear, like he was talking with someone on his comm.

With him only thirty feet behind, she made the right turn into the alley.

Yes!

Once he turned there, he looked around him. They were alone. He pulled the scarf up around his nose to hide the lower part of his face, unzipped his jacket, and pulled out his garrote.

By now, the adrenaline flowing in his arteries rushed full force. All his senses were sharp.

This is the time.

He rushed up behind her, made a loop in the garrote, slipped the short rope over her head, and pulled on the two wooden blocks to tighten the loop around her neck.

She dropped her bags and rushed her hands to her neck. But it was too late. He pulled tighter as she struggled to breathe. Not once did she reach over her head to pull on his face. Most of his victims' immediate concern was getting air in their lungs.

He imagined her rush as she realized her life was coming to an end.

Just like Mom.

This one was strong. She struggled for fifteen seconds before her body went limp. He eased her to the ground and continued pulling for another ten seconds until he was sure she was dead.

He removed his garrote and looked around. No one else entered the alley.

Good. No witnesses.

Standing tall, he walked back toward the entrance to the alley and pulled his scarf down from his mouth. His whole body shook with excitement.

What a rush!

As he made his way back to his car, he smiled to himself. He was on top of the world.

His comm vibrated on this wrist. He tapped his nostril. It was from a client, Guy Coocher.

"I have a job for you."

CHAPTER 16

I tagged my daughter but had to leave a voicemail. Next, I tagged her dorm and learned she had moved to a professor's house. I tagged there next.

"Mrs. Albert? I'm Jake Dani, Alena's father. Is she home?"

"Oh. You're the father. I'm sorry to say but Alena is in class right now. She left hours ago."

"I'm trying to get hold of her. Do you know which class?"

"No, I'm sorry, but I can't remember. Something about mathematics, though. She rushed her breakfast saying she had to finish cramming for a math test."

"Thank you. Would you tell her I'm trying to reach her?"

"Sure thing, Mr. Dani."

I flared my nostrils to disconnect.

The temptation rose to tag Leanna next but she was at work and I'd probably have to leave a voice mail.

Oh well. Alena's probably studying and doesn't want to be disturbed.

* * * * *

Alena looked up as the woman approached her table. Despite the chill in the air, she had chosen one of the outdoor tables so she could enjoy the view of Central Park across the street. She pulled the jean jacket closed and snapped its buttons. Underneath, she had clothed herself in total blue jeans, including shirt and pants.

Being from another planet, she enjoyed being outside here whenever she could. She hoped to "soak up" what life was like while on Rossa. After all, she intended to spend the rest of her life here, close to her parents and the alien species she wished to study.

"Hi, Alena," said Leanna Stone in her green slacks with a beige overcoat.

"Hi, Mom."

Leanna pulled out a chair and sat.

"Thanks for inviting me for lunch."

"I hope you don't mind paying. I don't get much spending money on my scholarship."

"No problem," replied Leanna. "It's good to see you." She reached out her hands and the two women clasped and smiled. They were buddies again.

"I sent another paper yesterday to 'The Journal of Rossan Biology'."

Leanna squeezed her daughter's hands. "I'm so proud of you. Can you tell me what was in it—in plain English, this time?"

Alena grinned. "Sure. I analyzed samples of mercon DNA and found several SNPs in common with human DNA and nape DNA."

"In English?" said Leanna as she sat back.

"Oh, sorry. SNPs are single nucleotide poloymorphisms. They are small sections of DNA. There is no reason for such a match with human or nape DNA. Unless they came from a common ancestor."

"Are you saying humans, mercons, and napes have a common ancestor?" asked Leanna with wide open eyes.

"Yep," replied Alena with a big grin.

Her mother sat, maybe stunned by this revelation.

"Where'd you get the mercon DNA?" asked Leanna.

"Oh. That was easy. I bought a doll at the mall."

"And the nape DNA?" asked Leanna.

"From artifacts in Dr. Albert's collection."

"Who's Dr. Albert?"

"He's my advisor at the university. His specialty is xenoanthropology. I have a room at his place."

Leanna asked, "And the artifacts came from?"

"He has a collection of dolls and tools from napes. He got them on his expeditions to Braco."

Leanna sat back.

"Are you sure? About the ancestors, I mean."

"Oh yes. I double checked my tests. This is going to wreak havoc with all theories of human evolution." Alena smiled at her mother. "I'm going to be famous."

Leanna changed the subject. "Have you seen your father lately?"

"Mom! Did you hear me? I'm going to be famous!"

"Yes, dear. I heard you. But you haven't answered my question."

Alena didn't see any reaction on her mother's face. Maybe it would take time to sink it.

Oh well.

With a sigh, Alena answered, "I tagged Mrs. Albert when I got out of class. That test was brutal! She said Dad was looking for me."

"Have you two connected yet?"

That's all she can think about. Me and my father. I'm sitting on the most important discovery in my professional career and all she can think about is my relationship with my Dad.

Alena sat, disappointed in her mother.

"Hey, let's go to the Mall," offered Leanna. "We can get a bite to eat there."

Oh well, might as well. Maybe she just needs time.

The two women got up from their outdoor table and headed towards the Franken Mall.

"Vin and I would like to invite you to dinner at our place, some time," said Leanna.

Alena walked to the right of her mother, on the street side along University Avenue. She saw the tall man dressed in all black and standing next to the building and wondered what he was doing here. He was too old to be a student.

As he walked by her, she naturally turned to see him turn toward her.

The next thing Alena knew was. A loud gunshot came from somewhere on her left side.

"Mother!"

Someone grabbed her from behind and she kicked out at her assailant. She heard a man's voice groan. Strong arms grabbed her and her legs kicked in the air as she found herself airborne. Next came a scream in her mother's voice. Alena continued to kick and strong hands grabbed her ankles. It all happened fast and soon she felt a sting in her left thigh.

Her face crashed onto a hard surface. She struggled against someone laying on top of her. A door slammed shut. But she didn't have much time to think as she blacked out.

The next thing Alena became aware of was sitting upright in a chair, with her hands tied behind her. She opened her eyes but couldn't see much with a dark mask over them. She tried to kick and discovered her ankles secured beneath her.

A man's voice said, "The younger broad is awake."

Younger? So there must be an older woman nearby. Mother?

It was impossible to tell with this damned black eyeshade. Alena struggled against her bonds and her arms separated a couple inches.

"She's getting loose!" said another man.

Another male voice yelled behind her, "Amateurs! Grab those wrists!"

But before she could break free, strong hands grabbed both wrists and forced them closer together. She felt something wrap tightly around her wrists.

"There. Let's see you get out of that one!" said the same male voice to her rear.

"What do we do now? Hoskins said to take the student."

Hoskins? Student?

So her kidnappers wanted her, not her mother.

"Idiot! Don't use names!" said one male voice.

Apparently that one was the boss.

Alena said out loud, "Mom?"

A slap to her mouth from someone in front of her was her reward.

"No talking!"

* * * * *

That evening while rinsing my dinner dishes in my apartment, I got a tag from Vincent.

"Leanna didn't come home. She sometimes works overtime, so I called her comm. It's not answering. I tagged her office and she did not come back after lunch. Her coworkers said she was looking forward to lunch with her daughter from Earth."

"Did you try tagging Alena?"

"Yes, but the same thing. I had to leave a voice mail. Neither of them has called back."

"Strange," I replied. "Maybe they went shopping. You know, girl stuff."

"Maybe. But why would both of their comms be off?"

"Could be they wanted some time alone," I suggested. "They haven't seen each other in a long time."

"You don't think something's happened to them?"

"I doubt it. Give them a few more hours."

But I hadn't totally convinced myself. After disconnecting, I tagged Mrs. Albert.

"She's not here. My husband tagged me to say she did not show up for his afternoon class in biology. That's was unusual enough for him to notice."

"Will you tag me when she gets home?" I asked.

After I hung up, I pondered this new development. *Now what the frick has happened?*

CHAPTER 17

At nine the next morning, while I ate my breakfast in my apartment, I got a tag from Vincent.

"Lee didn't come home," he said. "She knows she should tag me when she's spending the night somewhere else."

"Did you check her work?" as I munched on my scrambled eggs.

"Yep. She didn't show up this morning."

Oh dear. My worst nightmare may have begun.

"Let me call around," I added.

After we disconnected, I sent a message to Acorn to tell him of the disappearance of Leanna and Alena. The last we knew they were going to lunch at a deli on the north side of the campus yesterday.

I tagged Dr. Albert and he informed me of her absence from his class. Which was very unusual since she always attended his lectures on xenobiology.

"How's she doin'?"

"Alena's my best student. By far. Her research is 'over the top.'"

Then I tagged my team members for a virtual meeting. Ron couldn't make it because he was working. It was important that he keep up his job at Stenno's. Zetto was at another HO rally. But Vincent and Andy showed up on my wall.

Vincent and I brought Andy up to speed on what we knew.

Vincent said, "Jake, what did Dr. Albert say?"

"He said Alena presented a draft of her next paper and it was a looloo. In it, she claimed a common ancestor for humanity and the mercons. It was so controversial that he wouldn't put his name on it."

Andy added, "If that gets out, the HO guys are gonna hate it."

Vincent said, "Do you suppose HO is involved?"

"Let's not leap to conclusions just yet, guys. Vincent, can you meet me at the ops center ASAP? We need to trace their last steps, starting at the deli where they had lunch."

* * * * *

I kept an operations center in the Marino Office Suites on Main Street. Kerle Company managed the property, which included rentals on the first through fifth floors. What I reserved was the full basement.

My hardware expert, Andy Warden, provided the security we needed. Andy had installed hidden cameras and secure access to the entire basement. The basement was not listed in the elevators, nor was there an entrance to the elevators. Visitors had to walk down the stairs.

There were four doors in the basement. The first was a small room used for electrical power and maintenance.

Our shooting range entrance stood opposite it on the right. The second and third doors on the left led to the main operations center.

To gain access to either the ops center or the shooting range required keying in the password and pressing one's palm on the flat rectangle to the right of the keypad. That palm reader was painted the same color as the walls. Anyone entering the basement had to know it was there.

There were no windows on any wall of the basement. I didn't want anyone peering into one of our rooms.

Our operations center consisted of three large rooms. The doors to the dorm and the planning room opened to the basement hallway.

The first room consisted of the dorm, with an adjacent bathroom and shower stall. The dorm held six bunk beds, stacked in pairs. All of us could sleep there and often did while planning a spy operation.

The next room held the kitchen and dining room, with a small jail and pantry for storing non-perishable foods.

The jail room of six foot by eight foot had its own bunk hanging from the wall, a small sink, a toilet, and a shower, all of stainless steel. To reduce the chances of anyone escaping, we used metal fixtures everywhere, including the walls. The door to the cell opened onto the dining room and on the outside of the door we installed a sliding panel over a one-way mirror so the occupant could not see or hear who might peek, but we could see in. As long as the dining light was out, that is.

As a precaution, I had hidden cameras installed looking at all four walls of the jail. They connected to our ops center AI, Ruta. If anything happened on any wall, Ruta would alert anyone in the center, as well as Acorn and anyone currently outside.

We planned our operations and sometimes ate on a large table in the third main room. The evidence oven took up part of the space where we could burn body parts, clothing, disguises, etc. It had a vapor scrubber connected so even the fumes were thoroughly burned. Next to the oven was the lathe we'd use to file the numbers off guns. Sometimes we used acid to remove the last of the numbers.

On the four walls of the planning room rested whiteboards connected to Ruta. I chose a large space so we could put a hospital bed there if we needed.

Ron and I had installed an escape stairway in a narrow passageway from the dormitory room that allowed us to exit onto the parking lot in the alley behind the building. The exit door had no handle on the outside. I made sure each of the six of us knew how to escape from the ops center via the hidden stairs.

With the railroad just behind us, and Bagel Joe's Deli across the street, we could feel comfortable in this run-down section of Zor.

* * * * *

I arrived at the parking lot of the ops center before Vincent. He had to travel across the Oreo River through downtown and I had to cover only a few blocks. When he pulled his car into the parking garage, I tooted my horn. He climbed into my car, wearing a beige shirt, jeans for pants, and a gray jacket. We left at once.

I drove slowly past the eateries along South Central Avenue.

Vincent pointed to one and said, "Let's check that one."

I pulled into their parking lot.

The owner wasn't delighted to see us. Too busy behind the register. With a nod of his head, he pointed to a waitress.

"Ask Shirley."

Shirley, dressed in a yellow and white uniform that ended just above her knees, reported two women being abducted yesterday.

She said, "I tagged the police and they came. Asked a lot of questions too.

"It was just after lunch. They were at a table outside. I noticed them because the shorter woman gave me a large tip of ten sols. For a pair of sandwiches and two Blackstone iced teas? I rushed after them to ask her if she'd made a mistake."

"Did you see where they headed next?"

"No, but I don't think they expected what happened."

I looked at Vincent.

She continued, "I saw two guys rush up to both of them, put black hoods over their faces, and shove them into a van. Then they tore off."

Shit. My nightmare had come true.

"Did you see anything unusual about the van?" asked Vincent. "Did it have a sign on its side?"

The waitress shook her head. "Nope. And I didn't get the plate either. It all happened so fast. In front of Scarlett's. They sell women's clothing."

I asked, "What color was the van?"

"Black, I think. Or maybe a dark gray. It all happened so fast."

"How many guys did you see?"

"I saw three of them. Two grabbed the women and a third opened the van door for them."

"Did you see a driver?"

"No, but there must have been one," she replied.

"Can you describe the men?"

She shook her head. "They wore all-black clothes. Even their heads were covered with something black. All I could see were their eyes."

"Were they white, black, tall, short, lean, fat?" I asked.

"The cops asked the same questions. White, I think. I tell ya, it all happened so fast."

"Tall, short, lean, fat?" asked Vincent.

"Kinda tall, like you guys. Not fat—though they were big. Lots of muscle maybe. I'd hate to meet one of them in an alley."

CHAPTER 18

I had Vincent tag Andy and Ron as I drove back to the ops center.

Ron said his shift would be over soon but he needed to take a quick shower at his home.

Andy said he could come right away.

Then I had Vincent tag the cops to start a Missing Person's report while I stopped to refuel.

An hour after we returned to the ops center, Ron sat in the planning room in a pink shirt, gray slacks, and gray jacket. His hair glistened so he might have just washed it.

Andy sat in one chair in a gray business suit, his ear pressed to his comm as he spoke to someone.

I tagged Deek Tanny, my friend and head of the Homicide and Robbery Department of the Zor Metro Police. I put the conversation on one wall of our ops room. My comm would transcribe our conversation and display my words in red and Deek's in blue.

"Alena Dani is missing."

"I know," replied Deek. "I saw the MP report."

"Do you have any leads?"

"Jake, we may be friends but that doesn't mean I work for you. I can't report on the progress of an ongoing investigation."

"She's my daughter, damn it! Would you like my help if Marcie and Doreen turned up missing?"

A sigh greeted my ears. "I see your point. The black van could be anybody's. The wit did not see the plate. Her description of the three men was vague too. Could be anybody."

"Do your snitches say anything?"

"I haven't had time to ask them yet. But this has all the earmarks of a professional grab."

"That must narrow the number of suspects," I added.

"Yep."

"Who are the crime bosses?"

"Morentoss, whom you know. Big Rick, Gregor, Slippery Steve, the list goes on. There's a lot of crime in this city. But I doubt any of them ordered it."

I asked, "Why?"

"We can't find any reason for them to do this."

"What if it's political?"

"What do you mean?" asked Deek.

"Alena was going to publish a paper connecting human DNA to mercon DNA. She suggested we both have a common ancestor."

"Holy crap! If that gets out, we won't be able to contain the riots."

"So somebody might have a motive to prevent that."

"Hmm. This is a new line of investigation. Thanks."

"I suggest, merely suggest, since as you pointed out I'm not your boss, that maybe the police ought to look into HO or RUFF."

"How do you know your daughter was going to publish that?"

"I talked with Dr. Albert, her advisor at the university. He refused to put his name on it."

Silence.

"Deek, who are the key players for HO or RUFF who could do this?"

"Hmm. I see your point. We'll look into it but the chief is not eager to start a pissing contest with Coocher. After all, the guy may be our next PM. As in my boss's boss's boss. That's all I can tell you."

"I understand."

"Do you? Jake, I know you're a PI. One with some skill too. But if you get too close to Coocher or Horton and I hear about it from the chief, you'll be burning bridges I don't think you want to burn."

"Got it. But she's my daughter. I can't stop looking for her. You wouldn't stop if it was Marcie and Doreen. And you'd break some rules, too."

With the silence on the other end, I added, "Goodbye, Deek." I flared my nostrils to disconnect. I looked around the room and settled my eyes on Vincent just as he stood in his gray suit.

"And where do you think you're going?"

"Lee's gone."

"So?"

"I'm gonna squeeze those bastards until one of them talks."

"Sit down!" I ordered. "We have a much better chance of getting both of them back safely if we act as a team. After all, Alena is my daughter."

Vincent glared at me. He glanced around at Andy and Ron, but in the end sat down.

I said, "Computer, retain a copy and erase the wall."

After the blank whiteness appeared, I pointed to one wall and said, "Guy Coocher." His name appeared at the top.

I pointed to another wall and said, "Craig Horton." His name appeared.

I turned to my team.

"Now, let's find out what we know about both men and organizations."

To Vincent I said, "You can start by tapping into the comms of Coocher and Horton."

"That's Zetto's area," Vincent answered. "He hasn't finished training me. I'm not sure I know how to do it."

"How's he doing, by the way?"

"Don't know. I'm supposed to meet him," he raised his left arm, "in ten minutes."

"You'd better get going then," I replied.

* * * * *

Zetto Teasely entered the small diner and heard a bell tingle as he closed the door. He strode past the tables, went directly to the door marked "Employees Only," and pushed it open. No one seemed to notice him. Maybe it was his gray long-sleeved shirt and blue-jean coveralls. He might work there. The diner was small but busy. Like many small businesses, employee retention was a problem. If another job offered fifty cents more an hour, workers hopped.

Two men sweated over on a metallic table, with pots and pans hanging from nails on the walls. They didn't say anything to the intruder, being busy with their heads down and attention focused on their cooking. Besides, their backs were to him.

Zetto noticed a row of partially filled dishes in front of one man.

Zetto went to the back door and out into the alley, closing the door behind him. He studied the assortment of opened boxes and a large trash bin with rubber lid. He leaned next to the trash bin and waited.

Two minutes later, a man entered the alley. He walked up to the bin.

"Have a light?"

Vincent Stone asked with both hands turned down in front of him.

"Sorry. Don't smoke. Have you the time?"

Zetto stood erect and raised his right hand.

Satisfied that both had used the coded phrases and motions showing they weren't tailed, Vincent stuck his palm out and Zetto placed a small data cube in it. Vincent closed his fingers over the cube and put his hand into his gray jacket. The air was cool, but not enough for their breaths to show.

Zetto added, "I read something about a surprise. And then the code."

Vincent nodded. "I'll check it out. Are you in any danger?"

Zetto shook his head. "They don't suspect a thing."

"Want a gun?"

"No. That would alarm them. They search me every time before a meeting."

"Careful, eh?"

"Very."

* * * * *

Vincent returned to the ops center and placed the data cube in a slot next to his computer. With practiced fingers, he examined the list of files. Fifteen minutes later, he leaned back. The BIS decryption software was good—very good.

There were fourteen messages between Guy Coocher and Stenton Duran. Three of them used the word 'surprise' and asked if the materials were ready but Vincent still had no idea what that referred to.

And four messages from Duran to a guy with a last name of Hoskins referred to a package, but once again, no explanation. Maybe the two of them knew but Vincent had no clue what they talked about.

One thing was evident though. A message from Hoskins asked if he should dispose of the package. Duran passed it on to Coocher who replied, "No. I want to find out what that girl knows first. After that, you can do what you want with them. Just don't leave any traces to you or me."

Another message from Durant to Hoskins said, "It's time to find out what she knows."

Is "she" Alena?

* * * * *

Hoskins observed as the last of the lights went out in the residential neighborhood. With a black glove, he lifted his sleeve to uncover his comm and stole a glance at its lit face. Nine-thirty p.m. He raised his binoculars and scanned the back yard for evidence of a dog. No fence, no doghouse in the yard.

He smiled. *This will be easy.*

With his black clothing, he didn't expect anyone to see him in the bushes. He waited another half hour to make sure the woman got to sleep. He pulled on his night vision goggles to get his eyes adjusted to its green colors. No lights came on in the house by the appointed time so he left his hiding place and proceeded to the back door.

Unlocked.

Jeesh. These folks are trusting.

He wouldn't have to use his glass cutter and suction cup this time. With a turn of the handle, he cracked the door open and waited for the sound of barking from any house dog. Silence greeted him and he smiled.

Piece of cake.

He closed the back door slowly and snuck along the carpeted hallway on his athletic shoes. He climbed the stairs carefully, testing each step for any creaky boards. At the top, he peeked in three of the doors. A pantry full of towels and whatnot. A bathroom. An unoccupied guest bedroom.

That leaves only the end door.

Everything was dark behind him so he would not have to fear a light penetrating the room and showing his shadow as he approached the door.

Using his gloved hand he slowly turned the knob.

In his night vision, a woman with eye shades lay on this side of the large bed. All but her head lay underneath the bedding.

Good.

That would make it harder for her to get her hands to her face.

He inhaled and exhaled several times to hyperventilate. From his jacket pocket, he removed a cloth and from the other pocket, a small narrow bottle of liquid. After taking a deep breath and holding it, he unscrewed the bottle, and poured a portion of the liquid on the cloth. He still detected the aroma of chloroform.

He approached the bed and held the cloth over the woman's face. She struggled but in less than ten seconds, her breathing returned to its steady and slow pace. With care, he screwed the cap back on the bottle and waved his hand to clear the air before he exhaled. He turned his head to one side and took a breath. Then he reinserted the bottle in his pocket and leaned over the reclining woman.

He pulled her nighttime mask up over her head and removed the covers to reveal she was in her nightgown.

An old fashioned woman.

With both his arms, he lifted her off the bed. The aroma of chloroform lingered and he needed to get her out of the room before he breathed too much of it.

With less care this time, he descended the stairs with the load in his arms and took her to the kitchen. First he pulled her nightgown over her head, exposing her flabby and aged body. Then he tied her hands behind her to the back of the chair. Then he knelt on the kitchen floor and tied her ankles to the legs of the chair. He tied a gag across her mouth and secured it behind her neck.

With the kitchen still dark, he kept his night vision goggles on. It would not do to have a neighbor notice the light. Besides, keeping the room dark would add to her fear.

From one pocket, he removed another small bottle and opened it under her nose.

She jerked her head and turned away from the ammonia. He followed her nose so she had to breathe in the vapors.

Mrs. Albert's eyes opened and got wider when she saw him in his all-black outfit. She struggled and tried to scream but only her muffled voice came through.

CHAPTER 19

At eight the next morning, I rose for the last time, glad to be free of the dreams. Kept having nightmares of watching my daughter die while I was stuck in mud and couldn't get to her.

I jogged at nearby Ally Mason Park and took a shower. Got dressed in brown slacks, white shirt, and brown jacket. Barely made it to the kitchen where I intended to get a quick drink of orangette juice. Orangettes were the Rossan equivalent of oranges. My comm alerted me to a tag and I looked at the clock on it. Ten in the morning.

Who could call now?

I opened my nostrils to answer.

"Deek Tanny here. Do you know a Mrs. Albert?"

"Yeah. Alena was staying there. Why?"

"Mrs. Albert bought it. Care to come look over the scene?"

"Yeah," I said. Instantly alert. "Gimme fifteen."

"Know the address?"

"Oh yeah."

I looked at my new pet on the floor.

"Take care, Monk."

When I got to the scene, it wasn't easy finding a parking space. Cop cars with flashing lights filled the street.

I rushed up to the front door. A uniformed cop stopped me. He came to within two inches of my height.

"Can't let you in here, sir. It's a crime scene."

"Deek Tanny tagged me to come here."

"Your name?" he asked.

"Jake Dani."

The uniform tapped his nose and spoke. "Sir, I have a Jake Dani at the front door."

While he was on his comm, I glanced in the living room. Lots of equipment. It's amazing how they can shrink electronics to a portable size.

A minute later, the uniform stepped aside. "Captain is in the kitchen." He pointed.

Careful to stay on the brown paper, I proceeded into the kitchen. There I saw the back of a woman's head, angled down, hands tied behind her back. I walked around to her front and saw the red marks on her.

Deek looked up at me in his cheapest gray suit. It didn't fit him well. I figured it came from a discount store. Cops can't afford to wear expensive threads while on duty.

The homicide captain said, "Hi, Jake. Sorry to get you to see this. Figured you'd be used to it. Cleaning lady called the precinct when she found the body. Guy was careful. No fingerprints anywhere, even with all the blood. Probably wore gloves. No shoe prints in the blood on the floor."

He looked at Mrs. Albert in the chair.

"The vic was tortured and then choked to death," he continued. "There are slash marks on her belly, naked thighs, and lower legs. Closely spaced, just deep enough to draw blood. Not deep to the muscles. Just deep enough to cause pain."

The victim sat bound and naked in the chair. Poor thing was sleeping when her nightmare began.

"Why'd you tag me?" I asked.

"One of my detectives found Alena's name in the guest bedroom."

"It's unusual for a captain to be on a crime scene, especially at this hour."

"All of my other guys are busy. Besides, I like to keep my edge."

I looked at the victim's bloodied body. "Why was she tortured?"

"Dunno. Any guesses?"

"The killer wanted to know what she knew about Alena's paper."

Deek looked at me. "And why would the victim know that?"

"Maybe Alena told her."

"Why here, though?"

"Maybe the killer also knows who took Alena. Maybe he did it himself. Could be he tortured Alena or Leanna and found out about a second paper but Alena wouldn't tell him more. So he tried Mrs. Albert."

I looked around. "Where is the professor?"

"I dunno. Good question."

"Any sign he was here?"

Deek shook his head. "The bed looks like only one person slept in it."

"Could Dr. Albert be on leave?"

"You'd think he'd take his wife."

"Not if he were going on a research expedition. University professors do that, you know."

Deek nodded. "I can find that out."

"Any sign that Alena was here?"

Deek added, "There's a bed in a small bedroom off the living room. Somebody slept there until recently."

"Recently? How do you know that?"

"Smelled like a female too."

"Alena said she was staying here."

"And she can't tell us any more till we find her."

I looked the body over. "This looks like a professional job. Not a crime of passion."

"Why kill her though?"

"To keep her from testifying as a witness. Or telling the cops what she knows."

"Pretty cool guy," said Deek. "Killed her in cold blood."

I paused.

Deek continued, "He knew he was going to kill her. He tortured her to find out what she knew. Then he put something thin around her neck and choked her to death. See here?" He pulled her hair aside to show red marks on the side of her neck. "Narrow rope of some sort."

"Find it?" I asked.

"Nope."

I replied, "May be a professional's garrote and he took it with him."

I looked around. "Knife?"

"The perp used a kitchen knife, from the drawer over there." He pointed to an open drawer. "Left it on the counter. We bagged it."

"Time of death?"

Deek replied, "TOD was less than twelve hours ago."

"How do you know that so soon?"

He sighed and shook his head. "I opened her mouth and took her temp. Also under her arms. The ME can check her bottom."

"So she died last night."

"Looks that way, doesn't it?"

"How'd you know so soon?"

"Cleaning lady called us. She's in the living room. Pretty shook up."

A crime scene tech walked into the room. He spotted me and wouldn't speak.

Deek said, "It's all right. He's an ex-cop and a consultant on this case."

I looked at Deek.

Consultant? So he has decided to share with me.

Deek turned to the tech. "What is it?"

"We found a white cloth on the floor next to her bed. Smelled of chloroform, so I bagged it."

"See if you can find out if the blood on the knife matches the vic's."

The tech left. Twenty minutes later, he returned. "It's her blood, all right. Same DNA."

I marveled at the speed of modern detection. They didn't even know about DNA or fingerprints in the nineteenth century during the times of good ol' Sherlock Holmes. And now they can compare fingerprints and DNA on the scene—in an hour.

* * * * *

I got home in a half hour. It took longer than a straight shot because I took loops to check on a tail. While I stood in front of my open refrig to get the rest of my orangette drink my comm vibrated with another tag from Deek.

"Dr. Albert is on Braco, out of contact on the nape reservation."

"Did you contact Ranute Fallow?" Fallow was the head of the Alien Protection Society and had exclusive rights to allow anyone to visit the nape reservation.

"Thought of that too. Fallow said he gave Dr. Albert permission to go on the reservation, but on a fact finding expedition. As far as Ranute knows, Dr. Albert is still there."

"Have you told him his wife is dead?"

"Not yet," replied my favorite cop. "And don't you tell him. I'll do that."

"One of the perks of your job as IO, eh?" I teased.

From my years as a cop in LA, I dreaded having to relay the bad news as the Investigating Officer.

"Worst part actually," he replied. "I think we may have a serial killer. Two days ago, we found a woman choked to death in alley near Grand Central Station. Now Mrs. Albert. The two murders don't seem to have anything in common except the MO. Marks on their necks hinted of a garrote."

"Nothing before?"

"Not in the last three months."

"You might check immigration. See who came from Earth recently."

"Already did. Nothing popped out. Say, Marcie asks when are you going to stop in for dinner?"

"Not soon, I'm afraid. Gotta find my daughter."

"I think she'll understand that."

I added, "By the way, thanks for the consulting job. Does it come with any pay?"

"Sorry."

"You scratch my back. I'll scratch yours. Don't ask me how I know but HO is planning some kind of surprise. I don't know anymore, so don't ask."

"Huh. Probably another demo. Maybe with a boom."

After I disconnected, I noticed Monk staring up at me. I must seem like a giant to him.

After checking for bugs, I sat at my computer with the door open. Monk climbed up into my lap while I checked emails. Clever little bugger. I tapped my index finger on the table top in a pattern of five taps and repeated it, pausing to look at him.

He looked at my hand and back to my face several times. Then he tapped his finger on the surface in the same pattern. Both of us grinned. Playtime.

My monitor showed an incoming message. "Our sympathies on your daughter. Can we help?" It was signed Detter.

The mercon ambassador.

How the hell did he find out so soon?

"You know, Monk. It's a small town."

The little critter's head turned toward the office door. I heard it too. A click.

"Computer. Lights out everywhere."

I pulled out my Snap, snuck as quietly as I could to the top of the stairs in the middle of my apartment. Tut sat there with his head tilted to the right. We had an intruder. I looked down at the door.

A man's face looked up from bottom of the stairs just before he closed the door.

I took three steps at a time. The back door was wide open so I ran in that direction. When I got into the parking lot, a lean guy rushed toward the street and I took off after him.

Despite his head start, I caught up with him at the corner of Cierto and Abby Lane. This was one time when my jogging came in handy. When I came close to him, I dove into his waist to tackle him. Down we went.

I got up first and pointed my Snap at him.

He raised his hands in front of him.

"Roll over. Spread your arms and legs. You know the routine."

The son of a bitch had a .38 in the small of his back. I took the .38 in my left hand. Then I tagged 911 and asked for the police.

A lean male bicyclist dressed in colorful clothes and with a white stripped helmet stopped twenty feet from me, his eyes opened wide. At the sight of my gun, he turned around and pedaled off fast with his head leaning forward.

I put my Snap back in its holster. The wind was chilly. I had not had time to dress for this weather.

My wait didn't last long though. Which was good because I shivered.

An unmarked car pulled up and two guys got out.

I recognized Barney Maston and his new partner, Stu Jamesly. Both had on cheap brown suits. Barney used to partner with Deek before the latter got promoted.

I handed the perp's .38 by its barrel to Maston, who put it in a bag.

"What happened?" asked Maston.

"Guy on the ground broke into my apartment." I pointed.

"Your apartment is over there. You're here. Want to explain?"

I tapped my nose and tagged my apartment. "Tut, download the vid of the intruder."

When it came in, I touched Maston's comm and copied it.

"I chased him and tackled him."

Maston squatted to look at the perp's face. "Well, well. If it isn't Jacky Storey. Hands behind your back. You know the routine." The cop reached behind his back and placed a set of cuffs on Storey's wrists. "Up."

He led Storey into the backseat of his car and looked at me. "Want to file a complaint?"

"Yep."

"I'll need your statement."

"I'll send it in. But first, I'd like to ask him a question."

Maston waved his hand toward the open door. I went to it and leaned over.

"Who sent you?"

"Huh. Nobody," replied Storey.

Maston shut the door. "That's your one question. We'll squeeze him at the station."

As the cops drove off north on Cierto, I turned to go back to my place to get out of the coolness but stopped when I saw Sing Sing Cullen, my landlord. She held a shotgun aimed upward. Today she had on dark slacks, but that was normal for her. She was not a skirt or dress kind of woman. Most gay women aren't.

She aimed upward and her shotgun barked as she fired into the trees. A bird fell to the ground. She turned to me and yelled, "You okay?"

I nodded. I made a motion of pushing my hands downward.

"Oh," she said as she lowered her gun.

When I walked up to her, I asked, "What the hell was that about?"

She pointed. "I bagged a four-winger. They're not allowed in the city. So they're open game." She walked up to the base of the tree and picked up the bird by its feet.

Sure enough, a four-winger.

We plodded back to her real estate office on the ground floor. On the way, I filled her in with the details.

Then I went up to my apartment. When I got inside, despite the warmth, I pulled on a sweater over my head. In the next fifteen minutes, I typed a full statement on my computer and sent it to the police HQ, care of Maston.

When I finished, I got a cup of coffee when a tag came in from Maston.

"Thought you'd like to know. An assistant DA bargained for a lower sentence and Jacky coughed up a name. Borner Hoskins. But on condition we not connect Hoskins to him. Said Hoskins would kill him if he knew. Do you know Hoskins?"

"Nope."

"I ran a search," said Maston. "Works for Stenton Duran."

CHAPTER 20

I sent a message to my team to meet at the ops center ASAP. When I got there, only Vincent waited. Today he had on a yellow shirt with thin vertical blue stripes and blue jeans.

"Ron can't make it nor can Andy," he said.

We both knew Leanna and Zetto were busy elsewhere.

"Ron works tonight," he added. "Andy had to go to La Seille soon and will be gone for a couple weeks."

I studied the walls with Coocher's and Horton's names. On the Coocher wall below that of Stenton Duran, was a new name. Borner Hoskins. So I walked up and spoke a few words.

"Hoskins hired Jack Storey, who broke into my apartment." I added the date. "I chased him and Maston arrested him."

My words appeared on the wall.

Next, I explained the morning's events to Vincent. He went to work on his computer and came up with an address for Hoskins and a photo.

"The cops may pick up Hoskins for questioning."

"They can look for him but the guy's invisible," added Vincent. "He's never home."

I thought about that for a few seconds.

"Let's go visit Keepen. Maybe he knows something."

"Who?"

"Jat Keepen. He replaced Fondero. Owns Uzzo Martial Arts now. He took over from Fondero to run the south side of Zor."

Sometimes crooks popped up and down like popcorn as it's cooked. That's the trouble with running a criminal empire. The longevity wasn't great. Until you got to the top, that is. With many layers between you and the action, it becomes harder for the cops to nail you. And you could afford more hired guns to protect you from your own people. If the cops didn't nail you, your own people could. If it wasn't for the money, most wouldn't try. But then again, most of us do a lot of things for money. Things we don't necessarily like.

We had to run to Vincent's car because of the rain. When it rains on Rossa, it can come down so hard it stings. When we got to Uzzo Martial Arts, we used our extra-sturdy umbrellas. No man could be called a sissy on Rossa for using an umbrella. Last year, a tourist thought he could brave it and a hailstone cracked his skull. He died before the ER people could get to him.

The rain dried up but we still carried our umbrellas just in case.

As we walked from the parking lot next to Uzzo's, I said, "When I shrug my shoulders, get ready. When I slap my hand on the desk, that's to distract the big guy there. You use the opportunity to pull out your gun."

Uzzo was Keepen's cover business. The Sunblocker in the black suit, sized super large to fit his massive frame, sat behind the reception desk. His face lit up when he recognized me. I swear they must hire guys by measuring how big they are. The guy who blocks the most sun gets the job.

When he eyed Vincent, his right eyebrow went up.

I pointed with my left thumb. "Vincent. Works for me."

Sunblocker nodded. "There's a new guy in the office now."

"I know. Jat Keepen. He's the one I want to see."

"Appointment?"

I shook my head. "Courtesy call."

I shrugged and slapped my hand on the table top. Sunblocker jumped as his eyes went to my hand. In the corner of my vision I saw Vincent pull his Snap out and point it at the man.

Sunblocker turned to look at Vincent's gun.

"That's my appointment," I added with my left thumb pointing to the gun.

Sunblocker kept his gaze on the weapon and blurted out, "Keepen won't like this."

I went behind the counter and when Sunblocker raised his hands, I frisked him. Only found one gun, a big .38, which I closed the safety on and put in my waistband.

I reached down and pressed a button. A buzzer went off and I heard a click. I rushed up to the door and kept it open.

"Bring him along," I said to Vincent.

I saw Vincent wave his Snap in my direction and Sunblocker moved out from behind the desk with his hands in the air.

"Put your hands down," I ordered.

"I ain't supposed to leave the front open," he said as he lowered his hands.

"Tough. Make an exception this time," I replied as I held the door wide open.

We three walked the narrow hallway, Sunblocker in front, then me and Vincent. I paid little attention to the view through the windows on my left side as I kept my focus on the big buy in front of me. As we approached the end door, I drew my Snap and held it in the back of Sunblocker.

"Just say one word, 'Visitors'," I ordered.

When we got to the door, Sunblocker knocked and a panel slid aside. A fat Oriental looking face appeared and seemed surprised to see Sunblocker.

Sunblocker said, "Visitors."

The panel closed. I heard noises from behind the door and shoved the gun forward to get Sunblocker's attention.

"To the right," I said. "Kneel. Keep your head down and stay there."

Vincent and I leaned on the left side of the door and waited while Sunblocker did as he was told.

"Who is it?" yelled a voice from behind the door.

"Dani!" I yelled back.

"Who?"

"Fondero's friend."

More silence. I motioned with my right hand for Vincent to step back and I followed him. Two holes appeared in the door at my waist height, accompanied by two gunshots.

Then nothing. I raised my Snap and aimed it at the upper part of the door.

The panel slid aside and that same Asian face appeared. Not a smart move.

I aimed for his face and when he saw my gun aimed his way, he slid the panel back. Then I put two slugs in the panel on the side where he might have stood and heard a thud.

I hastened to the door and slammed my foot at it. But it didn't budge. So I fired three shots at the handle and tried again with my foot. This time it swung open.

A huge flat surface greeted my eyes. Fondero's desk. Or rather Keepen's now.

I looked at Sunblocker, who had his hand over his face, palms out. His eyes were wide open as he looked at my gun. I think he expected me to shoot him on the spot.

From the hallway, I shouted inside the room, "Keepen?"

A voice from in back of the desk replied, "Yeah. What the hell do you want?"

I glanced back at Sunblocker to find him kneeling on the floor where I had left him. This time his hands were on his knees and his head was bowed. Must not think I would kill him after all.

I called out to Keepen, "Know anyone named Borner Hoskins?"

I pulled out a photo I got from Vincent's hacked police records. "Got a photo."

"Put it on the desk and shove it forward."

I did and the photo slid across the surface, coming to a rest a foot from the edge.

A pair of eyes peeked over the top, looked at us and the photo, and went back out of sight. Next a hand reached up, grabbed the photo, and pulled it forward and down.

The voice said, "Ah, the Rat. Doesn't work for me. Who's your friend?"

"Vincent Stone. Works for me part-time."

"Big guy like you. Looks like he can handle himself."

I glanced at Vincent and he and I both grinned. That part was right.

"Why should I talk to you?" said Keepen.

"Fondero was my friend. I have no bone with you." Even though I did Fondero myself, I thought it best to claim ignorance. So I added, "Did you kill him?"

"Nah."

A pause. "The Rat works for Duran now and then," said Keepen. "That's all I know. Where'd you get the name?"

"Jacky Storey visited my place. Or tried to. But I was in it."

"Storey's a punk." A pause. "You shot one of my men."

"Get another one. They must be cheap because they don't have any brains," I said.

Another silence.

"Why are you looking for the Rat?" asked Keepen from behind his desk.

"My daughter and his wife are missing. We think Hoskins had something to do with it."

"So if I provide you with some information, you'd owe me a favor?"

"You sound like you already know."

"Just thinking."

"Well?" I asked.

"Well, would you owe me?" said Keepen.

"Yeah."

Noises came from behind the desk. Then Keepen gave me an address.

* * * * *

Vincent drove his car back to the ops center with me in his passenger seat. I got a tag from Deek and put it on broadcast so Vincent could hear it.

"Heard you had a visitor this morning," said Deek.

"Yeah. An amateur."

"You got that right. But you don't have to worry about a repeat visit from him."

"Why?"

"Somebody knifed him at the jail," said Deek. "Then they cut out his tongue."

"Wagging tongues don't live long, eh?"

"Something like that. Barney and Stu paid a visit to Hoskins's apartment."

"He wasn't there," I added.

"Of course not. Hey, how did you know that?"

"I heard he was invisible. As in never where you think you can find him."

I added, "Any record on Hoskins?"

"New York said he spent five years for assaulting a guy in a bar," replied Deek. "I suspect he's a pro though. Only a pro would know enough to have someone workin' for him."

When I disconnected, Vincent said, "We find Hoskins. I'll bet we find our gals."

"Kinda looks like that."

"Damn! Where the hell are they?"

As he turned left on Moss Street on our way to the ops center, he added, "I hate to say this, but if we don't find them soon..."

My thought exactly.

* * * * *

Vincent and I trekked into the ops center.

Both of us placed our used Snaps in a box in the large planning room, pulled out a drawer, and picked up new ones from the assortment. Somebody would wipe our used Snaps, clean them, and make sure they got their barrels redrilled so slugs couldn't be traced to them. After each time, when the barrels couldn't be drilled again, the Snap would be tossed into a box for disposal. We got new Snaps from a dealer in the southside.

We kept a supply of untraceable Snaps on hand with their serial numbers filed down and etched with acid. We used them whenever we stepped out of the office.

Vincent inquired, "What do we have to eat around here?"

Before I could answer I got a short tag from Zetto.

"K2 at 5 today?"

Before he went undercover, we had agreed on four possible meeting places and had assigned a letter and a number to each. K2 was the gofer section of the Franken Memorial Park.

Gofers were the Rossan equivalent to Earth's lions. Except they had six legs and excellent eyesight and hearing. They were at the top of the food chain. I'd rather run up against one gofer than a pair of greepers or a pack of those damned screechies. Built close to the ground on those six legs, they could sprint to their top speed of twenty miles an hour in five seconds. That was faster than most humans could run but not as fast as a cheetah from Africa. The males were solitary creatures and bigger but the females were the more dangerous and did most of the hunting. Just like the big cats in Africa on the home planet.

I grabbed three strips of bologna, two slices of sourdough bread, and shoved them in a plastic bag. On my way out, I picked up a brown jacket with a liner to stop the wind. The air was chilly so I put the jacket on while holding the bag in my teeth.

"Chima, zoo at Franken Memorial Park.

I wolfed the food down along the way.

Fifteen minutes before five I rested my arms on the wooden guard rail in front of the outdoor gofer cage. Not sure if Zetto would be inside or out, I waited outside in the fresh air. The sky was cloudy and the wind off the Oreo River was brisk and chilly.

Now and then the breeze changed direction and I'd get a whiff of the body odor of the two gofers I watched as they lay on the rocks. The gofers had to live in that odor. Maybe they were used to it.

One was larger than the other. Probably a male. Since I was the only visitor, they watched me with lazy eyes. They knew they couldn't get through the iron fence. I suspect they watched me out of instinct. As in 'any prey will do'.

These two wild animals belonged in the open plains of York, not confined in a cage like this. I figured the bored look in their eyes was real. I'd be bored too if I were I in a cage. That brought back memories of my time in solitary. Depressed, wishing to die just to get the frickin' boredom over.

I felt a nudge on my right shoulder and saw a familiar pair of hands in front of me.

Zetto said in a voice so quiet I could hardly hear him, "I saw plans to pollute the main water supply for Zor. What I didn't see was any mention of how."

I didn't react with a nod or anything. If anyone was watching us, they'd think we were just two guy nestling close to keep the wind off.

I replied in a similar quiet voice, "If you need out, just give me or anyone on the team a call. Help can be there in fifteen minutes."

"I'm okay," Zetto replied, "for now. I think HO plans to blame it on RUFF."

He shivered and pulled the lapels of his beige jacket to his neck before he left to go inside the nearby building.

I waited another five minutes of staring at the two beasts while they stared back. Made me wonder what they were thinking. Probably what I tasted like.

I spoke to the eyes of the larger of the two of them.

"Is anybody home in there?"

When I didn't get an answer, I straightened up and strolled toward the entrance.

On my way, I thought I'd better inform Deek. I tagged him and got him in his office.

"From my sources I've learned that the Zor water supply may become contaminated."

"What with?" asked Deek.

"Don't know."

"Well, when you find out, let me know."

"You want me to give you enough details and names so you can arrest someone?"

"Jake, look. I can't alert the Water Works on just what you gave me. I need more."

"Okay, I understand. Will work on it."

We disconnected.

Damn! Now I've got a dilemma. Rescue Alena and Leanna—or save the city.

CHAPTER 21

When I got back to the ops center, I went straight to the dining room. Vincent sat in front of a laptop. I relayed my visit to Zetto.

Then I strode into the large planning room. Since I hadn't used my shoulder Snap, I didn't bother to replace it. Nor my ankle one.

First, I sent an encrypted message to my team telling them the gist of our discoveries. After that, I sent a message to Acorn updating him on Zetto's news and our search for Leanna and Alena.

Vincent walked into the room.

"Which is our first priority? Save the folks in the city or our gals? I hope you're going to say Lee and Alena."

I moved my head up and down.

"L & A come first. We know they're at risk. The other is merely a threat at this point."

Feeling the need for more food, I returned to the kitchen and fixed myself a sandwich of ham and grilled Swiss cheese. Well, the closest to Swiss cheese we had, something called Swiss-o. And a bowl of chicken noodle soup.

Halfway through the meal, I got a tag from Keepen.

"He's stayin' at Duran's house. He heard the cops are looking for him."

"Got it."

"You owe me one."

"Got that too."

Time for some serious thinking.

Ten minutes later, I went to Vincent.

"Find the home of Stenton Duran, Coocher's second in command. Get the layout if you can. We're gonna pay him a visit tonight."

Then I lay on a lower bunk and tried to sleep so I would be fully awake on the op. I set an alarm on my comm to wake me at seven forty-five. But I couldn't stop thinking about Alena and Leanna, so I practiced my spy training technique to force myself to sleep. Relax all my muscles and try to focus my mind on the static inside my eyelids. I kept repeating to myself, ever slower each time, "My brain and body are slowing down. My-brain and body are...sl-oo-wing...do-wn."

The vibrations of my comm interrupted a nightmare of being locked in a cage with two hungry gofers. And no Snap. Some guy fumbled with the door. Unfortunately, the door was between the animals.

A trip to the AutoCook in the kitchen and a minute later I had a cup of coffee.

On the planning room wall, Vincent displayed an aerial view of Duran's property in Beverly Hills north of the Oreo River.

Luck was with us this time. It was not in a gated community.

While putting on moustaches and bushy eyebrows, we laid out scenarios of our approach in case we didn't get what we wanted by the front door approach.

A trip to the website of the Homeless Aid Fund and I had what I needed. I painted a metallic cup with their logo and put three sols and some change in it so it would rattle.

At dark, we put on sports jackets and bright yellow caps with the Zor Screechies logo. The Screechies were a football team and were up for their second All York trophy. After putting our night vision goggles, gloves, and other gear in sports bags, we walked to the BIS van. We'd leave the bags in the van since we didn't want attention on our walk to Duran's house.

I put on my gloves.

"Chima, manual drive. Put the logo of Zor Screechies on your outsides."

I glanced at my comm to get the time. Eight forty-five.

I drove to within two blocks of Duran's house in the Beverly Hills part of Zor. When we passed his place, lights were on in the living room.

We tried the frontal approach first. Vincent kept to the left side of the door out of sight while I knocked on the door.

After fifteen seconds, I wondered if anybody was home.

It was possible he left a light on in his living room so some scum casing his house would think somebody was home.

If the house was vacant, we'd have to try another approach. Luck was on our side. The front door overhead light came on. A French window opened in the door behind a screen.

"What do you want?" asked a tall white man. He had a large pistol in a chest holster. He looked at my jacket and said, "Don't you guys keep regular hours?"

I shook the cup with the Homeless Aid Fund logo. "We're from the Zor Screechies, sir. Have you made a donation to the Homeless Aid Fund yet?"

A sigh was our answer. "Come in. I'll get my wallet."

When the screen door clicked, I opened it and pushed the main door open. In the living room, Duran bent over a low table loaded with a remote, two empty mugs of beer, and a pile of tablet readers.

"Are we interrupting something, sir? We can come back later."

"Nah. Let me get this over with." Duran bent over the table.

I glanced behind me and saw Vincent close the front door and lock it quietly.

Duran opened his wallet and took out a ten sol note. "Will this be enough?"

I drew my Snap at the same time as Vincent.

When Duran saw them, he said, "What is this?"

"Your guest wouldn't be Borner Hoskins, would it?"

With that, Duran pursed his lips and lowered his eyebrows. The stubborn act.

I shoved my Snap in his belly and pulled a .40 caliber from his holster, which I put into my jacket pocket. "Into the kitchen, Duran."

He raised his hands and asked, "Do you know who I am? You're in serious trouble."

I waved the tip of my gun and he looked at it.

"I'd just as soon shoot you," I said. "Your choice."

Duran shook his head, sighed, and walked into the kitchen. There, I motioned with my left index finger to a wooden straight back chair. After he sat, I wrapped duct tape around his legs and fastened his wrists behind his back. Vincent kept his Snap pointed at his chest from three feet away. I stuffed a washcloth in our victim's mouth and a piece of duct tape over it. When I finished, I pulled my gun out and pointed it at the man's head.

"Where's your guest?"

He shrugged his shoulders.

I looked around and spotted a door. I motioned to Vincent and we went through it and down to the basement with our guns out. We left the lights out, not wanting to disturb anyone.

A sofa lay against the far wall, with a blanket tossed aside and a white pillow on one end. In front of the sofa lay a table with an empty glass. I picked it up with my gloves on and sniffed. Beer.

We went back upstairs to the kitchen.

When I got to Duran, I swiped my Snap across his face and drew a streak of blood.

"You work for Guy Coocher. Where's Hoskins?"

That brought a narrowing of his eyebrows and a squinting of his eyes. I don't think he expected that.

"Now, we're going to apply a little pain. If you want it to stop, all you have to do is nod your head. But I warn you, if we remove the gag and you don't answer the way we want, the gag will go back on and we'll try more pain."

Duran glared back.

Vincent ripped open the man's shirt to expose black curly hairs on a pale white chest. Duran's chest rose and fell with each rapid breath. From his jacket, Vincent brought out an electrical heating rod, the kind used to melt solder, and plugged its long cord into a wall socket. When the red light went on, he stuck the business end to the man's chest.

The singe of flesh greeted my nostrils, along with a muffled scream.

Vincent pulled his rod away.

"Now," I asked, "Is Borner Hoskins staying here?"

When I didn't get a prompt answer, I waved my left hand and Vincent applied the rod. When he stopped, I could see from Duran's face he believed more would come.

"We can keep this up a lot longer than you can bear it, Duran."

The man's wide-open eyes looked at me. He nodded.

I grabbed one end of the tape over his mouth and yanked. Duran winced.

Then I pulled the cloth out.

"Is Hoskins staying here?"

"Yes."

I asked, "Who ordered the kidnapping of Alena Dani and her mother?"

At the mention of a name, Duran straightened up.

"What's it to you?"

"I'm Alena's father."

I raised my hand to signal Vincent to apply another dose.

But Duran blurted out, "You can't tell anybody I told you. If you do, they'll kill me."

I paused.

Duran looked at me with wide open eyes and furled eyebrows.

"Promise?" he asked.

I nodded.

"Coocher ordered them taken."

Vincent asked, "When?"

"A week ago."

"Why?" I asked.

"Coocher read Alena's paper," Duran said. "He wanted to prevent her from doing more research."

"Who did you give the job to?" asked Vincent.

"Hoskins."

"So he was the one who kidnapped both women?" Vincent asked.

"I told him to take only the daughter. He must have felt it necessary to take the other woman at the same time. I swear I didn't know she'd be there."

Vincent asked, "So you gave the order directly to Hoskins?"

Duran looked down. "Yeah. Sorry about that."

Vincent turned to me. "I believe him."

I nodded. "So do I." I looked at Duran. "Do you have any kids of your own?"

He shook his head.

"Then you don't know what it feels like to think your own kid may be tortured, raped, and killed by scum."

Vincent said, "I say kill him. We got what we came for."

I looked at Duran. This bastard ordered my daughter taken. I pulled his .40 out of my pocket, made sure the safety was off, and pointed it at Duran's temple. It took two pulls on the trigger, the first to load a bullet in the chamber, the second to do the job. One bullet was all it took.

He collapsed with blood splattered on the wall behind him.

Vincent looked at the corpse. "If you wouldn't do it, I would."

I pointed at the corpse. "That bastard ordered my daughter kidnapped! She was an innocent victim!"

"You're preaching to the choir here."

"Yeah, I know."

Then Vincent added, "Oh look. He's dead. I guess that means you're released from your promise."

I grinned. "Yep. You can't keep a promise to a dead man."

Even though I used gloves and couldn't leave any fingerprints on the gun, I decided there was some risk. I didn't know if the man had taken steps like we would to hide the grooves in the barrel. So I put the gun into my jacket left pocket.

We left before the cops might arrive. A neighbor might have heard the shot.

On the way back over the Ambassador Bridge, I stopped and went up to the edge in the middle of the Oreo River. I waited until there no headlights. After checking to see if anyone was looking and there wasn't, I flung the gun way out from the bridge. Not as far as I could but as far as a woman might toss it. With the river flowing fast and muddy, I figured the silt would cover it so it might be undiscovered for another fifty years.

When we got back to the ops center, we both showered and put our clothes and gloves in the wash. I didn't want even the best forensic technician finding any gun powder residue. I turned on the clothes washer to get rid of any evidence.

* * * * *

We hit the sack. Nothing takes it out of you like killing someone. Surprisingly I didn't have nightmares about it. But it was the first thing on my mind when I woke up.

I ate breakfast across from Vincent. Both of us wore the same clothes as the day before. I had a feeling I'd be seeing more of him until our gals were safe. And if they weren't.... well, I don't know what I'd do. It's hard to think that far ahead, especially when each day brought new information.

"Lee and Alena depend on us to find them," said Vincent.

"I understand."

"Where could Hoskins be?" asked Vincent before he inserted a forkful of steak in his mouth.

"We may have exhausted one underground source but I still have another."

He stopped chewing and said with a mouthful, "Gancha?"

I nodded.

We adjourned to the ops room and sat at the table. I tagged Gancha Morentoss. Not surprisingly, I had to leave a message. She would naturally screen her calls.

We studied the wall on Coocher. Having the confession of Duran made our jobs easier. We could ignore Horton and RUFF.

A minute later, my comm vibrated.

"Yes?"

"I got your message," said the voice from my past.

"I need information."

"What?" asked Gancha.

"I need to know the current location of Borner Hoskins, also known as the Rat."

"And in exchange?"

"Maybe dinner."

"If you can make that a definite dinner, I'll see what I can do."

"Okay, make that definite." I had to smile at that one. But at least she didn't mention what came after dinner.

"Tag you back when I find out."

She disconnected.

If it were anybody but Alena, I wouldn't go to Gancha. Her inheriting a crime empire meant she had access to lots of people. I hoped she had the right ones.

I'd have to decide what to do when the time came. My first priority was getting Alena and Leanna back.

Over the next four hours, Vincent and I went over several plans but nothing popped out as doable. Time was running out. It had been four days since they disappeared. Each day increased the odds that when we found them, they'd be dead.

Then I got a tag from Gancha. I put it on Vincent's comm.

"Two Moons Hotel. Room 234. Now about that dinner."

"Let me check it out first. I promised you, Gancha, and you know I keep my word."

"Luv ya," she said just before she disconnected.

I looked at Vincent. He had one eyebrow raised. I added, "No, I don't plan to kill her."

"Then let's get hopping on how to hit that hotel," he said.

CHAPTER 22

Ron walked in wearing blue jeans, a matching jacket, a light pink shirt, and brown cowboy boots.

"I got off shift. Took some leave so I won't have to go back there for a while. Thought you might need some help."

"Thanks."

I sent a message to Acorn to update him.

Vincent found the address and then an aerial view of the Two Moons. To think, they were just a block and a half away, across the street from Uzzo Martial Arts.

From public records, Vincent showed the layout of the motel on the wall of the planning room. Room 234 was just above the registration desk and not far from the inside stairs.

I filled Ron in on our recent activities and findings. When I got to the part about killing Duran, he didn't flinch.

I fixed my gaze on him.

"A man's gotta do what a man's gotta do," was his response.

I smiled as did Vincent. Ron was a true buddy and a true spy.

Ron volunteered to go along on the op to the Two Moons. As a matter of fact, he insisted and I couldn't think of any reason to deny him. Besides, having an extra gun might help.

We spent the next two hours getting dressed in black and going over different scenarios and escape routes, while we cleaned our guns.

When nine o'clock rolled around, it was dark outside and I decided it was time. Our gals might be dead by now.

You could cut the tension in the air. We would see Alena and Leanna in a few minutes and we wanted to be ready for any contingency, including finding their bodies. Both Vincent and I hated that part but we had to face reality.

Next, we loaded our gear into the BIS van and headed out, Ron behind the wheel.

"Chima, look for a tail," I said.

It was easier when your van could track not only vehicles but also who might be in them. From the sixteen cameras we installed on the van, three on each side, six in the rear, and four in front, we enabled Chima to get a good all-around view. She need four in front to plan where to turn. Four more cameras peered inside. And she had an impeccable memory when it came to license plates, models, and who might be in a given vehicle. She could tell if the same car followed us two weeks ago, even if they changed plates.

It didn't take long to cover the block and a half to the Two Moons. We parked in the underground parking and pulled our face masks down. We wore rubber masks of old men. Ron and I wore bald-headed masks. Vincent chose thin gray hair.

"Silencers."

We screwed silencers on the ends of our Snaps.

To help communication without our Z helmets, we kept our comms on broadcast.

Ron led the way to the lobby on the ground floor.

We wouldn't have bothered with visiting the registration desk except room 234 was on the other side. Plus we needed a key to the room.

Ron went first. Next came Vincent, who shot out the camera behind the desk. I stayed out of sight until then. The less information they had the better.

Ron hopped over the counter and pushed his Snap into the throat of the sole male clerk. Then he injected him with a sleeping solution.

"This means you'll take a nap. We'll be long gone by the time you wake."

He also took the master key card.

The stairs were just beyond the registration desk. I stepped out from behind a pillar in the lobby and led the way. We took the stairs two steps at a time.

When I got to the second floor, I peered down both hallways. Nobody was in sight.

"Hallways clear."

Room 234 was on my right and we soon came upon it. Vincent and I stayed on different sides of the door while Ron swiped the master key card and turned the handle.

We three barged into an empty room. In front of the two King sized beds sat two chairs. Strips of duct tape hung on the legs of the chairs and the backs.

Ron checked the bathroom and shook his head when he came out.

We were too late.

* * * * *

Ron drove on the way back to the ops center. No one said anything but I expected that.

Once inside, I got another tag, this time from Zetto.

"Botulism in the water. Midnight tonight. I'm done here. I need an exit. Meet me at Fourth and Moss."

Shit.

"Any hurry?"

"Yep. They suspect me."

One in the hand versus two in the bush.

"We're on our way."

I disconnected. "Zetto needs extraction."

Vincent, Ron, and I donned our armor. We had to change shirts to a larger size. All three of us chose dark blue. I screwed a silencer on my Snap.

Ron drove this time. When we got to Fourth and Moss, out in the countryside on the west side of Zor, Zetto was nowhere in sight.

Shit.

We drove up and down the parking lot aisles, scanning every vehicle.

"He's not here," said Vincent.

"Ron, let's go to the Water Works."

Ron stayed in the van for a quick escape while Vincent and I rushed inside.

I had to use my silenced Snap on the lock on the glass doors. I pointed. Vincent took the offices on the right side and I the left.

When we got to the end of the first floor, I saw an Exit sign next to the Basement Sign. I motioned to Vincent. We entered the stairwell and walked with our Snaps in front of us.

After scanning the rooms in the basement and finding them leading to water treatment tanks, we approached the only other door.

We took each side.

"On zero. Three. Two. One. Zero."

We burst through the door to find a large room. Four men stood around a chair with Zetto sitting in it, his hands secured behind him, his head bowed.

Vincent and I exchanged fire several times with the men around our guy. The other guys must not have been wearing armor because they took hits. When all four lay on the ground, I noticed Vincent was down.

"How bad you hurt?" I asked him.

"Flesh wound, I think. My leg. I'll put a StopIt patch on it. Go help Zetto. I'll be all right."

I rushed up to Zetto. His head hung down and I could see blood on his face. His eyes looked puffed up but at least he was awake.

The bastards.

I untied him and tagged Ron.

"We got him but Vin took a hit on a leg."

I had to carry Zetto up the stairs. Vincent limped alongside but made his own way.

When we exited the front door, Ron had his Snap out and opened the rear doors of the van. We placed Zetto in the back seat and Vincent sat next to him.

I ran around to the passenger door and Ron took the driver's seat. We tore off and headed back on Moss.

I watched as Vincent placed StopIt gray goo on Zetto's bleeding wounds.

The poor man said from his puffed up face between breaths, "They found out about me. Thanks for the rescue."

I said, "We'll take you to the doctor's office. Hang in there, buddy."

Ron drove up to Doctor Alicia Newton's office and I carried Zetto inside. Vincent limped alongside me.

Dr. Newton wore a white long-sleeved blouse and black tight skirt. I noticed because she was in different attire from when we usually met. Gone was her white lab coat and a DetectIt hanging from her neck.

She put on her lab coat and DetectIt before she examined Zetto.

"I have to keep this one overnight."

After she looked over Vincent, she asked, "I noticed a StopIt on your leg. Can you walk?"

He nodded.

She said to me, "I still need to keep the other guy. He's hurt much worse than this man."

So I left Zetto in her care while I helped Vincent get into the van.

I tagged Sheila at Channel One News. "Break into any program. Botulism in the public water. Don't drink tap water. Humans Only is responsible."

She responded, "We already did. Got an anonymous tag. Why do you think HO is responsible?"

"We can provide a witness but you need to disguise his appearance."

"No problem. Jake, sometime, you'll have to explain why you are always in the middle of everything."

"Yeah. Sometime."

When we got back to the ops center, we three suffered downer moods. We had rescued Zetto but not our women.

Vincent rested on a bunk while I brought Acorn up to speed on the latest developments. The failed mission to rescue Alena and Leanna was the biggie. I also mentioned our rescue of Zetto and the poisoning of the water.

I had to face the possibility that Lee and Alena were dead and buried someplace where we would never find them.

* * * * *

In the dorm, I thought over my options. I had burned my bridges with Keepen and was on the hook with Gancha. Which wasn't a bad thing.

What the hell could I do?

Everything I had tried had failed.

Was I going to find the bodies of Alena and Leanna somewhere?

The thought tore me up.

Hoskins was out there with Leanna and Alena. Coocher was king of the media.

What chance did I have?

The only lead I had was Coocher.

So, go with what you've got.

"Vincent, can you get me the layout of Coocher's place?"

He looked up from his laptop in his bunk. "Sure."

I swear the guy had a laptop growing out of his hip.

Ron, Vincent, and I went into the planning room and went over several options.

Deek tagged me. "I thought you'd like to know this before it hits the news. Stenton Duran, second in command for Humans Only, was killed yesterday. The killer tortured him beforehand. You wouldn't know anything about that, would you?"

"Nope."

"I hope you don't mind my asking. Where were you yesterday?"

"Well, you're my witness for part of the time. I visited Uzzo Martial Arts and took a walk at the Franken Memorial Park."

"Anybody vouch for that?"

"I didn't know I needed an alibi. Jat Keepen may remember me at Uzzo. Most of the day I spent alone, but that's normal for me."

"A witness reported two men going into the house. Both had facial hair but that could have been part of a disguise. Both were large men."

"That's it?" I asked.

"That and they wore uniforms that made them look like the York Screechies."

When Deek didn't respond, I asked, "Am I a suspect?"

"One of hundreds," Deek said with a sigh. "Duran had many enemies. He was pressing for tightening the laws."

"Tightening the laws won't do much good," I said. "What we need the most is enforcing the ones we have."

"You won't find any argument here."

After we disconnected, I turned on the telly to see if Duran's death had made the news. Sure enough. Channel Four didn't mention it but the other three did. Channel Two sympathized with HO so I expected them to make a big deal about it. The part I liked the most was the police didn't have any clues. But that could be a lie. Cops do that.

The news on Duran mentioned he'd been killed by gunshot. The fact that he was burned and bloodied first never came out. I figured the police withheld that part.

Channel One was the only one that mentioned poisoning the water. That story was not repeated on the other channels.

I didn't see any mention anywhere, even on the Net, about Alena and Leanna being missing. That irritated me. A minor male politician gets killed and it spreads, but when two women go missing, not a word. But Zor was a frontier city and women went missing often.

CHAPTER 23

I grabbed a Snap and put it in my holster.

"I need to visit Zetto."

Andy was still out of town. Vincent insisted on tagging along, despite his leg wound. He limped to our van while I drove with Ron in the passenger seat.

"Chima, whenever one of my team drives, check on a possible tail."

"Affirmative," replied the female voice.

"Report any suspicions."

"Affirmative."

"Oh, make that when any of my team is in the van."

"Affirmative."

"And plan a route that includes looping around a block."

"Affirmative."

Most cars and vans used automatic driving. Since it might arouse suspicion if I drove, I gave Chima the address of Dr. Newton's office and let the AI pick a route.

Chima drove around two blocks and I was pleased that she understood my instructions. When we arrived at the doc's office, we went in.

I spoke to the receptionist.

"Dr. Newton? I gotta see her personally."

Ten minutes later, she came out in her white lab coat with a DetectIt hanging from her neck. A DetectIt could analyze breath, sweat, or blood. It ran hundreds of tests and gave near-instant readouts to the doctor. When held to the patient's chest, it could also detect heartbeats and breathing irregularities.

She took us into her office and closed the door behind us.

"Dr. Newton," I asked, "Where's my friend?"

She took her seat.

"My place. I thought it best to take him there. My staff here might wonder why I hadn't reported his injuries to the police."

"We can take care of him on our own. We have a place that won't arouse suspicion."

"Can I visit him?" she asked.

"If you're willing to wear a blindfold during your travels. We can't let anyone know where that place is."

"I understand. And agree."

She knew about our work for BIS. As a matter of fact, that was a major reason why she helped us.

With her agreement, I replied, "Can I take him now?"

She rose from behind her desk. "You'll have to wait until closing time, I'm afraid."

"When is that?"

"Five. Come back at five thirty and you can follow me."

"Your address?"

She gave it to us.

When we returned to the ops center, I put a stack of twenty sols in my jacket pocket.

At five, Vincent and I left for her office. At five twenty-five, we waited in her parking lot.

I looked in my outside rear view mirror to see Dr. Newton walk out the side door of her clinic.

Gone was her lab coat. Instead she wore a beige long-sleeved blouse and black full skirt. And a long coat, open at the front.

"Here she comes now. You sit next to her and give her driving instructions. Make sure she takes many turns. I'll follow and check for a tail."

We took twenty minutes to cover the two miles to her home, doubling back twice.

When she pulled in her driveway, I parked on the street and joined them.

She lived in a two-story house with a peaked roof of red slates. That would come in handy when it snowed, which it often did in the winter.

I followed Vincent and the doctor as they entered through a side door.

As we progressed in her home, I used my comm to scan for broadcasting.

We made left turns all the way through the kitchen, into a dining room, and then into the living room. I spotted a door off to the left of the living room. We had traversed a full circle. I figured the side door to the outside lay beyond a closed door. Sure enough, when I opened it, there was the door. Another door lay on my right, just left of the front door.

"Number one," said Vincent. Out of habit, he referred to me by my number when in the presence of strangers. He had never been introduced to Dr. Newton.

It was time to correct that. I turned to her, standing beside him, and said, "Dr. Newton, you know me as Jake." I pointed to him. "He's Vincent, part of my team."

"And the man on the bed?" she asked.

"Zetto," I replied, "also part of my...."

"Team," she filled in as she nodded.

I looked around me. Opposite the front door was a staircase.

She pointed. "Upstairs is my bedroom and a small office. And the public bathroom."

I walked into Zetto's room and saw him lying on a large bed, white bandages over most of his body. He must have been hurt in places I didn't see.

Those bastards must have worked him over.

His eyes were closed.

I walked up to his bed and shook the mattress. He opened his eyes, focused on me, and smiled.

"Feeling up to a ride?" I asked.

Zetto looked at Dr. Newton and Vincent when they walked in.

"If the doc says I can," he replied in a hoarse voice.

She turned to me. "It will be dark soon. Care to eat here before you take him? I usually eat alone but could use the company."

"That might be a good idea. Moving him in the dark. Can you make sure any outside lights are off?"

"Okay. You three visit while I fix dinner. I started a slow cooker before I left." With that, she walked out of the room.

I looked at Zetto. "They did quite a job on you."

"I don't think they liked having their communications sent out," he added. "Have you found our two women yet?"

I put my index finger to my lips. "Let's not talk until we're in a more secure environment." I glanced at Vincent and tapped my comm.

He took the hint, held his comm up, and walked around the room holding it in front of him. Zetto and I waited in silence until he stopped and said, "All clear."

Zetto asked, "What about Leanna and Alena?"

I looked down and Vincent replied, "We haven't found them yet. But we know who did it."

"That's great!" said Zetto. "Are the police on the case?"

Vincent answered, "The confessor didn't survive."

Zetto looked at me. "Oh."

A look can tell paragraphs.

I added, "We can talk more at the center."

Zetto said, "You'll find them."

I looked down at the floor. "I'm afraid we may be too late."

Dr. Newton peeked in the door. "Dinner's ready. Hope you guys like split pea and ham."

I said, "Beggars can't be choosers."

She smiled before replying, "You're guests, not beggars."

I answered, "Then guests can't be choosers."

She grinned again and walked out of the doorway to her left.

Vincent and I helped Zetto get up and walk.

Her dining room had six tall-back dark wood chairs. Zetto sat on the end opposite the doctor and rested his limbs on the arms of the chair. Vincent sat to his right. Behind Vincent rested a dark wooden case with glass doors. On the shelves of the case, I saw stacks of dishes.

I sat to Dr. Newton's right in a chair without arms and said, "I hope you don't mind. We'll fill you in more when you come to visit Zetto. There are just too many possible ears."

I pulled the thick pile of twenties out of my jacket and handed them to her. "For groceries, and such," I said with a wink.

She smiled and took the money.

After dinner, we adjourned to the living room. We needed to wait until darkness would cover our exit.

We watched the news on the telly. The artic jet stream was due to dip south in a week, bringing cold weather. Just what we needed.

I pulled her living room curtains aside a crack to check on the weather. The sky was dark.

"It's time to go."

Under a black sky full of clouds and with the side door light out, we transferred Zetto to the passenger seat of our van. Vincent kept a lookout from the back of the van while I drove around the university and the railroad station to check for any tails.

CHAPTER 24

I received a tag from Ron on the way.

"I'm in the center."

"Vince and I are bringing in Zee. Can you set up a bed in the planning room?"

"Got it."

Zetto moaned.

"Can I have another pain pill?"

Vincent handed him a morphine pill and a bottle of water.

When we got to the ops center, I told the now sleepy Zetto, "Put your arms around my neck."

His eyes drooped as I lifted him up and carried him. Vincent limped ahead to open the doors.

Once inside the dorm room, Ron met us and led the way past the bunk beds. I glanced and saw that one bed lacked its top counterpart. We went through the kitchen and into the planning room. There rested the missing bed.

How he got a bunk bed from the dorm I didn't know. With the beds stacked one on top of the other, it must have been a chore to remove the top one. But he was half-Binger.

Zetto laid down on the bed and Vince covered him up.

Zetto's eyes drooped. Having a full meal, a ride, and the morphine must have worked their magic.

Before he nodded off, he mumbled, "I overheard of a meeting with some bigwig and Coocher to take place Saturday at noon."

"Did you find out where?"

"Yep," said Zetto as he fixed his eyes on me. "In the parking lot of Franken Mall at noon tomorrow."

Vincent said, "Odd place for a meeting."

I noticed the time. "It's getting late. Why don't we all get some shuteye and start fresh in the morning?"

Zetto closed his eyes. Ron, Vincent, and I left the room. As I made my way out the room, I flipped the switch on the wall to turn the lights off.

At breakfast the next day, I swear you could cut the tension in the air. An op always does that.

After nine in the morning, Vincent and I headed to the mall in our van. Ron stayed to take care of Zetto.

"Chima, change your outside color."

"What color would you like?"

"Gray…er, light gray, until we get within a block of the mall. When I park in the shade, change that to all white. And gradually, in case anyone is looking."

A block away, I turned into an alley. Shade came from the nearby buildings. "Chima, it's time to change colors. Change our license plates too."

"Affirmative."

Then I headed to the mall's huge parking lot.

We had plenty of time to set up six remote viewing cameras and at eleven-forty, one of them showed a black van parking in the southeast corner of the lot. Two men sat in the front and kept the engine running. Two other guys looked out the back windows.

That seemed odd. Might be our target.

I slowed to let Vincent out. He left via the back doors with a backpack.

I drove two rows over from the van and out of its sight. As I drove by, a guy standing outside looked at me and unfolded his arms.

Oh oh. He's alert.

I drove by, appearing to look for an empty space. When my head turned away from the van, I spoke into my comm.

"Vince, the guy outside the van watched me."

Luck was not on my side that day and I could not find a parking space. Maybe lots of folks shopped on this Saturday morning.

At this mall.

To avoid arousing further suspicion, I drove by the front of several stores and around the edge of the mall, out of sight of the guy in front of the van. Didn't have much choice. Couldn't find a parking space.

"Chima, put on the colors and logo of..."

"I haven't used Maria's Produce in a while," replied Chima.

I nodded. "That's a good one."

Unfortunately, I had to wait while oncoming traffic cleared before I could make a U-turn. I thought of poor Vincent alone back there. If the guys in the van thought he was connected to me, his life could be in danger.

I said in my comm, "Vince, are you okay?"

"Sure," came a quick reply. "Snug as the proverbial bug."

I wondered where that phrase came from.

Chima reported, "I've changed my colors and logo to Maria's Produce."

"Vince, how's your leg?"

"Some slight pain but I can handle it."

I headed back. This time I spotted the guy outside the black van on my left as I drove two aisles over from him. A man and a woman loaded bags into the boot of a car. I waited a safe distance behind them. Behind me and to my left was the black van with the guy still outside. I turned my inside mirror to check on him. He busied himself lighting an ecig.

It seemed to take the guy in the car a half a minute to back up. Eventually, the car pulled out and I took its spot.

I pressed the button and opened the disguise kit. Then I put on a full beard and black hat, picked up a sport bag with the Stacy's emblem, and left the van keeping my eyes on Stacy's Department Store.

Vincent reported on my comm, "I'm here, behind the target. And with a good view, too."

"Keep alert to anyone coming up on you."

I walked up to the store and entered. After visiting the restroom of Stacy's, I removed my disguise and put on a larger nose. I inverted my jacket to present a beige color.

Then I strode back to the second row from the one with the target van, where I ducked and ran toward it while keeping out of sight. When I got between two SUVs, I could peek out and see the van but they'd have a difficult time seeing me.

"In position," I reported to Vincent.

I waited another fifteen minutes like that, crouched in front of two SUV engine compartments, before a limo pulled up in front of the black van.

A big guy in a gray suit and a buzz cut on top went from the limo to the van and back. Then Guy Coocher exited the limo, walked over to the van with the same big guy, and entered as a side door slid open.

I couldn't see the inside of the van from my position and said on my comm, left open to Vincent's, "See anything?"

"Beautiful view, right in the front window. Coocher is talking with a guy."

"Can you get his photo?" I asked.

"Sure thing."

"See if you can determine who he is."

I waited for another five minutes before I got another tag from Vincent.

"Ash Getner, head of YSA."

What the hell was he doing talking with Coocher?

Five minutes later, Coocher left the van, returned to his limo, and it drove off. The black van waited another ten minutes before it left.

My legs ached from crouching so long and I stood up after the last of the two vehicles drove out of sight.

Vincent rose from his hiding place. I could see why he had such a beautiful view. He had been right in front of the van in the bushes. More bushes lay behind him.

I went directly to our BIS van and drove to Vincent's spot. He got in.

"What do you have?"

He tapped a few buttons on the side of his camera and we both looked at the view of the front of the van. Coocher and Getner sat opposite each other. We couldn't get any sound but at one point, Getner passed a small package to Coocher. The men shook hands before Coocher left.

I looked at Vincent with a big grin. "That shot of them shaking hands is a beaut!"

As I drove my mind went into overdrive thinking of how we could use this vid. Coocher shaking hands with Getner would undermine his credibility with his Humans Only organization. Here was the top guy of a hate campaign against "hybrids" shaking hands with a man with artificial legs. And that man was the head of the spy agency YSA.

"Don't let that recording get lost."

Vincent replied, "I've already sent a coded copy to my office."

"You might send one to our boss, too."

"Will do, later," he replied.

It took fifteen minutes to get back to the ops center.

Zetto cheered at the good news.

Ron was the spoilsport.

"All that is fine, but we still need to find Lee and her daughter."

I slumped my shoulders and nodded.

Vincent looked up from his equipment, "Hey, guess what? That guy who walked between the limo and the van? I thought he looked familiar. Take a look." He displayed the still view on the wall.

It was the Rat.

"Found you, you son of a bitch," I said.

You could cut the excitement in the air.

"I think Hoskins is staying at Coocher's house," said Vincent. "And I'll bet my wife and daughter are there, too."

I pointed to Vincent. "Get me his address, aerials of his home, and anything else you can find."

Ron beamed. "Are we going in?"

I turned to him.

"Yep."

With Vincent still lame in his leg and Zetto lying on a bed, I had only Ron on the op.

Coocher's home was a fortress. He had a ten foot wall around his thirty-acre property, guards from El Libro Security, and six Rossan wolfhounds. The main house sat in the middle of the property, a good hundred yards from the main gate. I'd bet the house had security up the wazoo. And it was huge with at least a dozen bedrooms in its three stories.

"With all that security, makes you wonder what the man is afraid of."

Ron answered, "Maybe he fears reactions from those he hates so much."

CHAPTER 25

We expected at least twelve shooters, including Coocher, Hoskins, and several guards. I didn't like the odds. Twelve to two. But I had few choices.

Even wearing full-body armor and packing lots of firepower, we'd be in close range of many guns. I suggested semi-automatic rifles. Ron carried a shotgun too. Both of us had our regular Snaps, two other guns, and knives.

Since there were so many guards, we would try subterfuge. That meant wearing outer clothes. With the weather getting cooler that should not be a problem.

Vincent pulled out a pair of eyeglasses.

"Andy dropped four off before he went to La Seille. They have the same night vision and instant shutters we have in our Z helmets in case of glaring lights. They also have the same communications."

Andy's Z helmets had come in handy many times. When one person speaks, his helmet will select slices of the voice, encode the information into a scrambled packet of data, compress it, and send it out over the next channel from a preselected list. The other guy's helmet will receive the burst, acknowledge receiving it, slow it, unscramble it, and send to his earpiece. In this way, it would be next to impossible for anyone to detect and decode the conversation.

The radio waves will be of short duration and the frequencies changed according to the preset sequence of 240 channels out of a possible ten million in a short burst of less than a thousandth of a second. In addition, the low power of the radio waves made it unlikely that anyone over sixty feet away could detect the conversation.

I pulled on a pair of the glasses and noticed right away they had side and top covers. Our eyes would be fully protected from glaring lights.

"Flip the switch on the left side," said Vincent.

I did and my vision returned to normal. I removed the glasses.

"Tell Andy thanks."

"You can do that yourself. He's coming back next week."

We discussed what subterfuge to use and Ron suggested we pretend to be HO people. We went over several scenarios. All had inherent risks, even with Vincent and the BIS van parked outside the guard gate and in constant touch.

Zetto would have to be alone for a few hours, but he was okay with that. "I'll load up on pain killers. Have a little party of my own here." He patted an automatic rifle and a Snap next to his legs. "And I've got my friends here."

The big issue was when. I didn't want to wait until dark. That would mean another half day of Leanna and Alena maybe being tortured. They could even be dead already.

I ended all further discussion.

"Let's go in there."

Zetto showed us the HO logo of a glaring male face scowling down at a smaller man with artificial arms next to a robot.

I went to work on adding that logo to two light blue jackets that were a bit large, even for Ron or myself. We'd be wearing armor underneath our dress shirts.

Ron got out two pairs of pants with pockets hidden inside. We'd add another layer of light blue pants to match the jackets. We donned rubber-soled dress shoes.

Fearing recognition, I insisted the three of us wear moustaches with heavy sideburns, the rave now in men's fashions. We put on wigs of light hair and contacts to change the color of our pupils to blue. And the magical glasses. We had kept our light colored skin. Coocher might be suspicious if our skins were dark.

"Ready?" I said.

Ron nodded and Vincent stood. We waved to Zetto. "Don't open the doors until you see our natural faces. I'll send a warning message using the code word 'alphabet'."

On the side of the van, Ron slapped a magnetic name plate with the HO logo. Vincent drove and Ron and I sat in the back.

"Ron, when I pull my gun on Coocher, you take out any guards nearby. Then move back and forth so nobody else could get a clear shot."

I sat back, lost in thoughts. On every op, there was a chance one of us could die.

* * * * *

When we arrived at the guard gate at Coocher's place, Ron and I left the van. Not sure if we'd be allowed in with our rifles, we left them. Both of us wore two larger Snaps plus the smaller ones on our right ankles.

I told the guard who approached us, "We gotta see Coocher."

One older mean looking guard shook his head. "Not without an appointment."

"Call him. I'll tell him why when he's on the phone," I said.

The guard examined us and went inside his little guard station. He left the door open and I walked in. Ron stayed outside to chat with the other two. While the older guard was distracted, I reached in my inner pants pocket and pulled out a package. Ron had engaged the two other guards in conversation and stood so the other two had their backs to me.

They laughed while I tossed the package under the desk of the guard on the phone.

When the guard passed the phone, I said, "Mr. Coocher?"

"Yeah, what is it?"

"I saw something about that communications guy. Thought you'd like to see it yourself. I don't want to give any names but his first name starts near the end of the alphabet." I figured they would know his real first name since he may have spurted that out under torture. Even so, his cover name was Yates Smythe.

After five seconds of silence, Coocher said, "Put the guard back on."

Not sure if he bought it, I tensed. I'd have to shoot the guard if he refused us.

He put the phone down.

"It's okay."

I relaxed my muscles.

He went outside and talked to the other guards.

"Let these two in. The van stays out."

I looked at Ron.

This is it. We're on our own.

The gate opened slowly and one guard held his hand palm up to Vincent to show he could not enter.

Vincent nodded and backed up the BIS van.

Ron and I walked through the opening gate and onto the crushed stone walkway. We kept silent, not sure if anyone would have microphones aimed at us.

The house looked even more intimidating than on the overhead.

Three stories tall, the lowest floor had no windows except near the front door. I saw men with rifles moving on the roof. Visitors had to walk up cement stairs that split in two before coming to the front door.

After fifty yards of walking up the driveway, I said, "Jeesh. This guy sure keeps a strong house."

"Yeah he does," said Ron.

I chose the stairs on the left and when we got to the front door, we met two more guys carrying rifles. Behind them, the door opened.

There stood Coocher, dressed in a gold-speckled purple jacket tied with a gold-colored waistband over his large belly. He wore purple slacks and black shoes. He stood at my chin height and must have weighed at least two hundred pounds. The top of his head was bald. But something was wrong with his posture. The guy was bent sideways, something that never showed on his camera appearances. But I remembered his face from the many vids I'd seen.

"Mr. Coocher," I said as I extended my hand in greeting.

He didn't return the shake. Guess he didn't like mingling with common folk.

"Inside," he said. "Show me what you got and leave."

"Yes, sir," I replied.

Once we got inside, we looked at a long hallway. Coocher stayed behind us and motioned with his hand that we should walk farther. One guard closed the door. Two of them walked behind Coocher.

Not sure if someone was watching, we kept up the subterfuge.

"The library's on your right," said Coocher from behind us.

We entered a room filled with book shelves. And hundreds of books. Then I remembered this guy liked old-fashioned stuff.

Once all five of us stepped inside the library, Coocher closed the door.

I pulled out a Snap, rushed up to him, and jabbed it in Coocher's neck. Ron fired twice and the two bodyguards went down. Then he looked upwards and shot out three cameras.

"Where are the women?" I asked Coocher.

"What women?"

"Don't make me ask twice. One of them is my daughter. I'm willing to give my life to get her back."

Sweat formed on his fat forehead.

"I don't know what you're talking about."

I fired my Snap beside his head and watched him jerk in surprise. His manner changed immediately. Now he believed me.

"Downstairs," he replied. "In the basement."

"Lead the way," I said.

"You won't get away with this. I have guards all over the place. They're watching us right now."

"I figured that. That's why I'm holding a gun to your neck. They won't risk killing you. Now go!"

Ron and I stayed close to Coocher. But Ron moved back and forth to make it more difficult to get a shot at him without endangering Coocher. We walked the hallway and entered the stairwell. Four men with guns pulled followed us but with my Snap at their boss's neck, they didn't dare open fire.

"Drop your guns," I yelled.

They complied.

"Stand back or I'll shoot him first, then you," I yelled.

The four guys stayed still as we walked. I figured them to be ex-cops. There was no sense in getting killed for a few sols.

I kept my gun on Coocher's neck. Ron busied himself by shooting out several cameras on the way with his Snap. We approached an elevator.

I shook my head. No way was I going to get stuck in a box, even with Coocher as a hostage. Too damned many things could go wrong, included knock-out gas.

"Stairs," I ordered.

Coocher looked at me and my gun, aimed at his head. He turned and walked to a door under a red light with "Stairs."

I pointed with my Snap and he pressed on the door to open it.

We went through the door and down the stairs. I heard footsteps behind us and glanced back to see four guards follow us.

"Tell your guards to keep their distance."

Coocher looked at them and yelled, "Keep your distance."

The guards stopped moving. Orders are orders.

When we got to the basement, we came upon a door with a keypad. Coocher hesitated.

I pressed the gun farther into his neck. "I'm damned serious, Coocher. Hesitate now and you're dead. We'll shoot our way out. But you'll be a goner. At this close range, I can't miss."

The man's hands shook while he pressed the keypad and then placed his palm on the glass rectangle.

The door slid ajar.

"Who sent you?" asked Coocher.

Apparently his confidence had returned.

"None of your business," I answered. "Your first priority is staying alive."

Ron popped his head in the doorway.

"Another frickin' hallway," he said.

"Lead the way," I said in Coocher's ear.

Ron stayed close and shot out four cameras as we walked.

We stopped at the last door on the right.

"They're in there," said Coocher, with his eyes wide open and staring at me.

The man shook. I'll bet this was the closest he had ever come to facing death. Gone was the self-confidence I had seen on the telly. But then again, bullies usually were afraid of getting hurt. That was my advantage.

Ron raced around us and tried to open the door.

I motioned to Coocher. "Open that door."

Once again, his hands shook at he pressed on the keypad and then the palm glass.

When we heard a click, Ron opened the door and crouched down.

Sure enough, we weren't alone. Three guys faced us, wearing casual clothes, not uniforms. Ron fired while I stayed behind Coocher. All three went down. They were fools not to wear armor.

In two chairs sat Leanna and Alena, blindfolded and tied with their hands behind their backs and their heads bowed. Neither had a shirt on so they were naked from the waist up.

I noted the blood on their clothes.

Bastards!

CHAPTER 26

Both women had gags on their mouths.

Ron rushed up to Alena first and took off her eye mask and gag while I stayed with Coocher. Then Ron went to work on Leanna.

Alena exclaimed, "I knew you'd come! I knew it! I told Mom you'd come."

I could see burns on their chests. Some son of a bitch had burned their right nipples. I could see little dark spots on their arms and legs. It was enough to make me gag, but I had a job to do.

"Sorry 'bout taking so long," I said. "We had to find you first."

Alena's face held tears. "But you got here. I knew you would. Thanks, Dad!"

I held Coocher close me to and kept my Snap at his throat as Ron untied both women. Sweat poured down the fat man's neck.

"After what I've seen of your handy work, I'd just as soon kill you right here."

Coocher's eyes opened wider and he shook.

With my eyes glaring at Coocher, out of the side of my mouth, I said to the women, "I hope you can walk on your own."

Leanna stood first—and fell. Ron helped her get to her feet. She looked pale and hesitant.

"Easy, Lee," I said. "Take your time."

I said to my open comm line, "Vincent, we got 'em. We're in the basement. Shoot your way in."

The next thing I heard was a boom. The package I had left in the guard gate must have gone off. It was strong enough to level both the guard building and the gate. But it might make a hole, preventing Vincent from driving his van through the gate.

In five seconds, I heard the faint rapid chatter of gunfire. Vincent's drones must be closing in on the front door. The sound of glass shattering in the distance came next.

I kept my Snap on Coocher's neck as Ron help both women walk to the door. They were an ugly sight as they both had bloodied legs and chests. He helped the two walk, one on each of his shoulders.

In the hallway, we met a group of ten guards with guns pointing at us.

"Lay down your weapons!" I shouted. "Or I'll kill Coocher and then you."

The guards looked at each other.

Ron took advantage of their hesitation. He let go of the women, unstrapped his shotgun, and fired at the armed men. One went down. That did it.

A young guard laid his gun on the floor and raised his hands, his eyes wide open. The others followed suit. I would remember for a long time the look of fear in their eyes. I didn't like scaring them but it couldn't be helped. If they were scared, they were less likely to act brash.

I brushed my hand to the side as we approached them. They all moved to one side of the hallway, keeping their hands up. Four of them stared at Coocher, the rest kept their eyes on me.

As we walked by them, I wondered if one of them would get brave at the last moment.

"Make one sudden move and I'll shoot your boss," I yelled. "And then we'll shoot you."

The warning must have helped because they stayed motionless with their hands up, their guns on the floor.

We got to the main entrance at the same time as Vincent entered the door carrying an automatic assault rifle and wearing one of our special helmets. He could control the drones by voice with it.

He used the strap on his rifle and pulled it over his head. Then he lifted Leanna up into his arms. Ron picked up Alena the same way. I followed them with Coocher as they walked the hundred yards to our van outside the guard gate.

This was one time I appreciated our Binger greater strength.

Overhead two drones aimed their cover fire at the building, continuing a constant chatter of gun fire shooting out windows on the two upper floors.

As we walked, I saw four guards come around the side of the building on my right. A drone sprayed fire in their direction. Two dropped. The other two ran for cover.

That hundred yards seemed like a mile, especially since I had to walk backwards. Vincent led the way to our van.

Our drones stopped shooting and a shot rang out from the building. Coocher fell from my arms, exposing me to fire. I saw his back ooze blood. Some brave son of a bitch had hit him instead of me. I left Coocher on the gravel, his eyes staring at me wide open. I think he expected me to kill him on the spot.

A drone lowered itself between the building and me, providing some protection. As it chattered away with its automatic fire, I saw guards with guns duck behind whatever cover they could find.

I turned and ran after Vincent and Ron. They had gotten Leanna and Alena in the van. I hopped in after them and pulled the sliding door closed. In seconds, Vincent got in the driver's door and drove off.

Several pings told me our van had been hit. Two loud explosions followed.

"I blew up the drones to prevent them from getting into the wrong hands," said Vincent. "Figured it might shake them up too."

Which was a good thing since their electronics came from Andy's Mourtan Security.

"They will burn with Pyronex, destroying all evidence," Vincent added.

I looked at Leanna. Ron was busying putting StopIt bandages on her open wounds. I got busy doing the same on Alena's.

We drove a devious route to lose any tail.

Ron asked, "Do you think we should take them to Newton?"

I looked at Alena, then Leanna.

"No. You can bring her later. Let's get them to the ops center."

On the way, I remembered to send a message to Zetto. "We're coming in with our gals." Then I remembered to use the password. "And an alphabet soup."

At our headquarters, Vincent carried Leanna and Ron Alena. I rushed ahead to the basement door. I keyed the sequence on the pad and pressed my palm on the plate, to be greeted by a loud click.

When we got inside, they laid the women on lower bunks and covered them.

"Ron, get Dr. Newton."

He rushed out the door.

Vincent and I put StopIt on each woman's wounds. Then we handed them morphine pills and bottles of water.

"Thanks, Dad," said Alena. "I knew you'd come."

I nodded with my head and looked up to Vincent.

"Get some sleep. The doctor is coming."

I turned toward Vincent.

"Let's leave them alone on their bunks."

We moved to the planning room. There, Zetto sat upright in his hospital bed.

I wanted a drink but I needed to remain sober until the doctor arrived.

Nobody said anything. I felt enormous relief that we had rescued Alena and Leanna. They would need medical care but help was on the way.

We had lost Coocher. All in all, it was a successful op.

Then why did I feel so lousy?

Maybe it was the way Alena and Leanna looked, naked, burned, and bruised.

A half hour later, I heard the buzzer at the dorm door. On the monitor I saw Ron and Dr. Newton. She had on a black blindfold that covered the top of her head while wearing blue slacks and a white blouse. Her straight brown hair was visible on the edges of the blindfold.

When they entered, Vincent and I walked into the dorm. Ron removed her blindfold and she looked around, dazed. Then she spotted the two women on the lower bunks. She set her medicine bag on the floor, kneeled, and pulled the cover off Leanna. She turned her head to one side and I saw her wince. It was not a pretty sight.

"Who put the StopIt on her wounds?" the doctor asked.

Vincent replied, "We both did."

"You did a good job. You may have saved her life," replied Dr. Newton. She got out an injector and loaded a vial in the bottom. She pressed the injector on Leanna's hip. In seconds, compressed air hissed as the medicine rushed into her body. Newton reloaded from a vial and pressed the injector to Leanna's hip a second time.

"What are you using?" I asked.

"A combination of pain killer, cortisone, and electrolytes," said the doctor. "Ron told me their condition when you found them. I figured they were malnourished and would need cortisone to cut the inflammation."

Next she pulled the covers back up over the now sleeping Leanna and turned to Alena on the opposite bunk. She loaded her injector again and with one hand, pulled the covers back until she had exposed Alena's chest. She pressed the injector above her right breast and reloaded for the second injection.

Alena opened her eyes wide, probably in fear of more torture. When she saw me, she relaxed and smiled.

When Newton finished and Alena closed her eyes, the doctor pulled the covers back up and stood.

"Got any coffee?" she asked me.

I led the way into the kitchen. "Vincent, block the other room."

Vincent stood by the door to the planning room. She didn't need to see our plans on the walls.

When the AutoCook finished, I poured her a cup of coffee while she sat at the table.

"I appreciate your help, Dr. Newton."

"They're in a mess. Must have suffered a lot of pain. Frickin' bastards!"

"I know."

I could see her hands shaking while she drank the rest.

"Want something stronger?"

She shook her head.

"No, I have to get back to my patients. In my work, I've seen a lot of wounds caused by humans on others. But this is the worst."

When she finished her coffee, her hands no longer shook.

I said, "Ready to go back?"

She nodded and Ron led her to the dorm.

Through the open door to the kitchen I saw him place the blindfold on her head. He grabbed the doctor's arm and put her black bag in her hand.

After they left, I studied my two sleeping women.

I wish I had gotten to them earlier.

I went into the kitchen, closed the door, and sat at the dining table. Vincent looked at me with one hand on a cup of coffee.

"At least we got them," he said. His eyes were red and his face was wet.

I nodded, then shook my head. "Bastards."

A half hour later, Ron came in the kitchen and touched my arm. "Shall I pour you something stronger than coffee?"

I still had adrenaline rushing in my blood but that would go away. I bobbed my head.

In less than a minute, Ron set a tray on the table. The tray held a bottle of Yarley's and four glasses, each three-quarters full of a light brown liquid. He placed a glass in front of me.

"Zetto?" he asked.

"Let's adjourn to Zetto's new bedroom."

I carried the bottle and the tray of glasses into the planning room. Ron handed Zetto his glass.

I led the way by raising mine.

"To our gals!"

Three glasses clicked with mine and Vincent clicked his with Zetto's.

Images of Leanna's and Alena's bare chests, riddled with burn marks, flooded my mind. I gazed at my glass and drained it in one gulp.

CHAPTER 27

I tagged Dr. Newton. I suspected she would keep her mouth shut but the look on her face after seeing Lee and Alena told me she might let something out. Or somebody might press her for more information once they saw her face.

"What you saw today may be hard to keep under wraps. But many lives depend on your doing just that."

"I understand. I'm so sorry they had to go through all that."

"Yeah, we're all sorry."

She added, "I hope you catch the bastards who did that."

"I will. That's a promise."

We disconnected and I took another sip of my drink of Burbock.

After every major op, I went through a period of winding down. I thought over what we had. We had Leanna and Alena back, Duran was dead, and Coocher was wounded. We had won more than they did.

But we still had to find Hoskins.

Granted Vincent still walked with a limp, and Alena, Leanna, and Zetto would take a long time to recover. But we were all alive. Sometimes that's the best a spy can hope for.

I sat at my computer and sent an encrypted message to my Mom, Maurine. At first, I wanted to send an "open" message but since YSA might get copies of all courier messages, especially right after our rescue, I encrypted it.

Mom would be worried sick about her granddaughter. I thought of including a photo of Alena and Leanna, but their conditions would only cause Mom to worry more. So I included a photo of Ron, Vincent, and me, all smiling.

Naturally, I included a clock in the photo so I could embed a message to Acorn.

In that message to my spy boss, I told him details of our rescue and Coocher's wounds. As an afterthought, I included Zetto's rescue.

The news stations were alive with the damage at Coocher's house. Eight guards had died and Coocher took a bullet. Vids showed the damage to the guard gate and a dozen rent-a-guards standing behind walls in front of the house. We saw photos of the men who had died and two others who had been shot.

Vincent shook his head.

"No mention at all about the basement or who was in it."

Channel Four had a vid of Coocher in a hospital bed.

"We didn't get a look at who did it but they were big, I can tell you. Probably Bingers. I'll bet the mercons and hybrids were behind them, too. This took planning, especially with them drones."

Who else were they to blame?

Unfortunately, the polls showed sympathy for Coocher and the fallen men.

I thought of the risk of poisoning the water but figured that as long as Coocher was in Gerges Hospital, he wouldn't risk adding anything to the water supply. He didn't want to die himself. No. I figured he'd wait until he could run back to his home town of Chester on the western edge of York.

* * * * *

Everything was quiet. The espionage business can be like that. Weeks of boredom or healing. Then a mad rush to deal with yet another crisis.

The next day, Alena sat across from me at the breakfast table, wearing a pink top and blue jeans. Her face was puffed up.

"Now can I join BIS?"

That was the last thing I expected out of her mouth.

"I think you'll find your research to be more compelling. It's what you are good at. So go with that. Being a spy is a full-time commitment. We go into dangerous places and risk our lives and torture. I think you'd be much happier as a researcher."

Leanna limped into the kitchen wearing a white blouse and blue slacks. Her face looked bloated too.

I hoped the swelling on both women would go down soon. They didn't look like themselves.

My daughter asked, "Then why do you do it?"

I was grateful for the distraction. Two parents against one would be better. Besides, I didn't want to answer her question.

"Your father's right," said my ex with a blurred voice. "Think of what we went through. It could've gotten worse."

"How?" asked Alena.

"We could be dead," answered her mom.

Alena turned to me.

"Dad, I want to help. My research means nothing compared to fighting the bigotry we Bingers face."

"I understand your feelings. But it helps us a lot more if you focus on research and gain traction in the scientific world. If what you have found out so far bears up under scrutiny, it will have a greater effect on increasing the understanding between humans, Bingers, mercons, and even napes—than anything you could do as a spy."

Alena was quiet.

I knew she was thinking it over.

"Would you like to meet the mercon ambassador?"

Her eyes lit up on that one. "Can you arrange that?"

"Let me work on it," I said. "Would you be interested?"

"Yeah. That would be great!"

"Are you willing to focus on your research and give up becoming a spy?"

Alena looked down, lost in thought for a long time. "Is that a condition?"

I nodded. "'Fraid so."

* * * * *

Guy Coocher wasn't too groggy to utter "No amputations!" over and over again.

Dr. Roger Steiner, dressed in a white lab coat with a DetectIt hanging from his neck, patted him on the right arm.

"I assure you, we won't take off any part of your body. We know full well how you feel about that. But—I'm going to have to operate—to get that bullet out. X-rays show it is lodged close to your spine. If we don't remove it, it might migrate and cut off the nerves in your spine. That means you wouldn't be able to move your legs."

Dr. Steiner placed an etablet on Coocher's lap. "But before that, I need you to authorize the surgery."

Coocher glared at the doctor. "No amputations!"

"I understand that. I won't amputate anything, I assure you. But I do need you to sign this form."

Coocher looked down at the etablet and raised it so he could read it.

"Can I have a moment with my assistant?"

"I understand," said Dr. Steiner. The doctor turned and walked out the door.

Coocher motioned with his finger for his assistant to come closer.

Coocher whispered in the man's ear, "I want you to go in the hallway and call this hospital. Be persistent. Find out if they use fifty nanometer filters on their water. Then come back and tell me. And don't tell anyone I told you."

The assistant nodded. "Right away, sir."

After the man left his bedside, Coocher raised the etablet and read the form. It showed a standard disclaimer that if anything should go wrong, neither the hospital nor the doctor would be responsible. He waited to sign it.

Two minutes later, the assistant came back in with Dr. Steiner. The assistant nodded his head.

Coocher raised the etablet and signed the form.

* * * * *

I watched the six o'clock news on all four stations report that Guy Coocher would undergo surgery to remove the bullet next to his spine and would recover in Gerges Hospital. Eight bodyguards would stay either in his room or outside it. He'd be in the hospital for at least a week.

That means he won't be going to his estate in Chester anytime soon.

I got another message from Acorn.

"Glad to hear your rescues worked. Can you talk with G about Bs visiting Ensam?"

CHAPTER 28

Alena took a tag. Her head went up and down in a nod.

I shook my head.

Callers can't see a nod.

When she disconnected, she turned to me.

"Can I get a ride to Dr. Albert's place?"

"Is he back?"

"He got home this morning. He said he got a tag from a cop and took the first flight back to York."

"Why did he tag you? He must be busy with funeral arrangements for his wife."

"He said the house seems hollow without her. He wants me to move back in with him. Says he thought it over and wants to be my advisor. Thinks I might become famous after all. He invited me to move back into my old room."

"I don't think that's a good idea."

"Why?" she asked with wide open eyes and a dropped jaw.

That was too much. I shouted, "Because it would be too damned easy for someone to recapture you if they knew where you slept every night, that's why! You want to go through all that again? The next time, they'll be more cautious and we may not be able to rescue you. You could be tortured until you give up all the information you know and beg them to kill you."

She fixed her gaze on her hands for a long time. "I can't stay forever, you know. Besides, I miss going to class and my research."

At least she didn't say she missed being a spy.

"Let's talk it over with the team."

She turned her eyes up at me. "I thought you made all the decisions."

"Only the little ones."

Not true, but she'd find out soon enough.

We assembled the team in the planning room. "Alena, you want to tell them what Dr. Albert said?"

She repeated what she had told me. Then she said, "And I'm going to live in his house."

"Oh, no, you're not!" exclaimed her mother. "I'm not going to have you taken again and it would be damned easy if you lived there."

"I agree with your mother," I said. "It's too dangerous."

Alena slumped in her chair.

Like a little girl.

Ron spoke next, "I think they're both right. It's too dangerous."

"You could be my bodyguard," Alena said as she regarded him.

Ron shook his head. "I have to work."

"Dad?" Alena asked.

"And I have some PI business to take care of."

She turned to Vincent.

"Not me," he said. "I have a business to run."

She looked at Zetto. By now he had recovered enough that he could walk with crutches.

"You gotta be kidding."

She scrunched together her eyebrows and looked at me with that look of pleading that most girls use with their fathers.

"I think you'd better stay here a little longer," I said. "At least until we can find a safe place."

"I need to go to class," Alena said with a whimper, just like a kid. "And I'm going nuts in this place. There's nothing to do! I need my lab work."

I answered, "As long as Hoskins is loose and Coocher is on the warpath, I think you better stay here."

With that, I walked into the empty dorm room and shut the door.

There must be something I can do.

Like magic, it occurred to me.

I sat on a lower bunk and tagged Gliituk. Zetto had arranged a secure line from his server to the mercon embassy, via servers at the university.

"Yes, Jake?" said that voice from my past.

"Do you want to meet the author of that paper on humans and mercons having a common ancestor?"

"Yes. That would be interesting. She your daughter? I noticed she has same last name."

"Yep. When could we come?"

We set a time and disconnected.

I returned to the planning room. Everyone was quiet, so I guessed I hadn't missed much. After turning to Alena, I said, "I made arrangements to go to the mercon embassy. Care to come along?"

She jumped out of her chair, her face lit up.

"When?"

"Now would be a good time."

She rushed up and put her arms around me. Being an inch taller than me made that easy. I embraced her and kissed her cheek. I had not hugged her since she arrived at the airport.

"Ron?" I asked.

He got up and followed Alena and me out. We took the BIS van with Ron behind the wheel.

The steering wheel remained recessed in the dash and we pulled out of the basement parking lot.

On the way, Alena and I held hands in the back seat. Every minute, she squeezed my hand as if to reassure herself that I was there.

"What do I say?"

I chuckled. "He's a decent guy. Don't worry about what to say. Follow my example if you get stuck."

"You've talked to him?"

That one I decided not to answer.

"You do get around," she added.

When we got to the parking lot of the hotel, we three walked to the basement and entered room 43. I pulled the rug aside and opened the hidden door, using the same code I had used before.

I went into the small room and the walls glowed, driving away the darkness. When Ron followed Alena in, he closed the rug and door behind him.

"We're here," I said to the empty room. "We don't want to be drugged this time."

Nothing happened. I walked around the room, pushing in spots to check for hidden doors.

"Be patient," said a voice with a mercon accent from the ceiling.

It took two more minutes before I heard a rumbling noise. Part of the wall opposite the rug slid aside to reveal three small railroad cars.

I took the lead car, Alena the middle one, and Ron sat in the last seat. The door slid shut, casting us in darkness. Occasional lights appeared overhead. The cars moved into the round dark hole in front of us and we went up and down, left and right, turning around so many times I lost track of where we were. It felt like I had taken a ride on a roller coaster in a dark tunnel.

At last, we came to a stop next to a lighted platform where four uniformed mercons waited. Three had rifles and the fourth a handgun in a waist holster.

When our little train stopped, we got out.

Alena stared at the mercon guards above us.

"Alena."

She shook her head and got out.

The guy with the handgun said, "Follow me."

I noticed all four wore plugs in their elongated nostrils. I had forgotten about their supersensitive smell. We must reek to them. We got out of our cars and walked along a hallway, ducking to get under the low ceiling. It might fit the shorter aliens but each of us was over six feet. We went up a stairs, through a door, and along another hallway. Our mercon leader opened a door and motioned that we were to enter while he and his escorts stayed in the hall.

Gliituk rose from a chair in his iridescent orange cape. He gestured to three other chairs. "Have seat. Hope you don't mind my not shaking hands."

Alena stared at him and I had to push her to her chair.

"So this is researcher," said Gliituk looking at her.

I looked at Alena and saw her eyes were wide open. She didn't say anything.

"Alena, it's polite to respond."

She jiggled her head. "Oh. Sorry."

She stared at the shorter Gliituk.

"Nice to meet you."

She winced immediately.

"Where did you get samples for your research?" Gliituk asked.

"Ah, I got some nape DNA from a doll's hair and mercon DNA from another doll from a merchant at the mall."

"And the Binger DNA?" he asked.

She looked at me.

"I gave her some," I said.

"You are part Binger?" Gliituk directed the question at her.

She nodded.

I don't think she was used to being in the presence of a world leader.

They discussed her research, and he told her of the Mattons and the history of his species. She sat through it all without saying a word.

Then she exclaimed, "Oh dear. I forgot to record all this."

"Never mind, my dear. I will send summary of recording," Gliituk responded with a smile.

I smiled. It was good to see him taking a liking to her.

"I'll send you copies of my new papers, too," she replied.

"Gliituk," I interrupted, "my boss asked me about our visiting Braco some time. Would it be okay for us to visit Ensam?" I used the mercon name for their colony on the eastern edge of the island continent.

He nodded. "Yes. I will make arrangements and tell you."

Next, he reached to the floor beside his chair and picked up a small box wrapped with a red ribbon. He must have studied human culture to know how to present a gift.

He handed the box to Alena and she took it with a big grin. She looked at me.

"Should I open it?"

I nodded.

She tore the ribbons with nervous fingers. Her eyes opened wide and her jaw dropped. She reached in and pulled out a small mercon doll.

"Oh, this is terrific!" She glanced at Gliituk and put a gigantic grin on her face. "Thank you."

Her eyes went from me to him. "Ah, we forgot to bring a gift for you."

Gliituk waved a hand of his five little black fingers. "It is fine."

On the way back to the ops center, Alena examined her gift doll in great detail, turning it over and over again by its lower pant legs. She avoided touching most of the hairs and fabric.

"Maybe I can get DNA from two separate mercons."

She glanced my way.

"Thanks, Dad—for everything."

Those words were magic to my ears. I had to grin.

Why are fathers so vulnerable to their daughters?

* * * * *

Back at the ops center, Alena showed off her gift to her mother.

"Jake," Zetto interrupted, "you need to see this."

He displayed Sheila Fish's report on the telly on one wall of the planning room. The vid showed Coocher in a wheelchair being pushed up a ramp into a large white limo van.

"Guy Coocher recovered enough from his ordeal to be released from Gerges Hospital. He has not healed from the surgery on his lower back. Mr. Coocher told us…"

The screen changed to show Coocher standing with a cane in front of a podium in the Gerges Conference Room.

"Stan Curling of the York Federal Police," he smiled while he looked back at Stan Curling, "is investigating the invasion of my home by the team of kidnappers who tried to get me. One of my guards shot me. I fell to the ground and the kidnappers escaped. Mr. Curling, the Special Agent in Charge of the Zor Office, assured me they will pursue this investigation until all three kidnappers are caught and punished.

"I will stay at my home in Zor for a few days. Then I'll travel to my home in Chester. Frankly, I was going nuts with boredom in the hospital."

The next scene showed Coocher getting into his large van.

Sheila Fish appeared. "Mr. Coocher will journey to his estate in Chester in another week. Chester is on the western section of York, close to a thousand miles away. Next up is local news."

Zetto turned off the recording.

I sat in a chair and bowed my head. When I raised it, I said to Zetto, Ron, Vincent, and Leanna, "This means we need to lie low for a few more days. With Coocher traveling to his western estate, we can expect him to contaminate the public water soon."

I turned to Vincent. "Can you show us on that wall the vid you made of Coocher meeting Getner?"

When the recording got to where Getner handed Coocher a package, I yelled, "Stop!"

The image froze.

"Makes you kind of wonder what's in that package. It could be something Coocher dumped at the Water Works. Have there been any reports of illnesses?"

Zetto shook his head. "I've been monitoring all four news channels. Nothing so far."

CHAPTER 29

Ambassador Gliituk stepped up to the podium. Not an easy feat since he had to work his way up two steps on the stool first. He took care to pull up his iridescent orange cape from in front of his feet before going up. Today, his nyteen hurt his back more than usual. Thank heavens his doctor found that propanoic acid, otherwise known as Naproxen, made the pain diminish to the point where he could perform his public duties without wincing. It would not do to have the mercon ambassador narrow his eyes in pain.

He turned his eyes upon his audience, assembled in the auditorium of the Zor Water Works. Except for the first row, all were human faces, some pale and some darker, but none as dark as the six short mercons in front. The purple cape of Zanuck, Picka'tor's wife, was easy to spot among them. Gliituk's personal assistant was sure to report this talk to her husband.

The invitation to speak had come as a surprise but he was not one to miss a chance to speak for interspecies tolerance. He began.

"Ladies and gentlemen…"

* * * * *

While Gliituk spoke, Hoskins marched through the door leading to the lower levels where the public water was treated. Today he dressed in a policeman's dark blue uniform, courtesy of the good folks at Humans Only. Wearing the uniform of a cop might mean fewer questions about his wandering the halls.

He walked past the four huge settling tanks, each the size of a football field and covered with a white round metal top. If it weren't for the covers, he would have smelled the odor of raw sewage, including human fecal matter.

Hearing voices, he stopped and scanned around for a door. Even wearing a policeman's uniform might not be enough. Seeing one labeled "Electrical maintenance," he ducked into the small room. Despite the switch near the front door, he kept the room dark to lessen the likelihood of someone noticing a light from the bottom of the door. He stepped to one side and listened in the dark.

After the voices had passed by, he waited another ten minutes before carefully cracking the door open and peering out. No one walked the halls.

Trusting his memory of the layout of the huge facility, Hoskins proceeded through two more doors and down three hallways. He sauntered without jarring, ever careful of the glass vials in his jacket pockets. He didn't want to break any of them or he might get the disease himself. At last, he got to the final outlet tank where calcium and magnesium carbonates and silicates were added for water "hardness."

Humans didn't like their water to taste too purified, claiming it was too bland. So the Zor Water Works added back in some of the hardness. Fortunately, the water for Zor came from the nearby Oreo River and the Orca Mountains and was high in natural water hardness, so not much needed to be added.

When he approached the inlet tank, Hoskins glanced in both directions to make sure he was not observed. He donned gloves to protect the skin of his hands and looked around him often. Next, he pulled off the protective top, exposing the bronze-colored screw cap on the vial. He unscrewed the cap and poured the murky liquid into the tank. The color disappeared in the gently swirling water.

One down and three to go.

After he had finished with all four vials, he smiled and stepped away from the tank. He placed the last vial in its protective case in his left side inner pocket and strode to the door leading upstairs.

He chuckled over the planning of his boss, Guy Coocher. Arranging the invitation of the mercon ambassador prior to Hoskins' poisoning of the public water supply was pure genius.

Let's see you get away with all your talk of tolerance now, Ambassador.

* * * * *

Two days later, the first reports came in. Sheila Fish of Channel One had the most detailed coverage.

"All the hospitals and medical clinics in Zor report a surge of patients coming in with difficulty breathing."

A vid showed people of all ages sitting in chairs lining the hallways of Gerges. The smaller ones in the arms of women had droopy eyelids and gasped for air while their mothers wept.

"Doctors said several infants have died of this strange new disease. The Center for Disease Control reported this is a serious epidemic and they are investigating the cause."

The image changed to show people in white lab coats bent over microscopes. Next came an image of a squiggly "something" in a round white circle.

Sheila Fish said, "The illness appears to come from a virus the CDC says matches the Viral Botulism virus that recently spread on Earth. The virus mimics the effects of the botulism bacteria. In the expectation that this is the same virus, the CDC warns people not to drink tap water until they have boiled it for at least five minutes at one hundred and eighty five degrees or higher. The same goes for food. Cook it first. Don't eat any food that has not been cooked, including salads.

"Children under the age of one and the elderly were the most vulnerable but people of all ages can come down with difficulty breathing."

The screen changed to display a male teenage patient sitting in a hospital bed. His eyelids drooped and a technician used his fingers to raise both eyelids.

Sheila reported, "This patient was fully conscious. He was not sleepy and had no fever. His breathing may become difficult as carbon dioxide builds up in his lungs. That's the critical stage. If he continues to be ill and the virus stays in his body, he may pant. Soon after that, he may tire and expire."

The screen changed to show long lines outside the hospital emergency room.

"So far, the CDC estimates about fifty people have been infected. CDC investigators are seeking the identities of all people who have come in contact with those who have become ill with the virus."

Sheila Fish appeared behind her desk at Channel One News. "If you know of someone who has symptoms of this viral infection, please call the CDC or your local police immediately. Advanced cases have constipation, difficulty speaking, and weakness in the chest muscles, arms, and legs. No fever is expected and patients usually have full consciousness. There is no reason to panic at this stage. We now bring you Dr. David Reener of the Center for Disease Control in Zor."

The image changed to show a man in a white lab coat in front of a podium. "We have contacted the Center for Disease Control in Atlanta. Even though they are in the midst of a major pandemic themselves, they have put on the next fast flight to Rossa 200 doses of the only known vaccine effective against VB, along with vials of the active virus. We received information on manufacturing the vaccine. However, we have to wait until live cultures of the virus arrive in Zor. Orion

Pharmaceuticals has assured us they are ready to scale up the manufacture of the vaccine as soon as that arrives. The good news is that the vaccine cures the disease as well as prevents it. So even those infected can benefit."

He looked up at the camera. "In the meantime, it is important to not panic. If you leave Zor, you risk spreading the disease. Stay where you are. Help is on the way."

The image changed to show Sheila Fish. "Demonstrators marched in front of the Parliament Building today against the food price increases expected with the passage of the new Farm Labor Bill…"

"Telly off!" I ordered.

I looked around at my team. "Anyone experience any weakness or difficulty breathing?"

Heads moved left and right.

"Then let's assume none of us have VB. Ron, can you report on our water purification?"

Ron spoke next, "When we set up the operation center, we anticipated someone might poison our water supply. Per Jake's instruction, I have made the changes so our drinking water goes through reverse osmosis and then through membrane filters set to fifty nanometers. That should be enough to trap the VB virus."

I added, "So we have no reason to expect contamination here in the operations center. We are safe as long as we stay here."

No one spoke.

I remembered Monk. Tut would make sure he had enough food but it was the water I was concerned about.

I drove to my apartment while Ron kept a lookout for any tails. Traffic was light. When we got into my place, Tut and Monk stared at us from the top of the stairs in the middle of my apartment. They were both glad to see us. Tut reported no visitors with a tilt of his head to his left.

"Tut, I will take Monk with me. I want you to keep alert for visitors. Tag me if anyone shows up, even Sing Sing."

Sing Sing was my landlady and was the manager of the real estate office downstairs.

We gathered up Monk's water and food dishes. The water in my apartment went only through reverse osmosis. I wondered if he had contracted VB.

"Ron, take Monk's toilet too."

While he went into the bathroom to take care of that, I played with my new pet. Monk purred as I petted him. He'd have plenty of company at the operations center.

We left my place and drove the long route to the ops center. Spotting tails was a lot easier with so little traffic.

When we entered the ops center, I set Monk down. He began exploring every room.

I put Monk's toilet in our small bathroom and connected it up. Ron took his food into the kitchen. I told my team that Monk may experience symptoms since he had only reverse osmosis water to drink in the last few days. The next morning, when I could not find Monk, I grew worried. I found him lying on the floor of the planning room.

Don't tell me he's got it.

When the little critter opened his eyes and saw me, he yawned, smiled, and reached out his arms. I picked him up and hugged him.

He did not show symptoms. Just sleepiness. Which was normal for him since he was part cat.

Alena played with Monk a lot and I worried I may have lost a friend.

Would she argue with me over him when it was time to move out?

The next day, all four news channels showed the main roads out of Zor clogged with traffic. Apparently few paid attention to the caution to avoid panicking as they tried to leave the city.

Sheila Fish came on the news.

"If you think of leaving Zor, we caution you that doctors in the outlying areas will not have access to the vaccine for another week. Assuming Orion can scale up its operations, you are better off staying in the city where help is on the way."

I kept an eye on several newscasts over the next few hours but saw no drop in the number of vehicles leaving the city. The downtown and the malls reported an eighty percent drop in foot traffic. I had never seen such a low level in my life on Rossa. If this kept up, Zor would become a ghost town.

The newscasts reported that over half of the animals at the local zoos were dead. Bopum, screechies, greepers, gofers, and four-wingers were all vulnerable to this human disease.

Would it be better if they had been turned loose?

I wondered if the two catlike gofers I had seen at the Franken Memorial Park Zoo were still there.

* * * * *

In the planning room, I gazed upon the news on the burials of those who died of VB.

The view showed a row of open pits, lined with plastic. A huge claw dumped dozens of bodies in black plastic bags into the pit.

"Mass burials of bodies that died of the virus are first dissolved in acid. The process takes two to three days. The resultant slurry is then poured through steel filters to catch any remaining metals that might come with such things as implanted medical devices. The collected metals parts go through a purification process to isolate the metals.

"Then the slurry that comes after the filtration process is distilled to recover most of the acid, which is recycled back to dissolve more bodies. All that remains is a sludge of calcium and magnesium phosphates. The sludge is dried, treated with lye to neutralize any remaining acid, and used as fertilizer on crops.

"Scientists from CDC state that all the virus is destroyed by this method of burial. None can survive this harsh treatment. Because there are no remains left and since so many bodies are disposed of in batches, there are no markers identifying any individual. This is a true mass burial method."

When the news changed to show local weather, I turned off the telly.

Alena came up to my chair.

"Dad, I'm going nuts staying here. There's nothing to do!"

"I can't help that, Alena. I have the same problem. Have you watched all the movies you're interested in?"

She bowed her head and nodded.

"Dad, I can't go back to my lab at the university. Can you find a place for me to do my research?"

"Let me check."

After she left for the dorm, I tagged Ranute Fallow. He was a client from my earlier days and was now head of the Alien Protection Society, which looked out for the welfare of napes.

"Hi Jake. What can I do for you?"

"Have you read my daughter's paper on human and nape DNA having a lot in common?"

"Is she your daughter? I wondered when I saw her last name was Dani. And yes, I've read her paper. Very interesting."

"Can I ask a favor?"

Silence greeted my ears.

"And?"

"Can Alena set up a lab at the Nape Museum to continue her research?"

"I don't know. There's a lot of controversy surrounding it."

"If she can get verification, it would help reduce the prejudice against the napes," I said.

Silence.

"Hmm. You may be right. Let me get back to you on that."

"How are you faring the pandemic?"

"Candy and I—she's my wife now—have been staying home. How are you? You live in Zor."

"I'm staying with some friends. We have a water purification system."

"We do too at my estate. Say, Jake, let me get back to you on your request."

"Got it." We disconnected.

He tagged me back an hour later. "Sorry, Jake. I don't think that's practical."

"I understand. Thanks for considering it."

We disconnected. That would have presented a problem anyway. The Nape Museum was on South Central Park Avenue, on the other side of downtown from the university. It wouldn't take long to get there, but commuting would be a problem.

And she would need bodyguards.

Oh dear. This is getting complicated.

Vincent piped up with "Have you considered asking the mercon ambassador about Alena setting up her lab at the embassy?"

"That's an interesting idea. I wonder what the downside is."

I hesitated to ask Alena her opinion. The way she jumped to conclusions bothered me.

Did she do that in her research?

One thing was clear. We would not have to provide bodyguard service if she could live at the embassy. The major drawback was our human odor. Could the staff tolerate her presence?

One way to get an answer. Ask.

I tagged Gliituk. He was not available and would return my call. I didn't want to ask my question in a voice mail.

It took an hour before I got a tag back from the ambassador.

"What do you want?"

Might as well spit it out.

"Could my daughter set up a residence at your embassy and do her research in a lab there?"

A pause followed.

"Let me ask Picka'tor."

CHAPTER 30

Leanna came up to me.

"We need to restock our food. And toilet paper."

She handed me a list.

Since I felt I could not ask her or anyone on my team to risk exposure by going out to a store I went alone. I wore a blue breathing mask for whatever good it might do. I hated to rebreathe my hot air but catching the virus was my greater concern.

As I pressed along on University Avenue, I had to stop three times at military check points to explain my reason for being on the road. Prime Minister Pierre Klava had declared a curfew beginning at six in the evening and ending at eight in the morning. He had brought in the military reserves to police the streets and prevent looting.

At one stop, I spied military escorts in front and back of a Walker's delivery truck. Every person in every vehicle I saw wore breathing masks, either pale blue or white. All the soldiers at the checkpoint had them on.

At the store, empty shelves stared back at me when I strode the aisles looking for bottled water and beverages. Even the milk section had few choices. I smiled when I saw the alcohol section was empty—beer, wine, hard liquor, you name it. Looks like some folks planned on partying until this epidemic was over.

After a minute of searching, I found a clerk who wore the uniform of the store, along with a white mask.

"When do you expect more bottled water?" I asked.

"Don't know," he replied as his mask bobbed up and down. "We get some in every morning, but they're gone by ten."

"What do you do for water?"

The edges of his mask moved upwards. Was that a smile behind the mask?

"As an employee, I get first choice."

"What about ordering online?"

"You could try, but with the looting going on, most of the delivery trucks are bare by noon."

The shelves had half of their usual offerings so it didn't take me long to get what I came for. In my mind I thanked Vincent for stocking up on canned goods. Zetto claimed we had enough to last three weeks of a siege. I had gone shopping to pick up the perishable items.

When I got back to the center, Vincent met me outside the security door in a full coverage contamination suit of light green.

He passed each item under a tray with radiation before putting them on a table. We didn't want to bring the virus in with us.

"Take off your clothes," he said.

After I stripped, he ran a hose of filtered compressed air over my clothes and every item I brought in while I stood outside the security door. After that, he placed each item of clothing under the radiation.

"Turn around."

He blasted my naked body.

When he finished, I redressed and helped him carry my purchases inside.

Even the air inside felt used. I'd seen enough of these walls to last a lifetime and we had maybe a week to go. Faces everywhere bore the strain of being cooped up. No smiles, no joking or teasing. Just "grin and bear it" was the code of the day.

I had to do something to get their minds off being stuck here.

"Any ideas on casualties?"

Zetto said from his chair, "So far fifteen percent of those who came down with VB have died. The police have blockades set up on the major roads out of town. Barricades block the rest. But most of those who want to leave claim they have nowhere to go."

When I finished putting food away, I said, "If everyone is here, let's have a meeting."

The two tables in the planning room soon filled up. Monk sat on Alena's lap while she stroked him.

I looked at the members of my team. "We need to think about our next step."

Alena spoke up first, "Let's get Coocher and Hoskins."

I glared at her. "This is a not a democracy. I need your advice but I have to make the final decision."

I walked over to the walls, which still had information on Coocher, Hoskins, and Craig Horton of RUFF. On the wall behind the tables, Zetto had put the current status of VB, with the number of new cases spreading out from around Zor. It looked as if those who fled in the beginning brought the disease with them. That wasn't a surprise.

"With so many people in the city dead, we can expect HO to press for more restrictive laws on immigration."

As if the plague wasn't enough of a deterrent.

I looked at my daughter. "Alena, what progress have you made on your discoveries?"

"Well, since I can't do any more lab work," she said, "and my next paper is held up by reviewers who don't want to see it published, I'd say none. Dad, when can I get a lab set up?"

"I don't know. Let me think about that," I replied.

Leanna piped up next.

"Craig Horton was released this morning. The police said they didn't have enough evidence to hold him. And the lawyers for RUFF made a motion in Superior Court for habeas corpus."

"Jake," added Vincent, "what about sending a copy of the recording I made of Coocher and Getner? That is bound to raise concern."

"Does the vid show Getner's face?"

"At one point, yes. But when he passed the package, only his legs appeared. And those were covered with pants.

"That may not be enough."

Vincent added, "I think you should tag Sheila. The rest of us should stay out of sight."

"I agree on that," I replied. "The question is—is this the right time?"

"If we don't act soon," said Ron, "Coocher may get a law passed banning criminals, hybrids, mercons, Bingers, and napes from entering York. He's entered a bill into Parliament called the Freedom from Aliens Bill."

"When did this happen?" I asked.

"This morning," Ron replied. "I saw it on Channel Four."

I asked, "So Coocher is back in Zor from his home in Beverley Hills?"

"He came in just today," replied Ron. "Attendance in Parliament is low. Maybe because of the pandemic, he hoped to get the bill passed into law with fewer votes."

"So what do we have so far? Any news from Earth on who started the VB scare?"

* * * * *

I tagged Sheila at a time when I knew she wouldn't be on the air.

"I'm concerned about the rising popularity of the Humans Only organization."

"So am I," she replied. "But you wouldn't call unless you had something. Whatcha got?"

"I have a vid recording of a strange meeting."

"Who?"

"Of Coocher and a man, who I know from other sources is a hybrid. And the hybrid passed a package to Coocher two days before the outbreak of VB."

"Come on, Jake. I can't suggest what you're thinking."

"But you can show the recording."

"Where'd you get it?"

"I can't tell you that, but you can have your technicians verify the vid is real."

She was quiet for a few seconds. "Send it. I'll need the original, not a copy. I'll look at it."

After we disconnected, I went up to Vincent.

"Can you make sure none of your fingerprints or DNA are on the vid of Coocher and Getner? The original, not a copy. Make copies for us. And drop the original off at the Channel One station. Mark it for Sheila Fish."

"All right!" Vincent smiled. "We're fighting back."

"Jake," said Zetto from his hospital bed in the planning room. "I think you ought to see what's on Channel Four."

"Put it on," I said.

The wall opposite him lit up with his recording. The telly showed large pumps and several tanks bearing the words "Zor Water Works." A man dressed in a gray suit and wearing a white hard hat with the organization's name spoke to the camera.

"We installed four radiation beams over streams of water. We looked into using reverse osmosis and carbon black filters but found them too expensive. Radiating the water kills all the bacteria and viruses. We assure you that safeguards are in place to protect all our citizens from VB contaminants in the water."

Yeah right. And what about the few viruses that survive the radiation treatment? Are we training the virus to mutate?

Zetto said, "I'm not sure how much to believe him."

I agree.

One broadcast showed a reporter asking people on the street what they thought.

One lady said, "I think it comes from some damned terrorist. Have they arrested that guy at RUFF yet?"

Craig Horton of RUFF was taken in for additional questioning by the Zor Metro Police. I saw a guy speaking on the steps to the justice building.

"Mr. Craig Horton protests he is innocent. He has threatened to sue the city. But the police assure me he's not under arrest at this time."

Two hours later, Channel One showed Horton himself as he walked down the steps of the justice building. A reporter thrust a microphone at him and he said, "Has anyone looked at Humans Only? Or is Coocher's being a minister in Parliament affecting their judgment? RUFF is not a terrorist organization! HO on Earth is. Has anyone looked at HO here?"

So much for the palsy-walsy relationship between RUFF and HO.

* * * * *

Over and over again, I thought of how I could fight HO and keep my name out of it. I reached a decision and tagged Sheila Fish.

"What about my writing as Albert Poors? Poors had a good reputation after his interviews on Channel One as a slave. He could write a series of columns to express his opinion? It could be just opinion pieces. That way Channel One would not be responsible for what was written."

"Hmm, I'll have to think about that."

"You'd have to take extra precautions to protect his identity."

"Yeah, I know. That could get to be a problem," she added.

"How so?"

"The biggest shareholder by far of Channel One is Venisio Enterprises. If they say no, I can't do it."

That meant Gancha Morentoss, James Venisio's heir.

"Maybe I can get that threat off your back," I added.

"How so?"

"Never mind, Sheila. Let me get back to you."

After we disconnected, I tagged Gancha.

"I have a favor to ask you."

"Well, well," she replied.

I could almost see her grin in my mind's eye.

She added, "Favors cost favors."

I sighed.

"What kind of favor do you have in mind?" I asked.

"You know that. Dinner at least. I'm buying. Say seven this evening?"

Oh boy. Solve one problem and get another.

That would be the third time in as many weeks.

A guy could get used to this real quick.

CHAPTER 31

I viewed Channel Three, the York Broadcast Corporation, or YBC for short. They seemed to favor the opinions of the rural folks. It was best to get a wide range of opinions. Somewhere in between them hid the truth.

I read with special interest the long article by Guy Coocher in which he blamed the poisoning of the public water on the mercons. He did not come out directly blaming them. After ranting about the evils of aliens amongst us, he wrote, "Who gave a talk just before the water was contaminated? And who had a team of bodyguards, any one of which could have slipped the virus into our public drinking water? Who would have the nerve to kill off thousands of humans in one fell swoop? Who wanted the planet Rossa rid of human presence so they could claim it as their own? We don't have far to look to find the mercons."

"Vincent, see if you can find out who owns Channel Three."

Vincent nodded and turned back to his laptop.

An hour later he reported that YBC was owned by a shell of companies, but it appeared that the Humans Only organization owned sixty percent of the station.

Well, I'll be darned.

* * * * *

I put on my best blue suit and pale yellow shirt for my dinner date. No tie, of course. Guys stopped wearing them decades ago.

Before Gancha and I entered the main dining room of The Top of the Town, I read the notice, "Prepare for a blast of air as you enter the dining room."

As we crossed the threshold, my hair got tossed.

At least they were taking some precautions, even if for only the benefit of those customers who wanted to believe the air blast kept out the virus. Since they didn't ask us to strip, I knew some viruses might sneak in on the folds of our clothing.

Oh well. I guess many customers wouldn't strip anyway.

Booths lined the outer walls of the restaurant, most with windows that provided a view of the city below. At this hour, lights glowed in most of the buildings. Rivers of white and red snaked through the streets, revealing headlights or taillights. We sat on the side opposite the Ambassador Bridge and I could make out the double arc of lights on the suspension bridge over the Oreo River.

In the middle of the room rested a dozen tables, each a little rectangle of white table cloth with tubes of black indicating tableware in front of each chair.

I estimated that half the seats were filled. Maybe more diners would come later. But with the virus spreading, maybe this was as full as the Top of the Town would get on this midweek night.

Our waitress came to our table and stood by my arm. A little too close. I knew my body was eye candy to most women, but, for crying out loud, I was sitting with another woman dressed to the hilt.

Come on. Have a little sense.

Gancha had a light blue evening dress on that showed cleavage. We looked like brother and sister in blues.

It was all I could do to keep my eyes level with hers. They kept slipping down to her cleavage.

Hang in there. I know you're hungry, but this is dangerous.

"Care for anything to drink?" said our waitress with the super long legs with most of them showing just inches from my eyes.

"I'll have some Yarley's," said Gancha.

"Same here," I added.

Our waitress turned and left.

Whew! One down and one to go.

Gancha had the barest eye make up on, the current fashion. Except for the young. I had watched old movies in which girls in their late teens wore a lot of dark makeup around their eyes. They might have been trying to look serious but all that said to me was "Look out! I'm jail bait."

I have to say Gancha had a nice tone to her skin. She must be close to fifty by now and must work out because I didn't see any wrinkles.

"What favor did you have in mind?" she asked.

Back to reality, boy. And the reason for this dinner.

"In the next few days, Channel One online is going to publish some articles of opinion," I said. "Sheila Fish has asked me to ask you if you will assert the independence of Channel One."

So I lied. Spies do that.

She looked at me with her head titled. "Is that all?"

"For now."

She looked down at my chest.

Was I the only one who did that?

"You're a man of many mysteries, Jake."

Why do so many women say that?

I smiled back. "Well?"

"Sure, I can do that."

"Would you be willing to send a message to Sheila Fish saying that?"

She nodded. And smiled as she looked at her menu.

The next question hung in the air. Would I be willing to go to bed with her? I had to give her credit though. She didn't say it.

We gazed at our menus when the waitress came back with two tall drinks. After I sipped mine, I looked at her.

"We didn't order doubles."

Our waitress looked back at me with the most lustful stare I've seen in a long, long time.

"It's on the house."

I must have stared at her beautiful legs or something because the next thing I heard was from Gancha.

"Jake?"

I turned to her.

"One at a time."

I closed my mouth and swallowed.

"Sorry. Was it that obvious?"

"Yes."

Gancha ordered first. "Chateaubriand, red potatoes, green beans." She looked at me.

"For you, ma'am, or both of you?" asked the waitress.

Gancha pursed her lips. "Yes, damn it! For me!"

I hurried to order. "Make that two, if you will." I handed my menu to the waitress to distract her. She kept staring at Gancha. Maybe she wondered where Gancha would put all that food.

When we were alone, Gancha said, "I hate it when they ask that."

Gancha was a big woman. Big for her gender, and from the definition in her arms, I suspect she worked out with weights.

The view this evening was the kind to write home about. Across the room, I could see lights along both sides of the Oreo River. The Ambassador Bridge was lit up with strings of lights, too. That contrasted with the ink black of the river and the distant black as the river spread out to join the Bay of America.

I could see why this Top of the Town restaurant on the roof of the Embassy Suites was so popular.

Gancha spoke. "Why would Sheila ask you to ask me that?"

So she guessed that.

"Good question. I think she's shy about it herself. I must have let it drop I knew you."

"Right." She took a sip of her drink and set it down.

"How's your daughter?"

"Alena? She's fine. Anxious to do more research."

"I read her paper. Very interesting. I had the impression she wanted to suggest more."

I had to remember this woman had a high IQ. She was half Binger, like me. I took a long draw on my drink while I thought my response over.

"Jake, do you remember the time when we walked on the pier in Santa Monica?"

I nodded.

She added, "The fog, a deep throated horn in the distance, the lights, the sense of being alone in the universe, just the two of us out there?"

I added, "Remember when we petted the goats at the LA Zoo? And dinners at Gargon's?"

Those were the better times. What she didn't mention was our many arguments. And the times we talked over our relationship. At the time, I was interested in a more long term living arrangement, but she wanted her freedom. When she became a guest of the state for a few years, I lost track of her. That's when I met Leanna and got married.

Gancha just couldn't stay within the law and I was a cop at the time.

What was I to do? Sacrifice my career for her?

"Have you ever stepped outside the law?" she asked.

She had a point. I had killed men and done breaking and entering. By any definition, I was a career criminal. But I never did it for profit. It was part of my job as a spy.

"I see by your hesitation," she said, "I may have hit on a nerve."

"That you did."

"Care to talk about it?" she asked.

I shook my head. "Can't."

"We used to tell each other anything."

"That was then. This is now."

"We had something then. We still could."

I could see the hurt in her eyes.

She wiped her eyes with her cloth napkin.

We sat in silence until our orders arrived. Even then we didn't speak for several minutes.

"Gancha, I've been doing a lot of thinking about the two of us."

She nodded her head the barest amount. At least she acknowledged hearing my thoughts.

"I'm going through a rough time right now. Now is not the best time."

"It never seems to be for you."

She had a point—again.

"Listen, when this whole VB thing blows over, maybe we can talk again?"

I cut and took a piece of meat in my mouth.

That brought a turn to the corners of her mouth.

"Sure. Can I tag you later?"

I nodded with my mouth full of Chateaubriand.

After our dinner, I walked her back to her car in the basement. Then was the awkward moment. Do I kiss her or not?

I elected not.

"Till later, Gancha."

She jerked her head up and down a few times.

"Till later."

She wasn't happy about that.

When I got back to the ops center, via a trip around Beverly Hills to spot any tails, I went to the kitchen and poured myself a stiff one of Burbock, the only booze we had plenty of. Well, we had some Yarley's, but I was not sure when we could buy more so I kept those bottles for special occasions.

I put ice in my glass of Burbock and sat at the dining table. Ron sat across from me. "Girl trouble?"

I nodded.

"You know, you'll never get over the last love until you get a new one."

"Dated any girls lately?" I asked.

"That's cruel."

"You're right."

I tipped my glass upward. When I had taken a long drink, I added, "Sorry."

"Jake, we've been through a lot together. Braco. KL Farms." He leaned forward. "I mean it. You need a new gal."

I thought over what he'd said. Made sense.

"You're right."

"What you could use right now is another black op," said Ron.

That would do it. The tension of a break and enter job. The danger of getting killed if I made a wrong move. The unexpected that always happened.

I downed the rest of my Burbock.

CHAPTER 32

The next morning I tagged Sheila.

"I talked with the new owner of Venisio Enterprises. She will guarantee the independence of Channel One's views." I didn't mention having dinner with that owner.

"That's interesting. How did you do that?"

"For another time, Sheila."

"You know, you're building up a heap of curiosity about you."

"Can't be helped. Will you publish Poor's articles?"

"I'd have to see them first."

"Agreed."

We disconnected.

I typed an article, printed it, and sent it by Ron to the drop station outside the Channel One building.

That afternoon, I read my article on the site of Channel One. The piece was in the opinion section under "What was in that package?"

The top of the article presented the grayscale photo of Coocher when Getner passed a small package.

"You know me from my interviews on Channel One. First off, let me say this is my personal opinion. It does not represent the views of the management of Channel One.

"Ever wonder what was in that package passed from the hybrid to the guy in the van?

"First off, what was he doing having a meeting with someone he professed to hate?

"That package was small. Small enough to contain vials of the damned VB virus, wouldn't you say? I'm not saying it was VB. But it could have been.

"What if that same guy added the contents of those vials to our public water supply?

"By now, we've read of the Humans Only organization on Earth being suspected of being a terrorist organization.

"How did the virus get from Earth to Rossa? Some folks claim immigrants brought it. But in the eleven days of one-way travel, someone should have shown symptoms of infection by VB. Since none was reported, we have to consider an alternative source.

"What if HO on Earth has passed VB to the hybrid?

"Makes you kinda wonder, doesn't it?"

The article was signed, Albert Poors, ex-slave.

Not once did I mention names. That way Channel One could not be sued. Coocher's face was easily recognized though.

A half hour later, Sheila Fish tagged me with the sound of glee in her voice.

"The article by Poors received the highest number of views of any article on the Channel One website."

I could hear the happiness in her voice.

"You did it, Jake! You started them thinking."

After we disconnected, I brought Vincent up to date on this development and thanked him for the idea.

Vincent said, "You're paying a hefty price. You must love your daughter a lot."

"Do you love your wife?"

He grinned. "I see what you mean."

That same day, I got a tag from Gancha.

She started with, "Albert Poors, I presume?"

"Ah, sorry. Wrong number."

I was about to hang up when she blurted, "Jake!"

"Yes?"

"I'm sorry about the other night. We got off on a wrong foot. Can we try again? Only this time we'll focus on the positive."

"I don't know."

Silence. That damned dead kind of silence when you wonder who will speak next.

She said, "I still think we have a chance. I have enough money for both of us."

"I couldn't be your gigolo."

Another frickin' silence.

"Look at it this way. Go anywhere you want. Anywhere. Except the home planet."

"Gancha, I don't think you understand. There's been too much water over the dam since those old times. We've both changed."

Silence.

Then I said the big words. "It's over. Face it."

She said nothing.

Heaven knows what was going on in her mind.

"Jake, I've changed. I sold all of my grandfather's empire. Put the cash into investments and even bought a few legit businesses."

That pregnant silence again.

Damn! Why did I use that word?

"I still think we have a chance," she said. "It might not be easy but we're both strong people. We can do it."

I had to nod at that one, knowing she could not see my gesture. She was right.

"Can I join your team?" she asked.

She'd be quite an asset with her money and her skills. But could I stand having her around?

"That might be possible."

Finally, she broke the silence with "Can we at least remain friends?"

Why do they always ask that?
"I suppose," I replied.
Coward.
"Can I buy you a dinner?" she asked. "Salia's this time?"
A guy has to eat. "Sure."
Then I realized I was too eager. Her voice was music to my ears.
Damn! What was going on in my mind?

* * * * *

I put on a light gray suit, custom-tailored to allow room for my shoulder Snap. Then I picked Gancha up at her new house.

She came to the door wearing a tight red dress with spaghetti straps. Her breasts strained against their bounds. I noticed she wore low-heeled matching shoes and purse.

I drove to Salia's. With loops, of course, to check on any tails. We didn't speak much on the way.

I could cut the tension in the air. When we got to the parking lot, I went around to her door and opened it. Once again, she showed her gorgeous legs.

When we got seated, she said to the waitress, "I'll have a double Yarley's."

When the waitress looked at me, I nodded.

While our waitress was getting our drinks, Gancha added, "I sold off all my grandfather's crime network. I assumed a new identity for the house. My investments are in my real name. Thought it might be better that way."

After a silence, I said, "This is awkward."

"It doesn't have to be," she replied. "Just act natural."

She had veal parmesan with spaghetti and broccoli. I had chicken parmesan, rigatoni pasta, and broccoli.

She told me her memories of our romantic times together. I let her do most of the talking.

When our waitress came by, Gancha tapped her empty glass. I looked up at our waitress and nodded.

After we finished our meal and went to my car, I drove her to her new home.

When I got around to her side of the car to open her door, she put her feet on the pavement and showed a lot of gorgeous leg. She stood close to me. Maybe a little too close.

Without saying a word, she put her arms around my neck and gave me a slow kiss.

Oh dear. That magic happened again.

I felt as if I belonged here.

She broke away and opened her eyes. "I think you felt it too."

She had me there.

I grinned.

She put her arms down.

"Care to come inside? For just a drink. To celebrate what we had."

I nodded with a grin and followed her into her kitchen.

She opened the glass door to her liquor cabinet and got a tall bottle of Yarley's. After she poured generous amounts in each glass, she looked in my eyes and raised her glass.

I acknowledged her drink and drank a generous portion of mine.

She placed her glass on the dark marble counter, as I did.

She came up to me and put her arms around my neck.

Naturally we shared a kiss. A damned good one too.

Without saying a word, she pulled the two straps of her dress down her shoulders and let it fall to the floor. Her breasts hung loose and she had on a bright red half-slip. Next, she put her two hands on the top of the slip and let it fall to the floor.

She stood there in black garter belt, red bikini panties, black nylons, and red shoes.

She reached up with her arms around my neck and pressed her lips to mine. Those beautiful two mounds of flesh pressed on my chest.

Hormones took over and Junior was more than willing.

I reached down, put my arms around her bare back and red-pantied buttocks, and lifted her.

"Which way?"

She kept her left arm around my neck and pointed with her other hand, with a smile.

Afterward, I lay on her bed.

A guy could get used to this real quick. Maybe I'd better reconsider.

She turned over and looked into my eyes.

We both smiled.

"We can do this as often as you like," she said.

CHAPTER 33

The next morning, I showered and when I returned to her bedroom, she lay still with her eyes closed. I picked up my clothes and went into the living room, where I got dressed. Making as little sound as possible, I left her home.

I drove to the ops center and barely got into the kitchen when my comm vibrated. A tag from Gliituk.

"Jake?"

"Yeah."

"It's okay. When can she move in?"

Whoa. This guy moved fast.

"I'll make arrangements."

"It would be best if she didn't arrive at front gate," he added.

"I agree. Any suggestions?"

"Can she move her belongings to waterfront?" He gave me an address. "After that, she can come by same route you've used before."

After we disconnected, I went into the dorm and sat next to my daughter.

"How are you feeling?"

"Rotten. Bored to death."

"How would you feel about moving into the mercon embassy?"

She looked at me. "Come again?"

"And you'd have space to set up your lab equipment."

"You serious?" she asked.

I looked at her without responding.

Her eyes bounced from my left eye to my right.

"Really?" she begged.

I nodded.

Her face lit up. "Wow!" She jumped up and into my lap. She planted a kiss on my cheek and gave me the tightest hug I'd experienced in a long time.

It's good to be a dad.

Since it was a weekend and the streets might be crowded with people stocking up on food and water, I decided this was an ideal time to move Alena.

When we got to the BIS van, I said, "Chima, can you disguise your outside to have racing stripes in a black background?"

"Consider it done."

Not her usual "Affirmative." I saw that Vincent had been busy with her programming.

Ron had on blue jeans and a yellow shirt and drove the van. Alena wore a green pantsuit while we helped her load empty boxes and two of her suitcases.

She sat in the back with me in the passenger's seat as we went in the van to Dr. Albert's house.

At the front door, the professor greeted us, wearing a dark gray suit. Guess he must lecture today.

"Is there any way I can convince you to stay, my dear?" he asked as he faced her.

I interjected. "I'm sorry, Dr. Albert. Alena would be at risk of being kidnapped again if she stayed here. We're taking her to a safer location."

Alena piped up.

"Professor, I realize how you must feel, but my father is correct."

"He's your father?" asked Dr. Albert with wide open eyes.

Alena looked at me. "Yep. And a mighty fine one too." She looked at her advisor. "I trust him."

"Well, in that case, come in," asked the professor. He looked at Ron. "Who's he?"

"Ron," I replied, "is a friend who came to help."

Dr. Albert turned and led us to her room.

Ron and I carried empty boxes which Alena filled with her personal stuff.

How did she pick up so much stuff in the short time she's been on the planet?

Once we had the van loaded, Alena gave Dr. Albert a hug.

"Heard anything about my paper?"

"Some idiot on the review panel thinks it needs more data," he replied. "I think it's just a stalling tactic. I'll see what I can do about springing it free."

"Thanks," she replied, followed by a big grin and a quick kiss on his cheek.

Yep. She was definitely feeling happy today.

We prodded along on a twisted path to check for tails and then headed up Franken Boulevard to Shoreline Drive and east to warehouse row on the waterfront. We were the only car on most streets.

I had never seen Zor this empty.

"Chima, park in the shade if you can. Then change your color to orange on top and green on the bottom."

"Consider it done."

That phrase again. Vincent must have added his sense of humor.

Ron pulled into the address that Gliituk had given us. We dropped off eight of her boxes to human workers. I wondered why there were no mercons there but since they expected us, I figured we had the right place.

Then Ron drove us to the parking lot next to the Harper Hotel.

When we entered Room 43 and got into the room behind the rug, Tettar sat reading a tablet. He rose from the chair and greeted us. I noticed he had nose plugs.

"We'll take a more direct route."

"You have time to just sit and wait for us?" I asked.

"The warehouse people informed me you had dropped off her boxes. I've been here for only ten minutes. Time to catch up a little on my reading."

His Amerish was flawless. But I would expect the head of the mercon spy agency to polish his skills for speaking with humans in York.

After we each got into four small railroad cars with Tettar in the lead car, we went a short distance before stopping. A new portal opened. Since there was little light in the tunnel, I couldn't tell where it was.

We had to disembark from our cars and get into new ones on the other side of the portal. Once on board, Tettar pressed a button on his waist and the door to the room closed.

So he's coming with us.

This time, we went around a corner and then straight for a hundred yards before coming to the same exit place where we met four alien guards. I couldn't tell if they were the same mercons we had met before.

Dang it. They look alike. I need to develop a more discerning memory soon. Which means I had better pay closer attention to the details of their faces.

We went to the large room where we had met the ambassador before. Same dark colors, same paintings on the walls, same fireplace, same tall-backed chairs opposite the one with Gliituk.

I recognized his iridescent orange cape and his gray hair, what little there was on the top of his head.

Gliituk spoke to Alena. "So, my dear, you're coming to stay with us." He pointed to the mercon we came with. "Have you met Tettar? He's head of our security."

Alena and Tettar shook hands. If she had any surprise at having a five fingered hand with two thumbs shake hers, she didn't show it.

"We are honored to have such a brilliant researcher," he said.

That brought a big grin to her face.

Tettar extended something in his hand.

"Here is another comm like the one you have. You can use it to call your housekeeper for anything you should desire. By the way, she speaks Amerish. She will show you your lab space after your possessions arrive. I'm afraid the room is bare. You'll have to tell us what you need. It may take a few days to get some of it but we will try to accommodate your wishes."

Before I departed, I gave my daughter a hug. I whispered in her ear, "Tag me after you get settled in. I'd like to know if you're satisfied."

"Will do," she whispered back in my ear.

Tettar stayed behind while Ron and I took the rail to the room on the other side of the rug. This time there were only two railroad cars.

Ron took a route around Parliament Building and by Gerges while I kept a lookout in the mirror for anyone following us. Chima worked fine but sometimes we need to keep up our skills using the old-fashioned methods.

* * * * *

At the ops center, I tagged Deek Tanny, my friend and captain of the Zor Metro Police Homicide and Robbery Division. Despite it being a Saturday, I suspected he'd be at work. You can't keep good cops away from their jobs.

"I have a suggestion for your investigation of who started the VB attack on Rossa. You might check into who ordered fifty nanometer membrane water filtration systems in the month before the first victim came down with the disease."

"Why those systems?"

"Because anyone who knew there was going to be an outbreak would want to make sure he was protected. Fifty nanometer membrane filters would trap the virus."

"How do you know that?"

"Deek, anyone who has access to the Net can find out what filtration would work on water to screen out the virus and make his drinking water safe."

Ron had installed a membrane filter over a year before the outbreak of VB. So I was sure his name wouldn't show up on recent purchases.

Deek said, "So you're suggesting that anyone who ordered those membrane filters would know the virus was coming."

"Not exactly," I answered. "Other than hospitals and special laboratories that might need such precautions, you could form a list of suspects. The filters are expensive. I'll bet HO ordered several membrane filtration systems. Why would that organization need the extra protection?"

"You think HO is behind it?"

"I'm suggesting an avenue of investigation, that's all."

"I'll look into it. Thanks for the idea, Jake."

We disconnected.

* * * * *

I scanned every room in the ops center but couldn't find Leanna.

"Where's your wife?" I asked Vincent.

"Taking out the trash. And getting some fresh air on a short walk."

"I don't like her going out. Someone might recognize her," I said.

"Relax, will ya?" he replied.

I shook my head. One of the problems of hiring bright people is their tendency to have independent minds.

I sat at a monitor and drafted my next article for the opinion piece on Channel One under the byline of Albert Poors. This one was to be titled, "Who is up to their old dirty tricks?"

"I suggested earlier that the virus VB was deliberately brought onto Rossa. Any immigrants with the disease would not only have come down with symptoms, many would have died during the eleven-day voyage from Earth. That was bound to be noticed.

"But if a package of the virus were frozen and kept separate from the other cargo, it would arrive on Rossa intact. And ready to do its deadly deed.

"If Craig Horton and RUFF are innocent, then who else has an interest in damaging the images of aliens, hybrids, etc.? What other organization is large enough to back such a devious plan?

"The Humans Only organization on Earth has been implicated in several terrorist attacks. Even though Coocher claims that HO on Rossa would never resort to terrorism, can we believe him? Especially after he was seen taking a package from a hybrid? By the way, the head of the York Security Agency is a known hybrid.

"And what was in that package anyway? What business did he have taking anything from anyone, let alone a hybrid? Especially after he expressed hatred of them so many times.

"If you ask me, I think Coocher has a lot of explaining to do.

"Albert Poors, ex-slave."

I deliberately mentioned that last question to keep the fingers pointing at Coocher.

I printed my article on paper and sprayed it with chlorine bleach to destroy any DNA and fingerprints. Then I placed the paper inside an envelope I sprayed with bleach. After replacing the top papers in our printer with bleach-sprayed ones and letting them dry, I printed the name "Sheila Fish." Then I put on a pair of rubber gloves, cut her name out, and taped the rectangle on the outside of the envelope.

Vincent took it in his gloved hands, drove it to the Channel One building, and left it in the overnight drop box.

Two down, an unknown number to go.

Four hours later, I read Albert Poors' latest opinion piece on the Channel One site. I sat back and smiled. My campaign was coming along fine. I was surprised to see it mentioned on Sheila's six-o'clock news in the "local interest" section of her program.

Sheila tagged me the next afternoon.

"The letter from Poors was our most visited webpage, topping even the front page of the sports section and those who just read the comics. This is dynamite!"

"What pressure has anyone put on you to reveal his identity?"

"Oh, the Metro, YFP, HO, you name it. But with Morentoss's assurance, I ignored all of them. That was a good move on your part. Someday, you must explain how you did that."

"Maybe." I couldn't commit to even setting a date to explain.

"Say, cowboy, you didn't have to trade favors, did you?"

"Come on, Sheila. You don't reveal your sources, I don't reveal mine."

"I suppose. Say, what are you doing tomorrow night? Care to share dinner?"

"Busy. Got two new cases this past week and they require a lot of my time. I don't know when I'll be free."

I certainly wasn't going to make it easy to commit to dinner with her, even if I had to fabricate a little.

"You're a slippery dog, Jake."

"Sorry, don't mean to. It just happens that way."

Vincent waved his hand and I said, "Gotta go, Sheila. My guy is on the move."

I disconnected as if in a hurry.

Vincent came over.

I said, "Good timing."

CHAPTER 34

After lunch the next day, I secured the exits.

"Ruta, keep all doors to the ops center locked until I give permission to open them. If I die in the next four days, then allow any BIS team member to open them. Open the front door to medical personnel who wish to enter, but get clear IDs first. Check with the dispatcher."

Ruta was the name we had given to our ops center computer. We gave "her" a name because it seemed natural. Most people give their smartest AIs names.

I strolled through the dorm and to the kitchen. At the dining room table sat Leanna, Vincent, and Ron, chatting.

"Let's have a meeting."

They got up and followed me into the larger planning room. There lay Zetto on his bed, with Monk sleeping next to his legs.

I sat in a chair and turned to my full team.

"The virus is running rampant outside. We'll stay inside here until we can get the vaccine."

Monk climbed into my lap.

Could he sense the tension in the room?

Leanna was the first to speak. "And what happens if one of us becomes ill before then?"

I looked at every person, one by one.

"I repeat, we stay here until the vaccine arrives."

The silence was deafening.

I said, "So far, only fifteen percent of those who come down ill end up dying. I know that sounds high. But it also means eight-five percent will survive."

Ron asked, "What happens if no one will bring the vaccine to us?"

"Let's find the answer right now."

I tagged Dr. Newton. Unfortunately, she could not answer, so I left a voice message and used the speaker phone so my team could hear.

"Dr. Newton, this is Jake Dani. Is it possible that someone from your office could have the VB vaccine available for pickup?"

After I disconnected, Vincent added, "And who will go pick up the vaccine?"

"That's a risk I could not ask you to share. I'll go."

I turned to Zetto. "I know you're still recovering, but can you fix meals?"

He nodded. "Leanna can be my backup."

"I suppose it goes without saying but I'll say it anyway," I said. "I want anyone who feels any symptoms to report them to me, immediately."

"What are the symptoms?" asked Leanna.

I turned to my communications expert.

"Zetto, what have you found?"

He clicked a few buttons and read from his monitor, "Muscle weakness in the face first. Then in eye movements, chewing, and swallowing. Double vision, drooping of both eyelids. Difficulty talking. Dry mouth and throat. The weakness spreads down to the arms and legs. Some get constipated. Most victims experience difficulty breathing. That is the major cause of death. Fever is not a symptom, nor high blood pressure."

"So we just fade away," said Leanna. "How long is a person sick?"

Zetto turned to his monitor. We waited. Finally, he looked up.

"From first symptoms to the worst stage is three days. If they survive on the fourth day, they'll live."

I asked, "What about the most contagious time?"

He read from his monitor, "Third day. When the symptoms are the strongest."

I asked, "And what is the incubation period? How long from first getting it to showing symptoms?"

He replied, "One day, at most."

Faces drooped and heads titled down.

"Listen up, folks," I said. "That's the worst case. We may never get it."

Vincent added, "Okay, now that that's settled, what the hell are we going to do while we wait?"

We spent the first day watching movies, reading books, or watching a telly. One telly showed on the far wall in the dorm, one displayed on the blank wall in the dining room, and one in the planning room on the fourth wall. None were in the shower or toilet. We all had readers which we could use for movies.

I noticed Ron preferred action books. The current rave in crime noir he read was Asterid's Bad Guy. Vincent favored books where the hero was at a disadvantage. He read Cavers' Last to the Wedding. Zetto preferred comedies. Myself, I preferred spy flicks, especially about a protagonist recruited against his will.

We didn't watch the telly much, except to catch up on the news. Prime Minister Pierre Klava declared martial law and enforced a curfew from dark to daylight.

Klava said, "Only ambulance personnel, nurses, doctors, and federal troops are allowed on the streets after dark. During the day, you need a pass, or carry a body bag of someone who had died and you are headed toward the burial pits or back home. You can have a body bag delivered to your home or you can wrap the body in a bed sheet.

"Everyone out on the streets must wear a breathing mask or they'll be arrested."

And does that include government people?

Klava answered my question.

"Only those whose jobs require a presence, such as police officers, soldiers, and medical staff, are exempt. But all must wear breathing masks. Folks, please stay home and sit this out."

On the screen I saw flatbed trucks with wooden sides, all headed in the same direction. In their cargo holds were body bags, some white, some of colored linen. No faces were visible as the linens were tied at one end.

One newscast showed a truck backing up to a pit and lifting its cargo bed. The view changed to show hundreds of body bags below. Some wrapped in white and most in different colors of bed linen, all tied at one end. Here and there the camera spotted a black body bag. Bulldozers stood by ready to push mountains of dirt into the hole. All the truck drivers, crane operators, and bulldozer operators wore full-body green HazMat suits.

Views of the streets of Zor showed only a car or two, even during rush hour. A military checkpoint blocked the road at every second light.

Even the shelves at Walker's, a major source of groceries for most people, stood bare. No workers showed up to restock them. Everyone obeyed the curfew.

Leanna said, "Jake, I don't know if this qualifies as a symptom, but I feel depressed."

"I understand. Having this over our heads is enough to make anyone depressed. Hang in there."

That evening, Dr. Newton tagged me back.

"Sorry I missed your tag, Jake. We don't have any vaccine yet. It's supposed to come in small vials that can be inserted into the injectors. I'll let you know when they arrive. How many injections do you need?"

Modern injectors used compressed air to move the drug under the skin. The person giving the dose would pump the injector between uses to build up air pressure.

"We are five here. No, make that six with my pet. He weighs only twenty pounds. I'll wait for your call. Once again, thank you, doctor."

"How are you feeling?" she asked. "Where are you staying?"

"I'm in the same place you visited before. We'll stay here in quarantine until I get your tag."

We disconnected.

On the second day, I noticed Leanna's eyes looked sad. She didn't move much.

"Are you feeling okay, Leanna?" I asked.

She nodded. And then broke out with a big grin.

I couldn't help but smile too.

"Great!" I added.

Zetto slept more than usual in his hospital bed. Ron, Vincent, and I didn't feel a thing and slept normal hours. Since Vincent snored, I moved his bunk bed into the storage room. That was easier than moving our beds into the planning room.

The next day, Leanna looked different. Her eyelids drooped and she breathed with difficulty. Ron took over in the kitchen. When Zetto dropped a dish, the clatter turned everyone's head. I stepped in.

"Zetto, go lay down. Ron and I will fix lunch."

He dragged his butt into his bed and soon fell asleep.

Vincent spent most of his time with his wife, trying to keep her awake. When he walked into the kitchen to get food for both of them, I noticed sweat on his forehead.

"How is she?"

"Not good. I think she's got it."

"Can I go get some vaccine?" asked Ron.

I shook my head. "None available."

Vincent and Ron looked at each other.

I got a tag from Dr. Newton in the evening.

"We don't have any vaccine yet and when we do, we'll vaccinate the staff first. How are you holding up?"

"We won't be needing it. Two of us have come down sick. Symptoms look like VB."

She paused before saying, "Oh. I'm sorry to hear that."

CHAPTER 35

We spent another day trying to entertain ourselves. Ron and I spent several hours treating our Snaps to the drilling, filing, and acid baths.

The next day, Leanna could hardly move. This was her third day of being ill.

I didn't want her breath to be taken in by everyone in the dorm so Ron and I wore breathing masks as we moved her bunk bed into the small storage room.

Since Vincent's bed was in there, we moved it to the dining room. It was a squeeze, but we made more room by transferring cans to the kitchen floor and removing two rows of shelves.

Vincent said, "But if she moves into the storage room, I won't be able to see her."

"She'll be close by and you can visit her any time."

He said, "You've given up on her already."

"Vincent, this is the stage where she is the most contagious. I have to think of the rest of us. You can spend as much time by her as you like as long as you wear full body protection. And no kissing of any kind."

He looked at me, closed his eyes, and nodded.

Ron moved a telly into her small room from the kitchen and put it on the wall opposite her head so she could watch movies. That meant we had two tellies left. One in the planning room where Zetto slept and the second in the dorm. Vincent brought Leanna her food at meal times. He wanted to check on her every five minutes but I wouldn't let him.

"Let her rest."

We watched a lot of comedies. Anything to get our minds off the depressing situation.

Zetto reported not feeling well. Ron came to his bedside every couple of minutes and yelled, "Breathe!"

The startled Zetto took a deep breath.

The aura of depression hung heavy. With two people ill, we had a death sentence hanging over us.

One day I noticed Monk seemed to sleep a lot, a sign of VB. Or maybe it was the cat part of him. He seemed to be energetic enough at meal time though and he still went to the toilet by himself.

At lunch one time, I asked Ron and Vincent, "How are you feeling?"

Vincent shrugged. "No problems."

"Ron?"

"Same here. How about you?"

I replied, "Nothing."

Vincent suggested, "All three of us have Binger DNA. Do you suppose our stronger immune systems could be what's protecting us?"

Hmm. Leanna and Zetto had no Binger DNA and were the only ones here to get sick. If you didn't count Monk. I had spent so little time with him I didn't know his habits yet.

* * * * *

On the morning of the fourth day, Leanna got worse.

Even though she claimed she was wide awake, her eyelids said otherwise. She spoke slowly and with much effort.

"Vin, I'm gonna die."

"Not on my shift, you're not!" I exclaimed.

That brought a short-lived smile from her.

"Hon, please hang in there," said Vincent. "Think of Alena. She needs your guidance."

With labored breathing, Leanna replied, "No. She's an adult now. Set on her own path in life. She doesn't need...my guidance. I can support her...but not guide her anymore."

"Let's have no more talk of dying. You're sick now but you'll survive," I said.

She looked her husband in the eyes. "Vincent, I want you to find another wife. You need someone to love you."

"Easier said than done," he replied with a half-laugh. "In case you haven't noticed, I don't have real legs."

Leanna gasped for air. "That doesn't matter. You found me, didn't you?" She gasped again. "I don't have long. Promise me you'll look for another wife."

Vincent looked down. I saw his body jerk. He was crying and trying not to show it.

Leanna reached out to him but he didn't notice.

"Vincent," I said. "She's trying to touch you."

Not me, damn it. You.

A lump grew in my throat.

Vincent looked up. His eyes were red and watery but he reached out to grab her hand.

I said, "I think you two need to be alone." I left the storage room and walked into the kitchen. Thank heavens it was empty.

I looked around for something to do and saw the sink had dirty dishes. So I rinsed each dish of any food scraps and placed it in it the warm soapy water. That kept me busy for ten minutes. To conserve energy we didn't use an automatic dishwasher. The power company had asked everyone to help since they were understaffed.

"Jake?" came Vincent's voice behind me.

I turned around. I could see he had trouble forming words. Something about his appearance told me the worst had come.

"Is she gone?" I asked.

He nodded. Then he puckered up and squeezed his eyes shut.

I closed the distance between us and held him in my arms. He sobbed on my shoulder. I wished I could join him but I was the boss. Somebody had to be strong. So I postponed my own reaction.

* * * * *

An hour later, I called for a meeting in the planning room, otherwise known as Zetto's bedroom.

"I think the worst is over but to be sure, we should stay here for one more day."

"It should have been me," said Vincent. "I'd give anything if I had gotten it and not her."

I looked him in the eyes. "You did all you could. You said yourself it may be our Binger DNA that helps us.

We watched the news when it came on the fourth wall.

Channel One's anchorman spoke. "Sheila Fish couldn't be here today. She's sick and is staying home. She refused to have a camera in her bedroom. We wish her the best of luck."

He was silent for five seconds, an eternity on television. He looked at his monitors, unable to speak.

Like thousands of viewers, I hoped Sheila would survive.

The scene changed to show a street view. Cars and trucks filled the streets. At least commerce was moving again.

A small crowd marched outside the Parliament Building with signs that read, "Stop the virus. Stop HO!" and "We've had enough!"

Too bad it took the threat of death to get people to wake up.

Zetto managed to keep breathing. Ron helped him go to the bathroom. I locked the storage room and wouldn't let anyone go in there.

"What's the point?" Ron asked. "We need food from there. Zetto probably has it. The virus is in every room by now."

I nodded and unlocked the door. Ron and I put sheets over Leanna's body and fastened them with clips. Ron retrieved a dozen cans. He passed each under a blast of filtered air and radiation, turning each can over several times. The larger freezer was in the kitchen, packed full of food for such an emergency.

Vincent spent several hours in the storage room before he came out. His head hung the lowest I'd ever seen.

I went to the dining room and tagged Alena at the mercon embassy.

She was excited. "They get me everything I ask for. These guys are great! I have a full lab set up here. So far, I've confirmed that humans and mercons have DNA in common."

My silence made her pause.

"How's Mom?"

That damned familiar lump formed in my throat and my eyes watered. I bowed my head and put my forehead on my right palm.

"She came down with the virus."

Silence.

"How's she holding up?"

When I didn't—no, couldn't—answer, she yelled in my ear.

"Dad! Tell me she's okay!"

I struggled to say, "She didn't make it."

This time a longer silence came.

"Are you okay?" she asked with a quivering voice.

I nodded and realized she couldn't see that. "Yeah, I'm okay. No symptoms. Vincent has a theory that Binger DNA means a stronger immune system. Which suggests you may be safe."

"Who's with you?" she asked.

"Ron's here. And Vincent. And Zetto. Zetto is sick, I'm afraid."

"Will you have someone call me if…."

"Yes. I'll have Ron or Vincent tag you if I get it. You should get vaccinated as soon as possible."

Then she broke down. I waited to the sounds of sobs.

I wish I could put my arms around my daughter.

She recovered enough to ask, "When?"

"An hour ago."

"Did she…?"

"No, she didn't suffer. She must have felt exhausted at the end and must have just given up."

God damned VB!

"Dad! Can I…?"

"No, you stay there. You're safer there. I'll visit you as soon as I can."

"Call me if there are any developments," she said.

"Okay."

"Oh, Gliituk said I should tell you the mercons seem to be immune. No mercon in the embassy or outside it has caught the virus."

"That's interesting. Thank you."

The next day, Zetto reported he felt better. That's when Ron told him about Leanna. Which may not have been the best time. Zetto became depressed.

"Zetto, it looks like you're going to be okay," I said. "What happened to Leanna won't happen to you. You're gonna make it."

I have to give him credit. He tried to put on a happy face. Which wasn't easy since his facial muscles were still weak.

Monk spent more time in my lap, wanting petting. Or maybe I needed him.

There was a small freezer in the storage room. Ron and I studied it but couldn't figure out a way to get Leanna's body in the small space. She would have to stay under the sheets on her bed.

The only good news was the crisis was over. We could leave the ops center. Except Leanna.

I tagged the police but with so many deaths, I had to wait a long time to get through. Their dispatcher finally said, "Sorry, fella. The morgue is overloaded and won't accept any bodies except those who died by violence. The cemeteries have large pits for those who have died from VB. I'll have a truck come by your place. Where are you?"

I didn't want to give him our address.

"Where are the pits?" I asked.

He gave me three locations, all in the south end of Zor.

I asked Ron if he'd help me take Leanna's body to one of them. Zetto wasn't feeling strong yet and Vincent couldn't help.

I approached Vincent. "We're going to take Leanna's body. Do you want to say goodbye?"

He nodded, went into the storage room, and closed the door.

Ron and I waited a long time for him to come out.

"Hungry?" I asked.

"Nah," he replied.

"Me neither."

Vincent came into the kitchen.

"You can take her now."

Ron and I put on rubber gloves and moved to the storage room. He carried one end of her bag and I the other. Vincent held the front door open and looked at the white sheet over her body as we carried her out.

We carried the bag up the stairs and into the back of our van. I gave Chima the address of a burial pit. When we got there we saw a truck raise its container at the edge of a pit. When we got out, a man with a rifle and dressed in HazMat green came out.

"Where are your masks?" he said through his light blue face mask.

Dang. I forgot.

Ron smirked and whispered.

"Let's see you get out of this one."

"Don't have any," I replied to the man.

He sighed, went to his car, and brought back a dozen masks and handed them to me. "Dump the bag here and leave. We'll take care of it. Who is it anyway?"

"His wife."

That got a pause from Ron. He quickly recovered, put on his sad face, and lowered his head.

As Chima drove away, he said, "My wife?"

"Now we're even."

A grin spread over his face.

As he drove our van away, I looked out the back window. I hated to leave her in a mass burial.

As the burial site got smaller in the distance, I realized I would never see her again.

Goodbye, Lee.

CHAPTER 36

When we got back to the ops center, nobody spoke much. Each kept to himself. Leanna was gone from our lives.

Zetto yelled from the planning room, "Hey, guys. The vaccine has arrived!"

Ron, Vincent, and I rushed into the main room and scrambled to sit in chairs.

On the far wall was the rectangular view of the Channel One newsroom. Across the bottom of the screen scrolled the words "Vaccine arrives at Meda."

A young woman sat behind the desk where I expected to see Sheila. She wore a blue low-cut dress with short sleeves. Despite her long wavy black hair, perhaps made to mimic the style of Sheila, it was obvious to me she was someone else.

"This news break just came in. We take you to our reporter on the island of Meda at the Space Elevator."

Two men dressed in green HazMat suits lugged a gray metallic case between them. White "smoke" poured down from the case as they walked toward the camera between rows of police dressed in black, rifles pointed upward. They faced the outside of the rows but I saw faces turn as the men walked by.

In the background, I noticed the exit doors from the bottom of the Space Elevator.

The next thing I saw was the case with two humans carrying it between them. All three boarded a small gray jet plane with the words York Air Force above the windows.

The scene moved upward to show two military jets as they roared overhead.

A male reporter came into view, wearing a white face mask. Nothing below his face showed on the camera but his hair blew in the wind. He spoke with a microphone held close to his mask.

"A case containing two hundred doses of the VB vaccine and two large tubes of the active virus arrived at the bottom of the Space Elevator this afternoon. A military jet is standing by to whisk the virus and vaccine to the Zor-Franken Airport."

Prime Minister Pierre Klava held himself erect in front of a dark blue curtain and behind a podium. The York flag was visible behind him.

"I have ordered a police escort from the airport for the two men and their valuable cargo of Viral Botulism and vaccine. Orion Pharmaceuticals and Omar-Kadish Pharmaceuticals are standing by to receive the live virus and will prepare additional vials of the vaccine. The first two hundred doses of the vaccine will go to medical personnel who treat the sick. Officials from Orion and Omar-Kadish told me it would take two days to prepare the first vials of vaccine. Please don't call them. They'll be busy.

"When police and military personnel are vaccinated, I will lift the curfew and martial law."

The view changed to show the young woman as she spoke to the darker skinned man next to her. "Any news on Sheila Fish?"

He replied, "I'm afraid not." He turned to the camera.

"Next is our coverage of your local news."

The scene changed to show a woman racing down the gray steps in front of a glass building. A car pulled up in front of her and she stopped to look at it. Another car commercial. The wall went all white again before it got further.

Zetto was the first to raise his left thumb up and yell, "Yeah!"

Ron and I joined him.

"The crisis is over," I said. "And Zetto is feeling better."

Ron, Zetto, and I looked at Vincent, whose head remained bowed.

Can't say I blame him.

"I'm declaring the quarantine over. Anyone can leave at any time. Ruta, disregard my previous instructions on locking the operations center. Maintain normal security."

That should have brought smiles to every face, but it didn't.

"Now we have to think about the future. Vincent, what do we know about the Humans Only headquarters?"

Ron broke a smile. I looked at him and nodded.

Yes, we're going on a B&E.

Vincent looked up.

"Why there?"

"Those bastards took Leanna and killed thousands more in the city. We need more evidence of their complicity and that's the best place to get it."

After a pause, I added, "Besides, we owe it to her."

Ron and Zetto moved their heads up and down. Vincent stared at the floor but said nothing.

* * * * *

This time luck was our side. Mourtan Security had the contract for security at the Alton Building where Humans Only had offices. The snag came when Vincent found the HO office used the highest level of Mourtan Security.

Even though I owned most of the shares of Mourtan, I was reluctant to pull my weight to get the HO plans. But we had to get in there.

I tagged Andy using our security encryption.

"Hi, Andy. How are you doing?"

"As well as could be expected with half my workers gone on sick leave."

"You?"

"No. Neither grandma or me is sick."

"Andy, I need to gain access to your security at the Alton Building. Specially the HO offices. Can you tag Elsie to give me access?"

Elsie Mourtan was his grandmother and the firm got its name from her.

"Why? What do you want to do there?"

"Do you really want me to tell you?"

"Hmm. Maybe not. I'll tell grandma."

Vincent and I waited for twenty minutes before I tried to access the HO security on the computer in the ops center. Sure enough, I got in easily. Vincent copied the floor plans and the security plans to our ops center computer.

We studied the plans and went over seven different routes of access. HO rented the entire sixth floor, which made it easier. If we could get into one office, we could access all of them.

Ron stole a van and he and I spray painted the outside to hide its label of Keller's Grocery. Then both of us removed our stained white painter's clothing and put on our casual wear. Ron wore blue jeans, white shirt, and black shoes. I had on brown slacks, white T-shirt, brown sweater, and black shoes.

This time Ron and I went on the op. We both wore full beards and moustaches, long hair, and bushy eyebrows. He chose brown and I black. We packed an extra set of all black clothing in sports bags, along with a pair of Z helmets.

Ron headed out first in the Keller van and I followed in my car. The first thing I noticed was the absence of military checkpoints. All lanes were full of cars and a few trucks but I supposed many folks were visiting the stores for the first time in a week. The parking lots we passed were jammed full.

The news said workers spent overtime restocking shelves from bulging warehouses.

With the stolen van in front, I drove to the countryside at the end of Moss Street, where I parked under a walnut tree and hopped into the passenger seat of the van.

As Ron drove to the Alton Building, we passed a side street I heard a burglar alarm and the flashing lights of patrol cars rushing to the scene.

"Guess the cops'll be busy tonight."

Ron drove into an alley and parked. In the van, Ron and I changed into black clothing from the bags we brought with us. Then he drove to the parking lot behind the Alton Building, where we put on a pair of Andy's Z helmets, the ones with communications that allowed the two of us to share conversations in private. I put on a dark blue backpack for whatever we'd find.

The only lights on in the Alton Building came from the tenth floor. Somebody was putting in overtime, or the cleaning people had left the lights on.

I used my gloved fingers to key in the combination from Mourtan to gain access to the building and Ron placed a cover over the keypad. When we exited later, he'd issue a wireless command and the cover would explode, destroying evidence of tampering. Of course, that was tampering itself but we didn't want the police to think we used the combination. Let 'em guess.

We entered the building and used our flashlights to go up the stairs to the sixth floor. I keyed in another combination on the keypad on the glass doors leading to the lobby of Humans Only. Ron adhered a cover over it as well.

Ron took one hallway and I another. We weren't sure where to go. Fifteen seconds later, Ron's voice came in my helmet, "Will Records do?"

"Be right there," I replied.

We encountered a smaller keypad at the beige door to the room with the label Records. Ron attached two wires to the keypad and held a black box in his left hand.

"Douse the flashlights," I ordered.

Soon we stood in the dark while we waited for the red numbers on the box as they changed rapidly. And waited. In forty-five seconds, the numbers stopped changing and a button changed to green. Ron pressed that combination on the pad. I pulled the handle down and the door opened.

Our flashlights illuminated a safe at the far wall and one locked file cabinet on the right wall. I examined the labels on each drawer of the cabinet. We didn't know what we wanted but when I found one labeled training vids, I wondered if it held any secrets.

"Ron, try your opener on this one."

Ron came beside me and placed the electrodes on the locked cabinet. In thirty seconds the button turned green. He used the combination on the lock, opened the cabinet, and shined his light inside. Besides training manuals in binders, we found eight training vids on disks.

I pawed through the first file but couldn't find anything obvious.

Ron asked, "Shall I pack the vids?"

"Might as well."

He pulled the vids out and put them on top of the cabinet.

We spent another ten minutes searching through other drawers of the cabinet but nothing popped out.

Damn! I had hoped we'd find something incriminating.

I looked at the timer on my wrist. "We've been here long enough. Pack the vids."

Then I turned around and presented my back to him. He slipped the vids into my backpack and zipped it closed. Then he tapped me on the head.

We reversed our path out of the building and entered the van.

I took off the backpack and put it on the floor in front of me.

He drove the van to the countryside to the tree where I had parked my car. There, Ron tossed a package through an open window of the van while I carried the backpack into the driver's seat of my car. After Ron took the passenger seat and I drove away, I saw a flash of light in my mirror.

Good ol' Pyronex.

When we returned to the ops center, Vincent let us in. I showed him our take and we divided up the eight vids among the four of us, Vincent, Zetto, Ron, and me. I took the dorm monitor, Ron, the kitchen, and Vincent and Zetto used those in the planning room.

Three hours later, Zetto yelled, "Bingo!"

I yelled across the doorways, "Whatcha got?"

"A doozy," he replied.

When I got to the planning room, Ron and Vincent had already taken seats.

Zetto projected the image on the far wall.

Coocher spoke in front of eight people, five men and three women, in a classroom.

"I shouldn't say this," said Coocher, "but we have plans to wipe out enough damned liberal voters in the city to change the votes."

"What do you mean?" said a feminine voice.

"I can't tell you specifics," said Coocher, "but think illness. And don't worry about catching it. We've installed filters on our water supply to make sure nobody in this building gets it."

He continued his lecture on how to recruit volunteers to join the organization.

"Off," I said. I turned to Zetto. "Can you make copies of just the incriminating portion?"

"Sure," he replied.

I looked at the three men.

"Folks, this is the smoking gun we need."

I wrote another letter from Albert Poors and included a video of the part of Guy Coocher talking about an illness. After wiping everything to avoid leaving any fingerprints or DNA, and spraying it all with bleach, I labeled the package "To Sheila Fish, from Albert Poors." This time Ron wore gloves when he took it to the Channel One office.

The next morning, I saw the vid in the opinion part of Channel One's website.

Two hours later, Sheila tagged me.

"Damn! That latest vid of Coocher was over the top. Where the hell did you get it?"

"Can't tell ya," I answered.

"Will you ever?"

"Can't say. Ever is a long time."

"Right. Well, anyway, thanks buddy."

"It's good to hear your voice again," I said. "I take it you're over your illness."

"Yeah. Back at the grind."

I heard a voice in the distance yell her name.

"Gotta run," she said.

We disconnected.

The news said twelve percent of the population of the city now resided in those burial pits. Hardest hit were the news staffs, medical staffs, and government offices. This was the greatest disaster on Rossa—ever.

When the polls showed the Freedom from Aliens Bill would pass by a narrow margin, I sighed. The number of rural voters outnumbered those in Zor and La Seille. My efforts had not been enough.

The news was a downer, to say the least. None of us in the ops center had much to say.

CHAPTER 37

The next day, I put on jeans and a white short-sleeved T-shirt.

Then I tagged Dr. Newton's office. Much to my surprise, she answered right away.

"Yes, Jake?"

"We lost one person here. Can I pick up an injector and one dose of vaccine?"

"Why not four doses?"

"Can't tell you that."

"Did anybody come down with VB?" she asked.

"We lost one woman and another man is sick. He's the one we need the vaccine for. Oh, and another dose for my twenty pound pet." I thought of Alena. "Ah, we might need another dose too."

"The vaccine is best used on those who don't have symptoms yet," she said. "But we've been instructed to vaccinate everyone except those who caught it and survived."

"I learned the mercons seem to be immune."

"Hmm, that's interesting. Where'd you hear about the...others?"

Her avoidance of the word mercons alerted me to the presence of staff around her.

"I can't tell you that. Maybe later, in person."

She added, "There might be some protection if you've been exposed to the virus. It works differently in some individuals."

"Maybe you're right."

I made a mental calculation. Ron, Vincent, Zetto, Alena, Monk. Oh, and me.

"Can you have an injector and five and a half doses ready for pickup?"

"I can have them available in an hour," she replied. "We're swamped here with patients who are afraid they have VB. In half of them, it's just fatigue from nervous tension. Why five and a half?"

"Can't answer that. I'll come by in an hour. And thanks, doc. I really appreciate your work."

"I know. See you then."

At the appointed time, I drove myself to her office.

"Do you have an appointment?" asked the chubby female receptionist.

"Yes, with Dr. Newton."

She looked me over. "Are you Jake?"

I nodded.

"Have a seat, please. She'll be with you in a minute."

People sat on every chair in the waiting room. When one became available, I noticed a woman with two small girls standing and I let her take it. I stood against one wall.

After twenty minutes, a nurse came through a door with a bag. She glanced around at those waiting and locked eyes on me.

"Are you Jake?"

I nodded and she handed me the bag. I peeked in it and saw an injector and some vials for it.

The nurse added, "Sorry about the delay."

"Thanks again."

I drove around several blocks before heading up Ambassador and left on Shoreline Drive. When I pulled up to the gates of the mercon embassy, several human soldiers in camouflage uniforms checked my ID.

"Why the guards?" I asked.

The man with the gun on his hip looked bored and tired when he answered, "Demonstrators."

That made sense. I had seen on the telly that some folks blamed the mercons for VB. Conspiracy theorists were having a field day.

The same response came from the mercons guards inside the gate. I presented my ID. After one look at it, the officer in charge let me in.

I parked in the small courtyard parking lot and entered the front door.

And everything changed.

The walls glowed white, which I expected, but what I didn't expect were the statues. In recessed places around the walls rested a dozen busts of mercons. In front of each bust I could make out a name. Since they didn't mean anything to me, I glanced over them.

In front of a desk sat a small dark mercon receptionist. I couldn't tell the gender.

"Can I help you, sir?"

"Can I speak with Alena Dani, please?"

"And you are?"

"Her father, Jake Dani."

"One moment."

He or she, whatever it was, pressed a few buttons on a console on the desk. "There's a Jake Dani to see you." It nodded and looked at me.

"She'll be here in a minute." It pointed to a row of seats.

I didn't have to sit long before Alena came through a set of the double doors, wearing dark blue slacks and a light brown shirt.

She rushed up with open arms and we embraced. We were all we had of a family on Rossa now. My parents and grandparents were on Earth and Leanna had lost both parents.

We held the hug for a long time. Neither of us seemed willing to end it. Finally, we separated.

"How are they treating you?"

"Like royalty!" she replied. "I get everything I want."

"I brought you something," I said as I stooped to pick up the bag on a seat.

"What?" Alena asked.

I opened the bag and extracted the injector.

"Raise your sleeve," I instructed.

She did.

I loaded the injector with a vial of vaccine and pumped the handle several times until it resisted. Then I pressed the injector to her forearm, activated it by the button, and heard a hiss as the vial emptied.

"Feel anything?" I asked.

"Only a full feeling under my skin."

"You may be protected against VB with your 'special' DNA but we need to make sure. You are now vaccinated against VB."

She lowered her sleeve.

"Can I see your quarters?"

"Sure," she replied with a smile as she fastened the button on the end of her sleeve.

I repacked the injector in the bag and followed Alena, as she led the way through the double doors and down a hallway. The ceiling was low but then again every mercon I knew was much shorter than most humans. Only human children were consistently shorter. My daughter stooped as she walked, barely avoiding scraping her head. She was an inch taller than me but I stooped too.

When we got to her suite, I wasn't surprised. She had decorated her suite much like I expected of her, as in not much. She was a researcher first and not interested in housekeeping. Everything looked like it had one purpose. A bed, a refrigerator, a dining table, a closet. In one room, I saw an upholstered chair with a telly in front of it. Next to the chair was a small table with a half glass of brownish liquid.

"Care to see my lab?" she asked with a big grin.

"Wouldn't want to miss that."

We went down the same hallway to another room across the hall, ducking as we walked. She opened the door. I didn't know what to expect. On hard black surfaces above rows of green drawers lay an assortment of instruments. From my university days, I recognized a centrifuge but not the bigger machines.

"This is where I extract DNA," she said as she pointed to the glassware. On the surface of the table in a glass-covered enclosure rested several mercon dolls. Rubber gloves extended from the inside front of the glass cage.

"From here, I put the samples in the centrifuge," she pointed again. "Then I extract the residue and inject it into here." She patted a metal box.

"It replicates the portions of the DNA so I get enough of a sample, which I then inject into here." She pointed to another metallic box.

Then she traveled on foot to the end of the row and pointed to a monitor and chair.

"The results come out here."

"What are you working on now?"

"Mostly additional data to support my thesis."

"And what revelation do you have next?"

She looked at me. "You'd better sit down for this." She pointed to a stool.

I sat on it and gave her my attention.

"I've examined ancient mercon DNA that the ambassador was so gracious to provide from their museum and have narrowed the time window down. Dad, I think modern humans and modern mercons have a common ancestor, from about two million seven hundred thousand years ago. I think they were mercons but their DNA is slightly different from what we see today."

* * * * *

When I returned to the ops center, I carried the bag inside.

Vincent said, "We still don't have any idea where Hoskins is. Coocher is on his way to Parliament."

"How do you know that?"

But he just grinned in response.

"I want Ron and you to come into the planning room," I ordered.

There I used the injector to give Vincent, Ron and Zetto a dose of vaccine. I handed the injector to Ron and rolled up my sleeve before he gave me a shot too.

Ron added, as he pumped the injector and queried, "Have you seen Alena?"

I nodded. "She's fine. Having a good time at the embassy. I vaccinated her too."

I grabbed the injector.

"Where's Monk?"

Ron answered, "I saw him napping on your bunk."

I went into the dorm and sure enough, there lay my little furry buddy. I took out the small bottle labeled "for twenty pound pet" and loaded the injector with the bottle. Then I pushed aside his fur on his back and pressed the injector close to his skin. It didn't take long and as it hissed, Monk's head turned to see what was going on. I finished and put the injector back in the bag and smoothed his fur.

"Hope this works on you, Monk. I'd hate to lose you so soon after you came into my life."

He lay back and closed his eyes. Guess naptime was not over.

I picked up the bag and headed out the door, saying to Ron as I left, "I'm headed to Dr. Newton's." It was standard procedure to keep the other team members informed whenever anyone left the center.

When I got there, I carried the injector bag inside.

"Your name?" asked the receptionist.

"Jake Dani. But I don't have an appointment."

"Do you want to schedule one? The waiting time may be a couple hours, I'm afraid."

I put the bag on her desk.

"Can you make sure Dr. Newton gets this?"

"What is it?"

"An injector she loaned me. And some empty vials."

The gal took the paper bag and said to an aide as she handed over the bag, "This needs autoclaving."

I didn't stick around long enough to hear any more.

Instead of heading back to the ops center, I stopped at my apartment to pick up clean clothes. The same three outfits in the center bored me by now.

Tut reported no visitors but I checked every room anyway. After grabbing several items from my bedroom, I headed to the stairs in the center of my apartment.

"Monk's doin' fine, Tut. We should come home in a few days."

CHAPTER 38

"Hey, gang! They're passing out the vaccine!" yelled Zetto.

Ron, Vincent, and I rushed to the planning room where Zetto displayed the newscast on the wall.

An aerial view showed a snake of people waiting in line for blocks at the public high school. Other lines wound their way out the door of the university basketball court.

The scene changed to show an apartment manager unlocking a door as several cops in the blue of Zor Metro Police waited in the hallway. Two guys went in wearing the same all-green outfits I'd seen so many times before. Others stayed outside the apartment. The scene changed to show a man in the hallway with a breathing mask speaking into a microphone.

"The police have made door-to-door searches to find those who had died of VB."

One guy came out and waved to the reporter that he should come inside. The camera view jiggled as it entered the apartment. It came to rest on a bedroom scene where an old man and an old woman lay in an embrace. Neither moved. Blood spread from the man's head. A pistol rested in his hand.

"Sometimes we see a suicide as one partner ends their life when the other died of VB. Especially when the wife died first."

A team of men put each body in a black bag and carried them outside. Others in HazMat suits sprayed the areas with disinfectant.

That was the worst scene. It was different elsewhere.

Smiles were everywhere on the news, on the streets, and in the stores. The worst was over.

After it barely got dark, fireworks exploded in celebration.

I felt something pull on my right leg as I ate dinner. I looked down to see Monk. His eyes opened wide, and he shivered every time a loud boom came. I picked him up and held him close. Poor little guy didn't understand what was going on.

"It's okay, Monk. Just us humans shooting off some fireworks."

I stroked his fur. It seemed to help. At least his shaking stopped.

Zetto spoke, "Klava said he would lift the curfew in two days. Merchants demanded it end sooner saying they got a lot of customers in the evening. Over seventy percent of the employers report allowing their workers to take time off during the day to go shopping."

Later that same evening, I got a tag from Sheila.

"Can you come to a meeting here tomorrow morning at ten with a representative to the Rossan United Freedom Fighters?" she said. "RUFF wants to make it clear they are not responsible for the campaign of anti-hybrid attacks."

"Me—or Albert Poors?"

"Poors, actually," she answered.

"I can be there but how will you protect my identity?"

"I will meet with the RUFF rep in one room and you will remain in another room. We'll communicate by intercom. I will visit you and then go into the room with the RUFF rep to verify that Albert Poors is in the next room."

"Sounds good."

"Thanks, Jake. I've lost track of how many favors we've each done for the other. But on the off chance I'm behind, can I take you to dinner?"

"You never stop trying, do you?"

* * * * *

Ash Getner, head of the York Security Agency, picked up the tag from the prime minister.

"Yes, Mr. Prime Minister. How can I help you?"

"I want you to find out who's behind the VB virus getting into the public water," said Pierre Klava. "Make this a top priority project. If you need funds, let me know."

"Yes, sir. Right away."

After they disconnected, Getner wondered who he could blame this one on. His nemesis came to mind. But who to do the dirty work? He smiled.

After all, the guy may become my boss in the next election.

He tagged Guy Coocher on a secure line.

"This is your friend at the federal building. I just learned that a certain Jake Dani is a Binger and the father of Alena Dani, the researcher."

"So she's a Binger too," replied Coocher.

"Stands to reason," Getner added. "And Jake Dani has visited the mercon ambassador at his embassy."

"Son of a bitch! I knew it! The mercons are in cahoots with the Bingers. I wouldn't be surprised to learn this Jake was the one who poisoned our water."

Getner smiled at the reference to someone else poisoning the water. Coocher was laying out his strategy for him.

He added, "Oh, by the way, he's a spy for the Bingers back on Earth. And I have reason to believe this Jake is the real Albert Poors. Listen, I have a plan for how to get rid of him."

After a few seconds, Coocher asked, "Hmm, what's your plan?"

Getner told him. "I also learned that Jake Dani will be at Channel One tomorrow morning at ten o'clock."

"How do you know that?" asked Coocher.

"I have my sources."

"Right."

"Can you take care of your part?" asked Getner.

"I'll see what I can do."

* * * * *

Guy Coocher tagged Borner Hoskins on a secured line. This was one operation he didn't want to use normal Humans Only personnel on.

Hoskins replied, "Yes?"

"Talk to me some more so I recognize your voice."

"I see. Mary had a little lamb. Will this be enough?"

"Yep. Somebody broke into our office last night. I think it's time I fight back. I need you for a special assignment. You'll need to hire some muscle. I want to teach Albert Poors a lesson."

Coocher explained what he had in mind.

Hoskins replied, "This will take time to set up. Do you have any idea how we can find this Poors?"

Coocher explained his plan for that too.

Hoskins added, "Brilliant!"

CHAPTER 39

A half-hour before the appointed time at Channel One, I left the ops, my mind busy on ways to convince RUFF they needed to cooperate with the cops and Channel One, so they could find out who was responsible.

As I ambled toward the Channel One building from the parking lot, I noticed two big men walking from between parked cars. One guy held a camera on the left side of his head and the other had held a recorder to his mouth so I couldn't see his face. They looked like they worked at the news channel, so I ignored them.

Ten steps from the side door to the building, my right backside erupted in pain. It was so strong I fell to my knees. I felt a shove from my right shoulder and down I went. I rolled over to see who my attacker was and saw three men with ski masks over their faces. Two held baseball bats and I held up my left arm to protect myself. They let me get to my feet and I pulled my Snap out.

Then darkness descended. Total pitch black. From the light coming near my feet, I figured they used a black sack from behind me.

Rough hands grabbed me and pulled the black fabric tight. My Snap was useless.

I heard the screech of tires as a vehicle pulled up near me.

The same rough hands pulled and pushed me left side down onto the floor of something. A van.

I had better get free soon or I was a goner. So I pushed my Snap in front of me and fired three times.

Rough hands grabbed my right hand and held tight.

"Son of a bitch pulled a gun out."

The black fabric lifted from my feet and two pair of hands seized the Snap in my right wrist. I struggled to hang onto it but it was four hands against one.

In less than four seconds, my gun was ripped from my grip.

More blows came to my back and arms. A sharp pain came to the back of my skull and I blacked out.

I woke to find myself stark naked and lying on a cot with only a linen sheet over me.

From the vibrations and the curvature of the walls, I suspected I was in a small airplane and airborne.

The back of my head ached. My back didn't feel so good either.

I sat up on the cot and looked around. A very small room with only one door. There was a small window covered in black paint. I tried scratching the paint with my fingernails but could get not get much traction. All I got was a small scratch and that cost me a torn fingernail. I put my eyeball to the opening and looked out. It was daylight outside but I couldn't see much. Some clouds in the distance that didn't move much.

All I could tell was it was daylight. I was airborne and flying high.

"Hey! Anybody hear me?"

* * * * *

Ron worried every time Jake failed to show up at the ops center as expected. A tag to Jake's comm went unanswered.

Since Jake was supposed to go to the offices of Channel One, he tagged Sheila.

"Have you seen Jake?"

"No, and I'm pissed. He failed to show up for his appointment. Where the hell is he?"

"That's the sixty-four thousand dollar question." Part of him wondered where that old phrase came from.

"Listen. If you find him, tell him he needs to apologize."

"Will do," said Ron as he disconnected.

Next he tagged Jake's comm again but didn't get an answer. So he tagged the computer at Jake's apartment.

"Jake's residence. He's busy right now. Can you leave a message?"

Ron asked, "This is Ron Boscoe. I need to talk with Jake immediately."

"I recognize your voice, sir. But Jake is not here."

Crap. He's missing again.

He disconnected and tapped his fingers on the table in the planning room.

Who should I inform next?

Zetto rested on his bunk in the dorm and Ron told him first.

"Oh shit! Let me know what you want me to do."

"Come to the center ASAP."

Next, he tagged Vincent at his home.

"Jake's missing again."

"Shit! Here we go again. I'll be there in an hour. Have you told your dad?"

"He's next."

"Gancha might want to know too."

Jake had told Ron Vincent that Gancha would be joining their team. During that conversation, Ron had learned that Jake and Gancha were dating but it was an on-and-off relationship.

"I agree. I'll let her know after I tell our boss."

Ron went into the planning room and composed a message to his father. Inside the image of a clock, he sent a separate message.

"Our boss is missing."

The shorter the message, the better. Besides, he didn't like "talking" with his father.

It would take time to get a reply. While he waited, he tagged Gancha.

She replied, "Oh-oh. All I can tell you is he's not here. We didn't have plans either."

After a pause, she added, "Shall I come to the center?"

"Not until I need you," he replied. "I need to trace his last steps."

After he disconnected, he yelled to the dorm room, "Zetto, you need to erase Jake's comm. Where's Andy?"

"I don't know. It's not my day to watch him."

"I'll ask him to come," said Ron. A tag to Andy got the message, "I'm away from my office on a business call. Please leave a message and I'll get back to you as soon as possible."

Damn it!

He left the message, "My boss is missing."

Then Ron disconnected. He sighed and helped Zetto fix dinner by setting the table.

Vincent came in the front door and joined them. He had on a black suit and pale yellow dress shirt.

When they had finished the meal, Ron got a tag from his father.

"Trace his last steps. I can't join you this time. Onta is six months pregnant and can't travel by the fast method. I can send Gerhi though.

Ron sent his reply.

"I thought of tracing his last known steps. I could use Gerhi."

* * * * *

Gerhi Oman got the orders while lecturing a class at the training center. He acknowledged his new travel and left an assistant in charge. Then he rushed to his apartment and packed in a mad dash. He drove himself to the BIS airport and hopped on the waiting private jet to Macapa, Brazil.

You'd think by now I'd get used to this sudden change of plans.

A Navy Seal before being discovered as a full Binger, Gerhi prided himself on his ability to survive on almost nothing. He could dismantle and assemble his Snaps in fifteen seconds each while blindfolded. An expert marksman, he could hit the center of the target five yards farther away than most anybody else. At six foot three, Gerhi was muscular. From the look of his body, anybody who opted hand to hand combat with him risked his life.

On the flight over the ocean, he pondered his near future.

Guess I have to get drowned again.

After landing in Brazil, he learned there was a two-hour wait before he was scheduled to go up the Space Elevator. He didn't want to eat a meal for fear he might lose it later. So he drank two doubles of scotch in the lounge while waiting and recalled his earlier experience with the fast method of travel.

Then he carried his suitcases while walking the long corridor separating the main airport from the Space Elevator. He arrived at the prep room fifteen minutes before his appointment.

"Mr. Smith," said the attractive young woman behind the counter, dressed in a crisp gray suit with the logo of Macapa Space Elevator on her right lapel. "You're early."

"Yep," he replied. Gerhi was not known for his chit-chat.

"Do you want to wait or shall we get started?"

"Might as well."

She pressed a button and he heard a click on the door to the prep room.

"I can take your luggage, sir," she added.

He dropped his bags, squared his shoulders, and walked through the door.

Let's get this over with.

Despite his earlier experience, Gerhi didn't look forward to this.

He took the sedative injection on his right forearm. Combined with the scotches, his mind was in a blur as he stripped. Next he placed his arms in the slits in the rubber suit and lifted.

"Place your organ in the hole," said the technician. "It's for draining your bladder."

He didn't feel like telling the technician he had traveled this way before.

Next the male technician pulled the cap over his head.

"Nod if you can you hear me," came a voice into his ears.

He nodded.

The other guy said, "Good." He wore beige rubber gloves as he attached a drain to his groin.

"We're done. Mr. Smith, you may walk forward now."

Not that walking was easy with the extra padding of a diaper between his legs.

He followed the technician to the pool and his heart sped up when he spotted the wire cage.

This is it.

Despite having done this whole thing before and viewing for a second time the vid of the procedure, the real thing was so damned real. And scary. When the chair descended, he held his breath as his face went beneath the liquid.

He looked up to see the bubble of air recede out of sight just as a man closed the lid over his cage. He tried to inhale the liquid but nature took over and he held his breath.

"Relax, Mr. Smith. It will be over in less than a minute," said a male voice in his ear.

"Take a deep breath. When the liquid fills your lungs, you'll see you can breathe it and remain awake. You're not going to die. Thousands of people have done this and lived to tell about it."

Gerhi gritted his teeth and pushed the air out of his lungs. *Here goes.*

He braced for dying, just like he'd done before and coughed as the fluid filled his lungs. He resisted the urge to press on the lid to his cage, knowing it would do no good at all.

CHAPTER 40

A hissing noise told me that gas was pouring into my room on the plane. I tried to find the source but dizziness overcame me.

I woke to total darkness again. But this time, my mouth held a breathing tube. My hands were cuffed behind my back and I felt the restriction of movement in my ankles. From the vibrations, I suspected I was being transported in a vehicle on a road.

I decided to wait for an opportunity to escape. Couldn't do much else.

Then a pinprick on my right upper arm, followed by a full feeling, told me I was being drugged again.

Naturally, I dozed off. Couldn't resist it if I tried.

* * * * *

Ron started the operation by stating, "Let's start with the most likely suspect, the Humans Only organization."

Vincent nodded and Zetto joined him. Together, the two managed to get into the private server for HO comm chats. Ron and Andy busied themselves preparing the gear that might be needed for a special op.

"Ron," queried Vincent as he looked up.

"So far we've learned that Coocher tagged Hoskins and told him of a plan from your old buddy, Ash Getner. Hoskins hired some guys to kidnap a big guy in the parking lot of Channel One. We figure that was Jake. Then they turned their captive over to someone named Ben Portal, an agent of YSA."

"See if you can hack into the YSA servers," ordered Ron.

"Won't be easy," added Vincent.

"Nothing is easy," said Ron. "Get started."

Vincent shook his head. "I've tried to hack into the YSA servers before."

He took eight hours and fifteen tries, each with a different idea. The BIS decryption software was good but YSA had better.

Andy suggested an idea.

"How about we try to get into the van Getner uses to tap into the YSA database?"

Getner used three vans, all parked in the city building lot. Zetto picked one and Vincent was able to get into its database of codes. From there, another try to get into the main YSA servers worked.

Vincent read on and eventually looked up.

"Ron, Jake was taken to Fairport Base for interrogation."

"Ruta," Ron told the ops center computer, "show us what you've got on Fairport Base."

The base was located northeast of Zor inside the Orca Mountain range. At first, the overhead of the base was blurry.

"Let me try," said Vincent, as he went to work on their map software.

Fifteen minutes later, he said, "Gotcha!"

They now had a detailed view of Fairport Base, even its own landing strip in the valley. The overhead image showed several buildings.

"See if you can find out where they do interrogations," said Ron.

After several taps on Vincent's laptop, the view zoomed in on one building.

"I think this is it," added Vincent. He pointed.

"Jake is probably held here."

The building was a two-story one at the corner of Second Avenue and B Street. The team spent the next two hours debating four different plans to get through the two fences surrounding the buildings on the base.

Ron got a tag from Gancha.

"Can I help?" she asked.

Ron thought it over. She was a newbie on the team but Jake had told him of her skills.

"Maybe you could. You haven't finished your training but we could use more guns on this op."

"You have an op in mind? By the way, where's Jake? Why am I talking to you instead of him?"

"Jake is missing. That's what the op is for."

"Oh-oh! I must help! Where do I go?" she asked.

Hmm. Maybe it would be a good idea to get more firepower on this op.

It would not be a good idea to give the location over a comm tag.

So he said, "I'll meet you at the corner of Main and University."

"How will I recognize you?"

"Just be there. Jake has told me enough about you for me to recognize you."

They disconnected.

"Vincent, I have to step out for a while," he said, "to bring a new member of our team here."

"Who?" asked Vincent.

"Gancha."

After leaving the ops center, he walked to the corner of Main and University. Ten minutes passed and he was about to leave when a car pulled into the nearby alley. A tall dark woman stepped out.

"Gancha?"

She nodded. "And you are?"

He grinned.

She didn't volunteer any information and turned the question back to me. Just like a spy.

"I'm Ron."

He got into her car. "Drive down Main. When you see Marino Suites on the left, turn into the alley beyond it."

Fifteen minutes later, he piloted her past their security and into the planning room.

"Gang, this is our newest member, Gancha Morentoss."

* * * * *

While still immersed and able to see through a clear window, Gerhi's cage tilted backwards and moved along rails. He focused on breathing in the fluid with his fingers wrapped around the bars of his cage.

When his cage came to a monitor, it stopped. From the prior vid, he knew he was in the final position for the duration of the twelve hour flight—flat on his back. The ship would travel from an orbit above Earth to the jump gate at the L4 Lagrange Point sixty degrees ahead of Mars in its orbit around Sol. Without the special fluid in his lungs to help him breathe while under high acceleration, he would arrive with collapsed lungs.

And dead.

Over the next twenty-four hours, he tried to get as much sleep as possible, expecting he'd be sent on an op soon after he landed in Zor. Several times, an alarm rang and he'd wake. It usually interrupted a dream of his being wounded and left to die.

"Snack time," showed on the screen.

He sucked on the tube on the right side of this face. The menu consisted of different flavors of shakes, each containing the electrolytes his body would need over the next twelve hours. He chose strawberry this time.

Not bad tasting.

Despite the fluid in his lungs, or maybe because of it, he knew when he slowed down on the way to the Jump Station.

A voice came in his ear. "If you feel like throwing up after the jump, remember to put your lips around the round tube in front of your face. Otherwise, your barf will fill up your vision and you'll smell it for hours. It stings the eyes, too."

Gerhi embraced the vomit tube in preparation and watched the animation of the jump on his monitor, but the nausea was not as bad as he had remembered.

Then he sped up, endured weightlessness at the turn around point, and slowed down again as the small transport spaceship approached Rossa.

He whiled away the time with one of his favorite daydreams, the one where he won the lottery, and with enough money, quit BIS, bought his dream home on an island in the Pacific, and spent his days on its beach. This time he met a female surfer. Of course, she was good looking. Loved to have him do it to her, too.

It dawned on him how many times humans had nothing to do while waiting. They must all daydream, from the highest to the lowest of IQs. He wondered how much of his life he had spent daydreaming. Probably years.

The last time he slowed, he received a warning.

"We'll soon arrive at Rossa."

Time to cough up the fluid and get back to breathing air.

* * * * *

I woke to find myself resting naked on a cot. You might call it a bed, but it consisted of only green canvas over a hard surface. But at least my hands and ankles were free of the shackles. The air was cold and I shivered.

The room was tiny by any measurements, maybe six feet by six feet. I stood and found my head just under five inches or so from the ceiling. I saw a stainless steel sink and toilet on my right.

Some jail. About as tiny as the one in the ops center.

The small window, high up on the wall over my "bed," was closed. I could not tell if it was daylight or night time.

I wondered who had brought me here and the only one I could think of who had the resources to do this was YSA, the York Security Agency. Ash Getner's organization. I had often wondered when I'd come face to face with my nemesis.

I sat on the "bed" and rested my forehead in my palms.

Who knows know many hours it would take for my team to rescue me, if they could. I braced myself for torture. And death.

* * * * *

Ron got the tag while in the ops center. Hoping it was Jake, his hands shook as he tapped his nostril to open the comm.

"Gerhi here. I'm at Zor-Franken Airport. Who is this?"

Ron sighed. "Ron. I'll come pick you up. Are you ready to go on an op?"

"I expected as much. How soon can you get here?"

"I'll be there in less than an hour."

The comm disconnected. Ron stared ahead. He'd have to get used to Gerhi's abbreviated conversations.

After telling his team where he was going, Ron looked at Gancha.

Dressed in a brown pantsuit with yellow lace blouse, she said, "I can pick him up while you stay here and plan the op. Just make sure I have a spot on the team."

Ron nodded. "Okay. Take the van. Ruta, tell Chima Gancha is going to the airport."

When she departed, he tagged Gerhi to let him know.

* * * * *

Gancha asked, "Chima, why the two loops?"

Her answer came back from the overhead speaker. "Possible tail. False alarm though."

She smiled at the efficiency of the van's onboard computer system.

Soon, the van slowed as it passed by Baggage Claim. Gerhi was easy to spot as the only big man and more muscular than anyone else waiting outside. He waved as he spotted her in the van.

Ron must have called ahead.

Gancha offered to help put his luggage in the van but, as usual, Gerhi declined.

She asked, "How was your trip?"

Gerhi shrugged.

Ron had warned her he didn't talk much.

Right.

* * * * *

I lost track of the days as hunger gnawed on my stomach. I banged on the door.

"Any food in this joint?"

But only silence answered me.

Two hours later, I couldn't tell exactly when, my cell door opened and in walked three huge guys.

"Time for a little pain," said one. "Are you going the easy way, or do we have to drug you?"

That's when I saw the injector in his right hand.

What the hell? The pain can wait.

I stood from my bed and extended my wrists outward. Two of them put iron bracelets on me while the other placed anklets on my legs.

The lead guard pressed his injector to my upper right arm. Much to my surprise. I thought I was cooperating and wouldn't need it.

In seconds, my brain wobbled.

I walked barefoot and naked down a long hallway, walking as fast as my anklets would allow me. The air and the floor were cold. My cell was on the end and as I passed two other cells on each side, I wondered who might be in them.

We stopped in a small room with only bars on the door, all the better for my screams to be heard by fellow prisoners. The only feature was a chair with wrist and ankle straps.

"Sit," ordered a guard.

After I took the chair, two of my guards fastened my forearms with leather straps. Then they secured my lower legs the same way. The three of them walked out to leave me alone and in suspense.

I didn't have to wait for long when in walked a short and thin man, dressed in blue jeans and a white dress shirt.

Oh crap.

The smaller guys had something to prove by inflicting pain on a bigger man.

The Little Man carried a small briefcase, which he put on something behind me.

"You and I are going to get to know each other. I'm going to get to know just how much pain you can tolerate before blacking out."

With that he presented a scalpel to the right side of my vision.

Shit!

CHAPTER 41

In the planning room, Ron, Vincent, Zetto, and Gancha went over three plans for the op. Vincent would stay behind to act as the focal point if anything went wrong. It usually did.

Since they were going to hit a YSA training center, they could expect lots of trouble, both as they went in and on the way out. So Ron decided to take Zetto, Gancha, and Gerhi.

The more firepower, the better.

Every plan included driving the van to the small town of Fairport on the western slopes of the Orca Mountains. The team packed a lot, including heavy clothing.

Gancha drove the first shift. Snow peppered the roads, making high speed unattainable.

Hang in there, Jake!

They stopped at a gas station and restaurant on the nearside of the Seintz River. Gancha filled the van with gas while Zetto and Ron stayed inside. They couldn't get very far on one tankful of gas because of the extra weight in the van. Gerhi went in the restaurant to order take-out food. Gerhi was the only one who could risk not being recognized. Ron couldn't bear to have a customer of Stenno's remember him this close to Zor.

They drove off with Ron behind the wheel this time. He crossed over the bridge and slowed as the snow came down harder. They couldn't risk an accident or Jake might never be rescued.

Twice, they passed flashing lights behind cars and trucks parked on the side of the road.

Nightfall came and Ron turned on the headlights, which only made driving more difficult. The flakes seemed to come right at his eyes.

They stopped for gas and changed drivers. The rest of the team slept as much as possible.

Ron had difficulty getting to sleep.

I hope Jake isn't suffering too much.

* * * * *

The pain in my thighs never ended as my torturer dragged his scalpel from my hips to my knees in parallel lines, going only deep enough to draw blood. And pain, of course. That was the whole point.

At first I gritted my teeth and tried to hold my screams in. But the Little Man kept it up until I yelled out.

Eventually, the pain got so bad I blacked out, only to come to in my cell and flat on my back. I didn't dare touch my thighs. Once was enough.

I never got to sleep because of the pain in my legs. Didn't get any food either.

The next day, the Little Man grinned when I was dragged into the small room. And dragged I was. I couldn't walk.

Every hour, after the Little Man cut two ridges in my legs, a second guard, dressed in dark green slacks and shirt, walked in with a bucket, which he proceeded to pour on my thighs to wash away the blood so my torturer could see where to cut next.

I screamed with the pain from the salt water and pulled on my wrist straps.

"I'll kill you for this," I said to the Little Man between gritted teeth.

My torturer responded with a chuckle.

"If you live through it."

On the second day of pain, the Little Man shifted to using his scalpel on my left thigh.

"Remember, all you have to do to stop the pain is talk."

* * * * *

I actually dozed off for a few minutes when I heard a hissing noise. I opened my eyes just in time to see a man in a green guard's uniform holding an injector as he pulled away. Another frickin' injection.

Sleep eluded me as the pain in my thighs kept me awake. I had to lie on my back because any other position hurt.

I wished they'd turn off that damn overhead light!

This time, when they came for me my whole body didn't want to cooperate. My knees felt weak and they had to lift me off my hard bed.

What's that smell?

That's when I realized I needed a bath. It's amazing how much you can sweat when you endure pain. My guards didn't seem to care much as they lifted me, one man under each shoulder. My feet dragged behind me on the floor as they carried me down the hallway to the small room with that stupid chair. I didn't resist as they strapped me in. Couldn't, as a matter of fact.

My head bowed low toward my chest and I only saw the shoes and dark blue trousers of the stranger when he came in. My whole body begged to be allowed to fall to the floor and sleep.

"I am your best friend," said a voice in front of me. "The only friend you have. I can order the pain to stop. All you have to do is tell me your name."

I really wanted to and almost blurted out my name when it dawned on me that the injection I had received was truth serum. My tormentors were using the best tricks.

I knew that if I spoke even one word about me that would unlock the dam in my head and I might blurt out something that could hurt those I love. After all, if one word was enough to stop the pain, why not give it to them?

What did my BIS training say about this?

Keep repeating a mantra over and over again in my head. Don't tell them anything! Don't tell them anything!

It didn't surprise me when the dark blue trousers left and the Little Man returned.

Oh dear. Here we go again.

The first cut flooded my brain with pain. I jerked my head up and gritted my teeth.

Son of a bitch!

I heard a voice say, "You will tell us everything before we're done. Then you'll beg me to kill you."

I swear he smiled when he made first cut of the day and I screamed.

"After we finish your thighs, we'll start on your manhood. I'm sure we can find lots of pain there. Remember: All you have to do to stop the pain is give us your name."

* * * * *

Vincent sat at a table in the planning room with his laptop in front of him when he received the tag.

"You'd better leave the ops center," said the voice of Ron.

"Got it," said Vincent with a sigh.

Ron must be taking no chances that Jake might blurt out the location of the center.

Vincent closed his laptop and went into the dorm. His next meal might be several hours off so he returned to the kitchen and drank as much milk as he could and grabbed two sandwiches, which he put in a bag. Then he returned to the dorm and packed what clothes could fit into the one suitcase he had there.

"Ruta, after I leave, can you sterilize all the rooms of the ops center, including the shooting range?"

"Affirmative."

He had programmed the ops center computer to recognize his use of the word "sterilize." From canisters stored for this purpose, Ruta would spray bleach in all the rooms to destroy any residual DNA.

Not wanting to leave by the front door in case it was watched, he pressed the wall where the escape stair was located. The fit was tight as he climbed the spiral stairs with his suitcase and exited another door to come out on the basement parking lot.

* * * * *

The team arrived on the outskirts of Fairport on the western side of the Orca Mountains, and stopped before coming to the fence around the town. Fairport had maybe two thousand residents, in separate homes snuggled close together. Each was visible under a plume of white vapor.

Ron sat in the driver's seat and stared straight ahead at the snow-capped peaks of the mountains. Since it was daylight, he could see a long distance. He looked in the mirror and saw the van's tire tracks were visible. Snow had stopped falling and he put on sunglasses to cut the glare from the white stuff on the ground.

Gancha sat in the seat next to him and yawned.

"Where are we?" she asked.

"Just outside Fairport," he replied. "Chima, wake the others and get ready for driving off the road. Change your outside color to white."

The weather forecast said more snow in the next hour or two.

Good. That should cover our tracks.

Ron turned the wheel to the left and drove over rough ground. The van bounced as they traveled.

Zetto was the first to respond.

"Where are we?" he asked.

"Just outside Fairport," Gancha replied.

Ron followed the path that Vincent had outlined but even so, the ride was rough.

It took two hours for Ron to drive with the fence on his right before he turned left again to head toward Fairport Base on a dirt road. Ron only knew the road was there because the tree line stopped and the land was flat. Snow fell on the van's tracks.

He followed the road as it climbed up the side of a mountain and stopped when he leveled off with the outer fence of the base visible ahead. There was a guard shack at the only opening in the fence around the YSA base but he could not see any vapors coming off its roof. Hopefully that meant no guards.

"Chima, can you paint the outside toward the shack with camouflage to match the bushes and trees around here?"

"Consider it done."

He drove off the road a hundred yards and stopped.

"We park here," he said to the others.

He didn't want to alert the base to their presence.

Gancha and Gehri busied themselves putting up a tent on the side of the van away from the fence.

Zetto and Gerhi carried their equipment to the tent. The wooden polished rails were the heaviest.

The team slept and ate in the BIS van.

Ron had trouble getting to sleep.

I hope Jake can hang in there a little longer.

* * * * *

This time I felt the injection but didn't move. I was so tired I didn't want to move at all.

"Come on, big fella. Up you go," said a voice.

But I couldn't open my eyes to see who it was.

Rough hands sat me up and put my two arms around their shoulders. I tried to get some more sleep, but it was difficult as they dragged me down the hall.

I repeated the mantra in my head.

Don't tell them anything! Don't tell them anything!

I hope my team will get here soon. I'm not sure how much more of this I can take.

* * * * *

Ron tested the rope harness as he descended the tunnel in the tent. Down he went fifty feet. As he exhaled each breath, he could see the fog it created.

At the bottom, he said, "Looks good. Let's get moving."

Using the equipment they ferried from the van, they dug a tunnel just wide enough to lay two rails of track over crossboards. It wouldn't hold much weight but it only had to carry three hundred and fifty pounds at most. After a hundred yards or so, they created a small rest area and dug another tunnel at a right angle to the first. The plan called for this diversion in case they were discovered.

The tunnel was only wide enough for one person to pass at a time. Fans blew fresh air from the tent down a tube and into the tunnel. It would come out at the far end to push any stale air out to the tent. Every twenty feet or so they placed a light bulb. Since they would use this tunnel only once, each bulb glowed naked.

Ron pushed them to work harder.

"If you think this is hard, try to imagine what pain, relentless pain, Jake must be going through right now."

* * * * *

The technician at Fairport Base shook his head. It was getting harder to tell what came from natural vibrations versus a Rossaquake. The needles on the seismograph jiggled. Something was going on under the mountains. He looked up at his bookshelf as he watched the needles show a Richter-scale five point two. The books did not vibrate. Nor did the light bulbs sway.

No quake yet. Wonder what could cause this?

CHAPTER 42

After another fifty yards of tunnel, Ron's measurements showed they must be about ten feet outside the building where Jake was held. And inside the double fence.

"Let's go up now," he said with water vapor showing as he spoke.

Gerhi worked the tunnel machine. As he filled a bin, it would move along the rail to the tent and another bin would take its place.

When the tunnel showed daylight coming in, Gerhi said in his Z helmet, used to protect his face from falling dirt, "I see daylight."

Ron waited just behind Gerhi and passed the periscope up.

Using it, Gerhi scanned the ground outside in all directions.

"Nothing. We are close to a building, though."

* * * * *

Loud noises woke me from a short nap. That was about the most I could get in and I was grateful for the break. I couldn't tell if it was day out.

But one thing was clear. That was gunfire.

"Jake! Stand back from the door!"

My name? Who knew my name? Did I tell the Little Man?

All I wanted to do was get more sleep so I closed my eyes and turned my head as best I could from the blinding overhead light.

An explosion woke me.

Smoke poured into my small cell. I coughed and felt rough hands under my armpits.

Here we go again.

But this time, the hands belonged to two men with helmets on. I couldn't see their faces but who was I to resist their lifting me off my hard cot? It was all I could do to stay awake.

They carried me through the smashed door of my cell and down the short hallway. My thighs screamed with pain.

When they got to the torture room and turned to go through a hole in the wall, it dawned on me that the two men were rescuing me.

"Stop!" I said.

My carriers stood still. I tried to get my feet under me but failed. So I pointed.

"Kill anyone in there."

One helmeted man spoke but all I heard was a mumble. One man bore most of my weight while the first man entered the room with that damn chair. He came back seconds later and grabbed one of my shoulders. They carried me through a door to the outside. It was dark. The first thing I experienced was intense cold all over my naked body. I heard gunshots. Or thought they were gunshots. Couldn't be sure.

* * * * *

Ron turned his head at the sound of a groan from Gerhi. His partner was on the floor with a widening circle of dark red expanding under his head.

He dared not let go of Jake though.

"Get outta here!" yelled the voice of Gerhi in his helmet. "I'm hit bad and will die soon. Get Jake outta here. I'll explode myself after you leave."

What a dilemma!

Carry Jake or help Gerhi? If he let Jake go, all might be lost. But wait, there was one more option.

"Gancha!" he said in his Z helmet. "Where are you? Gerhi's down and I have Jake. We're on the surface."

He decided that carrying Jake would be easier since he could barely walk and was dead weight. So he propped his boss up against the wall and put his left arm under the man's knees. Jake's eyes squinted shut. Blood seeped from his thighs. Ron decided he didn't have time to put StopIt on Jake's thighs.

The voice of Gerhi came through loud in his helmet.

"Get outta here! I'm fading fast and must activate the bomb."

Ron entered the cold air of the outside and the glare of snow on the ground. He carried the naked body of Jake several feet from the closed door when he heard the explosion behind him.

Pressure came to his backside and he fell down with Jake in his arms. Ron stood up at once, lifted Jake's limp body, and carried him to the triangle of wood holding the sling over the tunnel exit.

Gancha rose from the canvas chair. She brushed snow off Jake's legs and winced when she saw the cuts. She took Jake from Ron.

Ron turned around to see if he could help Gerhi, but thought better of it. Gerhi was gone in the explosion.

He turned again to see Gancha sitting in the small chair under the tripod they had erected over the hole. He kneeled and stood guard over the hoist as Gancha and Jake descended. Two guys came around the edge of the building from which they had taken Jake. Ron aimed and fired at both men, who went down in the snow.

Must not have had time to put on armor.

Fortunately, no one came out of the nearby buildings. Surely they heard the explosion. Any second now he could expect dozens of armed men to appear.

Ron crouched alone at the exit of the tunnel for what seemed like forever. Finally, the canvas chair came up. He climbed into the seat and aimed his rifle up as he went down, ready to shoot anyone who stuck his head over the small circle of light which grew smaller as he descended. Pieces of dirt hit the faceplate of his helmet and he swiped his gloved hand to get a better view.

When he arrived at the bottom of the pit, Gancha was not in sight. Jake lay unconscious on the ground. Gancha must have fled on the flat bed of the railcar and slid herself into the escape tunnel.

Was she trying to protect herself?

Ron kept his rifle pointed upward as he stood guard over the inert body of Jake as he thought of his options.

* * * * *

I shuddered from the cold as a guy in white carried me to a triangle of wooden struts and a canvas seat suspended just below the top of the triangle. I tried to stay awake and was glad of the cold. It helped.

One man, dressed in white, placed himself and me in the canvas seat. I watched as he pulled on a rope and lowered us into the dark space of the tunnel. I couldn't see the other two men.

"Ron?"

I heard a noise but couldn't make it out.

Soon I descended inside the walls of a tunnel while I hung on with my remaining strength to the straps holding the chair. The air was frickin' cold on my naked skin.

I heard more gunshots above me. The night air carried the sounds as I descended in darkness.

When I got to the bottom, someone lifted me and placed me on the freezing cold ground before picking me up again and laying me on a flat bed. Soon I disappeared into a tunnel.

I lay there shivering while the canvas chair ascended up the dark shaft.

Damn, it's cold!

Soon another man in white came down the same shaft. He lifted me and placed me on a canvas bed on rails. Soon I passed out of his sight. Only the occasional light bulb passed overhead as I shivered. The hard bed beneath me jarred as I moved along the rail.

What a helluva way to die.

After a long time, I came to a stop.

I looked up to see Gancha smiling down.

"You're a sight for sore eyes," she said

"So are you," I squeaked out between shivers.

She placed something on both my thighs. She covered me with a heavy blanket over my shivering body as the pain diminished.

Felt damned good. At least the blanket kept off the freezing air.

Was I dreaming of seeing her? I couldn't tell. It wouldn't surprise me.

I closed my eyes and slept some more. It was all I could do. Sleep felt good.

* * * * *

When I woke again, I opened my eyes and wondered where I was. I was certainly not in my cell. The only thing above me there was that damned frickin' light.

Instead, I saw a ceiling not less than three feet above me. Vibrations told me I was traveling.

"He's awake," said a voice.

I turned my head to see who said it. The face of Zetto stared back at me.

"Zee?"

He smiled. "That's right."

"Where are we?"

He looked to his left. "Just outside the town of Fairport, I'd say."

"I'm hungry as hell."

He nodded and reached to his right. He held up something.

It looked like food and I bit into it. A sandwich. Don't know what was in it but it sure felt good going down.

Ron said above my head, "Hey, buddy. We got you out of there. Did you tell them anything?"

I tried to shake my head but that required too much energy. So I swallowed and said, "Don't 'member much. Maybe I did. Don't 'member. My mind was in a fog. Still is."

* * * * *

"What!" yelled Getner into his comm. He listened as his agent-in-charge of Fairport Base told him the rest of Jake's escape.

When he heard the whole story, he added, "See if you can find where the tunnel came out."

He disconnected as he wondered if Coocher's network had a leak. Didn't matter much. Dani was gone and Coocher might be the next PM. Maybe. As long as Dani was loose, that was a question.

He tapped his fingers on his desk as he pondered what to say to Coocher. He had to be careful to not offend the man who might become his boss.

But Dani's escape could wreak havoc to both their plans.

* * * * *

I slept a lot on the way back from Fairport but when I was awake, I listened to Ron's explanation. Gerhi had come all the way from Earth and was one of the two guys in white who took me out of my cell. Gerhi was also the one who followed my orders to kill the Little Man.

Gerhi had been fatally wounded outside the building where I had been kept. He had fallen on the ground and blown himself up to prevent his being captured, and to scatter his DNA. He was a very good spy and had followed his training. But he would be missed.

I felt responsible for the man's death and wondered how I was going to break the news to Acorn.

I remembered how he had been wounded helping me escape when I was a slave. Back then, too, he had offered to blow himself up.

Ron said he had exploded several charges in the tunnel after they drove away from the tent, including one at the tent itself.

* * * * *

They took a secondary dirt road on the way back from Fairport. The main paved road would be too obvious. As Gancha drove, she stopped just before a mass appeared on the road ten feet ahead.

Gancha asked Ron, "What's next, boss?"

He looked on both sides.

"The road seems hacked right through trees. There is no way around either side. Everybody stay alert! It could be an ambush."

Ron put on a Z helmet and left the van.

On the greeper, flies busied themselves crawling in every crevice, the eyes, the open jaws, and the snout. But not on the fur.

Ron used the zoom of his helmet to scan the surrounding forest while he kept his face on the body. He didn't want anyone who might be watching to see him scanning. They might duck out of sight.

He said, "Gancha, I could use your help on this one. Bring two machetes."

That would leave only Zetto to guard Jake but that couldn't be helped.

He glanced at the van to see Gancha put on her Z helmet and pull a scope rifle from overhead. Then she checked both her Snaps.

Ron said, "Zetto, be alert as you can. Wake Jake and let him know. Take the driver's seat."

He watched as Gancha opened the driver's side door and left, carrying her rifle in her right hand and the two long knives under her left arm in their protective sheaths.

Seconds later, Zetto climbed over the space between the front seats.

Before she left the side of the van, Gancha scanned the nearby trees.

He said, "I checked with zoom and we are alone. The greeper seems to have died a day or two ago. So it's probably not an ambush."

Gancha walked up to Ron and stared at the body of the animal.

"What do we do with this?"

Ron replied, "Let's cut it in half and drag both halves off the road. Chima, be alert. Scan the entire area around us and you."

"I did already," came a voice in his helmet. "We are alone out here."

Ron laid down his rifle when Gancha handed him one machete. He took it out of its protective sheath.

"Hope this is sharp."

It was and cutting the huge carcass in half took ten minutes with both of them hacking away. The spine of the beast took several whacks.

But grabbing the fur and dragging each half off the dirt road took another ten minutes.

Gancha said as she strained, "This sucker is heavy!"

"Just pull," he said between his teeth.

When the body of the greeper was off the road enough to drive by, he fixed his gaze in the direction of the van.

"Zetto, can you drive through?"

The van crept past them. When it was five feet past the dead greeper, Ron and Gancha sheathed their machetes, picked up their rifles, opened the back doors, and climbed in. Jake lay motionless under a blanket.

Was he still alive?

CHAPTER 43

I opened my eyes in a bed but still felt woozy in my head. The ceiling didn't look familiar and I turned my head to see a tray. That brought a headache.

Gotta stop doin' that.

Next to my bed was an array of electrical equipment I recognized. At first I wondered if I was in a hospital. Again.

"He's awake," said a male voice from the foot of my bed and I looked to see Ron. On his left stood Vincent. The big surprise next to Vincent's left was Gancha.

Then I recognized the setting. I was in the planning room of the ops center.

Gancha came up to the right side of my bed, leaned over, and planted a nice kiss on my lips.

Ron raised his eyebrows. "Oh? Someone new in your life?"

He winked and I knew he meant did I have a new love life.

Vincent grinned as Gancha straightened up.

Ron asked, "What do you remember about your capture?"

Despite the cloud in my head, I replied, "Some thugs took baseball bats to my body."

Ron asked, "Did you recognize them?"

I didn't dare shake my head, since it might bring a massive headache.

"No."

Vincent turned to the sound of a buzzer and left.

"Where's Zetto?" I asked.

"Gone to get a doctor," replied Ron.

I lowered my eyelids and might have slept a few seconds, or minutes, I couldn't tell which, when I heard a voice.

Dr. Oberson stood by the left side of my bed. He pressed his DetectIt on my chest.

That sucker was cold on my skin.

He said, "Don't talk," while he studied the readout.

I waited in silence. Couldn't do much else. I remembered my thighs but no pain came from them. Maybe the fog in my head meant a painkiller floated in my veins.

"Blood pressure is down a little. Pulse is elevated," said the doctor. He looked in my eyes. "What's it this time?"

Before I could answer through my dry lips, Gancha added, "He was tortured. There are cuts on his two thighs. I put StopIt on both."

Dr. Oberson pulled the sheet down from my torso. He peeked under the dressings on both thighs and looked up at her.

"Good job. What pain killer is he on?"

Ron replied, "Synthetic morphine."

The doctor asked, "Anything else I should know about?"

"Headaches," I added.

"Have you lost weight?"

"Wouldn't be surprised. They didn't feed me."

He loaded an injector and pressed it on my tummy.

"What's that?"

"I figured you might be malnourished. That was vitamins."

He turned to the others and mumbled something.

I couldn't figure it out as their voices faded. I dozed off.

* * * * *

Ron watched the passenger outside mirror of Jake's car. Behind them, an old gray Tesla electric sedan followed as Gancha turned to the right and made a loop.

On their third day of Gancha's training, she had become a stellar student.

"Third car behind," she said from the driver's seat. "Old model gray sedan. Two people."

Ron tapped his nostril to open the connection on his comm. "She spotted you. Change cars." He tapped again to disconnect.

"Still think I need training in this?" she asked. "I was checking for a tail before you were born."

Oh cripe. Here we go again.

"You must have been pretty young."

"I learned before I was ten," she replied.

The gray sedan turned in another direction and disappeared from the rear view.

"Gancha, I realize you have been checking for tails for a long time. This is different. It's not just a matter of you avoiding the cops. The York Security Agency will have much better people. And they'll use more than one car."

Hint, hint.

"He's gone now," she added with her arms stiff and gripping the steering wheel. "Where to next?"

"Let's loop around Gerges and head back toward the center."

That will give Vincent time to catch up with us.

For this lesson, Zetto drove the gray sedan and Vincent drove the BIS van.

"When can I show you my shooting skills?" Gancha asked. "I'll bet you twenty I can score higher."

"No doubt."

She said as she drove, "Are you in love with Jake?"

"No," Ron sighed and shook his head. "I have a partner. And if you behave, you may meet him someday."

So that was it. She's jealous that I'm such a close friend of her lover's.

"Are you the girl or the boy in the relationship?" she asked.

"That's the heterosexual model. They think everyone must have one man and one woman. That does not fit gays at all. If you stop to think about it, you'll see that. What I like about my partner is his masculinity and vice versa. Neither of us is attracted to females. The same holds true for lesbians. Neither one wants to be the guy in their relationship."

"I knew that. I was just testing you."

He shook his head. "And how am I supposed to know what you're thinking? I judge you by your actions and your words, not your thoughts."

As they passed Grand Central on their right, Ron got a tag.

"I see you," said Vincent.

Now we shall see just how good you are.

"Make a left at Moss," Ron ordered.

Gancha turned as directed. As she headed toward Franken Boulevard, a green van passed them on the left. The single black driver had bushy hair and a full beard. His body moved in regular beats to music they could not hear. The side of the van said "Walkers delivers" with four bags showing garnot fruit, a bush of broccoli, and a stick of long bread sticking out the top.

They drove through the light at Franken. The green van turned left and went up Harken Avenue and its brake lights came on, as if it was looking for an address to deliver its cargo. It pulled into a driveway.

Gancha drove straight on Moss through several more sides streets. When she came to Indio Road, she slowed.

"Okay, boss, now which way do I turn?"

Ron looked out the mirror and saw the now-white van four cars behind them.

"Right."

When they turned, the white van moved up behind them. This time the driver looked Oriental.

They went a half mile more when Ron felt a bump as the white van collided with the rear of Jake's car.

"What the frick?" Gancha let out.

She stopped, got out, and marched behind the car. Ron exited his side and watched her. As she got up to the white van, the driver pulled his hat forward over his face.

She demanded, "Where the hell did you learn how to drive?"

Through the front window of the van, Ron saw the man. He watched her face drop when the driver removed his disguise.

"Hi, Gancha," said Vincent. "Thought you needed a bump to wake you up. I've been following you from the center to Gerges and now here."

Gancha glanced at Ron.

Ron grinned.

Gotcha.

* * * * *

I watched from the monitor on the wall of the planning room. I finally could wear my light brown slacks as my thighs healed. The BIS van pulled into the ops center parking lot, followed by my gray car.

Our team has arrived.

I grimaced from the stinging in my thighs while I sat in the planning room.

Only Monk heard me. Andy was on his way north from Mourtan Security near the airport. Zetto had returned to the center after driving the sedan with Vincent.

When everyone else assembled in the main room, I asked Ron, "How'd she do?"

"She passed." He wore his usual outfit of blue jeans and a yellow shirt open at the neck to show his chest. And of course, two earrings.

I looked at Vincent.

He nodded in his gray slacks and white dress shirt. "Not bad."

Gancha came up to my right side, wearing blue slacks and a matching blue shirt, open in front to show beautiful cleavage.

I looked at Ron.

"How'd she do on disguises?"

"She's okay. Might use a little more practice but that comes with time," he replied.

Gancha added, "Gimme a break. I never had to use a disguise before."

Vincent piped up. "We use them a lot. I fooled you, didn't I?"

Gancha lowered her gaze, as if admitting defeat. "From twenty feet away, yeah."

"Gancha, it's okay to admit a weakness," I added.

I raised my right hand.

"Okay, gang. Let's stop the chatter. Shall we begin?"

I wanted Gancha to see how we planned an op.

"When you do everything by yourself, only you are at risk. I want you to get a feel for being part of a team. As a team member, if you screw up, everyone on your team is at risk."

I turned to the wall with Coocher's information on it.

CHAPTER 44

The next day, I needed less pain meds and devoured all the food they brought me for breakfast and lunch. In between, I slept. Couldn't do much else with the medicine in my blood. Besides, I needed the time asleep to heal.

Vincent sat in a chair with his ever-present laptop. Ron handed me my new comm. I checked it and had a tag from Sheila. I tagged her back.

"Jake, I'm really sorry about what happened. I had no idea."

"I understand. You may need to check your staff. Someone leaked that information and the wrong parties got ahold of it."

"Trouble is, I have a large staff," she said. "We need to plan a lot."

"The more people you tell, the easier it is for a leak to occur. What elements can you keep secret until the last moment?"

She paused. "I see what you mean."

"I wonder how many people now know the identity of Albert Poors."

"Oh dear. I apologize."

Her voice sounded sorry.

After we disconnected, I heard a knock on the door of the planning room. Vincent got up, opened it, and in walked Ron and Gancha.

The three of them closed the door.

Something was up.

They circled my bed and leaned in. Ron spoke first.

"We haven't been idle when you've been enjoying yourself."

Vincent added, "I've gotten the floor plans for Coocher's estate in Chester."

"I asked around," said Gancha. "Found out who the four guys were that took their bats to you. Hoskins hired them."

"And I," added Ron, "have informed my Dad. Per your emergency orders, I've taken over the responsibility for operating the center. That means I've also coordinated the efforts of the three of us on a special op."

"Op?" I asked.

"We've decided," said Ron, "and our boss agrees, that these guys shouldn't—correction, won't—be allowed to get away with what they did to you."

I looked at their faces. Each seemed dead serious. I allowed a grin to appear.

"Can I say something?" I added.

Ron looked at me and nodded.

"I've decided, in my more lucid moments, that I've had enough of HO, Coocher, and Hoskins. Let's get the bastards. They've bullied the public long enough."

All three broke out in big smiles.

"But first I must heal. I want to go on the op."

Their smiles disappeared. Ron looked at Vincent, Gancha, and Zetto. He turned to me and nodded.

The days rushed by fast. Of course, it helped that I slept a lot. I figured I wasn't going anywhere, so why not take a nap? I had several talks with my body since I'm a great believer in bio-feedback.

Every evening, Dr. Oberson visited.

On the third day, he said, "Amazing. I've never seen someone heal so fast."

"Told ya," I replied.

By now I sat up awake most of the day. Vincent and Ron made a set of parallel bars that attached to the floor so I could walk to the bathroom, dining room, and back to bed. For the gaps between the bars, I used a cane.

After a week, I changed to walking around with just a cane. Two days later, I went without one. Slow at first, but at least I was on my own.

My one big problem was my right hand. It was still weak. So I tried to build up the muscles in my hands by squeezing a lot. Vincent gave me a tennis ball and I alternated hands. My fine motor skills were still off. I had difficulty hitting the target with a gun.

And that won't do.

* * * * *

We went over the different locations where we might expect Coocher to be, including his HO office, his campaign headquarters at the Embassy Suites, the Parliament building, and his estate in the western provinces at Chester.

I had a tennis ball in my right hand and squeezed it every minute.

The first thing we needed to do was find out where Coocher parked his limo. When it was on the road, he likely would be in it.

I ordered a break from the planning.

Ron said, "I saw you squeeze the ball. Ready for more shooting practice?"

"Yep."

After loading several guns and plenty of ammunition into their cases, we carried them across the hall to our shooting range. We entered our passwords on the keypad and stared at the security scan camera. We had installed the same level of secure access we used in the dorm and planning room.

I went first and put on the ear protectors. Ron dimmed the lights and lit up the virtual target in the distance. I emptied a Snap at the target and raised the gun. Ron displayed my results. Seven out of ten hit the target. That was not good enough.

"My hand shook when I fired."

He needed to know if I was ready. I was not.

We changed places, he donned the ear protection, and took aim. I doused the lights and turned on the virtual target.

He got all ten shots in the target. Three in the head and seven in the chest.

Next I tried a rifle and got seven out of ten on the target.

"Hmmph."

I am definitely not ready.

* * * * *

Guy Coocher studied the results of the latest polls and smiled. Every two years the MPs in the House of Commons ran for reelection.

Things are looking good.

If his party could gain a majority in Parliament, he would become the next Prime Minister. The virus had killed off many voters for the opposition and the precincts in Zor looked half blue and half red. The overwhelming majority of the rural districts could be expected to vote for his party, even though their numbers were far less than in the bigger cites of Zor and La Seille.

Yep. Things are looking superb.

Someone knocked on the door of his campaign office in the Embassy.

"Come in."

She cracked the door and said, "We got another poll. This time from Channel One."

Coocher looked up. She wore heels, a black tight skirt, and white blouse, opened to show her cleavage, of course. He insisted that his female aides showed femininity.

"Let me see it."

She entered his spacious office and handed him the plastic report.

He could tell from the overwhelming blue color that the voters of Zor might put his opposition in the head office.

Shit. Which poll to believe?

The only poll that counted was the final election result.

He studied the report, looking for cracks in its logic, and leaned back in his tall bopum-leather chair. He might need to drum up more votes after all.

"Get my car ready. I need to go home."

The aide nodded, turned, and rushed to the door.

He watched her behind as she walked away from him. Maybe it was time he tried her. He smiled. One advantage of being a bachelor was his availability. Every single woman approached him.

Not that being married would slow him down.

* * * * *

Ron put on a black outfit for this op. He drove his red two-seater sports car with Gancha in the passenger seat. As he prowlded around the parking lot of the Embassy Suites, they spotted a man guarding the only limo.

The man leaned on the long vehicle and white smoke came from his mouth and nose occasionally.

From fifty yards away, Gancha studied the limo with binocs. Today she had on a light brown pantsuit with a white lace blouse.

"License plate matches," she said.

Ron drove four rows over and slid into an empty spot.

"That guard puts a kink in our plans," Gancha said.

"Maybe we can do it anyway. Care to engage him in a conversation?"

She grinned. "Sure. That sounds easy."

"You may want an ecig."

She grimaced. "Gave them up, oh maybe five years ago."

"So pretend," Ron replied.

After putting on gloves and checking that their comms were connected, the two got out of his car and split up. Gancha walked toward the building and patted her pockets while Ron crouched and walked around the end of four rows of cars. He peeked up and saw Gancha look around and spot the only other person in the lot. She walked directly to the guard while Ron ducked again and made his way toward the limo. The guard was a big fella, probably six feet or taller, with bulging muscles, in a blue suit and white shirt.

Gancha's comm came in Ron's ear. "Hey, buddy. Got a cig?"

"Not for free," said a male voice. With the high cost of cigs these days, few gave them away.

"Will five do it?" said Gancha.

Ron heard nothing while he crossed several rows of cars.

"Got it bad?" said the male voice.

Gancha replied, "Enough. Didn't bring mine."

"Here," said the man.

Ron couldn't see what else happened but heard Gancha puff on the electronic cigarette and ask, "How about them Screechies? Think they'll win the pennant?"

"Naw. With Stoddard pitching, they don't stand a chance."

"God, this is good," she said as she exhaled.

The two of them talked sports while Ron approached the limo. He got down on the cement, slid his head under the car, and found a small crevice between the exhaust pipe and the transmission. He thanked the warm break in the weather, making the pavement bearable.

From his pocket, he pulled out a gray box and put it up over a small pipe. He secured the box with elastic tape so it was invisible with a simple scan under the car.

After backing out, he crouched as he made his way to the end of the row, across four rows, and up to his red sports car, while listening to the small talk in his ear. The guard must have been bored to talk with a stranger.

"I'm back at the car," Ron informed her.

From his vantage point, he could see Gancha wave.

"Thanks for the cig."

The big man nodded but didn't reply.

Ron added, "I'll be at the side door."

Once at that door of the large hotel, he waited while she headed his way.

After she got in the passenger seat, she asked, "Do it?"

"Yep. Let's go home."

Now the team would be aware when the limo drove out of the city to Chester.

CHAPTER 45

The next day, I watched both of them on the monitor. Gancha walked in the front door of the ops center wearing gray slacks, a white shirt, and a gray jacket.

"Did you see any tail?" Ron asked her from his lower bunk in the dorm room.

"No," she replied with a snap of her head and her eyebrows furled as if to say the question was unnecessary.

Ron sighed.

"Just checking."

He flipped his covers aside and stood. He was dressed in gray slacks and a white shirt. An observer might think he was her twin, except for their skin color. He put on his black shoes and followed her into the planning room.

There, he told me of their conversation. Today I wore a dark blue suit and white dress shirt.

Ron filled me in on their short conversation.

I turned my eyes to her.

"Ron's right. We can't afford to lead YSA or the cops here. Whenever you come here, you put us all at risk."

Gancha bowed her head. "I didn't mean it that way."

I walked over to her and put my left hand on her right shoulder.

"We're just trying to help you learn, Gancha. We've already lost one team member and don't want to lose you, too."

I referred to Leanna, of course. After I stopped talking I studied Vincent, who sat in front of a laptop. But his gaze was on the floor.

Oops. Hit a nerve. Gotta stop that.

I walked up to the wall where we had laid out several plans on getting Coocher.

"Jake?" asked Gancha.

"Yes?"

"I don't mean disrespect. Please don't take it that way. But you just cautioned me about endangering other team members. I don't think you're ready to go on this op."

She paused before continuing, "I'd like to go on this operation but I can't. I have a board meeting with one of my new acquisitions. If I go with you for such a long time, people will wonder."

Ron peered at me.

"Hmm. I see your point."

Damn! I could use her special talents on this op.

Vincent added, "I don't like the current plan at all. It all depends on our finding Coocher and depends on a trick. If he goes to his estate, he'll be surrounded by security. That raises the odds against success."

"Actually," I replied, "I think if he heads to Chester, he'll be overconfident."

Vincent shook his head. "I still don't like it."

"What about getting the cooperation of the feds?" I asked.

Andy spoke up this time. His business trips were over for a while. Today he had on a gray suit and white dress shirt. His suit was darker than Ron's or Gancha's.

Was gray the color of the day and nobody told me?

"Getner will oppose that. After all, we embarrassed him by the vid of him giving a package to Coocher."

Zetto interrupted. "But the vid doesn't show Getner's head."

Andy replied, "It's what goes on in the mind of Getner that counts."

"So could we get Prime Minister Klava to rescue Albert Poors?" I asked.

No response came immediately.

Andy said, "Klava will want to know why Poors was involved."

Vincent added, "That's a sticker. You'd have to reveal the ID of Poors."

From this angle, I could see he wore a white dress shirt and brown slacks.

"I don't think I want to do that just yet," I added.

Vincent added, "So that means no fed cooperation."

Which spoils the main part of our only surviving plan.

I looked at Andy.

He shook his head.

"I can't be away from my office as long as this op may take."

"I understand," I said. Andy had to keep up his appearance of running his security business.

I asked Andy for another of his special inventions.

"That's easy."

He smiled before he left for his office.

* * * * *

Gancha tagged Guy Coocher at the HO headquarters.

"You don't know me but I'm a big fan of yours. Name's Gancha Morentoss. I inherited the estate of my grandfather, James Venesio. I've sold all of his criminal empire as soon as I got it, and bought some legit businesses. I think we can help each other."

A pause on the other end.

"Are you there?" she asked.

"Just thinking it over," said a deep masculine voice.

"How about a million sols worth of donation to your campaign?"

"Hmm. You seem eager."

"I foresee your becoming the next prime minister. Can we meet?"

Another pause. This time she waited.

He asked, "Can you be at my office in the Parliament Building at two this afternoon?"

Gotcha.

"I'll be there," she replied

At the appointed time, she walked the hall toward his office. To her surprise, Coocher stood outside the door. He wore his usual medium blue business suit. What surprised her was his height. Kinda short and overweight. Big belly.

"Gancha?" he asked.

She nodded.

"I thought it best to meet you here, instead of in my office. Politics, you know."

"Shall we have coffee downstairs?" she asked.

"I think it would best to talk in my van," he added.

"Whatever you wish," she said.

As they walked, she noticed he was bent over a bit. Not a lot, but not straight either.

Once inside his van, she took a seat behind the driver's seat. Coocher got in beside her.

"You want to donate to my campaign?" he asked.

"Sure. I think you will be the next prime minister. My only question is: what would my donation buy me?"

Coocher spoke into his comm.

"I'm going to dinner with a donor. Cancel or postpone my appointments for the rest of the day."

He disconnected and turned to her. "Salia's?"

At dinner, Gancha sipped on her glass of Chardonnay. This conversation was tricky and full of potential land mines. She had to stay alert and could not afford to get drunk where she might say a wrong word.

He asked, "Where were we?"

"I had asked you what my donation of a millions sols might buy me. I have several businesses in Zor and…"

She stopped when his hand covered hers. This was getting personal, which brought a smile to her lips. All was going according to plan.

"Did I ever tell you," he said, "that I have a preference for tall women? Especially smart ones."

CHAPTER 46

The more I thought about Gancha, the more I made up my mind.

The most important op I've done and I can't rely on her. To hell with her. If she can't keep up with us, she might not fit on my team.

"Ron, pack food and water."

He grinned as he headed toward the kitchen. I couldn't tell if his grin came from having something to do or the fact we were going on an op.

"Vincent, can you detect the transponder?"

"Oh yeah," Vincent replied. "It sends a signal every minute. It's still at the Embassy."

"Let's take the van," I said.

I packed a rifle with a scope in a sport bag and exchanged my Snap in its holster with a clean one. By clean, I meant clean of serial numbers and barrel bores that might lead to any of us. Zetto made sure we had four cases of food and water. Ron hummed the whole time we prepared.

But the limo didn't leave the city. It traveled to the Parliament Building, to the HO HQ, and back to Parliament.

Vincent said, "If that guy doesn't go home in a week, the battery on the transponder will need replacing."

Andy showed up with his special invention. It sure looked like a button on my shirt, exactly like the photo I had sent him. The receiving end would rest in the BIS van.

The next evening, Vincent reported, "The limo is moving."

He looked up with a smile.

"This time it's heading south on Ambassador."

We watched the blinking icon on our wall as the limo approached the Zor-Franken airport.

"Might pick up somebody."

Then it kept going. When it got outside the city limits, I said, "Okay, Ron. Let's get movin'."

We had a long ways to go. Over a thousand miles.

He and I carried loads of food and equipment to the van. We had complete sets of black clothing and Z helmets in our sports bags. I packed three of the Pyronex small bombs and Ron another three. We also loaded six transponders, turned off to save their charges.

I said, "Chima, tell us where the Coocher limo is."

A map displayed on the dash showing a blinking light ten miles south of the city limits.

"Check your weapons?" asked Vincent from outside my passenger window. "Clean?"

"Yep. Packed."

"Good hunting," said Vincent with a smile and a wink.

Ron pulled out and drove around Grand Central Station while I kept my eyes on the rearview mirror and the overhead mirror.

While we were on the road we needed more current information.

"Chima, send a wireless signal to the transponder to set the broadcast rate at every fifteen seconds instead of a minute."

"Affirmative."

We headed south on Ambassador, fifty minutes behind Coocher. Since his cars had heavy armor, I figured they'd travel slower than ours and would have to stop more often for fuel. We had armor too, but we depended on fabric armor, not the sheet metal kind.

As we drove west on the two-lane road, darkness descended and snow fell from the sky. It was early this year. The white stuff that came in November was stubborn. It stuck around until March. Kinda reminded me of Earth when I visited Detroit. The locals there said that about their snow.

As we headed west, Ron said, "Better get some sleep."

I laid my seat back to a prone position.

The wipers went blink, blink, blink across the windshield. As Ron drove, particles of snow came right at me. I felt like ducking to avoid their constant onslaught. The red taillights of the car ahead of me glowed.

To my right lay more whiteness buried under a dark sky. Heading in that direction was insanity. That part of Rossa was too wild. In the distance ahead of us, I saw occasional lights, probably from farm houses, clustered together and inside a fence.

I checked my comm.

Another four hours to go before I could take the next shift.

With hot air coming out of the dashboard vents, I closed my eyes and thought of my daughter. Nestled back in the safety of the mercon embassy, she was safe for the moment. I doubted if anyone from HO would risk an attempt on her while she was there. The security at the embassy had to be top-notch to keep protesters out.

As for the rest of my team that was a different matter.

As the night wore on, I realized I was going deep into bigotry territory. Ron and I were half-Bingers. If that fact got out in this rural countryside, we might get killed for just that.

I shook my head.

Crazy thoughts. Can't go there.

I focused on the harm that Coocher and his Humans Only organization had done. Hoskins had tortured my friend Zetto, my ex-wife Leanna, and my daughter, Alena. Not to mention poisoning the waters of Zor with VB, resulting in thousands of deaths. That kind of bigotry had to end somewhere.

Then there was the question of Gancha.

Where the hell is she?

Ron had tuned the van's visual display to show the location of our transponder. Just three miles ahead.

Then the blip stopped moving.

I glanced at our gauge. Half full. As we passed a sign, I read "Fuel ahead."

Clouds covered the night sky, blocking my view of the stars. The onboard map showed a fuel station not far ahead. Maybe Coocher's cars had stopped.

We climbed a small hill and off in the distance saw a blur of lights. I reached over to Ron.

"Can't sleep. Too wired, I guess. Do we need fuel? The limo might be there. This might be a good time to change the battery."

Ron slowed the van. The red lights receded in the distance. No white lights appeared in my mirrors. We were alone out here with three limos of bigots in front of us.

"Chima, we're stopping at the station ahead. Turn off the dome light so you can't be seen."

I added, "Chima, kill the lights when a door is opened. Put the words and logo of Broadway's AC and Heating on the sides of the van."

I turned to Ron and said, "And while I'm inside, you fill up our tank, sneak up to one of their vehicles, and put a new transponder underneath."

"What if they see me?"

"Use a drone to distract anyone."

Three black vehicles parked next to the pumps. I could see the hoses leading to each. The occupants must have gone inside to relieve themselves and get food and coffee. Only one guy remained outside, a big guy in an all gray overcoat. Probably armed too.

Ron pulled up to the gate in the fence and waited while it slid open. He parked at the pump farthest from the three limos and got out.

I opened my door and emptied my thermos of coffee on the snow. Sure wished I had packed a warmer jacket.

While Ron connected a hose to our van, I huddled over and ran into the store as I got pelted with snow.

Movement on my right caught my attention and I glanced in that direction. Two small greepers sniffed the air near the trash cans. From the bend of the bushes, I figured they stood downwind from the cans. Then I spotted the momma greeper. Big thing. Her eyes focused on me. Thank heavens the fence stood between her and me.

I continued running. Once inside, six pairs of eyes watched me as I approached the counter and sat. They all wore dark coats and winter hats.

Coocher was nowhere in sight. The rest of the place was empty. But it was dark outside and few customers must visit this far from civilization. Mostly they came for the gas and food. As I entered the main restaurant, I passed kiosks of items for sale. Toys, and stuff for traveling, like coffee mugs, head rests, and blankets.

A chubby woman, with a flop of gray hair and wearing a mustard-yellow uniform, came up. "Coffee?"

I nodded while I shivered and placed the empty thermos on the counter.

She lifted a pot and poured the black liquid into a white porcelain cup. "From the city?"

"How'd you guess?"

"Folks around here know how to dress for this weather."

I had forgotten about how much colder it could be as we headed west toward to the ocean. Hundreds of miles of flat land lay around us. Except for the few farm houses and barns nestled inside fences, the rest was left to nature. Which on Rossa meant greepers, gofers, and reddoes. Screechies had migrated south to get away from the chilly weather.

Behind her rested a mirror, the bottom half covered in colored business cards. On the polished surface between them, I watched as the guys behind me continued their study of me. I wished she had not made her comment.

The coffee was steaming so I added ice cubes from my glass of water.

"Want me to fill up yer thermos?" asked the waitress with a pot in her hand.

I nodded and she poured the hot steamy liquid.

"Where you headed?" she asked.

I couldn't tell her my real destination. Not in front of those guys.

"Headed back. Visited my sister."

Two minutes later, I got the message I waited for. My ear piece spoke with Ron's words.

"Mission accomplished. I'm back in the van."

Coocher came out of the gents room with two big guys on each side of him, one in front and the other behind.

I placed my left elbow on the counter and put my hand in front of my face so he couldn't see me.

He took a seat with his back to me.

"That'll be three fifty," said the waitress.

I hauled out my comm and touched it to the outlet for the register. With a few clicks, I paid for the coffee in the name of Stan Broadway. That was one of my aliases. We kept small bank accounts open in each name. Every team member had an alias.

"Thanks," I said as I got up and turned away from the guards and Coocher.

The damned snow came down as I raced to the van and got in the driver's side. Once inside, I headed back toward Zor.

"Hey, aren't we supposed to go the other way?" asked Ron from the other front seat.

"I told the gal in there I was going back to the city."

When we got over the other side of the hill, I looked for place to turn around. With no one else on the road, I made the flip in direction, being careful to not let my tires press on the side of the road. Didn't want anyone to guess what I'd one.

"Chima, change the outside. Use plain gray this time."

The blinking light on my dashboard shifted. Coocher was on the move.

I kept a couple miles behind them. Several miles and hours later, when the transponder stopped again, I pulled over.

"Shift change."

I opened my door and got out. The snow had died to a light dusting.

Taking advantage of this opportunity, I grabbed a spare gas can, opened the gas cap, and tipped the spare can into the tank. The air had a chill to it and I wished it would hurry up.

But the time I finished, Ron had climbed into the driver's side.

CHAPTER 47

With all the time spent behind the wheel or waiting for my driving shift, I had plenty of time to think. I thought of what it was like to live on this planet. It was a frontier world for sure. Humans struggled to make a living, feed themselves and their children, and somehow survive.

Come to think of it, that was also true for most people back on Earth. Those in the developed countries seldom understood what daily life was like in the other parts of the world. Starvation, terrorism, corruption, war. And all too often, immigrants to Rossa brought with them their old cultures, which encouraged those behaviors.

The biggest problem we faced was not from the alienness and wildness of Rossa, but from other human beings. Earth shipped its poor and hungry and we had to deal with them.

Then I thought of York, where most immigrants from North America and Europe came.

I thought of my landlord, Sing Sing Cullen. She was a lesbian in a world that discriminated against them. Same for male gays and for Bingers like me. The same was true for those who tried to survive despite having an accident of birth. Such as fingers on one hand growing out of each other, ears that didn't work right, or any form of being born abnormal. Heaven forbid that someone made the mistake of being born with too dark a skin. Naughty, naughty. Shame on them.

Those who had grown up on Rossa were more adjusted to life here than their parents. "The young adapt, the old die off." Only those who spent the first twenty years of their lives on Earth would want to live with the old habits. Those who were younger adapted. Unfortunately, most of the immigrants were over twenty.

Which brought me back to the task ahead of me. Fighting discrimination was an unending battle. The people who lived in Chester had their limited attention spans focused on survival and being "normal." They had no idea how much they practiced discrimination. They tried to stay together in their struggles to survive and tried to get all those around them to conform to being the same, ignoring the fact that the few amongst them who were different could provide the answers—if only they let them.

They had no idea of the burden they put on those they discriminated against.

All the progress that mankind had made since we first tamed fire came not from those who conformed but from those who thought differently. We have no records from those prehistoric times but I suspected the first man who showed how to make fire met his death for daring to steal what belonged to the gods. The rest of his tribe reacted out of fear that the gods would punish them for his disobeying the rules. Rules they made up.

I thought back to the burning of the library in Alexandria, Egypt, so long ago. If the mob had not burned that library maybe humanity would have gone to the stars sooner. But then again, only the wealthy used the library and much of their wealth came from owning slaves. The mob had many slaves who burned the library in frustration.

The struggle to raise awareness had many bumps on its path.

On my turn to drive, I saw flashing lights. I slowed after the curve and spotted an ambulance and two cop cars, all with flashing lights. Then I saw the reason.

There weren't many cars on the road, so I slowed down to gawk at the damage.

A greeper in white fur lay off the right side of the road. A sedan with its front end smashed in rested off the side of the road about twenty feet from the greeper and turned around. Two men pushed and pulled a gurney to the ambulance. On it lay a white sheet over a body with boots sticking out.

A tow truck with a crane had its yellow lights flashing as it parked behind a police vehicle.

"Looks like someone hit a greeper.

Ron spoke next.

"Poor guy. Looks like he bought it."

"Looks that way."

Greepers were massive. Some weighed in at two tons. To hit one with a car traveling seventy meant the front end of your car was a goner. You too, most likely.

"From the damage, I'd say he was doing about ninety," Ron added.

I was tempted to slow down. It was a dilemma. Slow down to live but take more hours to get to your destination. So I compromised.

"Chima, keep a lookout for something on the road ahead. If you see anything, slow down. If you see a greeper on the road or about to go over the road, come to a full stop."

That should do it.

That was the only exciting thing on the long road. From my mental calculation, we were about a hundred miles from our destination.

On and on I drove. Quite boring really. Thank heavens the designers of this road built in curves every mile or so to keep drivers awake.

A white rectangle came into view on my right. Clumps of trees and open grasses spread beyond it. The ground was covered in snow. As a marker sped by, I read "Chester 10." Made of circular concrete, the marker looked like it could withstand greepers using it to scratch themselves. Built perfectly vertical, the cement rectangle faced oncoming traffic with a metal sign on the cement. Maybe it was to make the words visible, even if it snowed or rained. Must get a lot of both. No lights though.

CHAPTER 48

"Ron, wake up!" I yelled.

The seat next to me rose to an upright position and Ron blinked before commanding to the van, "Chima, coffee."

"We're coming up on Chester," I said.

When the tray slid out with a paper cup full of the dark liquid, adjusted to his taste and at a temperature he enjoyed, Ron lifted the cup to his lips.

To my left, off in the distance, I saw a white blob move. Staring at it more, I observed a white gofer prowling low. She must have seen something ahead of her. Female gofers do most of the hunting for food.

Sure enough, I spotted a greeper, also white. Must be a male to be alone like that. Female greepers, along with their young, had a tendency to be in herds.

The greeper busied himself with eating the branches of a bush, whose leaves had long since fallen to the ground. He must have enjoyed himself gorging on the food because he paid no attention to the danger sneaking up on him.

I watched in fascination as the gofer raced in a charge to the greeper. Both had six legs and were built close to the ground.

On one of its breaks from dining, the greeper must have seen the gofer because it faced its attacker and raised itself up on its two hind legs with claws from the four other paws waving, along with its abundant teeth. I could not hear anything from this distance but imagined the greeper let out a roar when the gofer charged it. The greeper fell over backwards as the gofer hit it and the two went down. The gofer was smaller but had momentum going for it.

The road curved and I paid attention to my driving. When I turned the wheel and held it steady, my gaze returned to the two animals off to my left.

But by now, nothing stirred. I switched my vision from the road to the animals, and back several times.

As the sight of the battle passed behind me, I saw the gofer stand over its kill, now lying belly up and not moving.

"Would you look at that?" said Ron.

I shook my head. Rossa was such a wild world.

It took several minutes for my heart to stop pounding. Only flat land separated my van from the two large animals in the distance.

A couple miles farther I came upon a fence surrounding the small town of Chester where three thousand people called home. A red and white striped board blocked the snow-covered road. Two guards in uniforms and carrying side arms strode up to both sides of my van, their faces exhaling puffs of white in the cold air. The guard on my side pointed to my front license plate for his partner. I pushed the button to lower my window.

My guard held his right hand on his weapon and leaned down to my level.

"Why are you coming to Chester?" asked the guard on my side.

"We're tourists," I said. "We came to find out what life is like in a small town. If we like what we see, we may bring our families to live here."

The guard on Ron's right looked us over and tapped on his window. When Ron lowered it, the guard asked, "You queer?"

I sensed Ron's shoulders dropping as he shook his head.

Ron replied, "Hey, I thought Chester was a friendly town."

If the guy hadn't worn a badge and carried a gun, I could have challenged him on that. But in Rome, do as the Romans do.

I smirked to the officer on my right. "I said our families. Both of us are married with kids. And I mean married to women. I have two kids, boy and girl. He," I pointed with my thumb, "has three kids, all girls."

"What's your wife's name?" asked Ron's guard.

"Arlene. But do I need to reveal that to go into Chester?" asked Ron. "That's not a friendly greeting. I heard this was a friendly town."

"Bring the virus with you?" asked the guard on my side.

"Nope. Everyone in both our families got vaccinated a week ago. How are the folks ahead? Been vaccinated?" I asked.

My guard nodded his head. "Four days ago." Then he looked at Ron before returning his gaze to me.

"You guys reporters or sumtin'?" my guard asked.

"No," I sighed. "I run a business, import/export. He's a waiter at a restaurant."

The guard looked over to Ron. "What restaurant?"

"Ever hear of Stennos?" asked Ron.

"Hmph," replied my guard. He straightened up, nodded to his partner, and walked to the shed, probably to get warm in this snow.

As the barrier in front of us raised, I drove through.

A mile beyond the guard gate, Ron said, "Damned suspicious."

"Gotta keep the narrow-mindedness pure, ya know."

He added, "Just give me the go ahead and I'll trim the reproductive tree."

"We gotta choose our battles. Remember what we came for," I replied.

"Arlene was your mother's name, wasn't it?"

"Yeah. It was all I could think of at the moment," Ron replied.

It took only fifteen seconds to reach the outskirts of town. Even in the dark, I could see the smaller rectangular glow of lights in windows. It was too dark to see any smoke from chimneys.

I had searched the Net for motels in this small town. So I kept an eye out for Motel Ten, the only place where visitors could find a room. Sure enough, its sign lit up the left side of the road as we entered. Chester had two stoplights on Main Street, the main drag. As I drove past First Street, I realized there was a third stoplight on First a block away to my right. As I drove by, I noticed a pickup truck went through the red light to make a left turn.

Must not get much traffic here. Either that, or the driver was related to a cop.

As I drove through the downtown, I swear mine was the only van on the streets. All the rest were trucks or SUVs. We endured stares from every turned face, in the trucks, on the sidewalks, or in the stores. Guess they don't get many visitors here. Just like that, we got to the other end of town. I made a U-turn and headed back to the motel.

* * * * *

Ron and I registered in adjacent rooms on the ground floor. From the lack of cars in the parking lot, we could have had our picks of rooms. I dumped my suitcase in my room. Ron came over and the two of us walked to the adjacent York Western Restaurant.

I selected a booth and slid in so I could keep my back to the wall. Ron sat opposite me.

Ron had the house special of spaghetti and meatballs. I had the rack of lamb. Yeah, the whole rack.

From the look on Ron's face, I said, "No competition for Stenno's, eh?"

My lamb wasn't much better. Tough. I wouldn't be surprised if it was mutton.

We ate in silence, enduring the stares of the other patrons. I noticed most of them wore clothing that suggested a rough life. Long sleeved shirts of either black, or checkered red and black, blue jeans, black or brown boots. Made me wonder if they kept their cowboy hats in their trucks.

We, on the other hand, had on city clothes. I wore a white shirt, gray dress pants, gray jacket, and black shoes. Ron was clothed in a blue and white checkered shirt, blue slacks, and black shoes. I noticed an earring in his right ear. That could be why the guard on his side of the van thought he might be gay. We stood out like New Yorkers in Podunk, Missouri.

I pulled on my left earlobe while looking at Ron and mouthed the word "remove."

He eyes rolled up but he detached the earring.

We avoided their alcoholic beverages and had coffee instead. Meaning we didn't drink their draft beer by the mug like most patrons did.

The music was awful. Pure country, complete with the twangy guitars and off-note singing of a guy or girl losing a lover. Or a pet dog. The sour notes came from overhead speakers.

At one point, the waitress collided with the right shoulder of Ron, spilling coffee on his lap. I saw my buddy purse his lips and look at me. He tolerated this rude behavior when he much preferred to beat not only the waitress but any of the locals who came to her aid. If only they knew how dangerous we were.

Once we finished, Ron paid and I put down a robust tip. Maybe the waitress would remember us kindly.

Back in my room, Ron said, "I'd just as soon..."

I shook my head and placed my finger to my lips. Our room might be bugged. After the greeting at the fence and the stares in the restaurant, I wouldn't put it past the owners of this place, figuring guests might let their guards down in the privacy of their rooms and say whatever was on their minds.

He nodded. "…take a nap after that meal."

"See ya, later. I'm gonna hit the sack too."

Ron left and I walked around my twin-bed room with my comm activated to detect any device that broadcast over the air. Nothing. That didn't mean it was clear though. So I checked all the light fixtures and the phone. There was no chandelier. Nothing again.

The air smelled of pig.

I set my comm to wake me at midnight and slipped under the covers. I don't know how much sleep I got when I heard a scream. Several more followed until they became a constant scream. With a sigh, I got up and walked in the chilly air to the front window.

I pulled down one metal blade of the venetian blinds and peered out to see the nearby pigs. They gathered near their enclosure and faced in the same direction. I looked there and saw a dark blob at the fence.

A shot rang out and I looked to the right to see where it came from. Another shot came and I saw the flash of light from the muzzle of a shotgun. A man walked from the main office of the motel while reloading. Another man followed with a rifle.

The dark blob retreated back to the woods, and the pigs stopped screaming.

I peeked at my comm. It was only ten. Maybe I could get some more shuteye so I climbed back under the covers. The warmth felt good.

* * * * *

My comm's vibration woke me in the dark.

I yawned, flipped the covers back, and stood in my street clothes. From my bag, I took a stim. Closing the bathroom door to keep the light in, I turned on the light and downed the tablet with a half-glass of water.

Next came rubber gloves. I applied black makeup to my face before removing the gloves. I doused the light and walked back to the main room where I removed my shirt, taped a transponder to my chest, and turned it on. Then I finished dressing in all-black, including shirt, pants, and athletic shoes.

A soft double knock on my door told me I had a visitor. I tucked my shirt in my waist, picked up my Snap, walked to the front door, and opened it a crack to see my fellow spy dressed in black. I opened the door to let him in.

He carried his suitcase inside and waited while I packed mine.

We each carried a suitcase and went to our van.

Once inside, I asked, "Chima. Have you had any visitors?"

The computer voice responded, "No one visited the inside or the outside of the van."

From the hidden compartment in the dash, we pulled out our Z helmets and put them on.

"Chima, stealth mode."

I drove out with no lights showing, not even the backup lights. If I pressed on the brake pedal, not even the red taillights would go on. Ours was the only vehicle on the street and I drove using the night vision in my helmet.

I headed away from the center of town. "Chima, show map on the dash."

The small screen lit up with Main Street. Above the screen was a metallic ridge preventing its light from being seen outside the van. I turned left a half mile later. Then I drove ten minutes at a slow speed on the dirt road. I stopped a hundred yards from the sign "Coocher Ranch ahead."

Using the zoom lenses on my helmet, I checked the guard gate ahead. Two guys with rifles.

To our right was a wooden fence five feet tall, topped with razor wire. It might keep screechies out but not greepers or gofers. Maybe the guards took care of them.

Ron removed his helmet, pressed a few buttons on his comm, climbed out, and walked to the guard gate. I followed the conversation via my comm.

"Helmet, activate forward camera and zoom."

Ron walked up to the guard gate.

When the younger guard heard Ron, he unshouldered his rifle and pointed it at him.

"Who is it?"

With his hands raised, Ron approached the guards. By now, the other one had his rifle pointed at him too.

"Where the hell am I?" asked Ron.

"Whatcha doin' walking in the night?" asked the older guard.

"I'm lost. I left my car way back there." He pointed behind him.

"Can you tell me how to get back to town?"

The younger one cocked his rifle and raised it to his eye level. Not a smart move. Must not be ex-cops. Maybe he was a wannabe who liked to carry a gun and wear a uniform.

"Headlights on," I ordered Chima.

The lights distracted the guards. Ron ducked and pulled his Snap with its silencer.

The younger guard fired at where Ron used to be.

"What the hell?" said the older guard.

With two quick pops from Ron's silenced Snap both men fell to the ground.

Damn!

I started the engine and drove up toward Ron.

He tossed something through the open door of the guard shack, another toward the fence, and lay on the ground. In seconds, the shack blew up, followed by the fence. If anyone watched in the main house, they'd sure be alarmed by now.

When the van got close enough, Ron got up, climbed in, and put his Z helmet back on. Ron had researched the kinds of bushes native to Chester and had chosen camouflage to match for our helmets.

I drove toward the house through the gap left by Ron's grenades.

CHAPTER 49

The three-story house was lit up, including floodlights around the outside. Everything stood in shades of gray or black. The ground floor had few windows. A split staircase wound up to the main doors. One staircase to the right and the other left.

In the windows on the second floor, I spotted silhouettes of men with rifles. In front of the house was loose gravel.

Ron ducked down beneath the dashboard.

"I guess our surprise is over."

"Looks like, doesn't it?" I answered. "Chima, dim all windows."

I pulled to the right and stopped.

"Out you go."

Ron opened his door and dove to the ground with his helmet still on.

"Chima, close the door."

I pulled off my Z helmet and returned it to its hidden storage compartment. With my passenger assured of not getting involved in the firefight, I drove up to the staircases of the house and stopped.

"Get out of your car with your hands up," commanded a loudspeaker I couldn't locate.

I kept a Snap in my holster. They would expect one and would look until they found it. With that little task taken care of, I opened my door and exited the vehicle with my hands raised. As I closed the door with my hip, I lowered my left hand to cover my mouth to prevent lip reading.

"Chima, security lock."

Now, no one could open any of the doors or enter through the windows except members of my team.

I walked out away from my car with my hands raised and my eyes squeezed narrow from the blinding glare of lights.

"Throw your gun away."

I hurled the Snap to my left onto the paved stones and stood, waiting further orders.

"Turn around slowly."

I turned to my left and completed the turn in fifteen seconds.

"Where's your buddy?"

"This doesn't involve him," I said. "I left him back at the motel." I pointed with my thumb back the way I had come before raising it again.

"Why are you here?"

"I have a score to settle with Coocher."

"You're not in much of a position to settle anything, mister. Who are you?"

"Jake Dani, father of Alena Dani. Coocher ordered her kidnapped and tortured."

"So daddy wants to play hero, eh?"

Two men approached with handguns in front of them pointed at me. I could see their breath. Saw mine too. The air was chilly, below the dew point for water vapor.

After a pause, one of them said in a puff of fog, "The only reason why you're still alive is the boss."

A pair of flashlights approached. I tried blocking the light with my right hand.

"Keep your hands up!"

"Then turn the damned flashlights off my eyes," I said as I kept my hand in front of me.

I heard voices behind the lights, which lowered.

"Turn around and stay there."

I did with my hands up.

"Put your hands behind your back."

After I obeyed that command, I heard the crunch of shoes on the stones approach behind me.

"My partner has a gun pointed right at your head in case you make any sudden moves," said a voice two feet away.

Rough hands put metallic handcuffs around my wrists. He slipped a black blindfold over my head. Then he fastened the blindfold tight behind my head with an elastic strap.

A little too tight but I was not in a position to complain.

Two hands grabbed each of my arms and led me back to the house. I smiled to myself but did not show it on my face. At least they hadn't thought to check me for the transponder.

I slipped once as we went up a stair and then walked a hallway. A door opened and rough hands shoved me inside. That happened several times. The next thing I knew, someone forced me onto a chair.

"Tape his ankles."

Two guys—I assume it was guys—obeyed.

One said, "Ah. An ankle gun."

He removed it.

Rough hands pulled my arms back and more tape secured them to the back of the chair. I wasn't going anywhere for a while.

Nothing happened for the next minute, at least nothing I could see.

Then a pair of hands tore off the tape from my left wrist and removed my comm. Then those same hands reattached my arm to the chair.

I heard a snap closure.

"Your comm is in a box. Now no one can hear what we say."

Then something happened I least expected. Someone removed my blindfold. The son of bitch Hoskins sat in front of me with Coocher to his right. Now I knew they intended to kill me. They wouldn't want to leave a witness.

I saw Coocher's arm cross his chest with a pistol in his hand. A sharp pain tore into my right cheek. That must have been what hit my cheek.

"Why did you bring another man along? Where is he?"

"I had to have somebody spell me on the long drive," I answered. "He's just a friend."

"How did you knock out my guards at the gate so fast?"

I looked at Coocher and saw he was winding up to give me another pistol whipping. So I quickly added, "I used to be a cop on Earth."

Coocher paused.

"Cops don't learn those kinds of tricks."

"Then I went into private practice."

The MP nodded. "Ah. Dirty stuff."

Who was I to argue?

I nodded.

"So you thought you'd just walk in here and shoot everybody, eh?" asked Coocher. He let me have another of his pistol whips.

Damn! That hurt!

After I caught my breath, I said, "I figured you'd be overconfident and lax on security. After I scouted the place, I was hoping I could get in, kill you, and get out before anyone knew something was amiss."

"Well, we may be country folks in your view but we know a thing or two about security. Had a good teacher."

"YSA?" I asked.

That brought another pistol whip to my face. Seconds later, I tasted the salt of my blood.

Hoskins stepped forward and ripped the front of my shirt open. He used a pair of green-handled scissors to cut the edges of my shirt and soon I was stark naked above the waist.

"Well, well. What have we here?" he asked.

I wish he hadn't done that. There went my plan. Now I was alone.

He yanked the transponder from my chest, ripping the tape from my skin. He placed it in the same box as my comm. Then he grinned as he put on a set of metallic loops with holes for his fingers. Good ol' brass knuckles. He raised his right arm behind him and let me have it in the gut.

Even though I expected it, I strained against the back of my chair.

That hurt worse than my face.

After that blow, came two more, also to my abdomen. If he kept that up, my kidneys would burst. I looked down and but didn't see any blood on my belly.

Hoskins stepped back. "Can I kill him now, boss?"

"Any last requests?" asked Coocher.

I blurted out, despite the searing pain in my gut, "People who do crime cannot talk about their accomplishments. They love to brag about what they've done but most of the time they can't tell others."

I looked up into Coocher's face.

"That was quite a bold accomplishment."

I paused "For the sake of my own curiosity, tell me how you did it."

"About what?" asked Coocher.

"How you got the virus into the public water, for one."

"Well, since you're alone and you're gonna die soon, why not? That was easy. Hoskins did it."

I turned my head to his henchman. I coughed up blood. "Care to explain?"

"Sure," the man grinned with his revolver pointed at my face. "I got the floor plan off the Net and went to the Public Water Works dressed as a cop, to avoid attention. It was easy to avoid prying eyes while your alien ambassador gave a speech. Nobody noticed when I slipped downstairs. They were all paying attention to that little dark alien. Some security! I poured four bottles of the virus in a large tank."

I looked at Coocher. "And you ordered this...killing thousands of innocent people?"

"They're not so innocent," replied the Member of Parliament. "Most of them are frickin' liberals."

"What about those who would have voted for it and died?"

Coocher shrugged. "Couldn't be helped. Call it collateral damage."

"One last thing," I asked my captors, "Who ordered my daughter kidnapped?"

Coocher grinned. "That was my idea. That bitch was swinging voters against my bill. I had to know what she knew."

"Then you planned to kill her, right?"

He shrugged. "Like I said, couldn't be helped. We weren't going to leave any witnesses."

"Okay, Q and A is over." Hoskins approached my head with his gun.

A voice called out, "Guy, can I speak with you?"

Gancha?

Coocher shook his head. "Not now!"

That same feminine voice said, "It may be better to keep him alive."

Coocher sighed before he looked at Hoskins. "I'd better hear what she has to say. Come with me. Leave him for now. We can always finish the job later."

The two men walked out of the room and Hoskins flipped a switch, leaving me in total darkness.

I had one chance. Maybe, just maybe, Ron could hear me. "Ron?" I yelled.

But I was greeted with silence.

Crap!

CHAPTER 50

I waited like that, in pain and in darkness for maybe two minutes. Then I heard a shot from the next room. Seconds later, the door opened and light flooded in. Whoever opened the door turned on the light. I bowed my head to protect my eyes from the glare.

Was it going to end like this?

I managed to raise my head to see who my killer was. Probably Hoskins.

Gancha rushed up to me and used a knife to cut through the tape on my legs and wrists.

"What the hell? Why are you here?"

She replied, "Saving your sorry ass. When Guy and Hoskins went out of this room, I pulled a Snap on them. I told them I had recorded their confession, and they had one chance to escape and they'd better take it now. Hoskins raised his hands but Guy made the mistake of pulling his gun out and I shot him in the leg. Hoskins helped him leave. Then I came through the door to your room. I would have preferred to shoot them on the spot but…."

"Why'd you call Coocher by his first name?"

"Can we talk later?" she replied as she finished with my ankles. "Can you walk?"

I stood but my belly hurt so much I groaned.

Gancha grabbed one of my arms as I tried to stand.

"Where's the exit?" I asked.

"Over there," she answered and pointed with one hand.

I looked at Gancha's furled eyebrows. I would have preferred to walk on my own but I hurt too much.

"Hand me your Snap," I said. "Can you carry me out of this damned house?"

She gave me her gun before placing her left arm under my knees and the other behind my back. I didn't resist her help and put my left arm around her neck. She lifted me up with ease. Her extra Binger strength came in handy.

"Can you tag Ron?" I asked.

"Not while carrying you," Gancha replied.

"Okay, put me down."

She did and I kept her Snap pointed in the direction we had walked.

She pressed a few buttons on her comm, and raised it to her mouth. "Ron?"

"Yeah," he responded. After a second, he added, "Gancha?"

"I'll explain later. First we need to get Jake out of here. We're in the basement."

"I'll shoot my way in," said the voice of Ron on her comm. "Keep your comm on so I can zero in on its signal."

She picked me up again and I kept her Snap pointed toward the doorway.

I heard the chatter of a machine gun in the distance, followed by an explosion.

Piles of boxes along the walls greeted us but Gancha carried me through them. When we got to the door to the stairs, she turned around to put her back against it.

"Watch behind me," she said as she cracked open the door.

We had the stairwell to ourselves and she lumbered up with me in her arms.

When we got to the main floor, she set me down and cracked the door to see who might be on the other side. Then she returned and lifted me again. She put her back to the door and swung it open while I pointed the gun ahead of us.

As we entered another hallway, I heard a loudspeaker in the distance.

"Jake! Where are you?"

I yelled back, "Coming! We're on the ground floor near the front door."

"Stand back! I'm crashing through the door," said Ron's voice from far away.

Gancha leaned against one wall with me in her arms.

I heard a bumptey-bump sound. Maybe from the van climbing the stairs.

In seconds, the front door burst open and I saw the front of our van. Ron sat in the driver's seat. When he saw us, he opened his door, and rushed up with his right hand carrying a semiautomatic gun.

"Are you hurt?" he asked.

"My stomach hurts like hell but I'll make it. Let's get outta here!"

Ron stood guard while Gancha carried me into the van and rested me on a bunk.

She closed the sliding door and soon I heard Ron get in the driver's side. In seconds, we moved backward. The van spun around and Ron drove us down the stairs. Bumptey-bump. My stomach hurt with each bump and I heard several pings on the back door. This was one time when I was glad we had reinforced the outside of the van with armor.

I lurched as the van tore off toward the gate. Gancha fell on her butt.

* * * * *

"Let's go back to Zor," I said.

"What about Coocher and Hoskins?" Gancha asked.

"I doubt…if we can catch them," I said between pants of breath. My stomach ached. "They're in friendly territory…and must have a place to hide. We're better off giving…their confessions to the news."

"Too bad our comms don't reach to Zor," added Ron.

Ron turned onto the paved Main Street and headed east toward Zor.

Flashing lights came behind us as I put on a shirt.

Ron drove fast without headlights. The road was curvy and that gave me an idea.

"Chima, spread oil slick behind us."

As Ron drove around one right curve, I looked out the back window. When the flashing lights came up to the curve, they slid to the right and went off the road. Two headlights went one on top of the other. The cop car was on its side.

"The police will have roadblocks."

"Where do we go?" Ron asked.

"Take the side road on the right."

We had mapped the escape routes but were not sure we had included all the dirt roads.

When we could see the flashing lights of the road block ahead, Ron slowed and took the right side road.

He said, "There's a car chasing us."

A hundred yards down the dirt road, I said, "Stop the car. Gancha, rifle grenade."

She said, "I'll get it."

When our van came to a stop, Gancha had a grenade launcher attached to a rifle and stepped out the back.

I watched her lift the rifle and aim at the curve we had passed earlier. Her grenade used rocket propulsion and had infra-red guidance. It would hone in on the heat of the car behind us.

She fired and the grenade left her rifle. It arched forward into the distance. Two seconds later, I heard the grenade explode. I couldn't see much from my bed inside the van.

Gancha got back in with a grin and closed the door. "That's a car full of people who won't harass anybody anymore."

Ron tore off down the dirt road and said, "Chima, activate shortwave radio."

"Activated."

He added, "Channel Nineteen." That was the channel that used our BIS encryption.

It took five seconds before the radio said, "Vincent here. Over."

"We need extracting," Ron replied. "Get a helo here ASAP. Jake's hurt from a beating. Coocher and Hoskins got away. We got a confession. Should be enough for the police to put the buggers in a cage."

Gancha yelled, "I shot Coocher in the leg. Over."

"Was that Gancha?" asked Vincent. "Over."

"Yeah," she replied. "I'll explain later. Over."

"Ron, would the York Federal Police be better?" asked Vincent. "They have a large helo. Over."

"If you can convince them to not arrest us, yeah. Over."

"What did you do over there?" After a pause, he added, "Over."

"Oh," said Ron, "a little thing of killing a few guards who may be on the payroll of Coocher. Over."

"Is that all?" asked Vincent, adding "Over."

"We need to get this confession on the news. Over," said Ron.

"I'll talk with Stan Curling of the YFP. Stand by."

I heard Vincent talking with Curling. He must have woken the detective up. I glanced at my comm. It was one in the morning here. That would be four in Zor.

We waited in the dark as we listened to the police band. The van tore down the dirt road. I felt like a criminal when they listen to the police trying to find them.

Vincent came back on. "He'll need a half hour to get to the helo. He'll call ahead."

I yelled, "Can you locate our beam?"

"No problem," replied Vincent. "You're coming through loud and clear."

I said, "How can you hear us?"

"Satellite," he replied.

At least the snow had stopped. Not that it would block our signal.

"Can you tell Curling we have a confession that will lock up Coocher and Hoskins?" I added.

"I did already," replied Vincent.

I wanted to know when they might arrive in the vicinity.

"Do you have an ETA?"

"It could be five hours," replied Vincent.

I turned to my buddy.

"Ron, stop the van. Can you lay a spiked chain across the road?"

"Got it." He stopped the van and left the driver's seat. He went in the back. Gancha opened the lid over one of the two bunks. She pulled out a chain in its case.

Ron took it in his gloved hands and exited the van, closing the door behind him.

I looked at Gancha.

"Any time you care to explain would be fine."

"You want the short version or the long one?"

"The short will do for now."

She sighed and looked down. "I wanted to prove myself to you. When I heard your plan, I knew this was my opportunity. Frankly, your plan sucked. It all depended on Coocher and Hoskins not detecting your transmitter. That was a big risk."

"But why?" I asked.

She looked me in the eyes. "Jake, I want to be part of your team. This was my chance to prove it."

Ron opened the driver's side door and climbed in.

"Done."

I turned toward him.

"Let's go a little farther."

Ron drove us another half mile around a bend.

"Let me have a Z helmet."

Ron pulled one out from the dashboard. Gancha grabbed it from Ron and handed it to me. Both my partners had theirs on.

After putting the helmet on, I struggled to get up. Gancha lent me her hand as I made my way to back window. My damned stomach ached.

Nothing appeared out there but the black of night. Then headlights appeared, followed by another set. When they got to the spikes, the lights slowed and when they got to the bend, they went off the road. Then they stopped. Maybe the trees got them.

"Chima, connect my helmet to the short wave. All of us."

"Consider it done."

Damn Vincent tampering again. I'll have to talk with him about that.

"Vincent, we'll try to hold out till the helo gets here. Tell them to rush."

"Did already."

I said to Ron, "Let's go another mile."

Ron drove without headlights and stopped.

I coughed up blood.

Crap! I'm hurt more than I thought. Will I live through this?

I glanced at my comm. "Helmet, start a countdown until the helo gets here. On Ron's and Gancha's helmets too."

In one corner of my vision, I saw a digital light displayed five hours and ten minutes.

Hope we live that long.

CHAPTER 51

"Helmet, show me the road ahead."

The dirt road turned left and right, mostly right. As we moved in the night, I noticed the countdown inched its way to four hours and forty-five minutes.

The road became overgrown. I could understand why. This far from the little village of Chester, road maintenance must take a low priority.

Thank heavens Chima could keep track. Most of the time, the road headed east. A dark mass appeared on the right.

"Chima, what is that dark stuff on the right blocking the stars?"

"That is Fortune Peak."

"Vincent, we're near Fortune Peak on our right."

I realized I didn't have a comm.

"Ron, can you give me a comm?"

He pulled one out of a compartment in the dash and handed it to me.

While I put it on, Ron yelled.

"Jake!"

"What?"

"Something's coming. In the air."

"Helmet, show me what Ron sees."

He zoomed the focus on the source of a searchlight. A helicopter, about six miles away and with its search light pointing at the ground.

"It's far too soon for our guys. It must be the Chester cops."

Gancha pulled down a scope rifle and checked its ammo. She went out the back door.

"Ron, can you use a rifle too?" I asked.

He got a rifle with scope from over his head, opened the door, and left.

"Helmet, split the view in half. Gancha's on the left, Ron's the right."

I felt a draft.

"And close the frickin' door. It's cold in here."

Soon I saw two beams of light coming from the sky.

The search lights moved left and right as I remembered the dirt road curved.

"They are looking for us. Get ready. Shoot out that damned spotlight. We can't be seen, even from a distance."

Two long and tense minutes later, the left side view in my helmet jerked. Gancha fired.

"Ron, can you lay another spike chain across the road?"

"Now? Or after I shoot?"

"After. There's time."

The searchlight came closer, maybe a half mile away, and then two shots, both from Gancha and Ron's rifles, jerked the view. The lights went out.

"They'll know we are close to that point. Better drive on."

Gancha opened the back door and took another spiked chain from its box. She held it up.

Mean looking sucker. Should shred any tires unfortunate enough to cross it.

Ron took the chain and lay it across the overgrown dirt road.

Then Ron got into his driver's seat. Soon the van lurched forward.

The damned road curved to the right again.

Ron stopped the van. "Where do I go next?"

"I dunno. Let's sit for a while."

Ron rolled down his window, turned off the engine, and looked outside. My view of his helmet showed hundreds of stars. So there was no cloud cover, which would have been nice.

Can't have everything.

With the engine off, a bevy of high-pitched clicks and other sounds hit my ears. A loud scream of pain came next, followed by silence. Then a loud roar. A gofer had taken down something. Maybe a bopum or a greeper. The roar was its bragging. Or maybe a signal to young gofers that dinner was ready.

Damn Rossa. Too frickin' wild for my tastes.

I was a city boy and being out here in the wild was not comfortable.

I struggled out of the bed and climbed to the back of the van. Gancha stood with her rifle pointed up.

"Think they'll give up?" she asked.

"I doubt it," I replied. "At least Coocher won't. He knows his bacon is burnt to a crisp if we get that confession to the police. If he had any influence on the local cops, they'll seek us out. After all, we killed several."

"The helo went away. I can hear it in the distance," Ron added.

"Now all we have to do is wait. Maybe the Chester Police will find another way to get to us. Chima, are we still in Chester County?"

"Affirmative."

I looked at Ron.

"So they might get the county sheriff to search for us. They know these back roads better than we do."

Gancha added, "You'd better get some sleep."

"As soon as the adrenaline wears off."

I got back in the van and laid on the bed. Gancha took something from the medicine cabinet and grabbed a bottle of water from the portable frig.

She handed me a pill and a bottle. "Synthetic morphine."

I hesitated.

"One will cut the pain and help you get some rest. Ron and I will stand guard. We'll wake you if we need you."

I took the pill and swallowed it with water.

It would need about thirty minutes to take effect. During that time, we three sat without saying a word.

I heard more clicks and screams in the distance. I had no idea when I fell asleep.

"Jake, wake up," said Ron.

I snapped my eyes open. I still had on my Z helmet.

"What's up?"

"It's daylight."

So it was. I glanced at the countdown clock in my helmet. Just thirty minutes to go.

"I checked with Vincent, who asked the helo," said Ron. "They'll be in the area in forty-two minutes."

That's a long time to wait when your life is at stake.

Ron munched on something.

"What are you eating?"

"I got hungry waiting for you to finish your nap."

I watched as he drank from a cup. Watching him eat made me hungry.

"Where's the food?" I asked Gancha.

She pointed.

Sure enough, there rested a gray box with a lid handle. I pulled it to my lap.

"Anyone chasing us?"

"The police band said the cops raised our last spiked chain. That was three hours ago. We can expect company soon."

"Spread another chain behind us and drive a little farther."

Ron replied, "Sorry, Jake. Wish I could. We don't have any more."

He drove us another mile but there were no bends, only a gradual curve to the right. He had to turn to get around boulders. We stopped at the bottom of a hill. I don't know how he followed any road. All I could see was grass. Thank heavens our van was built for rough travel.

I bit into a bologna and cheese sandwich and took a sip of coffee. Then I laid the sandwich and coffee down and got a rifle from the back seat, I unscrewed its silencer. Ron saw me and grabbed another rifle. Gancha did the same.

I got out the back door, despite the pain in my stomach.

We aimed our three rifles back up the road.

Sure enough. Flashing lights came around a bend. They couldn't make much speed with their tires shredded. I had to give them credit for trying though. They must have used the last cars in their arsenal.

"Aim for their grills."

As the lead car of the four turned toward us, less than a hundred yards away, the three of us fired. Steam rose from the front of the police car and it stopped. Four doors opened and four cops got out. In my scope I could see they had shotguns, which weren't much use at this distance. Three other cars pulled up next to them. Doors opened and cops emerged.

The guys in the lead car ran around behind it. The trunk raised. Other trunks opened too.

Must be getting better long-range equipment.

Sure enough, in seconds the trunk lids came down and I could see four cops with rifles. Only two had scopes though.

"Take out the ones with scopes first. Gancha, the one on your right, Ron the left."

Then Gancha groaned.

"Are you okay?" I asked her.

"Just a flesh wound," she replied.

My helmet microphone spoke next. "We are coming up on you."

I turned my head toward the east. "Helmet, zoom lens. Can you spot a helo?"

We had tied our Z helmets to Chima's AI and since she expected the air vehicles to come from the east, my view displayed two flashing bright spots against the black sky of stars. I waited while the helos got closer. A beam of searchlight came out of the bottom of one helo and blinded us.

I heard shots and two pings on the side of the van. The ground cops were trying to get us first.

"Better get inside. The walls of the van may help a little."

Gancha used one arm to help me get my butt on the floor of the van. I held my rifle in one hand and pulled up my legs. Pain shot through my abdomen as I rolled over. She got in beside me. In seconds, the rear door closed. Gancha used both hands to help me get up onto my bed.

"Let me see your wound," I said.

She had already put a StopIt on her left upper arm. I noted the white bandage.

My Z helmet still had a split view showing both Ron and Gancha's views.

"Helmet, clear the view."

I saw Ron fire his rifle from a rolled down window.

"We see you, Jake," said a masculine voice I didn't recognize.

The sound came in my ears in my helmet.

"Helmet, show what Ron sees in the upper half of my view."

Even without a zoom lens or my scope, I could see the cops run to the sides of their cars opposite the incoming helos, despite their exposure to our fire.

Silence came. Neither Ron nor the Chester cops fired any weapons. They must be waiting to see what the helo would do.

We waited too.

When the helos got close enough to show the letters "Federal Police" on their bottoms, the cops on the ground waved. Maybe they expected the helos to help them.

One helo stayed in the air while the second descended to a spot on the road between us and the Chester county cops. The helo in the air turned on its search light and aimed it at the cop cars, blinding anyone who looked up. The helo on the ground aimed its headlights on us.

My helmet compensated for the glaring headlights. I could see men in black with rifles jump down and aim at the cop car. That must have been confusing to the local cops.

The helo in the air descended between us and the cop car.

Three men in suits climbed out. Stan Curling walked toward us in a brown suit with white shirt and yellow tie. And a black armored vest with the white letters YFP in front. His hair blew in several directions as he bent over.

CHAPTER 52

When Curling got to the open back door of our van, he looked at me.

"Do you have the confession? We need it before we can go any further."

Ron raised his comm and pressed buttons. I added the vid from the camera disguised as a button on my shirt, now on the floor many miles behind us. Thank heavens it broadcast to the van.

"Chima, show the vid from my comms on the monitor in the van," I said.

My vid showed Coocher's lips moving in synch with his speech. I copied Ron's vid to my comm.

Gancha added her recording of the confession.

Hopefully the three would seal Coocher's fate.

When it ended, Curling nodded. "That's enough." He tapped his nose.

"We have enough evidence to arrest Coocher and Hoskins."

It took another half-hour for the YFP guys to talk with the local cops in the distance while Ron and I put our weapons and helmets away. The county police got back into their cars and the feds returned to their helos.

Curling said to me, "Want a ride home?"

I looked at Ron.

He said, "Gancha and I can drive the van back. You need medical attention."

I knew Chima could drive the van by herself but she would need a human onboard to buy gas. It was a long way to Zor.

I turned to Curling, "You heard him."

Curling tapped his nostril and gave instructions on his comm.

"Bring a stretcher to the van."

Two guys from the helo carried a stretcher. When it got to the back of the van, Curling and Gancha helped me lay on it.

Five minutes later, I lay on the same stretcher on the floor of the helo. Two men strapped me in and we lifted off. Curling sat next to me wearing a seat belt. I hated leaving Ron and Gancha but they were in safe hands with two YFP guys riding in the van.

One of the helo guys wore a medic's symbol on his dark green uniform. He gave me a pill.

"For the pain," he said.

I took the bottle of water he handed me, downed the pill, and lay back.

Then he wiped my mouth.

The medic jerked sideways as the helo turned.

I didn't see much because my eyes became drowsy and I nodded off.

When I woke, I glanced at my comm. It was an hour later. The noise dropped as the engine wound down. I must have looked curious because one fed, still in his black clothes, leaned over my left ear.

"We stopped to refuel."

I nodded and went back to sleep.

We stopped once more. Later, we landed on the top of Gerges Hospital.

It felt good to be back home, but I worried about Ron and Gancha. Knowing them, they'd pop stims and drive all the way home. They could be at the ops center in another day.

Four men in green hospital uniforms and a gurney rushed out of an elevator to greet us. Two helo medics moved my stretcher to the roof of the hospital. Then the hospital guys transferred me to their gurney and rushed me to the elevator. I could only see clouds above me.

As the elevator door closed, I heard the YFP helicopter whine up and take off again.

The elevator went down several floors and the door opened. I was rushed down one hallway and then another. You can't see much lying on your back. Mostly light fixtures.

Finally, we entered a room and two guys transferred me to a hospital bed. As best as I could see, I was the only patient in the room. One female nurse attached one end of an IV in my left arm.

Dr. Oberson arrived five minutes later.

"So you're back here again. What's it this time? Another beating?"

"Yeah, as a matter of fact."

The doctor looked at the monitors above my head.

"Blood pressure is normal. Heart beat looks good. Where on your body did you take the beating?"

"My stomach hurts. Probably from the brass knuckles."

"Hmm," he said. "We'd better check your blood." He nodded to a nurse.

She took three vials of blood from an outlet on the IV.

"Better leave some for me," I added to her.

"It's good to see you have a sense of humor," said Oberson. "I suppose you're gonna ask to be discharged in few days."

Something made me feel drowsy. Very drowsy.

The doctor said, "You need to sleep now."

When I woke, he was gone and Andy stood by my bed in his blue suit and pink dress shirt.

"How long was I out?" I asked.

Andy shrugged. "Don't know. I came in a half-hour ago."

"Anybody else guarding my room?"

"Two cops are sitting outside your door. I had to show ID as an employee of Mourtan Security. That wasn't enough, though. So I added my ID as a consultant to your PI firm."

He pulled a chair closer to my bed while I tagged Sheila.

"I got a big story for you."

I played back the confession and brought her up to speed on the story.

"Wow," she said. "A confession in their own words."

"Can you disguise my voice like you did for Albert Poors?"

"Sure," she replied. "But who shall I say is speaking?"

"Might as well be Poors."

She replied, "Folks will want to know how Poors got over to Chester."

"Can you be vague about that part?"

"Right. Thought you'd want that. Any chance we could share dinner?"

"Sheila, I'm in Gerges again. I took quite a beating back there. They may put me on a restricted diet. You know how the docs are."

"Okay, later maybe," she replied. "But I definitely want to buy you a dinner."

We disconnected.

I got a tag from Vincent.

"You back home all right?"

"Oh yeah. Sorry about not keeping you informed. I was asleep most of the time."

"That's all right. I heard the YFP got to the van and landed. Ron filled me in. I figured you were okay for a few hours."

"I'm in Gerges."

"Anything serious?"

"Just a little blood when I cough. Stomach hurts like hell. I'll let you know."

We disconnected.

An orderly came a few minutes later with dinner. As expected, it was all soft food.

Andy stood.

"I see you're busy," he said. "I'll go downstairs and grab a bite to eat."

Dr. Oberson walked in just as Andy walked out. The doc wore his usual white lab coat with a DetectIt dangling from his neck. Under his lab coat I saw the top of a blue shirt.

"Hope you don't mind but I put myself down as your primary doctor. Is that all right?"

"Sure. My first choice, actually."

I finished the vanilla pudding first.

He continued, "So far, everything looks okay. You had a tear on your stomach. That probably caused your coughing blood. You must have had quite an accident. Care to fill me in?"

"My stomach connected with a guy's fist. Remind me to dodge next time."

Dr. Oberson nodded. "From the blood tests, both your kidneys are bruised. Nothing serious, fortunately. And with your DNA, I expect you to recover in a few days. Eat only easy-to-digest foods for a week. Okay?"

I nodded. "Thanks, doc."

After he left and I was alone, I tagged Alena.

"Dad! Where are you?"

"At Gerges for a short stay."

"You okay?"

"Nothing serious. Like I told the doc, my stomach connected with a guy's fist. I should be as fine as ever in a few days."

"Can I visit?"

"Sure, but how are you going to leave," I almost said 'the embassy', "…your home."

"Vincent offered me a ride."

CHAPTER 53

Doctor Oberson kept me in the hospital for two more days. Two days of wearing those damned thin hospital gowns.

And the noise. My god, how do they expect anyone to sleep in the constant din of televisions, beepers, and conversations? I had the good fortune to be a room by myself with guards outside. With the door closed, the noise dropped. It didn't go completely away but was quiet enough for me to get some sleep—if I put earplugs in.

That evening, I watched Channel One as Sheila reported on Albert Pours' getting a confession from Coocher and Hoskins. The news said nothing about where the confession was obtained. It might have been in Zor or Chester.

Stan Curling of the York Federal Police said, "Many of you watching this had relatives who died from Virus Botulism. If you know the whereabouts of Guy Coocher or Borner Hoskins, please call the number on your screen. The number is different in different locations in York. Police are waiting for your call. Help us find these men and bring them to justice."

I wouldn't want to be Hoskins or Coocher right now. They might be holed up in Chester. The best chance for them would be to stay out of Zor. But that still left plenty of places to hide. It's a big country. The police must investigate thousands of tags.

After a brief nap, I tuned in again to see folks marching in front of Parliament. "Down with Coocher" said one sign. "Coocher is Dead!" said another. I grinned when I read one with "Poors for Parliament."

I watched my guard check the ID of everyone who came into my room. On one of my walks around the halls, I asked the older one how he checked everyone.

He wore a light blue shirt and dark blue slacks. But with his longish black hair, speckled with gray streaks, and a cap with a baseball pitcher winding up, it'd be easy to figure him for a visitor.

He said, "They don't let me download ID info to my comm so I have to send an image, name, and employee number to a computer. If I get back a green light, then I know that person is on the staff, a contractor, or a family member."

"You send a photo?"

"Oh yeah. It would be easy for someone who wanted access to your room to steal a uniform and maybe ID. But you can't fool a photo."

"And if they don't match?" I asked.

He grinned. "I pull out my gun and cuff them on the spot for impersonating."

We walked around a corner.

"What happens when you need to take a break?"

"There are always two of us on duty. You may not see the other one."

I had but I wasn't going to tell him everything. Spies are like that. We don't tell all we know.

I spent most of my time reading but found I could do only so much of that.

On my second day, I was busy with an ereader on my lap when I heard a voice.

"Ahem."

I looked up to see Alena and Vincent. She had on a red pantsuit and white lacy blouse. He wore his light brown suit.

"Wow," I said. "Thanks for coming."

My daughter came over to the edge of my bed and gave me a hug. Vincent offered his hand and we shook.

"How are you doin'?" she asked.

"My belly still hurts a little. It's getting better."

I raised my left arm to show her the IV. "They gave me something to stop the bleeding. And something to help the healing."

She said, "I heard the confession on the telly. They did a good job disguising the voice." She paused to look behind her at the open door. Then she leaned down to whisper in my ear. "If you hadn't told me, I never would have guessed who it was."

"Hey, we do what we hafta do."

Vincent interrupted our private chat.

"It's good to have you back, cowboy."

I had to grin at that one. It was a nickname for me at the ops center.

Alena asked, "When you going home?"

"Tomorrow morning."

"Good. Then you'll have time to attend Mom's memorial service."

"Oh, when is it?"

"Two tomorrow. At her house."

"That will give me time to go home, take a shower, and get a change of clothes." I turned to my daughter.

"How are you doin'?"

"Gliituk has been very helpful," said Alena. "He's provided everything I want."

"Have you published another paper yet?"

"Been too busy in the lab. It takes a lot of time to sequence a genome."

She sat in the only guest chair and Vincent stood at the foot of my bed.

"Do you suppose," she said, "that I could get a place of my own soon?"

"Not while either son of a bitch is loose out there," I answered.

My comm vibrated. There was a special newscast.

"Telly on."

The screen on the opposite wall lit up.

Sheila Fish said, "Federal Police raided the headquarters of Humans Only this afternoon. At the same time, several more Federal Police raided the home of Coocher in Chester on the western side of York."

The camera view changed to the front steps of the same house I had been in just days ago. Two men struggled to carry a stretcher down the steps. The stretcher held a body covered by a white sheet.

A male reporter spoke.

"Guy Coocher was killed by gunfire just a few minutes ago as federal police stormed his estate here in Chester."

The reporter turned to another man next to him. His name tag said Richard Brown, York Federal Police.

Brown said into the camera, "We tried to arrest Mr. Coocher. We broke down the door of his library. In the ensuing exchanges of gunfire, Mr. Coocher was fatally shot."

The reported asked, "Any sign of Borner Hoskins?"

Brown shook his head. "Nope."

"They'll catch him soon," said Vincent. "He can't hide for long."

I added, "Unless friends around Chester keep him in their basement. Lots of folks out there seemed pretty conservative. There's a reason why Coocher got elected, you know."

Then I added, "Anyone taking care of Monk?"

Vincent smiled. "Oh yeah. The bugger is making a lot of friends around the place."

He declined to use the words 'ops center.'

Alena glanced at her comm. "Oh shit! Oops." She covered her mouth. "Sorry 'bout that."

"What?" I asked.

"I have to get back to my lab. I have a sequence coming out soon."

"Sequence?" I asked.

"DNA sequence," she explained. "What the heck do you think I do?"

"Sorry. Forgot for a moment."

She stood and reached down to give me another hug goodbye. "Take care of yourself, Dad. You're all I have left."

"Ahem," said Vincent.

She stood and turned to him. "And my stepdad, of course." She gave him a hug too.

Before they left, Vincent shook my hand. "I'll see you at my house tomorrow."

"I'll be there," I replied. "You can count on it."

Alone after they left, I didn't get very far in my novel when I heard a rap on my door sill. I looked up to see Ron, this time in a light brown suit, complete with a pink dress shirt opened all the way down to his hairy chest.

"Well, it's good to see you," I said.

When he came close, I saw Zetto walk in. My communications expert stood tall, as usual, and wore a blue and white checkered shirt and blue jeans.

After handshakes, Ron said, "You're missed. You gotta get outta here."

"You got that right," I replied. "Zetto serves much better food than this place."

With that, Zetto grinned.

"Just tell me what you want and I'll have it ready for your first meal."

"Are you cooking at the memorial?"

Zetto shook his head. "No. It's catered."

"That sounds like Vincent. Where's Gancha?"

Ron replied, "Babysitting Ruta. Jake, I think she's gonna work out."

* * * * *

Ron and Zetto came at ten the next morning to take me home. The nurse made me sit in a damned wheelchair until I got to Zetto's car. At least he drove a decent sized vehicle. Ron's two-seater wouldn't do.

I got a surprise when I got in. A moncat jumped into my lap.

"Hey, little guy."

I rubbed his ears and fur. He jumped to my neck and gave me a hug.

As the hospital orderly returned the wheelchair to the front door, Ron climbed in the back.

Monk wouldn't let go, making it difficult to get a seatbelt on. When I managed, I held Monk in my lap.

We took off and Zetto drove around downtown while Ron and I checked for a tail. He drove on Main Street several times before heading on University Avenue to Cierto Road. When we got to my apartment, Zetto and Ron helped me get out.

Zetto took Monk while I limped to go inside. My stomach still ached. Climbing the stairs inside my place was a bitch and Ron pulled my right arm over his shoulders as we climbed.

Tut reported the apartment had no visitors.

"Want to take a nap?" asked Ron. "We have time."

"I'm all slept out. Let's get this show on the road."

It felt good to be back home in my own place. I had spent too many days and nights in the ops center, in a cramped van on the way to Chester, in a helo, and in the hospital.

The warm water from the shower was a touch of heaven, prompting me to hum.

Yep, life is good.

I washed the blood off my left hand from the IV before I checked my chin to see if I needed to shave. But it had been only a few weeks since I had last used Bristle Gone and I didn't need it.

Putting on my pants was difficult with my sore belly so it took longer than normal to get dressed. I pictured what it must be like to be old. The old advice, "Use it or lose it" came to mind.

As soon as my stomach heals, I'm going jogging again.

Ron helped me finish dressing in a blue suit with black shoes, undershirt, pale blue shirt, holster, and gun. Most of my shirts had two slits in the left breast so I could cover up the strap of my holster on my chest and yet get to my gun.

When we walked out of the bedroom and into the living room, I found Zetto watching the telly on one wall.

Sheila Fish reported that there had been no viable leads on the whereabouts of Hoskins. His image appeared to her right.

She said, "If you have any idea where this man can be found, please call your local police or the toll free number on your screen for the York Federal Police."

Since Hoskins was still at large, I said, "Ron, can you put my ankle Snap on, please? It still hurts to bend over."

While he wrapped the small holster and gun, I looked around. "Where's Monk?"

"In the kitchen," reported Zetto. "Where else?"

He pulled a black arm band from his jacket pocket and I stuck my left arm out straight while he slipped the black band up my arm.

"Better bring Monk," I said. "He'll stay with us at the center until Hoskins is caught."

Ron helped me down the stairs, but I insisted on walking alone to Zetto's car. Zetto had gone ahead and when we got to the back door, his car was waiting with an open back door.

CHAPTER 54

We passed over the Ambassador Bridge and I looked at a military ship docked below. Small. Must be a destroyer.

We parked in the huge lot at Vincent's house. Ron offered me a cane but I refused.

"I can make it on my own."

Vincent put on a grand display. We went to the living room, where photos of Leanna adorned the walls. A giant photo rested on one table.

She must have known lots of people because the room was full of folks, all wearing black or black arm bands. I spotted Sheila Fish with a drink in her hand and messed up eyeliner. Why is that women take death so hard? Maybe men do too, but they can't show it. Or don't want to. There were times when being a man was a burden.

Sheila spotted me and broke away from the group around her. She wore a black dress and black heels. She rushed up and put her arms around me while trying not to spill her glass of white wine.

I winced from her hug.

"Oops. Sorry," she added.

She glanced at the large photo of Leanna.

"I'm so sorry, Jake. I know she meant a lot to you."

Her breasts pushed against my chest. Her words echoed in my head.

Yeah. No one will ever know how much.

That damned lump came to my throat again.

When Sheila broke the hug and stepped back, her eyes were wet again.

"Got a tissue?" she asked.

I shook my head and looked around for a box of tissues. Every flat surface had one. Vincent had thought of everything.

I pulled one out from a box on the table by the door and gave it to her. She dabbed under both eyes. I don't know why. Her eyeliner was all over her eyes.

She took my right arm and led me to the large image of Leanna on the table. We stared at it for a minute.

The woman I had loved was now dead. She smiled in the photo. I recalled her face in the storage room, thin, gaunt even. The disease had taken a lot out of her. I preferred to remember her smiling.

Alena touched my left arm and I looked up at her. She stood three inches taller than me. Must have high heels on. Her eyes were wet too.

We three stood like that for several minutes, not saying a word, each lost in memories as we stared at the photo.

Vincent came up to us and placed his left hand on my right shoulder. He wore black too. I wondered why we still followed the old ritual.

He stood there looking at his wife's image.

Sheila got up on a chair. She spoke aloud to the crowd.

"This has not been released yet, but I thought you'd like to know. Leanna's sacrifice was not in vain. Parliament voted on the Freedom from Aliens Bill. It went down with 52 nayes. Klava said he hoped we could put this sour chapter behind us and move on. The House of Commons passed a bill declaring an annual Greet Your Neighbor Day. The bill goes before the Senate next week."

Hands clapped everywhere. She stepped down from the chair amid smiles and handshakes.

I turned to Vincent. "Got any food in this joint?"

He broke away from staring at Leanna's photo and pulled my right arm. We went into the adjacent dining room to a long table with a white cloth draped over it. On the surface were chicken and ham sandwiches, a stack of plates, a pile of green grapes, and apples in a basket, amongst a virtual cornucopia of food.

I saw a pile of garnot fruit, three different cheeses, sourdough and black breads, and two pink bowls of punch, one labeled "hard", with small glass cups stacked next to the bowls.

Sheila came into the dining room, went to the end, and selected a plate.

I grabbed a plate and followed her. The plates were small, so I figured I should avoid piling it high with food like I usually do. After all, it was a memorial service, not a picnic.

The ham sandwiches looked good, and I selected two, along with a pile of green beans and a half dozen wedges of potatoes. At the end of the table, I grabbed a knife, fork, and a paper cloth, which I stuffed in my suit pocket.

I turned to follow Sheila as a male server in a tuxedo stood behind a table and filled her glass with wine. When I looked at him, he turned a glass over for me and filled it.

I took the wine in my left hand and the plate in my right.

How am I supposed to shake hands?

I followed my favorite newscaster back into the living room. Sheila found a table with two empty chairs. I placed my food and drink on the small table.

With so many people in the room standing, it was impossible to see the large image of my ex.

I bit off a piece of ham sandwich and chewed.

Five minutes later, Sheila got up to get more wine.

I emptied my glass. The wine was good. I stood to get more. As I made my way toward the dining room, I turned around to see a man and a woman take the seats we had left behind. Oh well.

As I slid between one group of people and another, I saw a new guy come in the front door. Full beard and moustache with streaks of gray, bushy gray eyebrows, darker skin tone, gray hat, and a wearing dark gray suit. He walked with a stoop. Must be old.

How many people did Leanna know anyway? Must be in the hundreds.

His eyes looked out with intensity.

Where have I seen that look before?

Sheila was nowhere in sight when I got my glass refilled. I made my way back to the center of the living room when I spotted Alena.

I twisted and turned through the crowd, overhearing bits of conversation.

"…hear she was working for Channel One."

"She had good taste in flowers."

"…commodities are the future…"

A female voice said, "Come on, Larry, we've all heard that one."

I spotted Alena walking out to the balcony so I made a turn to join her.

She leaned against the wooden rail and stared at the night sky.

Clouds blocked half the stars. I came up beside her and grabbed the rail.

She turned to me and laid her head on my shoulder. I put my left arm around her.

"Hello, Alena. We meet again," said a voice behind us.

She spun around to look at the old man with the full beard.

She said, "How dare you show up here!"

He replied, "What luck! Both of you in the same place."

He pulled a gun out and pointed it at her.

My reflexes kicked in and I knocked the gun out of his hand. That's when I remembered where I had seen those eyes.

Hoskins!

He and I grabbed each other's arms, and he pushed me backwards toward the rail. I hit it with the low of my back but dared not let go of him. But no matter how I twisted or struggled, he held firm. My stomach hurt but I ignored it. I had more important things on my mind. Like surviving.

Then a shot rang out.

Hoskins went stiff and stared with a surprised look on his face.

In the moment of his distraction, I twisted out from his grip and pulled him toward me as I turned from the rail. He staggered forward and his upper body went over the rail, followed by his legs.

I stared over the rail to watch him fall. He made no sound as he receded in the distance to land with a thump on the pavement below. As he lay there, not moving, a dark pool inched outward from his body.

I turned to see what could have caused the gunshot sound and saw Alena holding a gun in both hands, pointed in my direction, eyes in a glaze.

I stepped aside and reached out to take the gun by its muzzle. She did not resist but remained staring ahead.

Where'd she get the gun?

Then I remember I had knocked it out of Hoskins' hand.

Ron and Vincent rushed out to the balcony with Snaps in hand. They stopped when they saw the two of us.

Conversation inside the other room had ceased.

"What happened?" asked Ron.

"Alena shot Hoskins," I replied.

"Here?" asked Vincent.

"Police! Stand aside!" yelled the voice of Deek Tanny as the man made his way through the crowd.

I wondered why his presence was a surprise. But he was short so I may have missed him in the crowd.

Ron and Vincent put their guns back in their holsters.

When Deek saw me holding a gun by its barrel and the dazed look on Alena's face, he said, "What's going on?"

"Alena shot Hoskins." I pointed over the rail.

"He fell."

Deek leaned over the rail. Seconds later, he looked at me and then down at the gun still in my hand. "Is that the weapon?"

I nodded and handed it to him. He pulled a plastic bag out of his suit pocket and opened it. I dropped the gun in it and he closed it.

Next, I put my arm around Alena as she buried her face and hands on my right shoulder. She shook as she sobbed.

Deek looked at her and me. "What happened?"

I filled him in about my struggling with Hoskin just before Alena fired.

He said, "Sounds like self-defense. I'll need your statements."

I nodded.

"In a minute."

Ron took Deek and Vincent back into the main room and closed the balcony door. I saw dozens of faces staring at me as the door closed.

Alena cried and trembled in my arms. Finally she raised her face and looked at me. Her makeup was a mess.

"I've never killed anyone before."

"And you wanted to be a spy, eh?" I said. "Spies sometimes have to kill."

She said nothing.

"You okay?" I asked.

Her eyes filled with tears as she put her arms around me and hugged.

"I know," I said. "I was shook up the first time I killed."

She said to my backside, "First time?"

"Yep. You always remember the first one."

She broke her hug and looked into my eyes with her hands still around my neck. "How many?"

I shook my head. "Can't remember."

She returned to her hug and said with plugged up nose, "Juss gib me a minute."

That minute lasted a long time with her in my arms.

The End

If you liked this story, how about hopping over to Amazon.com or Goodreads.com and write a short review of it with your comments? If you want me to write more of these adventures of Jake Dani, please reward me with your review. It takes only a minute and I'd appreciate it very much.

You may want to subscribe to my mailing list to receive an email when a new book is published. Go to www.crayne.com and sign up today while it is on your mind.

Excerpt from "Live Forever"

A Jake Dani/Mike Shapeck Novel
By Victory Crayne

Chapter 1

"Where am I?"

The room was new. I was certainly not at my apartment nor at the operations center. All I could remember was traveling to Earth and undergoing a nano-rejuvenation.

I glanced around me as I tried to figure out where I could be.

The walls sported a light blue on the top half and beige on the bottom. The bed I lay in was large enough, especially in the length. At six foot one, I often had difficulties in finding a bed I could be comfortable in.

The room contained only my bed, a light brown dresser of four drawers on the opposite wall at the foot of my bed, two upholstered guest chairs in a light brown print, and a small circular brown table between the chairs. No mirror.

On one wall rested a window but the dark blue curtain let in no light. The only door was shut.

I glanced down at my left wrist only to learn my comm was gone. Instead, I stared at the tattoo everyone received soon after they were born. In my baby years, the tattoo could be used to track my location in case I was kidnapped. Later, I got a comm to lay over it, powered by the heat of my blood. Comms became universal when everyone wore one and used theirs to communicate with others.

But no comm rested there. Only the tattoo from my childhood.

The red blanket on my bed didn't ring any bells. I flipped the cover off and looked at the sheet. White. I was dressed in thin light-blue pajamas I didn't recognize.

What the hell?

I pulled the cover back and sat up on the edge of my bed. In front of my feet I spotted black slippers of the type worn in hospitals.

None of this made any sense at all.

I put my feet into the slippers and walked to the window. "Open window."

But the curtain remained closed.

I looked for a cord to pull and found one of the left side. So I pulled it. That's when I noticed my fingers were different.

The curtain slid aside but that didn't help much. The window was covered with a black something. I touched it only to learn it was part of the glass or was painted on the outside. I could not scratch the covering. So I had no idea if it was daylight out or not or where I might be.

That did it. I wanted some answers and I wanted them now. I rushed to the beige door.

"Door open."

But it didn't. So I looked for a handle on the sliding door and slid the door aside.

One big guy in a green uniform turned toward me. Behind him stood three robots, dressed in the same green. It was hard to tell when a robot stood at attention. That was their normal posture. But one thing was clear. All four "men" were six foot or higher, and looked quite strong.

"Where am I?"

The guy lifted his left wrist to his mouth.

"He's awake."

He gazed upward into my eyes and must have been six foot.

"I'm sorry, sir, but you'll have to remain in your room until the doctor comes."

"Doctor?"

Behind them I observed another wall across a wide hallway. It too had the same color scheme as my room, blue on the top half and beige on the bottom.

I turned to the human male.

"Can you at least tell me where I am?" I asked.

He responded with "I'm sorry, sir. Everything will be explained by the doctor."

He looked aside. "Door closed and locked."

The damn thing slid shut. It wouldn't open on my command but closed on his.

I inserted my fingers in the slot and tried to slide the door aside as before, but it didn't budge.

I stared at the off-white color of the door for five seconds.

"Damn!"

I was a prisoner.

* * * * *

A glance around the room revealed no clock on any wall. Having nothing to do, I retreated to the bed for some serious thinking.

I recalled going to the rejuvenation center to get a template made, paid for by my boss and spymaster, Acorn.

For I was a spy, as were many Bingers. My father Petro's younger brother was Berry Dani. Berry preferred to call himself by his code name of Acorn.

In the Earth-Durr war of 2035-2043, Dr. Bing used snippets of DNA from captured alien mercons, supposedly to enhance human intelligence, strength, and healing abilities, and inserted the snippets into human embryos. The children born of such experiments became known as Bingers.

After the war ended, human prejudice against the hated mercons persisted and was directed onto the Binger children. Almost every Binger family had at least one member who had died. After hundreds had been killed, they went underground and changed their names.

Berry Dani was born in Omaha, Nebraska from Stetson Fulman and Margaret O'Malley, both full Bingers. They changed their last name to Dani to avoid persecution. Berry's older brother and my dad, Petro, were thus full Bingers.

Berry married Arlene Smith, a normal human, and had two sons, Charles and Albert.

After graduating from college, Berry went to work for the American CIA and had received promotion after promotion until he worked his way up the org chart to second in command. Along the way, he learned a lot about analysis, field operations and training. When the CIA purged itself of Bingers, he left before his own DNA was discovered.

Then he formed the Binger Intelligence Service, which became known as BIS. He tried to recruit almost every Binger as soon as they finished their education, either from high school or college.

When his son Charles graduated with a bachelor's degree, he joined BIS. Unfortunately, on a mission inside Russia, Charles Dani got himself killed. His brother Albert turned to a life of crime and on one poorly-planned caper, got caught while taking the jewelry of a rich man's wife. Acorn pulled a few of his influential strings and managed to get the sentence for Albert commuted, as long as he migrated to the new planet of Rossa and changed his name. Albert chose Ron Boscoe.

On Rossa, Ron and I became buddies and I used his help on several of my private investigator contracts. At one time,

Ron came to me to ask for my help on a spy mission. The idea was to rescue my father Petro. I did not know it at the time, but Petro had only joined BIS on condition that Acorn not recruit me. After I rescued my dad, and nearly got killed in the process, I made a deal with him. He was to drop out of BIS and go back home to Earth to care for my mom and run his engineering business. I would take his place as a BIS agent.

I didn't learn until later that Acorn could hardly believe his good fortune, for he had his eyes on me for a long time.

After several assignments on Rossa in which I excelled as a spy, I heard rumors of my eventually replacing Berry.

Six months ago, I got a coded message from Acorn that he was undergoing the procedure to get a template made in the rejuvenation clinic. Since there existed a small but not zero chance he would die during the process, he wanted me to take over BIS if he couldn't.

I breathed a sigh when he woke up. I didn't really want to go to Earth and be stuck behind a desk.

Later, he wanted me to come to the home planet and get a nano-rejuvenation made too. On a BIS nickel. It wasn't exactly a request. More like an order.

And who wouldn't want to get a template made? I could later return to the rejuvenation clinic and get a true rejuvenation done. I would have my body turned back to the age of my template but I'd get to keep my memories. Talk about the ideal solution to aging!

Things were quiet on Rossa at the time, so I made the journey from Rossa to Earth, covering the twenty-five light years in about eleven days on Second Class. Ron went with me so he could visit his parents. I left Vincent Stone in charge of the BIS team in York on Rossa.

When I arrived at the clinic, I changed into the blue pajamas and allowed the doctor to inject a sedative into my left arm. The only sensation I got was the full feeling under my skin after the injector hissed. Gone were the days of needles piercing skin. Injectors used compressed air to press a solution under the skin over an artery.

I went to sleep and woke up in this room by myself.

For free short stories, sign up for a free mailing list. This mailing list won't clutter your inbox since I'll use it primarily to announce new books. See www.crayne.com for details.

See www.crayne.com for links on where to buy a copy of "Humans Only."

www.ingramcontent.com/pod-product-compliance
Lightning Source LLC
Chambersburg PA
CBHW061302170626
46817CB00001B/18